continued . . .

ASTROPOLIS:

THE GRAND CONJUNCTION

Sean Williams

ACE BOOKS, NEW YORK

THE BERKLEY PUBLISHING GROUP
Published by the Penguin Group
Penguin Group (USA) Inc.
375 Hudson Street, New York, New York 10014, USA
Penguin Group (Canada), 90 Eglinton Avenue East, Suite 700, Toronto, Ontario M4P 2Y3, Canada
(a division of Pearson Penguin Canada Inc.)
Penguin Books Ltd., 80 Strand, London WC2R 0RL, England
Penguin Group Ireland, 25 St. Stephen's Green, Dublin 2, Ireland (a division of Penguin Books Ltd.)
Penguin Group (Australia), 250 Camberwell Road, Camberwell, Victoria 3124, Australia
(a division of Pearson Australia Group Pty. Ltd.)
Penguin Books India Pvt. Ltd., 11 Community Centre, Panchsheel Park, New Delhi—110 017, India
Penguin Group (NZ), 67 Apollo Drive, Rosedale, North Shore 0632, New Zealand
(a division of Pearson New Zealand Ltd.)
Penguin Books (South Africa) (Pty.) Ltd., 24 Sturdee Avenue, Rosebank, Johannesburg 2196,
South Africa

Penguin Books Ltd., Registered Offices: 80 Strand, London WC2R 0RL, England

This is a work of fiction. Names, characters, places, and incidents either are the product of the author's imagination or are used fictitiously, and any resemblance to actual persons, living or dead, business establishments, events, or locales is entirely coincidental. The publisher does not have any control over and does not assume any responsibility for author or third-party websites or their content.

ASTROPOLIS: THE GRAND CONJUNCTION

An Ace Book / published by arrangement with the author

PRINTING HISTORY
Ace mass-market edition / May 2009

Copyright © 2009 by Sean Williams.
Map illustration by Sean Williams.
See pages 315–317 for a complete list of copyrights for referenced lyrics.
Cover art by Scott Grimando.
Cover design by Judith Lagerman.
Interior text design by Laura K. Corless.

ISBN: 978-0-441-01713-3

ACE
Ace Books are published by The Berkley Publishing Group,
a division of Penguin Group (USA) Inc.,
375 Hudson Street, New York, New York 10014.
ACE and the "A" design are trademarks of Penguin Group (USA) Inc.

PRINTED IN THE UNITED STATES OF AMERICA

10 9 8 7 6 5 4 3 2 1

For the real Mr. Webb, with real thanks

For my ways are strange ways and new ways and old ways,
And deep ways and steep ways and high ways and low;
I'm at home and at ease on a track that I know not,
And restless and lost on a road that I know.

—Henry Lawson, *"The Wander-Light"*

Contents:
· ·

All quotes attributed to Robert Louis Stevenson are taken from Strange Case of Dr Jekyll and Mr Hyde *(1886).*

Once every twenty years or so, Saturn and Jupiter form a Grand Conjunction in the Earth's night sky. To astrologers, this symbolic union is one of great dynamic tension, heralding upheaval in both secular and religious circles. Seven US presidents were born under a Grand Conjunction. All died while in office.

The Muslim philosopher Albumasar believed that such conjunctions usher in prophets and new religious understanding, such as that wrought by the reformer Martin Luther, whose birth is associated with the Grand Conjunction of 1484.

Roger Bacon and Pierre d'Ailly went further, proposing that the world's last prophet would appear with a conjunction between Jupiter and the moon. Such an alignment would bring together elements of opportunistic expansion, the unconscious, justice, the past, and the hunt.

Many believe that this last prophet will be a false one, the Antichrist, and that the peace he brings will be but a precursor to the final war.

METAPSYCHOSES

When does recollection become history, memoir biography, and a name just words in a dead language?

Imre Bergamasc is a man widely known for changing his mind. As a mercenary in the Corps, he served his masters faithfully and well—until he turned on them, perceiving in their desire for long-term stability that the Forts were overreaching their responsibilities toward "lesser" forms of humanity. The bitter and bloody conflict that followed, known later in the galaxy-spanning Continuum as the Mad Times, was a bold gesture, perhaps even noble, but there could be only one winner. Imre's surrender sealed the fate of his revolution. His subsequent disappearance came as no surprise to many.

Few knew that he had entered into a pact with his former masters, a pact aligning his interests with theirs through a project called Domgard. Its purpose was kept from the majority of humanity; only Forts could be trusted with the secret. Imre Bergamasc became, therefore, identical to those he had spent 172,000 years fighting.

As part of their Graduations, Forts commonly adopted a new name, one based on the old but with multiple layers of meaning. Forts are wordsmiths as well as worldsmiths. Imre Bergamasc took over half a million years to choose his new name, but choose it he did. That name is presently known only to him.

The art of changing one's mind, like much in life, is easy to learn but hard to master. Imre Bergamasc attempted to preserve his reputation by systematically erasing or altering all records that might reveal the truth of his betrayal. Such records included the testimony of his former friends and allies, those members of the Corps who had faithfully served with him during the Mad Times and now regarded him as a traitor, or at best inconstant. The records also included the comprehensive backups of his life scattered far and wide across the galactic disk, from which a new version of himself could be created should some disastrous fate befall the original.

Imre Bergamasc is a man determined to survive whatever fate throws at him. He is not, however, omniscient. Even as he emerged once more into galactic society, apparently to resume his work as a servant of the Forts, he left loose ends behind him. One concerned the only living man who knows the truth of his betrayal. That man is the Old-Timer best known as Render, and he is the one man Imre can never kill.

Another loose end would cause him considerable grief in times to come. Of the many backups destroyed by Imre's own hand, a single example survived complete destruction. The Drum was discovered as a cloud of radioactive dust on the edge of the galaxy and reassembled by the group mind called the Jinc. An obsessive cataloger of extragalactic material, within which it hopes to find the truth regarding humanity's creation, the Jinc re-created Imre Bergamasc from the ruins of the Drum—a version of him, anyway, patched and imperfect, and briefly the wrong gender. It is difficult to say what went through his mind during this difficult rebirth, but the experience marked him as a very different man from his original, whom he ultimately rejected. Call this version of Imre Bergamasc Imre-Prime, not because he is in any imaginable fashion more authentic than other iterations of himself, but because he later turned his back on more advanced modes of being in order to appeal to the galaxy's common denominator: Primes, those multitudinous people most resembling our distant ancestors, the Old-Timers.

The template from which the Jinc "resurrected" Imre-Prime had been recorded by his original shortly after the end of the Mad Times. Imre-Prime possessed, therefore, no memory of anything that had transpired since then. He was unaware, for instance, that a weapon of considerable potency had recently destroyed nearly every Fort in the galaxy. The Slow Wave radiated out from Spargamos, a small planet near the galaxy's core, cutting off the drone-like frags that were every Fort's component parts. The only Forts to survive the catastrophe were those linked by means other than loop shunts—advanced technology that made the very existence of such galactic superminds possible, and which the Slow Wave specifically targeted. Imagine a human brain with the axons removed, leaving individual neurons isolated: such was the hammerblow to human cognition in the Milky Way. All advanced thought ceased. The great work of humanity came to an abrupt halt.

Imre-Prime was also unaware that his Fort-self had (a) ever existed and (b) survived the Slow Wave. (The Fort-self, of course, had contingencies in place—pockets of himself that operated without loop shunts—because you can never be too prepared for disaster.) Components of Imre Bergamasc swarmed across the galaxy in the wake of the Slow Wave, seeking by any means to reconnect and re-build the mind they were once part of. His priorities were, and remain, simple: the work of Domgard must continue, and whoever destroyed the Forts must not be provoked to mount further attacks on what remains of humanity. The long-term survival of the species is paramount.

By the time Imre-Prime escaped his Jinc creators and returned to the greater galaxy, several attempts to re-create the Forts had been interrupted by Imre Bergamasc and his band of saboteur Barons, plus another agency, the enigmatic Luminous, who manifested as swarms of silver spheres with lethal intent. The Luminous communicate via loop shunts, the same technology targeted by the Slow Wave, suggesting that they or their makers are responsible for the murder of the Forts. The two forces independently ensured that humanity remained in a kind of Stone Age, lacking everything the Forts had once provided: stability, unity, and the long view. Barons and Luminous coexist uneasily in the Milky Way, with unthreatening humanity caught between them, but there have been no major flare-ups for half a million years. The deadly phenomenon of the Slow Wave has never been repeated on such a large scale.

Imre-Prime, reunited with his former comrades, wasted no time returning to his correct gender and mounting a campaign to restore order to the mess that had once been his home. The First Church of the Return was his principal vehicle of reconstruction, with former lover and nominal-ally Helwise MacPhedron its high priest and he himself its figurehead, the First Prime. Together they fashioned a Returned Continuum and brought a large percentage of the galaxy under Imre-Prime's control.

He did his best to bring peace to the many ordinary humans of the galaxy, but a single Prime cannot possibly manage such a complex beast. Unrest was widespread. After an attempted coup by the more pragmatic Helwise, Imre-Prime abdicated, leaving his former bodyguard Emlee Copas in charge. To her he bequeathed: full control of the galaxy; responsibility for his unwanted son, Ra MacPhedron; his allies Render and Al Freer; and a considerable mess.

He could have managed his affairs more successfully had he not been distracted by other matters. Immediately prior to the coup, Imre-Prime was taken to Spargamos to see the ruins of Domgard. There he came face-to-face with his Fort-self, whom he had last encountered shortly after his "resurrection" by the Jinc—once to be attacked, the second time to be warned away from anything to do with Domgard.

On Spargamos, Imre-Prime was used as bait to trigger a battle between the Luminous and the Barons, a battle that served as a testing ground for new weaponry against the perpetrators of the Slow Wave. Imre-Prime was shot by his own hand, by his Fort-self, who had no further use for him. And that appeared to be the end of that.

Fortunately for Imre-Prime, death is not the absolute it used to be. Humanity is an infovore endlessly chewing the vast cud of data it has accrued down the millennia. We cannot forget, and we cannot let go. Baron spies in the Returned Continuum soon leaned that Imre-Prime had been resurrected from a hardcast record by Emlee Copas and returned to Earth via surreptitious means. There, during the attempted coup, Imre-Prime issued Executive Order KISMET, which resulted in the murder of every iteration of Helwise MacPhedron in the galaxy. For once, his mind was made up.

There is little the Barons do not know about the galaxy's would-be savior, although some details they have discovered only after the fact. They have learned, for instance, that Imre-Prime governed the Returned Continuum with the assistance of an advanced artificial intelligence, the Apparatus, and one sole remaining Fort, MZ. Both beings were written directly onto the fabric of space-time— using an arcane technology developed by the ancient minds of Earth, whose legacy Imre-Prime inherited. It was in the belly of this virtual Fort that Imre traveled to and from Spargamos, taking both the Barons and the Luminous by surprise.

The spies also learned that much of the unrest in the Returned Continuum was driven by a movement associated with the Veil, an alien parasite that allows the expansion and transmission of biological memory. They know that a former lover of Imre-Prime brought the Veil to Earth in the hope that he might use its unifying influence to bring peace to his troubled realm. They suspect that a trace of Helwise MacPhedron has survived in the Veil, and lurks there still, undetected by the Apparatus.

For all the Barons have learned, however, questions remain that they cannot answer. They do not know how much Imre-Prime has learned about the purpose of Domgard. They do not know what took place between Imre-Prime and the Luminous in the heart of Spargamos. They do not know where Imre-Prime is.

Perhaps most perplexingly, they do not know why Imre-Prime changed his mind about ruling the galaxy.

Official histories fail to explain why a man who has successfully quelled rebellion among his own ranks—and has in addition to that been offered an olive branch from the very forces threatening his regime—would turn his back on everything he worked for. Rumors were rife at the time, but none has withstood close scrutiny. It is possible that he realized the futility of his task and fled before the full consequences of his hubris came to bear upon him. (Fear would be his motivator, in that case.) Perhaps he felt regretful about Helwise's betrayal and the revenge he took upon her. (Guilt, then, would guide him into oblivion.) Another possibility is that he has struck a deal, such as the one his Fortself made with the Forts in the distant past, but this time with a power that has yet to reveal itself to the greater galaxy—more hidden Forts, perhaps, or a consortium of Old-Timers who have realized the truth about the fate awaiting us all. (Could hope possibly lie at the heart of his actions?)

Mercenary, Fort, First Prime, fugitive . . . No number of spies can tell us who Imre Bergamasc is now. Once declared to be anything other than a decent man, he remains changeable, unpredictable, and chaotic. That fatal flaw may yet be the undoing of all his plans. Until history has relegated him to the dusty drawer of oblivion, until his name is forgotten along with all who knew him, and until his deeds become mere footnotes in the vast list of humanity's great works, he remains a threat to everyone, including himself.

Imre Bergamasc is his own worst enemy.

The feeling, I suspect, is mutual.

THIS IMPOSSIBLE DREAM

> *If each . . . could but be housed in separate identities, life would be relieved of all that was unbearable; the unjust might go his way, delivered from the aspirations and remorse of his more upright twin; and the just could walk steadfastly and securely on his upward path, doing the good things in which he found his pleasure, and no longer exposed to the disgrace and penitence by the hands of this extraneous evil.*
>
> **—Robert Louis Stevenson**

The sky changed no less than three times on the way to the detective's office. First, as she stepped out the front door of the Iceberg building, a line of bright blue stars swayed erratically across the sky, casting sprays of sharply defined shadows down the length of Rammas Street. That wasn't a good start; blue days always put her on edge. She took every step in a hyperaware state, gaze directed down at the cracked pavement and mindful of every angular movement in her peripheral vision. The skin of her folded hands looked plastic, as though it might crinkle and peel away at any moment.

Fortunately the blue stars didn't last long. Magnificent, twisting nebulae, painted a thousand shades of orange and yellow, crossed the sky as she boarded the bus and headed downtown. As lulled by the aerodynamic vehicle's rumbling as by the warm light, she let herself be rocked ten blocks through the bumblebee traffic, thinking of anything other than why she was on the bus and not off to work, where she would normally be going were this a normal day.

It was anything but a normal day. The photograph of her sister, which she'd left lying facedown on her bedside table, had turned itself over during the night. On seeing it, she had thrust the portrait deep into her calfskin shoulder bag and resolved that the time had come, finally, to do something about it.

She almost failed to notice the single, lambent gem that had replaced the nebulae by the time she left the bus. Her attention was on the brownstone two doors up, whose address matched the one she'd torn from the telephone directory that morning. Only as she approached its glass double doors did she register how her hair turned golden in the soft light, making her look like something from a crime movie. How many posters for such movies had she walked past in her life? Hundreds probably, all featuring a busty blonde and a private dick. Almost she turned and walked away. She didn't like men looking at her like that.

The door was stiff. She shouldered her way through and into a stuffy, tiled foyer. A building directory on the wall to her left confirmed that she'd read the address correctly. She pressed the call button for an elevator, and concentrated on the conveyance's stained brass fittings as it carried her unevenly to the third floor. The farther up she went in the building, the more it stank of cigarette smoke and sweat— and something worse beneath it all. Not booze or rot, but definitely something corrupt, as though too many dark secrets had been carried along the same route as she was taking, indelibly tainting the air itself. Such corruption probably came with the territory.

The doors slid open. The elevator had stopped half a foot short of the floor, so she had to step up into a reception area from which three offices radiated. The carpet was green, darkest around the wooden baseboard and worn almost grey elsewhere.

The middle-aged receptionist's eyebrows rose at the interruption. "Yes?"

"Good morning." She held her shoulder bag close to her stomach like a shield. "I'm here to see Mr. Grimes."

The receptionist's cool iron gaze darted over her diary and back up again, knowing what it would find there before making the gesture. "You don't have an appointment."

"I'm hoping he can find time for me."

"Is this regarding a matter he's working on at the moment?"

"No." She wondered how few matters it took to end up in such a dive. "I'm a new customer."

At the word "customer," the receptionist's interest was kindled, although she tried to hide it. "Take a seat. I'll check to see if Mr. Grimes is available for new clientele at the moment."

"I understand."

"What name shall I give?"

"I can't tell you that." There was a moment's awkwardness. She twisted the calfskin of her bag so tightly she feared it might tear between her fingers. She would say nothing more. Of that she was determined. But it took all her willpower to stare down the receptionist's disapproval—which came with an amused edge, as though she thought she'd heard it all before—and turn away to take a seat. Three straight-backed chairs formed a triangle in the room's only bare corner. She took the one closest to the elevators.

There was a button intercom on the desk, but the receptionist forwent that option. Rising from her creaking seat, she walked briskly to the second office door from the right and tapped discreetly on the frosted glass. At a grunted monosyllable from within, she slipped inside and closed the door behind her. Black letters on the translucent glass spelled "M. Grimes, P.I." in strident block capitals.

The silhouette of the receptionist was faintly visible, like a shade in fog. Another joined it. They danced together for a moment, keeping time with a conversation that wasn't quite entirely inaudible, then the door was opening, and the gatekeeper emerged.

"Mr. Grimes will see you now."

A wave of dizziness passed through her. It was all she could do to stand and continue as she had planned: to walk into this stranger's office and tell him her troubles. The ones she could part with, anyway. Her sister. Her name. Not the dreams. Not the radio. The receptionist was looking at her strangely, and she wondered what could possibly be showing on her face. Fear? Anxiety? Dread?

"Thank you, Bea," called a rough male voice as she passed through the door and entered the office. He wasn't a big man, for which she was grateful, and his grey suit was rumpled. His hat rested on the "in" tray on the left-hand corner of his desk. The hair it normally hid was greyer than she had expected, almost white, and slicked tight across his scalp with Brylcreem, but his grip, when he leaned over the desk to shake her hand, was vigorous. He smelled like the building he worked in: of cigarettes and corruption. Like attracts like, she thought; or one begat the other.

Grimes smiled as she sat on the edge of a leather chair that, matching its sibling to her right, formed a set of five with those in the reception area. His chair looked more comfortable than hers, and thoroughly lived-in. A cigarette sent up a lazy banner of smoke from its perch in a glass ashtray near his left hand. Two parallel silver pens formed a perfect right angle with the base of his cobra-necked lamp.

"Mr. Grimes—"

"Call me 'Mac.' "

Nervousness, and perhaps a hint of disappointment, made her irritable. "Must I?"

"We'll get along much better if you do."

"It's not my intention to get along with you, Mr. Grimes. I want you to help me find someone."

His smile didn't slip a notch, but he did lean back in his seat and reach for the cigarette. Exhaling through his nose, he studied her through the silken miasma for a long moment.

"Why me?"

The question threw her. Not *Who* or *What for*, which she had expected. "I saw your advertisement."

"Where?"

She tugged the bag from her shoulder and reached inside. Her fingers brushed the photograph of her sister, but she ignored that for the moment in order to show him the fragment of telephone directory that had caught her eye that morning. The ad was simple, little more than a name, telephone number, and street address. She had been drawn to it by the border: a simple geometric pattern created from the letters *P* and *I*, which, combined with the utilitarian text, promised someone with a little more flair than the average private detective. Perfect, she had thought, for someone with more than the average problem.

Hope was a fine thing, frequently dashed. She offered him the fragment as answer to his question. He took it, looked along his nose at it as though he'd never seen it before, and then gave it back to her with a wink.

"You like puns too? That was my idea," he said, taking the last drag from his cigarette and butting it out in the ashtray. "Best ten bucks I ever spent."

She didn't know what he was talking about and was determined not to pursue the subject any further. "The person I want you to find—"

"Let me guess. Some guy who gambled your college fund away? Or a producer who promised you a part and didn't deliver? A pretty girl like you can get into all sorts of trouble if she's not careful."

"It's not like that. I know how to look after myself."

He reached into a drawer and pulled out a soft pack of cigarettes. He flipped one out with a well-practiced gesture, lit it with a Zippo lighter, and pointed it at her like a sixth finger. "You must be in some kind of trouble, lady, if you're talking to the likes of me."

She looked down, angry at herself for letting him focus on her an accusatory malaise he clearly felt for the world in general. The corner of the photo peeked out at her from the bag. She pulled it out, smoothed it on her knee, and gave it to him. "This is who I'm looking for."

He stared at the picture for a long moment. No posturing or playacting this time, just puzzlement. "This is—"

"Not me, Mr. Grimes. That's my sister. We're identical twins."

He nodded, took another look, and pulled an appreciative face. "Nice. When did she go missing?"

"A week ago."

"Do you think she's been kidnapped?"

"I—" She hesitated. "I don't think so."

"That makes sense. If it was me, I'd never break the set." His leer repulsed her, but she was glad to see his mind working, not just his mouth. "Could be an accident. I can check the hospitals for a Jane Doe with amnesia, see if that turns up anything."

"Does that sort of thing really happen?"

"Only when it's convenient for the missing party. Never fools anyone for long." He ran his right index finger along the edge of the photo as though testing its sharpness. "Did she say or do anything unusual before she left? If she left a message of some kind, that'd make it real convenient."

She shook her head, feeling a flush creep up her neck. The smoke was making her dizzy again.

His eye was incisive. "Are you feeling all right, Miss . . . ?"

"No. I don't feel all right, and I won't until my sister is found. She took—" She swallowed a sudden rush of nausea. "She took something very important to me."

"And you want it back." He nodded. "Sounds like a hundred stories I've heard before. You, like everyone else, want a happy ending." He rested the cigarette in the ashtray and pulled a notepad from the drawer. Picking up one of the reservoir pens, he uncapped it and paused with the nib hovering over the paper. "Let's start with the basics. I'm going to need a name. Yours or hers—take your pick. I'm easy."

"I can't," she said.

"Why not? There's no family in this city without a scandal or two hidden in the closet. Whoever you are, you can rely on me to be discreet."

"It's not like that," she said again.

"Then what is it like?" He tapped the nib to paper, releasing a bubble of ink that was immediately absorbed. "Come on, lady. You gotta give me something. Cruising the streets for nameless blondes is why my last gal left me."

"Mr. Grimes—"

"Mac."

"—please don't mistake my inability for unwillingness. If I could give you my name, I would." She took a deep breath. "The reason I can't is because she has taken it."

His gaze lifted from her cleavage, and his face assumed a blank expression. "Who took what?"

"My sister," she said, feeling like an idiot saying it aloud but refusing to balk now. "She took my name with her, wherever she went."

"Your twin sister took your name."

"That's what I keep saying, Mr. Grimes."

The pad went onto the table, and the pen, re-capped, followed. "Not 'took' as in she assumed it. She actually stole it, somehow?"

"I presume so."

"You don't sound so sure of that. I'd have thought that was something you'd remember." His expression hadn't changed. "Can you, ah, tell me the circumstances in which it went missing?"

"That's the odd thing. I can't. I woke up a week ago and it was gone. So was she. The two must be connected, don't you think?"

"I don't know what to think." He leaned forward and rested the weight of his upper body on his elbows. The desk made a hollow sound, like a laugh at a funeral. "Do you?"

"I think you don't believe me."

"I never believe my clients."

"Does that mean I am one?"

"You don't need a PI, lady. You need a shrink."

"Are you saying I'm crazy?"

"You're original, at least. That sometimes don't sit so well with the sane folk." His face broke with a smile that had a crooked cast to it. He eased back in his seat and reached into a lower drawer with his right hand, this time to produce a bottle of whiskey and two shot glasses. He poured a pair of well-practiced measures and offered her one. "You call me Mac like everyone else, or you'll be 'dollface' every time you drop by. And I'm paid by the day, plus expenses."

She picked the shot off the table and held it for a moment. The glass was oily and the liquor golden in the light coming through the blinds behind him. With one smooth motion, she cocked the glass and tipped its contents down her throat. The whiskey burned as hot as it shone in the light, and she closed her eyes for a second, dissolving without pleasure in the sensation.

"That's the last drink we'll ever share, Mac," she said. "While I'm paying your expenses, our relationship will be strictly business."

"Nothing friendly about drinking," he said with a weary kind of defiance. Nevertheless, he put the bottle away and picked up the pen again. "You'll find I don't do anything less than one hundred percent, when I set my mind to it."

"I trust your mind is on my problem now."

"Let's just say I'm thinking about the money. Why don't you tell me when exactly you think this . . . theft occurred? We'll work from there."

Her hands eased their grip on the shoulder bag, and she felt a tiny knot of tension unwind. Grimes had doubted her and cast aspersions on her sanity, but he hadn't turned her away. She wasn't alone in this anymore. That helped— more than any nebulous hope that the situation might be reversed.

She started at the beginning, at the moment she'd woken from a nightmare convinced that the world had changed, that something important was missing. She didn't tell him about the nightmare itself. He didn't ask, and she was glad for that. Curiosity danced in his eyes like a candle flame, but the dream was one thing she wouldn't talk of. It made her sweat to think of it even now, in Grimes's unhappy office, with street noise coming through the gap of the partly open window and his starch-collared receptionist just outside. She rarely had violent dreams—erotic ones either, for that matter—and to have the two combined, not just once, but almost every night since, was as upsetting as the mystery of her sister.

She kept a photo by her bed, and she had woken from the dream to find it staring at her with eyes cool and blue and cheerful facade intact. There were photos of the same woman scattered all through her apartment, alone and with other people she knew. There was even a photo of the woman with her parents. The woman was smiling, happy, and utterly unfamiliar. She didn't remember having a sister, but who else could it have been? The woman in the photos certainly wasn't *she*, although there was no disputing the resemblance. A sister she had somehow forgotten.

Her phone hadn't rung that morning, and no one had come to the door. That her name had gone missing with the forgotten twin sister took some hours to realize. Not just her name, but her identity too. On arriving for work—at the Grand Central Railway Company, where she maintained the clocks necessary to keep the city's trains on time—she was told she hadn't ever worked there. That was patently absurd, but no amount of protestation could convince anyone otherwise. People she had worked with for years were gone. Their replacements regarded her with puzzlement, then hostility, as she pleaded with them.

"Just give us your name," they mocked her. "If you really have worked here, you'll be in our files."

She couldn't comply with that simple request, so, stumped and humiliated, she had been forced to leave. There were no friends or bosses to appeal to. They were all gone, along with her name.

Outside the company headquarters, the sky had been a bright and painful green. She had shaded her eyes with her pocketbook and hoped the tears didn't show. Walking the streets with no destination, she had prayed for something, anything, to descend upon her and make everything right again.

Her prayers went unanswered, and she returned to her apartment that evening no closer to a resolution.

Darkness fell earlier than usual, and the stars seemed particularly restless that night. She lay in the dark with the radio on, barely hearing the actors' voices. She had been looking forward to Miram Graces's new version of *Brag Me a Crime*, but he had called in sick, and his part was being read by a substitute who didn't thrill her in the slightest. News reports of a union blockade of the docks registered only distantly; the death of a notable sportsman likewise. Someone was playing a gramophone too loudly across the way, and the words filtered through her emptiness in a way she couldn't immediately explain:

> *Listen, babe.*
> *Say you got no one*
> *Tonight.*

She wept when the song was finished and went to sleep with her pillow over her head.

That night, she dreamed she was a soldier wearing armor and holding a massive rifle in both hands. Wild colors danced across her vision, as though she were hallucinating, but the colors contained information about terrain, targets, and fellow troopers that prompted her to move in swift, decisive ways. Her gun pounded in her arms, convulsing her whole body. Distant figures jerked and fell to the ground. A bright flash lit up the world, and she was flying, flying . . .

Then she was back in her room, and the night had taken the form of an enormous black man who was pressing her down on the bed with crushing weight. Her legs were spread, and he moved forcefully between them. "I've been waiting here," he said to her in a voice like air over a catacomb. "Welcome to your savior." She cried out, frightened and unsure whether what she felt so intensely was pleasure or pain or a mixture of the two. He reared back like a god, and she looked down at herself in horror. Blackness was spreading across her pale skin like ink, turning her stomach and thighs as dark as his.

She screamed and woke. The photo of her sister mocked her from the bedside table. Thus ended the first full day of their estrangement.

"Photos probably won't tell me anything about her whereabouts and motives," Grimes said, underlining on the pad before him the few salient facts she had been able to provide. The office was becoming warm as the day grew older. She wished he would turn on the ceiling fan. "Have you asked anyone else about her? Friends or family is where I'd start."

"I tried," she said. "I rang everyone I know, but they didn't answer their telephones. So I went to see them, one after another. None of them were home. I sat outside one of their apartments, waiting for her to come back. I waited a whole day. The police eventually moved me on. The landlord had called in a complaint. I spoke to him. He said—" She became aware that she was talking too quickly again, and forced herself to slow down. The infuriation and shame of that encounter was still vivid in her mind. "He said my friend had moved on without giving notice or leaving a forwarding address. She owed him a month's rent. He claimed not to know me, at first, but then he thought he could get the money out of me, and I ran."

"It ended there? You weren't arrested or anything?"

"No."

"There might still be an incident report on file. I'll check that, if you don't mind."

She shook her head, knowing that she was under the spotlight too, not just her sister.

"Do you think this is some kind of conspiracy?" he asked her with a shrewdness in his eyes that she both respected and resented.

"I'm not paranoid, if that's what you're thinking."

"Don't worry about what I'm thinking," he said, exposing even, nicotine-stained teeth in something that might have been a smile. "What you're thinking is the issue here. You gotta admit this looks a little queer from the outside. If someone wanted to put you away for a while, in a sanitarium for your own well-being, say, they could mount a convincing case."

Her heart went cold at the thought. "Why would anyone want to do that?"

"I'm not saying anyone does. I'm saying they could, is all." He glanced down at the pad, and she could practically hear his brain shuffling through potential questions, looking for anything he had forgotten. He slipped the cap back on the pen and returned it where it belonged, in perfect alignment with its neighbor, then glanced up at her with something new in his eyes.

"Tell me about Imre Bergamasc."

She stared back at him, detecting a change in mood that made her think twice as hard about the question as she would normally have. Was he nervous, and if so, why? When she answered she was completely certain, within the limits of her memory, that what she said was the truth.

"I've never heard of him. Should I have?"

"I guess not." He searched her face in return. "I have another client, you see, another missing person case, and it's starting to look just as impossible as yours. Call me a fool, but I thought for a second they might be connected."

"Sorry."

His disappointment was palpable. "Thanks at least for not calling me a fool." He stood and came around the desk. His leather shoes squeaked as he walked. "Well, it's nearly noon, and unless you intend to break your no-drinking rule with this old gumshoe, I suggest you find somewhere else for lunch."

She felt drained and oddly reluctant to leave. Unburdening herself of her problems had exhausted her, and she was unwilling to reassume their weight so soon. Where would she go? What would she do? She hadn't thought beyond that moment and had, perhaps, naïvely assumed that simply bringing someone else into the matter might be enough on its own to resolve her situation.

"Thank you," she said. "I'll do that. Will you tell me the moment you find anything?"

"You have my word," he said, "and I have your number. You can't get more of a guarantee than that."

She stood.

"Payment in advance," he added hopefully, "provides an even stronger incentive."

She ignored him.

The receptionist glanced up at them as the office door opened and returned pointedly to her typing. The clatter of keys followed them to the elevator, where he pushed the button for her and shook her hand.

"Be seeing you," he said, with a two-fingered salute to his right temple, "either way."

As the floor of the elevator carrying her dropped, she was struck by a sudden concern that some of the building's reek might have stuck to her. It was all she could perceive, in her nose, her lungs, and her thoughts. Instead of going home, she walked downtown and bought a hot dog from a street vendor. She ate just two bites, having lost her appetite along with her name, but the salty sourness of the meat successfully drove the sense memory of cigarettes and sweat—and the lingering burn of Grimes's whiskey—firmly from her mind.

The city streets were becoming busier. Honking cars vied with policemen and hawkers for attention. Lights flared and flashed. Well-dressed executives strode past the mumbling homeless with eyes carefully averted. Clusters of two or three swept by in animated conversation. Shopkeepers hosed down sidewalks, set tables for the lunchtime rush, and dusted mannequins. Men and women looked endlessly at watches as the sky turned unpredictably overhead.

She felt like an alien, and kept panic at bay only by the greatest effort of will.

Determined to think about neither Grimes nor her situation for a while, she stumbled at random into the city library, a vest edifice of marble and iron, seeking quiet and calm in the midst of the metropolis. It was busier than expected, thanks to an exhibition of ancient books that had attracted a small crowd. She thought about leaving but couldn't face the roar of the traffic again. Soon, despite herself, she was lost in an apparently endless series of fragile folios—not just from the dawn of civilization, but from darker hours when all hope of regaining the light of civilization seemed dead. She pored over yellowed novels, crumbling diaries, and fragmentary Bibles. Handwriting both strange and wonderful hinted at meanings beyond the words, at lives long lost and sometimes forgotten. Others possessed sources that were well documented and lived on in contemporary knowledge.

She walked slowly down the aisles and peered with interest into every protective glass case, feeling slightly voyeuristic yet fascinated by words intended for other eyes, human or divine.

"Pious work, yet perilous presumption, to change the old

and aging language of the world, to carry it back to infancy," wrote an ancient translator and Doctor of the Catholic Church, "for to judge others is to invite judging by all of them."

In particular, one book, filled with huge, ornate letters that were the work of zealous artists unknown, captured her attention. Reproduced pages had been laid out flat so they could be viewed individually, and she wondered at the perversely dedicated hands that had produced such a magnificent but self-defeating legacy. She could barely decipher a single letter.

It was called the Book of Kells. So she learned from a series of signs accompanying the open pages. The name sounded familiar. It must be famous, she supposed, to be displayed so prominently.

Barely had she begun reading the explanatory signs when a man strolled by, softly whistling a tune through his teeth. She froze, dismayed. The song was instantly recognizable, and it shattered the contemplative mood she had enjoyed since entering the library.

She lifted her head and turned around, but the man was too far away to call back, not without creating a scene. Questions haunted her: why that particular song, and why just then?

The taste of hot dog was growing stale in her mouth. There were no answers in the restored silence of the library, and there were none to be found in the musty tomes surrounding her. Turning her back on the Book of Kells, she headed for the exit.

She bought a newspaper and stared blankly at the headlines while riding the bus back home. The ongoing blockade of the docks was increasing tensions all across the city. Several acts of arson had been reported. A businessman called Mr. Cambersea had been kidnapped and held for a possible ransom. The mayor had called for calm. Above an ad for a new brand of perfume—Sanctified Obsession—

the chief of police spoke ominously of suspicions that a well-known mafia hit man had broken the blockade. Why Anthony Archer, better known to his mob contacts as Rosy Tony, had chosen to enter the city illegally at that moment in its history was unknown to anyone but himself. He had a gruesomely romantic reputation for leaving a single long-stemmed rose on the body of every person he killed. Aces Barr, a gambler of uncertain reputation, had already been found dead with the trademark rose. No one doubted that there would be more deaths.

As she flipped one broadsheet page over another, she caught a stocky man farther up the bus looking in her direction. He glanced away too quickly, and she knew that he had been watching her. Because she was blond and sitting alone? Ordinarily she would hope not, but at that moment she preferred that to the alternative.

She kept looking at the paper, ignoring the words on the page and watching him carefully out of the corner of her eye. He wore an ill-fitting steel blue suit with a matching fedora and black tie. The suit's lines made him look impossibly broad across the torso, but the way his collar cut into his neck suggested that the bulk was real, and much of it was muscle. His hands were square and thick-fingered. Black hair poked out from the bottoms of his cuffs. Oddly, the little finger on his right hand was missing. He was clean-shaven but already sporting a five o'clock shadow. The time by the bus's clock was barely half past one.

She caught him looking at her twice more, fleeting, hooded glances that did little to put her mind at ease. They were hardly enough to cry foul, though, and she told herself to be careful. Grimes had wondered if she was paranoid. Indulging excessive fears was bound to make her so.

She forced herself to read. "Do you believe in heaven?" an advertisement asked her in bold lettering. "A grave waits for you at heaven's gate," it went on. "A doorway to heaven . . . your heaven . . . dead heaven . . ."

She screwed the paper up with both fists without seeing what the advertisement was for. The words filled her with an unaccountable dread, even though she didn't know what they meant. It felt like the paper had been talking directly to her, impossible though that had to be. Perhaps she *was* going crazy.

The stocky man stood up, and she physically jerked in her seat. He wasn't coming for her, though. He was simply getting off the bus. Her ears burned as he brushed by her and stepped onto the curb two stops before hers. The doors shut with a hiss. She watched the man walking down the street with a swing in his step as the bus rumbled past him. He had already lit a cigarette. He didn't look up.

Her brow ached from frowning, and the tendons of her neck were as tight as bowstrings. If Grimes had appeared and offered her another drink that second, she wouldn't have hesitated, even though it was far too early in the day for one drink, let alone two. She felt stretched thin and on the verge of tearing. Bad enough that she had lost her sister and her name. The thought of losing her mind as well was unbearable.

Clutching at normality, she stopped at the grocers on the way home and bought ingredients for a large, healthy dinner. Eating well, even though she was alone, was important, and she had subsisted for the last week only on what had been at hand. Her cupboards were bare of anything but scraps, and a raw heat that was at least partly hunger burned in her belly. Now that Grimes was on the case, she could begin looking after herself again. There would be no use in solving the mystery if she was too much of a wreck to get on with her life afterward.

Her apartment was sunlit and warm when she came home. A trio of bright yellow lights hung close together in the sky outside, casting thick-edged shadows across the room and sending dust motes dancing. She opened the drapes as wide as they would go and raised the windows an inch to let in some fresh air. Turning on the radio for background noise—tuned carefully to a station with no more music than the E. G. Mamba's McRib jingle—she set about preparing meat loaf with sweet potato puffs and a lettuce, celery and grape salad, with a Queen Mary sponge cake for dessert. It didn't have to take all afternoon, but she was in no hurry. The familiar routines of chopping, mixing, whipping, and baking pleasantly occupied her mind, and the homey smells coming from the oven touched a deeper part of her still, reminding her that even in a world where confusion and uncertainty reigned, there were still small things that could bring her comfort.

The night was growing cold when she laid out the components of the meal on the table and took off her apron. A cool breeze had come up, and she shut the windows one by one. On closing the last, she stopped, still with her hand on the latch, peering suspiciously into the roadway below. A man was standing in the entrance to the alleyway across Rammas Street. He was wearing a hat, and he seemed to be watching the entrance to the Iceberg building.

He was solid and muscular, and his suit was too small. Even from that angle, he looked like the man from the bus.

She forced herself to move casually away from the window, leaving the blind open as though she had seen nothing out of the ordinary. Her hands were shaking. She sat at the table, all appetite gone, and wondered what to do. She could shut the curtains and hide like a mouse in its hole, but that thought rankled more than it would have just hours earlier. She had taken matters into her own hands by approaching Grimes, and that had been an important step forward. She wasn't helpless and wouldn't give up her life to fears either real or imagined.

Keeping well out of sight, she pulled on an overcoat and hid her hair beneath a nondescript scarf. Leaving the food cooling on the table, she eased her way out of the apartment and took the stairs to the ground floor.

There was a trade entrance at the back of the building. She had never used it, but she knew where the super kept the key. Tugging at the stiff hinges, she peered into the alley outside and found it empty. She left the door ajar behind her and walked carefully around trash cans and piles of rotting boxes. The stench was foul but not unbearable. From the street ahead came the occasional flash and roar of cars going by. It wasn't Rammas Street; the alley ran parallel to the street she normally stepped onto when exiting her building. The man watching the entrance therefore wouldn't see her when she stepped into the open. Her mental road map of the area didn't include all the alleys and darkened ways, paths she would never normally have trodden on her own, but she could guess where they led. Moving hurriedly and keeping her eyes open for more sinister characters, she took a wide, digressive route around the man observing the Iceberg building, in order to come up on him from behind.

The stars spun above her as she inched around the last corner.

He wasn't where she had last seen him. The lane opened onto Rammas Street unimpeded. In the flash and blur of headlights, she saw no sign that he had ever been there.

"Looking for someone, dollface?"

She spun around. A dark figure stepped out of the shadows, bringing with it a whiff of cigarette smoke. She backed one step away, then stopped dead as the glowing-eye ember came up and cast a bright flare across the man's face.

"Grimes?"

"You expected someone else?"

"No—I—" She fumbled for words, confused by his unexpected materialization. "I saw someone watching my building—you, I presume?" she added, even though the resemblance was nonexistent.

"As a general rule, I don't stake out my clients. Besides: you didn't give me your address." He cocked his head across the street. "This is actually where you live? You're not messing with me?"

She didn't doubt that he could have obtained her address had he desired to and didn't let him turn the questioning back on her. "Tell me who he was—the man watching my home."

"Just some guy I was tailing."

"Is that all you're going to tell me?"

"I'm not sure yet. Client confidentiality, and all that."

"I *am* your client."

"You're *one* of them."

She studied the deep, orange-lit lines of his face as he sucked the last lungful of smoke from the cigarette. He dropped the butt to the ground. The toe of his shoe made a harsh, scraping noise, twisting the ember out.

The pounding of her heart had eased to a steady, driving pulse.

"Who was he, Grimes?" she asked in a low voice.

He moved in closer. "A thug by the name of Serge Maim. His friends call him the Crab."

"What was he doing here?"

"That's what I was hoping to find out. He was obviously on a job; that much I worked out. He was settling in for a long night." Grimes indicated a small pile of cigarette butts by the corner, where Maim had been standing. "We both heard you coming. Those heels of yours are as subtle as a shotgun in a registry office. He split before I could follow. Then you appeared, and I thought to myself: well, two and two ain't always four. Perhaps I ought to stick around to see what it comes to this time."

Her mind flashed through a dozen scenarios. One: Maim had been watching her apartment in the employ of persons unknown, keeping track of her movements and reporting when she came and went. Two: Maim had been pursuing her for his own ends and had been waiting for her lights to go out so he could move in on her. Three: Grimes was lying, and Maim didn't exist at all. The thug was a cover for whatever game he was playing, and she had walked right into it.

A car went by with its radio blaring. A snippet of song caught her ear:

"—this point of view appeals to me—"

She shivered. The night was cold, and she hadn't done up her coat. She hugged herself tightly and wondered if she hadn't inadvertently made things more complicated, not less, by involving someone else in her problems.

"Math is really not my specialty," he prompted her.

"I've told you everything I know."

"If that's true, dollface, it'd be the first time in history."

Putting aside her name, her sister, her job, and all her other worries, just for the moment, she had only one question that really mattered.

"Am I in danger, Mr. Grimes?"

He shrugged. "That depends on what you've done."

"Nothing. I swear it." She rubbed her temples with her left hand. His suspicion was relentless. Would he be so blatant about it if he was trying to gain her trust? "I'm going back inside," she said, "and you're coming with me. You're going to tell me about your other case."

Something crunched at the far end of the alley, where the gloom was deepest. Grimes stepped close and gripped her elbow tightly with his left hand. His right had slipped under his suit jacket, and stayed there.

"Okay," he whispered, "but we go in the front door, not back the way you came. We go in together, and we shut your blinds. I've got a reputation to think of."

Or a cover to maintain, she thought as the two of them walked out of the alley side by side, as close as lovers but a little too briskly to be entirely licit. Her neighbors were far from her mind. She glanced over her shoulder but saw no one visible standing in the shadows where they had been a moment before.

The smell of meat loaf hit her as she opened her apartment door. She had completely forgotten the meal she had cooked for herself.

"You really shouldn't have," Grimes said, as she hurried from window to window and finished the job on the drapes she had started earlier. The alley was still empty, but she knew better than to trust the evidence of her senses. When she turned back to the table, he was helping himself to a sweet potato puff. At least he'd removed his hat.

"I'll get you a plate," she said. "You can serve yourself."

That seemed to take him off guard, and she wondered if he had genuinely expected her to eat in front of him without making some kind of gesture. He removed his coat and laid it with his hat over the arm of her sofa, and with brisk, economical movements cut himself a slice of meat loaf from the baking dish, ladled on a small amount of salad, and replaced the puff he had stolen from her plate.

They sat opposite each other over their meals. Her appetite had not returned, but she knew she should try to force something down. The food sat heavily in her stomach, and again she surprised herself by wishing for some of Grimes's whiskey.

"No mirrors," he said through a mouthful of meat loaf. "This is the first dame's place I've ever been into that didn't have at least one in line of sight of the front door."

"I don't like them," she said. "Is this your brand of small talk?"

"Don't care for that either, huh?" He smiled. "The bathroom. There must be one in there, at least."

She shook her head and placed her knife and fork neatly across her half-empty plate. "Your other client, Mr. Grimes. That's what we're here to discuss."

"Only if you call me Mac. You keep forgetting that part of our arrangement."

"I fail to see why it's so important to you."

"Perhaps I was christened McGrimes."

"Were you?"

He shook his head. "It's from my first name."

She remembered the sign on his office door. M. GRIMES, it had said. That was as much as she cared to know. "Okay, Mac, tell me about your other client. Who is he—or she—when she's not paying your rent?"

"I don't know much. His name is Monsieur Li, and I've

never met him. I'm paid by wire and instructions come in the mail or by courier. He never uses the phone."

She imagined the world Grimes must inhabit, so she didn't feel asking, "Are you sure he's real?" was inappropriate.

Grimes shrugged and answered, "His money checks out."

"You must have taken it further than that."

"Oh, sure, but the man's a ghost. No one in Chinatown's ever heard of either him or the man he's looking for."

"How long have you worked for him?"

"One week."

He watched her as she absorbed that snippet of information. She kept her expression neutral. It might have been nothing more than a coincidence that the enigmatic Monsieur Li had hired Mac Grimes the very same day her sister had disappeared. Now that the case had led him right to her doorstep, a connection between the two cases wasn't out of the question.

"What have you managed to find out about this Inri whoever?"

"Imre Bergamasc." Again the disillusioned shrug. "He's a ghost too. Li's the one with the leads. Where he gets them from, I don't know, but I do as I'm told and check them out. A cigar importer; a nightclub; a sleazy dancer or two. I'm not saying the job doesn't have perks." He winked without humor. "The trouble is, the trail keeps growing cold."

"Cold how?"

"With a knife in its back kind of cold, or the like. Then late this afternoon a note arrives telling me to watch our friend the Crab, and here I am. Got any clues as to what that's all about?"

She had nothing. Every name he had mentioned was new to her. "Have you?"

His face became very serious. He leaned forward over his plate so his upper body was supported on his elbows and touched his fingertips together. His stare was disconcertingly direct.

"How many beds you got here?"

"That's none of your—"

"You don't need to answer. I know this kind of apartment. There's one bedroom through that door over there, and it's a small one. Enough room for a dresser, a cupboard, and a single mattress. A double, if you skip the dresser, but then you can't close the door. You'll note that the door is closed, and I bet you're not ever going to open it for me."

Her ears were burning. "You bet correctly."

"Don't think I'm angling for something well out of my league. I'm just asking because that sofa over there doesn't fold out into a bed. You mentioned in my office that you'd searched friends' places for your sister, but you never once mentioned that she had a place of her own. I assumed, therefore, that you berthed together. Now I see the place, I know I assumed wrong—unless you slept top to tail in that narrow bunk of yours, or were a lot friendlier than most sisters I know."

"If you're suggesting—"

"I don't know what I'm suggesting, dollface, but I'm getting that same feeling of chasing ghosts again." He leaned back and reached into his jacket for his cigarettes. He offered her one, and she shook her head. The complex aroma of burning tobacco and match smoke dispelled the homeliness she had tried so hard to restore by cooking.

She searched her memory while he smoked. It was true: she didn't know where her sister had lived. It had never even occurred to her to wonder. How was that possible when she spent the last week literally quartering the city, searching all the sprawling boroughs in the faint hope of stumbling across a clue? Shouldn't she have asked that question *first*?

"I rang a friend today," he said, dropping a finger of ash onto his plate. "Didn't mean anything by it. In my line of business, you've got to check every angle. He told me a bunch of stuff I'd never heard of before. He assures me it's genuine—sometimes things look like nonsense only because you're seeing them wrong—so I took notes and committed a few names to memory." He tapped his head with the filter of his cigarette. "I've got a good memory. It helps in my business. So does cultivating a good understanding of human psychology."

He leaned forward again. The smoke curled between them like a question mark.

"Have you ever heard of a Joseph Capgras? That's one of the names I recall." He raised a hand to cut her off as she went to answer. "No, you won't know him—or if you do, it might explain a lot. He's some fancy doctor from a whole other place. He has a syndrome named after him: Capgras syndrome, which is when a patient believes that a close relative or spouse has been replaced by an identical-looking impostor. Ever heard of that? I hadn't either. There are other syndromes like it, I'm told. Having a subjective double, say—when a person believes there is a doppelganger roaming the streets, getting up to mischief. Or clonal pluralization of the self. How's that for a mouthful? That's when you think multiple, identical copies of you exist, leading their own lives."

He drew on the cigarette. "The point is, I guess, that none of these impostors and doubles and misidentifications is real. All the shrinks like Joseph Capgras and my friend will tell you that, anyway. I don't think any one of them ever considered the possibility that what their patients tell them might be true. The professionals couldn't cope with that. That's where laymen like me have a role to play. My job is to know enough about people to tell when they're telling the truth about what's bothering them and find a way to put it right.

"I think *you're* telling the truth," he said to her, "and up until tonight I thought the best way to put it right was to show you, firmly but kindly, that your truth was all in your head. Now, I'm not sure it's so simple. Truth takes lots of different forms, and mine is this: you see one ghost, you assume you're dreaming. When ghosts start multiplying, you don't pinch yourself. You get an exorcist."

"I don't believe in the supernatural," she said.

"Vice versa too, I expect." He stubbed out the cigarette with bent-thumbed finality. "You'll take my meaning regardless, I hope."

She did, and she had tried to make light of his long declaration, but it hadn't worked, and for a long moment she could think of nothing to say in response. She found herself liking M. Grimes, despite his rough edges. The more he knew about the case, the less he hid behind innuendo and tough talk. He might actually be able to interest a gal, she thought, if she could see past the exotic dancers and strained analogies—and if she was serious about telling him everything.

"Would you think it strange," she asked him, hesitantly, "if I said that I'd been hearing the same song over and over? On the radio mainly, but other places also," she added, thinking of the man whistling in the library that afternoon. "It's like it's—yes, exactly like it's haunting me."

He stared at her, long and hard, as though she had called him a foul name.

"I feel stupid even mentioning it," she stammered, "but given the topic of our conversation—"

" 'You dream of something,' " he said, " 'like I dreamed of you.' "

The tablecloth bunched under her hands. "You too?"

He was suddenly on his feet. "To answer your question, dollface: yes, I would think it strange." He stared down at her with a harsh expression. "Suspicious, even."

The legs of her chair scraped across the floorboards as she rose to meet the accusation in his eyes. "What exactly do you mean by that?"

"I don't know. You tell me."

"You want me to read your mind?"

"Isn't that what you're doing?" His right index finger jabbed at her. "Tell me how else you could know about that damned song."

She was startled by the suddenness of his temper. "If you're accusing me of something, something real—"

"I ain't accusing anyone," he said, turning abruptly to scoop up his coat and hat. "I'm leaving."

"If you think this is some kind of trick—"

The door slammed shut in her face. Shocked by the sudden turn the evening had taken, she considered pursuing him. The thunder of his footsteps rapidly receding up the corridor outside persuaded her of the poor sense in that. With an exasperated noise, she chained the door, turned back to the kitchen, and began cleaning up the mess.

Shortly after ten o'clock, she peered past the drapes and saw that the alleyway was still empty. The reassurance was hollow but welcome.

"Shadows and pain?" the radio squawked. "Depressed and alone?"

She turned it off and went to bed.

Her dreams, when they came, were of a world covered from pole to pole with smoke. Not cloud. There was nothing natural about the phenomenon. Bubbles of febrile, red heat bulged upward from fires below, burning unstoppably through fields, cities, and mountains. The sight numbed her; she could barely grasp the scale of such a catastrophe; yet she knew, somehow, that she had caused it. She was responsible. The death of the world lay heavily upon her shoulders.

Then the black man came again, and his whisper in her ear was insidious. "I would swim across oceans just to talk with you," he said as he pressed her back onto a bed of burning stone. "I would climb a tall mountain just to look at you." His physicality was overwhelming and threatened to subsume her in a world of ecstasy and agony. "I would walk out of heaven just to be with you." She screamed when he opened his eyes and she saw nothing but stars staring back at her.

She woke crouched upright in bed, gasping for air. She was wet with sweat all over her body, especially between her legs. Thrusting one hand underneath her, she found a hot and subtle slickness. Two fingers slid easily inside her and she ground her pubis against her palm, making an almost masculine sound as she climaxed.

When it was over, she sagged forward, drained, and drew her legs together against her chest. What was happening to her? What was wrong with her? She wasn't like this. It wasn't her fault. Her sister had ruined everything—doppelganger, dream, or delusion, whichever she turned out to be.

She lurched onto her side, remembering the voice of the black man in her dream. *I would walk out of heaven . . .* That reminded her of the ad she had read in the paper that afternoon. *A grave waits for you at heaven's gate . . .* Were her paranoid fantasies becoming internally consistent?

Knowing that sleep was beyond her, she reached out and turned on her reading lamp. The sudden glare revealed the tangled mess of her bedsheets, which she straightened automatically before lying back down. She didn't realize that she had looked for her sister's photo on the bedside table until she saw that it was gone. In its place was a scrap of curled paper. She reached out and picked it up with tentative fingers.

It was Grimes's advertisement, the one she had torn from the telephone directory the previous morning. She had underlined his name and address in pencil. M. Grimes, Private Investigator. The border that had caught her eye marched with geometric precision around the text, and she studied it now with a frown. What had he said about it?

You like puns too? That was my idea.

The letters *P* and *I* marched around the border, angular and blocky. She could see now how the letters were sometimes rotated, so the *P* became a *d*. The *I* was unchanged, making *PI* effectively *ID*. That, she supposed, was where the pun lay: she was a woman who had lost her identity, and he was a private investigator who had made that word an essential part of his advertisement.

Her frown deepened as her eyes traced further permutations of the letters. They weren't just rotated, but reflected as well. A reflected *P* meant nothing, the *I* again remained constant, and all the *d*'s became *b*'s. *IB*, while not a word, could be initials.

Imre Bergamasc.

You like puns too?

She wondered if he really believed that an accident of design had brought him two clients in one week. More likely he was just being flip, talking because he liked the sound of his own voice. Later, when the cases had started overlapping, then the strange case of the song—which she still couldn't quite believe, and had begun to wonder if it could be trick on *his* part, to throw her off guard—what had he thought then? He hadn't seemed to be taking it lightly when he had stormed out.

She rubbed the scrap of paper between her fingers. It had ended up by her bed through mysterious means. She hadn't put it there. Like her sister's photo, it had appeared there while she slept. It was as though someone was trying to tell her something, but she couldn't imagine what—or how. Why slip into her bedroom at night and rearrange her personal effects when ringing her on the telephone or telling her face-to-face would be much simpler? The thought that someone was creeping around her apartment at night was so unreal and unlikely that it barely seemed possible, even if it did chill her to the bone.

She hadn't rung Grimes to make an appointment since she couldn't give his secretary her name. Now, though, under very different circumstances . . .

The possibility had hardly entered her mind when the telephone in her living room rang with a loud, startling jangle.

She answered it on the third ring.

"Dollface."

She collapsed into an armchair and put a hand over her face. "What do you want, Mac?"

"I want to know if I'm dreaming this."

She had been wondering the same thing. The room was dark. From the street below, she could hear muted shouting, as of a drunk staggering home alone, railing at the world. The cushions beneath her gave way in perfect accordance with the normal laws of physics—but how could he be calling her just when she had been thinking about him? It wasn't possible.

She could still smell the stink of cigarettes in the air.

"You're as awake as I am," she said.

"Excuse me for not finding that terribly reassuring." The noise of his sigh came clearly down the wire. "I ought to apologize for earlier. My temper got the better of me."

"Are you actually apologizing, or just acknowledging that you should?"

"Both, I guess. No, I don't guess; I am, positively. You've got a sharp ear, lady. You ought to be a lawyer."

"I'd be happy just to get my old life back. Is that going to happen anytime soon?"

He was silent for a long while. "It follows me everywhere, you know."

"The song?"

"No, a little black dog called Bertie."

She allowed him the retort. "Can you hear it now?"

"You know that ringing you get in your ears sometimes—after a loud bang or an explosion? Tinnitus?"

"I know what you mean." She wondered if he'd ever been in combat or merely knew people who had.

"That's exactly what this is like. It comes and goes, and although I can hear through it perfectly well, it never goes away. You say haunting; for me it's more like stalking."

"Is that what you're doing up so late?"

"It keeps me awake, yeah." He grunted. "What's your excuse?"

She didn't want to discuss her dreams with him. The savage excitement with which she had woken followed by her contemplation of him made her feel distinctly uncomfortable. "I don't sleep well anymore, either."

"Some pair we make. If we had any kind of style, we'd be at a dive somewhere, drowning our sorrows. Do you know the Crème Bar on Sigma Street?"

"You do remember, I hope, what I said about drinking on the job."

"Lady, it's unavoidable. Compulsory, even. No teetotaler lasts more than a day in my line of work."

"You sound completely sober to me."

"Not for want of trying."

She heard two sudden sounds from his end of the line. The first was a faint smash, as of glass shattering, followed by the distinctive creak of his office chair. She pictured him sitting suddenly forward at his desk, listening carefully.

"Mac—"

"Cigars," he said with his mouth pressed close to the receiver. "Remember."

Then the line clicked dead.

She jiggled the receiver, but got only the dial tone. He had hung up. She raced back into the bedroom and returned with the ad. When she dialed his number, it was busy. She glared at the tiny speaker, as though she could force herself down the wire by nothing more than willpower, and then firmly replaced the handset.

She dressed quickly and locked the door behind her as she left.

A Gem Cab stopped at her hail forty feet up Rammas Street. She gave the driver Grimes's address and told him to hurry. The name on the driver's taxi license, S. Mareri, conjured images of unknown shores and dangerous journeys, and she concentrated on that rather than what she might find at the end of her own brief voyage. She wasn't armed; she hadn't called the police; she had no idea what to expect. She was supposed to be the one in need, not the other way around.

Grimes's building was dark when they arrived. The front door was shut. She instructed the driver to drop her off around the corner, and paid him with a five. He said he'd wait a minute or two, just in case she needed a ride back. The late-night silence of the city was profound, and she could tell that he was worried on her behalf. If he wanted to stick around, she would let him.

Remembering what Grimes had said about her heels, she slipped her shoes off before getting out of the car. On stockinged feet with the shoes in one hand, she ran lightly around the corner and along the sidewalk. The sky was restless. Twisting sheets of faint white stars swirled back and forth above her, too faint to cast a shadow but distracting against the blackness of eternity. The air smelled electric, as though a storm was coming.

The door to Grimes's building was unlocked. She took a deep breath and slipped inside.

Both elevator doors were closed. She tiptoed past them to the stairs and ascended to the third floor quickly and quietly. There was no sound at all apart from her breathing. The landing on the third floor was as empty as the foyer below, and she took a moment there to calm the beating of her heart. It could be nothing, she told herself, and she would be pleased if she did find that she was jumping at shadows. She wouldn't be angry at Grimes for making her feel like a fool. Much.

She eased the stairwell door open and peered into the reception area. Fragments of broken glass were scattered across the floor like tiny, deadly stars. The source of the glass was a vase that had been knocked or thrown off its pedestal behind the secretary's desk. It had hit the floor and shattered into a thousand pieces. She slipped her shoes back on so she wouldn't cut herself on the jagged splinters. They crunched under her heels no matter how carefully she tried to step.

Grimes's office door hung slightly ajar. She could see nothing through its frosted glass. Fearing that it might burst open at any moment, she put her hand on the handle, gripped tightly, and pushed the door aside.

A sweep of stars chose that moment to cross the night

sky, sending a band of silver light across the room. It looked empty, at first, and only a single boardroom chair tipped on its side spoke of anything untoward. She took a step inside, feeling the lack of life within and knowing that she, at least, was safe. Whatever had happened there was long resolved, and her only task lay in reconstructing those events and working out what they meant.

She straightened the chair. Grimes's desk might have looked perfectly ordinary at a casual glance, but she remembered how particular he had been about the placement of his pens. They were out of alignment, which was an odd note but not necessarily alarming. None of the cupboards appeared to have been disturbed. His phone was off the hook, buzzing quietly to itself. Whoever had broken the vase and interrupted him didn't appear to have searched the place. If they hadn't done that, could they have had any real harm in mind . . . ?

She came around the desk to check the drawers and found him sprawled on the floor with a bullet hole through his left shirt pocket. His right knee was raised as though caught in the act of trying to stand. His eyes were open and staring at her in surprise and disappointment. On the dark stain that had spread across his chest and stomach lay a single, long-stemmed rose.

She gasped and turned away, pressing a hand to her mouth to suppress any further sound. *Dead.* How was that possible? She had been talking to him just minutes ago, and argued with him only hours before that. He was supposed to be helping her, not getting himself killed.

A name flashed across her memory. Anthony Archer, the mafia hit man who had broken the blockade. *Rosy Tony.*

An emotion she had never felt followed it. Like grief but more powerful—almost a breed of rage—it gave her the strength to turn back around. This wasn't something she could run from. For Grimes's sake, she had to meet it head-on and find the answers herself. Why had he died? What had he learned that made his life forfeit? What connection did it have to her?

Grimes lay heavy and unmoving. He wasn't going to be answering any of her questions. She stepped over his outstretched leg and crouched over him. His wallet lay next to him, tugged out of his back pocket by hands unknown. She flipped it open and saw his driver's license photo staring back at her. Without thinking, she read his full name. MACABRE GRIMES. No wonder he had preferred Mac.

A bubble of dismay rose up in her chest. She forced it back down. His jacket lay next to him, and she searched through it with shaking hands. He had been carrying a loaded pistol, cigarettes, and a box of matches. The weapon was cool and heavy in her hands. She put it behind her, on the desk, where it would be within easy reach while she searched. She had never fired a gun before, but she understood the principles. Point and shoot. Couldn't be simpler.

Grimes's notepad wasn't on his body or on the desk. She turned away from his betrayed expression and checked the drawers, as she had originally intended to do. There were four. She knew one would contain a whiskey bottle and two glasses. There was still a smudge of lipstick on the one she had drunk from the previous day. The level in the bottle had dropped significantly since then. The other drawer on that side held stationery and a box of bullets. She came around the body to check the other two, and found in one a checkbook and several unpaid accounts, and in the other a box of cigars.

Cigars, he had said. *Remember.*

She reached into the drawer and pulled out the box. It was garishly ornate and didn't strike her as the sort of vice someone like Grimes would enjoy, even as a luxury. He had clearly preferred cigarettes, and they were the only kind of butts she had seen in his ashtray. Standing, she tipped open the lid and peered inside.

The box was half-full. She didn't know the brand but

recognized the rich smell of tobacco leaf that struck her nostrils. The cigars were fat and long and rolled lazily from one side to the other as she tipped the box. The box was lined with paper. She could see reversed writing pressed into that lining. Delicately, with great deliberation, she reached inside and pulled out a sheaf of closely written notes.

She had never seen Grimes's handwriting, but she recognized it instantly: neat and blocky. At the top of the first page was the name Imre Bergamasc, double underlined. Below that was a list of public institutions, all crossed out: Births, Deaths, and Marriages; hospitals; police and union records; etc. Clearly these were places where Grimes had tried to trace the name, without success. Then came a list of other individuals and businesses that seemed to bear no relation to each other, some crossed out, others untouched. The company that made the box, Beammer Cigars, was on the list, and so were Serge Maim and the mayor. She flipped forward, seeking an explanation or at least a source, and found a series of wafer-thin notes in another hand. "Take another look at Sir Becamé," said one; the notorious playboy Gram Becamé had indeed been on the list. Another said, "Try Mirage." That name too had appeared, along with a note in Grimes's hand saying "E=Embraces."

Notes from Monsieur Li, she guessed, giving Grimes leads and instructions, some left unresolved.

The last note said simply "2 a.m.," the time Grimes had hung up on her.

A trap, she thought. And he had fallen for it.

Maybe the song had distracted him. Maybe she had.

The last page in the sheaf was a complex family tree linking many of the names on the previous list. Some lines connecting them were made in triplicate, so they stood out boldly. Other lines were dotted, with the occasional question mark for emphasis. Many of the names were crossed out, with words like "burned," "missing" or "murdered" scribbled next to them. In the middle of them all was *Imre Bergamasc* again, utterly unconnected to anyone.

No wonder Grimes had been frustrated. The trail, if there was one, was both convoluted and truncated. She stared at it until her eyes watered. The picture wavered in front of her. Then she was crying for Grimes and herself, and the fading hope that she would ever wind her way out of the ever-deepening maze. She leaned against the desk and resisted the urge to fold up next to the dead detective and wait for someone to discover them both. Maybe that someone could put things right.

She didn't cry for long. The stink of blood was like smelling salts, spurring her to move, to run, to hunt. Mac Grimes had been pursuing Imre Bergamasc, and it was that, presumably—for she had nothing else to go on—that had led him to an early grave. But Grimes wasn't the killer's only victim. Aces Barr, the gambler, had been killed by the hit man earlier that week, and his name was on Monsieur Li's list too. The only thing connecting the two men was Imre Bergamasc—and she too was now connected to him. Grimes had most likely been seen at her apartment earlier that evening. Who was to say Rosy Tony wasn't already looking for her?

Grief and rage rose in her again. If fate was coming to meet her, she wasn't going to hide in her apartment and wait for it. She had Grimes's gun now. Perhaps she would put it to better use than he had.

She checked the cigar box for any last scraps, then left it empty on the desk. Stepping over the body, she took the box of bullets out of the drawer and put it into her shoulder bag with Grimes's notes. She took one last look around the room, ready to sweep off into the night, and paused at the sight of Grimes staring emptily up at her.

She couldn't leave him like that. With a steady hand, she bent down and closed his eyelids, and swiped his driver's license for luck.

The taxi was waiting for her where she had left it, rumbling throatily into the night air. S. Mareri, however, was nowhere to be seen. She called out for him, twice, but no reply came. No lights shone in any of the offices or store-fronts. He had left no note.

Fearing the worst, she stopped the car and used the key in the ignition to open the trunk. It was empty.

Mystified, but unwilling to wait any longer—or to take her chances finding another cab at this hour—she slipped into the driver's seat and turned over the ignition. The warm engine restarted the first time. Cautiously at first—it had been a long time since she'd last driven—she pulled away from the curb and took the first corner.

Buildings swept smoothly by her. She wound down the window and breathed deeply of bracing, cold air. Grimes was dead, killed by Rosy Tony. She wasn't a witness to the crime, but she had his notes. By rights, she should take them to the cops—but what would *they* do? The mayor's name was on the list. They were hardly going to indict him or anyone else on the word of a dead flatfoot and a girl with no name. Besides, what kind of information was it, really? If the nuggets she had found comprised the sum total of Grimes's knowledge on the subject of Imre Bergamasc, it amounted to very little.

Five blocks away, she stopped at a public telephone box and stole the directory. Thinking that she couldn't be too careful, she drove another two blocks, then turned and pulled up under an incandescent streetlight. In the cab's glove box she found a well-thumbed street directory. Keeping the engine running, she set both directories side by side and began cross-referencing them against the list.

Some of the names were coming back to her. The executive who had been kidnapped was on the list. So was the dead sportsman, Magic Amberres. She regarded that death now with grave suspicion. Some of the companies she had never heard of, including one called Cimbaa Mergers, which had burned to the ground two days previously. She imagined Grimes feeling frustrated as his list of leads was gradually chipped away before him, and she sympathized with him. She could hardly walk up to Mayor Besmear's front door and ask him questions about ghosts, at any time of the day or night.

She opted, as she was sure Grimes had many times, for the path of least resistance. In the case of Sigma Street, that path was as circular as the uncial form of the letter it was named after, and narrow to boot.

The bar Grimes had talked about over the phone was little more than a slot in the wall, flanked by a boxing hall on one side and a movie theater on the other. The titles weren't of crime movies. On the way there, she had figured out how to flip the "engaged" flag, hoping that no one would notice her behind the wheel of the cab and think her an odd choice for a taxi driver. The blocks weren't numbered, but there had been plenty of signs. Some of those signs seemed to bear no relation to the business being conducted on the sidewalks outside. The streets were thick with hustlers, gangsters, and pimps, mingling freely with women in various stages of undress. It was with some relief that she had spotted the milky-colored sign of the joint she was after.

She took the next right and parked the taxi on the curb. Locking the door and slipping S. Mareri's keys into her bag, she stuck close to the walls and doubled back to the Crème Bar's entrance. There she was met by a bouncer, who looked her quickly up and down before waving her up the narrow stairs.

A lascivious beat grew louder as she ascended, making her nervous. She was relieved, then, to find the bar mostly empty, both on and off the stage. There was just one desultory dancer undulating in a corner for a trio of men staring into their drinks. A slight brunette was wiping glasses behind a stainless-steel bar. She looked up as her fourth customer approached.

"You're either lost or looking for someone."

There was no point prevaricating. Mac Grimes's license came out of her shoulder bag and slipped across the bar. "Seen this man lately?"

"What's he to you?"

"He was a friend of mine. He died tonight."

Warm brown eyes regarded her for a long moment. "Wait here."

The bartender put down her rag and headed through a door leading out the back. Her voice threaded through the music as though she was shouting at a closed door. "Hey, Ma. Some dame is here, asking after the dick. Says he bought it tonight."

The reply was inaudible, but the bartender returned a second later and handed her the license back. "Okay. Wait over there." She pointed at a booth in the club's darkest corner. "Want a drink?"

"It's okay." She changed her mind as soon as the words emerged from her lips. "No, wait. A whiskey. I don't care what sort."

"Bourbon. That's what he'd drink on a good week." The bartender didn't meet her eye as she dropped ice into a glass and poured two shots. "Old Oscar Pepper, on the house."

She nodded her thanks, not trusting herself to speak, and went to take the seat indicated. Neither the dancer nor the men paid her any attention, and she was fine with that. The beat throbbed through her head, making her temples pound, but the drink soon distracted her. The liquor's cold burn slid down her throat like bile and triggered a slow explosion in her stomach.

Mac Grimes was dead. Although he hadn't really been a friend, he had tried to help her, and they had been drawn into each other's problems because of it. He might not have been killed as a result of anything she had done, but the situation was too tangled to know what she should feel. Anger? Fear? Guilt? Despair?

"You're not his sort," intruded a rough-edged voice into her thoughts. "But with a little mussin' up, you might be."

She looked up, blinking. A weathered, hard-faced woman stood over her, wide of hip and as broad in experience, if her eyes were anything to go by. Her grey hair was cut short, little more than stubble, and her teeth were stained brown. She dressed in layers, like some kind of urban gypsy, and there were tattoos on her knuckles. Between the index finger and thumb of her right hand she clutched the stub of an aromatic Punch cigar.

"I'm sorry?"

"Don't be sorry until I find out you what you've done." The woman pulled a seat up to the table and sat astride it like a man, blocking her exit from the booth. "You didn't kill him, did you?"

"Who?"

"Mac, of course. Is that why you're here? You think he's been cheating rather than beating the streets? You blew him away, and now you've come down here to tie up the loose ends."

"No, no—nothing like that," she stammered, thrown completely off-balance by the woman's accusation.

"Quite sure about that? That bag's looking kinda heavy for makeup and a mirror."

She pulled the bag closer to her stomach, afraid it would be taken from her. "I didn't kill him. I found him in his office. He was dead before I got there. Shot. That guy who broke the blockade—Rosy Tony—"

"Hold it right there." Alarm rose in the woman's eyes. "Don't say anything you might regret later. If you say you didn't kill him, I'll believe you. You don't look the sort—either to let a guy like him put one over you or to fix a problem like that with a gun. That he's dead is all I need to be sure of." The cigar stub came up. "They got him too."

The sentence hung between them like smoke.

"Who are 'they'?"

"Before I answer that, oughtn't you know who *I* am?" The woman extended a broad right hand. "The name is Embers, but most people call me 'Ma Cigar.' This is my joint, and you're drinking my bourbon."

"I—" The woman's grip was strong and demanded reciprocation. "I can't tell you who I am. It's a long story. Mac was working for me, and I'm afraid I might have got him into trouble."

"Or the other way about. Right. Don't paint too kind a picture of our dearly departed. He was no saint, although I liked him well enough, and he tried to do the right thing when the chance arose. Like any gumshoe worth the name, he was looking for contacts around here and a safe place to drink. I was happy to offer him both, without being too free in the former department. A girl's got to keep her reputation." Ma Cigar's grin was as dark-stained as her humor, and didn't last long. "He came to me five nights ago, looking for one of my employees. As it happens, I'd been looking for her too. She'd been popular with the marks but had stopped showing up for her shifts. That happens often enough in this line of work, but they always collect their pay first. When they don't, or their fink boyfriends don't try to on their behalf, that's cause enough to worry."

"You think something happened to her?"

"Oh, I know it. That's where Mac came in. He was looking for her too, as I said. Some guy had given him her stage name, he said. He recognized it and came to me. I told him she wasn't around, and he looked into it for both of us."

She put aside the matter of the missing girl for the moment. "Did he say what guy gave him the name?"

Ma Cigar shook her head. "Just that it was in connection with a case he was working on."

She pulled out the list Mac had hidden in the cigar box and unfolded it under the table. It was hard to read by the dim light. Only one name looked like the sort of thing a dancer might call herself. "Was she 'Mirage'?"

Ma Cigar nodded soberly. "He found her in the morgue. She'd been dead two days. He ID'ed the body for the cops. Guess he knew it as well as most. No one claimed her."

"Mirage" was crossed out with a heavy double line on Mac's list. "How did she die?"

"Strangled. Don't suppose they'll ever find the killer. Cops couldn't care less about girls like her." Ma Cigar's stare was as hard and flat as a mortuary slab. "Mac poked about a bit, but the trail was cold. I owe him for trying."

She didn't doubt that he had been pursuing the killer out of something more than altruism. The girl's name had come from Monsieur Li, so whoever killed her might have known something about the mysterious Imre Bergamasc. That was reason enough for him to have pursued the lead a little further than he might ordinarily have.

That someone thought well of him didn't strike her as a crime, though, so she didn't speak the suspicion aloud.

"I found a list in his office," she said, understanding that Ma Cigar was waiting for her to explain. "I think it could lead me to his killer."

"If the man you named did kill him, you're heading in entirely the wrong direction."

"I don't have any choice about that."

"What, you want revenge?"

"No." She was clear on this point. "Answers."

"You think he'll just give them to you?"

She shook her head. "I'll find a way."

"You'll be dead before dawn, you mean." Ma Cigar laughed. "Show me the list."

She pressed it flat on the table and took another hard slug of bourbon while Ma Cigar looked it over. Her eyes moved from side to side, taking in every detail. "That's a whole lot of stiffs—more even than a good night in here. You need a live one to lead you farther than the cremato-rium."

"Not the mayor."

"No." The stub of the cigar sent a column of white smoke spiraling up to the ceiling. "Before I give you anything else, let me say this: Mac intimated to me that something was up, and I believed him. He didn't show me this list, but I had pieces of it already. I knew 'Gimme' Barr, and he didn't deserve to be rubbed out like that. He was small fry, not worth the cost of a bullet. So were the others. It doesn't add up, and I'm good at sums."

"You think the names are connected?"

"I'm sure of it. You can be sure that whoever's behind it won't take kindly to you sticking your nose into his business. I think we both know that about whoever 'he' is. He took care of Mac, and he'll take care of you too."

"I'll be careful."

Ma Cigar sighed. "All right. Here." One square finger jabbed at a name on the list. "Try her. She's still breathing, or was last I knew."

The name was *Marge Cambresi*. "Where do I find her?"

"The docks. She runs a game for one of the local kingpins. Here's the address." Ma Cigar pulled a pencil from under her voluminous layers and, with the smoking root clenched between her teeth, scribbled on Grimes's list. When she was done she slid the paper back with a perfunctory flick of her fleshy wrist. "Tell her from me to keep her head down. Broads like us have to watch each other's backs."

"I will." She raised the last of her bourbon and downed it in one.

"Broads like you shouldn't even be up this late." Ma Cigar smiled. "Come back to see me if you don't get your pretty ass—"

A disturbance from the stairwell cut her off. Raised voices could be heard over the music—men arguing, becoming quickly more heated. The distinctive whip crack of a gunshot had both women out of their chairs and heading in the same direction.

"No." Ma Cigar pushed her toward the bar with surprising strength. "You go out the back way. Gemma, show her."

The brunette was already halfway through the door. Heart racing, she hurried to catch up and was led through a cramped maze of STAFF ONLY signs and cubicle en-

trances. Alarming noises came from behind several of
them. Three more shots split the air, one a throaty boom
that sounded like it came from a small cannon. It sounded
like the sort of gun Ma Cigar might fire.

They reached a dead end, and the brunette fumbled on
a crowded ring for the key. The lock was stiff and the
hinges no looser. They both leaned their weight into opening it, and the door banged open, making a fragile-looking
iron staircase rattle below.

"Go on," said Gemma, indicating the stairs.

"Will you be all right?" Getting into a gunfight wasn't
part of the deal—especially one that might turn out to be
nothing more sinister than a neighborhood spat, given the
neighborhood—but still she felt guilty about leaving the
two women to it.

"Sometimes you gotta put up a fight regardless." The
brunette wrenched the door closed and locked it shut.

The alley below was empty of life, apart from a cat
picking through garbage and a bum who looked like he
hadn't moved for weeks. She descended as hastily as she
dared and followed the alley away from Sigma Street.
Moving quickly through the shadows, with her hand inside
her shoulder bag, gripping the butt of Grimes's pistol, she
hurried through the back streets to where she had left the
cab.

Someone had stuck an advertising bill under the wiper.
She pulled it free, glanced cursorily at the message—DARK
SALVATION COMES—and threw it away.

The night seemed about as dark as it was ever going to get.
She could see no stars at all from the inside of the cab, and
that small fact puzzled her so much she stopped halfway to
the docks, on the arc of a bridge spanning a nest of snake-
like train lines, and stepped out into the cold to see without
obstruction. Her impression was almost correct. Apart
from two bright stars hanging low to the east and a faint

wash of pale light to the north, sinking visibly, the sky was completely black.

It struck her as ominous, but she wouldn't let that thought hold her back from what she had to do. To avenge Grimes, and maybe Ma Cigar too—and to find out if there was any connection at all between the disappearance of her sister and the mysterious Imre Bergamasc. Perhaps they were lovers, she thought. Or bitter enemies. Either way, the quest for one had become profoundly wedded in her mind with the quest for the other, and she would see it through.

The docks at night were more brightly lit than the city, but its shadows were darker. She wound her way past mountains of containers, stacked up in their hundreds for the duration of the blockade and swarming with dock-workers. The shouting of men and the ringing of metal on metal filled the air. She felt even more out of place than she had on Sigma Street, and her anxiety deepened accordingly. This world was utterly alien to the one she normally inhabited. It undoubtedly had its own rules and expectations, almost its own language. She didn't belong at all.

She tried to imagine her sister in the port area, but could not. Not if her sister was anything like her. That anyone would flee there by choice was inconceivable. She must have been taken, then. Kidnapped. Perhaps by the same person who was behind the deletions from Grimes's list. Perhaps she too had been somehow connected with Imre Bergamasc and taken out of the picture with the others.

Perhaps, perhaps, perhaps . . . Her head spun with possibilities. If that theory was true, then why wasn't her sister's name on the list, crossed out with the others? Perhaps it was and she simply didn't recognize it. And where did the mysterious Monsieur Li fit into the picture?

Streets became back streets, many of which didn't appear in S. Mareri's directory. Light and motion fell behind her. The cab negotiated cramped lanes and its headlights illuminated corners that were normally never exposed after nightfall. It was like turning over a rock. She saw things she had never imagined and was unable to look away. In her rearview mirror, she occasionally glimpsed two faint yellow headlights, and for the first time she wondered if she was being followed.

Nothing for it, she told herself. The address Ma Cigar had given her wasn't far away now. There was no other destination open for consideration.

The cab jerked to a halt before a graffitied roller door, the entrance to a massive, ratchet-roofed warehouse. WELCOME TO DEAD HEAVEN, said the angular letters, and she knew that she had come to the right place.

She killed the engine. Icy silence rolled over her, making her shudder. The headlights behind her winked out.

Gripping the pistol tightly in her right hand, she stepped from the cab. The warehouse appeared as empty as a tomb, but when she moved closer to the door, someone stepped out of an alcove to confront her. More shadow than man, he seemed to have no features at all.

"Hold it right there, sister." His voice was surprisingly high-pitched, and inflected with all manner of gutter accents. "What you looking for?"

"The game," she said, remembering what Ma Cigar had told her.

"This ain't your scene."

"I'll be the judge of that."

"You got an invite?" His eyes gleamed at her in the dark, their whites the only parts of him that weren't completely black.

"Marge Cambresi," she said.

He nodded as though he had suspected already, and reached down to pull the roller door up. "Unnatural filth." He spat at her heels as she hurried through, and she fought a tide of shame she had done nothing to deserve.

The warehouse wasn't as empty as it had seemed from the street. A series of dim lightbulbs guided her deeper into the rambling brick structure. Murmuring voices came through the walls, an exclusively male susurrus that had an animal, primal edge. She didn't want to go any closer to the source of that sound, but she followed the lights without hesitating, concentrating on the clicking of her heels, and came to two closed doors.

One led to her right. The sound of the crowd seemed louder that way, so she turned instead to the door on the left. NO ADMITTANCE, said the sign. She reached for the handle.

It turned before she could touch it. The door swept open. A man in blue, pin-striped suit pants and a white shirt with sleeves rolled up stood before her. His eyes were wild, and sweat dripped freely down his face. Alarmed, she backed away a step and held the gun hidden in the bag before her, so it was pointed at his chest.

"What do you want?" he asked in a voice as cracked as an old record.

"Marge Cambresi." She repeated the password that had got her this far. "I want to talk to her."

"She—" He swallowed. "She's not here."

"I can wait."

"She can't do anything for you." He sounded angry, but the look in his eyes was all desperation. "Whatever you want from her, forget it."

"Is she all right?" The man completely barred her way. She could see only the edge of a broad pine desk behind him, covered in paperwork. "Has something happened to her?"

His jaw bulged. "Run," he hissed. "Run!"

A meaty hand reached from the behind the door and thrust him away. Another man took his place, a thug in a cheap suit with a cheap pistol to match. His hair was slicked back to the nape of his neck. A toothpick jutted from between his teeth. He didn't snarl or make any threats. With businesslike nonchalance, he brought his pistol up, obviously intending to shoot her.

The bang was deafening. She staggered backward. He dropped to the ground with half his head missing. A storm of paper blew up into the air from the hole in the bottom of her bag. The recoil numbed her hand, making it feel like it wasn't part of her, as though it had fired the shot of its own volition.

The man in the blue suit pants reappeared, staring at her as though she'd grown horns and a forked tail. She kept the gun up and stooped to salvage what she could from the bag without taking her eye off him. Grimes's list and driver's license, the remains of her purse, and the keys to the cab all disappeared into her coat pockets. The rest she abandoned. When she stood, she was holding the pistol in plain sight.

"Who was he?" she asked, stepping over the body without looking down at it.

"I don't know. He came with the usual crowd and forced his way in here during the game. Marge—" His eyes tracked to his right. She followed them and saw a woman's legs protruding from behind a second desk. There was a second pool of blood to match the one she had just created. "He didn't say why. He just did it, then he turned on me. That's when we heard you coming. He told me to get rid of you."

Her right hand had started shaking. She squeezed the pistol grip tighter to hide it. She wanted to close the door, but the corpse blocked the way. "Who are you, then?"

"Brice Mars."

"This your outfit?"

He straightened, seeking to regain some composure. "Who's asking?"

She took that as a yes, along with the assumption that she had saved the man Ma Cigar knew as a kingpin of the dockyards. He was Marge Cambresi's boss, and he probably murdered people for breakfast. But he had advised her to run, which said something about what character remained in him. He wasn't all rotten.

Ignoring his question, she said, "Tell me about Imre Bergamasc."

Something silver flashed over her shoulder. Mars reeled back, clutching at his throat and making a hideous choking noise. Bright red blood spurted through his fingers, around the handle of a throwing knife. She spun around and had the gun knocked aside by a powerful blow. Her numb fingers betrayed her. The weapon clattered to the floor. Brice Mars followed, kicking his last.

She backed away from the black-suited figure approaching through the doorway. This man was no cheap hood. His tie was impeccable and as red as blood. The silk band of his hat looked expensive. The vivid knot of a single red rose lay pinned to his lapel. His face above his upper lip was in shadow. His gloved hands held nothing at all.

"Same old line," he said. "I've read the book, and I know you well."

"Who are you?" she asked, even though she already knew the answer. He had to be Rosy Tony. "Stay back."

"Shut your mouth." He backed her into a desk and came close enough to pat her cheek, which he did firmly just once before she pushed his hand away. He laughed and came even closer. His eyes were still invisible, but she could feel his stare burning her where it touched. "This point of view appeals to me."

"What do you want?"

A slow smile spread across his lower face. It was as cold as ice. "Say you've got no one tonight."

Her heart stopped beating. It couldn't be, but it was—the same line from the song that had been haunting her and stalking Mac Grimes for a week. And not just that line, but every word Rosy Tony had said. She recoiled from the realization but couldn't fight it, just as she couldn't fight him off. He was too strong. His body pressed against hers, pinned her so she couldn't get free. His hands came up. She flinched at the feel of the leather against the skin of her throat, but she was paralyzed by her own powerlessness. Just moments before, she had killed a man. Now she couldn't even raise a scream.

Through her closed eyelids, he was a black silhouette blotting out the light.

She had killed a man. She deserved it.

"Don't cry," he whispered as he closed her windpipe with two strong thumbs. "Don't cry anymore."

She dreamed of a hole in the sky so deep it went forever. Its lip was steep, and she skirted the edge with great care, being sure not to fall in. Billions of specks of light turned with her, making her giddy, but she wasn't afraid. She didn't make mistakes. Her position was assured and her balance perfect.

A powerful shove knocked her off-kilter, and suddenly she was falling, falling at a speed too fast to measure. The walls of the hole were vertical at first, like a well, but then her inner ear rebelled, and she became a bullet in a barrel rather than a stone plummeting to the bottom. A wall of infinite blackness rushed up to meet her. She screamed in terror.

The blackness folded and unfolded around her. The wall became a man's stomach. His black skin was slick and shiny with sweat. He glowed with the reflected fire of dying stars.

"I looked deeper," he said, driving her down, driving his flesh into her. "I came closer, into dead paradise. I moved like a rumor, the ghost of a man. I walked into heaven. And now you realize: I am the Black Messiah. I am the truth."

"No," she said, the first word she had ever spoken in her dreams. "No, you're a lie."

"A glorious lie, cruel and divine." His laughter filled the universe. "Would you like to pay for all humanity?"

She tried to force him away from her, but that only made her grind against him more powerfully. "I don't understand."

"I give you the cure: choose heaven, or hell, or me."

She felt him growing harder inside her, more insistent,

and she groaned in denial. She didn't want him to climax.
She was afraid it would tear her apart. She struck blindly
outward with her right hand and caught him across the
face. Her fingers clutched for his eyes but found his mouth
instead. His lips opened for her, and she felt only coldness
where there should have been warmth, vacuum instead of
air. His emptiness pulled at her. He wasn't human, but he
wasn't a god, either, to make such promises. She didn't
know *what* he was.

He released himself inside her, and she blacked out.

When the tide of darkness retreated, she was being carried
by stretcher onto a boat. Her limbs were distant, as though
she had been drugged. For a moment she felt relief that the
mafia hit man hadn't killed her. There was hope yet, that
she might survive to find her sister.

Then she saw the name of the ship, picked out in white
capital letters on the tall metal hull, and she knew with certainty that any hope was premature.

Heaven's Gate.

"Be careful," the first of the two men carrying her
stretcher said over his shoulder to the second, who had stumbled over the leading edge of the gangway. "Li doesn't like
damaged goods."

She tried to raise her head. *Monsieur Li?* The movement, combined with her sudden anxiety, was too much for
her, and the brief window of consciousness abruptly
closed.

The next time she opened her eyes, she was lying on her
side on a metal surface, and the world was undulating beneath her, surging from side to side with the regularity of a
giant machine. She raised her head more cautiously this
time and was able to stay conscious. Her throat hurt. Rubbing it, she looked around.

The room was small, barely three feet across and two long. Lines of rivets pockmarked the grey-metal walls. A single naked globe burned down on her. There was a single door, sporting a high doorsill like the ones she had seen in movies set on naval vessels. There was no handle. Through a vent high in the ceiling, air smelling of oil and salt washed over her.

She was on a ship. The *Heaven's Gate*, presumably. A low, mechanical throbbing suggested that it was moving under its own power, but she had no way of telling where it was going. She didn't know how long she had been unconscious. It could have been days, judging by the gnawing emptiness in her belly. Her shoes lay next to her, blood-spattered and scuffed. Her stockinged feet were cold.

"Hello?" Her voice echoed from the impenetrable walls. "Hello!"

Footsteps sounded on the metal deck outside, but they didn't stop, and her door didn't open. They faded into the engine noise and disappeared.

She slithered backward across the floor and sat upright in a corner. She was still wearing her coat, and she wrapped it tightly around herself, afraid of the new, hard life she had woken into. In a period of twenty-four hours, she had been spied on, pursued, strangled, and imprisoned. She had seen three dead bodies and killed one man herself. She had not only learned nothing about her missing sister, but had been dragged into an underworld of mysteries and murder, from which she might not, now, ever escape.

The dream of the black man didn't seem so terrifying in comparison.

Searching the pockets of her coat, she found that nothing had been taken from her—apart from the gun, which she had last seen lying near the bodies of Marge Cambresi, Brice Mars, and the unknown assassin she had shot. If the police found it and traced her fingerprints, she would be in a whole different kind of trouble. She emptied her pockets and stared glumly at what were, apart from her clothes, her sole remaining possessions.

The purse was blackened by the shot she had fired from inside the shoulder bag. Its clasp wouldn't close, but there was little of value within, just a small amount of cash and the photo of her missing sister. Tucked into one fold was Mac Grimes's driver's license.

Apart from the purse, she had only Grimes's list, well thumbed and dog-eared, and S. Mareri's keys. That was all she had to show for one night of adventure, and the unremarkable life she could remember living.

She unfolded the list on the cold metal floor, if only to see what names remained once she mentally crossed off Marge Cambresi.

She stared at it in growing puzzlement, eyes tracking back and forth, then turned it over. The back side was blank, as she had known it would be, and did nothing to explain this new puzzle. Could someone have slipped a counterfeit list into her pocket while she slept? What purpose could such a substitution possibly have?

She turned the page back over and confirmed the evidence of her eyes. The handwriting was the same; the crossing-outs were identical; but the names on the list were very different. Beammer Cigars had become Acme Ambergris. The mayor's name was now written as Gabe C. Smarmier. Sir Becamé had transformed into Sir Mab.

The list swam before her eyes. A headache threatened to overwhelm her. Could her memory be failing, or was something else going on?

Staring at the last name, she realized something odd. The new, full name—Sir Graeme C Mab—was an anagram of the old. The same applied for Acme Ambergris and the mayor. It was the same for all of them. Once she had seen it, the rearrangement was obvious, even if the reasons behind it remained mysterious.

The list wasn't the only thing in her pockets with names on it. S. Mareri's keys had an identifying tag, and she raised it to see better in the dim light. It said A. MERRIS.

With hesitant fingers, she opened her purse and pulled out Grimes's license. SABER MACGRIM.

The flap of her purse, where she had written her own address, now said, "If found, please return to the *Carriage* building on *Bemms* Street."

With an involuntary, violent motion, she pushed everything away from her. The keys skittered like a metallic spider and came to rest against the far wall. The list lifted into the air, turned an ungainly pirouette and came down barely a foot away from her. Her purse tumbled like a stone.

The new address was written in her own handwriting.

Footsteps boomed outside. A lock clicked in the door. With a loud creak, it swung open.

Rosy Tony stood outside, an amused expression on his face.

"Same old smile that cracked a thousand hearts," he said, "but not mine."

She launched herself at him with fingers bent into claws. Her fury was complete. They—whoever *they* were—had drugged and brainwashed her in an attempt to drive her out of her mind. Having doubted her own sanity too many times in recent days, she wasn't going to give it up without a fight.

The hit man made short work of her attack. She wasn't a slight woman, but he was much bigger all the same, and stronger, and had obviously fought off many such attacks. He took her wrists in both hands and twisted. She found herself turned irresistibly, and pinned with her back to him, arms held at awkward angles between them. His lips were uncomfortably close to her ear. His breath was hot.

"What's this feeling? What's it for?"

"I'll kill you," she gasped.

"That I don't believe."

He spun her around and pushed her against the wall. Before she could think of attacking him again, he had a pistol at her throat, heavy and cold and smelling of oil. His eyes were like empty barrels, like the bottomless pit of her dream. She rose on her tiptoes, afraid of what would happen next.

"Listen, babe. Listen good."

He would have said more, but a voice called from the end of the corridor.

"Monsieur Li is ready."

The hit man turned to face the speaker, a man in sailor's uniform—dark pants and boots, a thick cream turtleneck sweater—and froze as though weighing his options. Eventually he nodded and turned back to her. A simple prod of the gun told her that she was to move. She dropped down onto the soles of her feet, relief warring with dread. She was about to meet Grimes's shadowy employer. The cold metal floor wasn't nearly as chilling against her flesh as that thought.

Rosy Tony marched her through the ship, past surly-looking crew members and pounding machines. The hit man walked behind her, keeping the gun firmly in her ribs. No one spoke to him. Few members of the crew even looked at him. Their attention was directed entirely at her, and the power of their combined gaze was distinctly threatening. As both an intruder and a woman, she could call on none of them for help. She was, once again, alone.

They came to closed door. The hit man banged on it, sending booming echoes rolling around them. It opened instantly, and he pushed her inside. She regained her balance directly in front of a desk as metallic and unforgiving as the walls. The chair behind it was empty.

She looked around. These quarters were much larger and more opulent than her cell, with a cot along one wall, a small cupboard, and two curtained portholes through which fresh air and a hint of purplish light entered. The engine noise was louder, as was the smell of the ocean. Men's voices rose and fell in the distance, their words inaudible.

"Do you believe in God?"

The question came from behind her. She spun around,

but saw no one. Turning in a slow circle, she took in every nook and cranny. The room was empty.

"Leave us, Anthony," said the same voice, "but please remain by the door. I will call if I need you."

Rosy Tony inclined his head and shut the door.

She folded her arms, feeling vulnerable and alarmed. The voice was that of a cultured, mature man, but its source was completely hidden from her.

"Where are you?"

"Please answer my question."

"Which question?"

"About God."

"What difference does that make to anyone?"

"If God is real, it would make a great deal of difference to Him."

"Or to Her."

"Indeed." When she didn't reply, the voice said, "Do you know who I am?"

She nodded. "Your name is Li."

"That is incorrect. I am Monsieur Zee. Monsieur Li has not yet arrived, but he is close now. You will meet him shortly."

"Why—" Her throat closed on the question. "Why can't I see you?"

"Can you not? I apologize. This side effect is unintended, and temporary, I hope."

"Side effect?" She guessed the answer as soon as she asked. "Of the drug you gave me. Right. It's been messing with my head ever since I woke up." She thought of the list of names and was relieved in part to confirm her suspicions that her confusion didn't arise from a physical switch but a mental one.

"I can assure you that it is not I who hypnotized you," Zee said.

"I didn't say I was hypnotized."

"Regardless, that is the truth of your condition. It is my fervent wish to restore you to full health."

Something moved across her field of vision. The suggestion of an arm, perhaps, or a hand waving before her eyes.

"Don't come anywhere near me," she said, retreating.

"I mean you no harm."

"No? What about the others, then? Your goon out there"—she cocked a thumb at the door—"has killed and kidnapped his way through half the city. Once you've finished with me, I assume I'll be poleaxed and tipped over the side. No one will ever find my body, out in the ocean."

Another hint of movement, this time on the far side of the room, by the desk. "Again you are mistaken, on both points. We have not left dock. The blockade is unbreakable. You are safe with us."

The sound of running engines belied his words, but she didn't protest the point. She didn't believe anything he said anyway.

"What's the deal with Imre Bergamasc?" she asked. "Who is he, and what did he ever do to you guys?"

"I fear that I know as little about him as you do."

"Then why are you looking for him?"

"He was looking for someone too. A woman. We believe he might have found her."

"So what? It's no business of mine."

"Her name was Bianca Biancotti."

It rang no bells at all, but one word Zee had used worried at her. " 'Was'?"

He made an irritated noise. "I have answered many of your questions, but you still have not answered mine."

"Oh, for Pete's sake. No, I don't believe in God. I never have, and I never will. Is that what you want to hear?"

"You don't believe there is a reason, or a purpose, to your life, to all this?" A ghostly limb waved, indicating the walls of the room and, by inference, the ship, the city, everything. Zee's voice took on an imploring tone. "You will not accept that there's something greater than yourself, beyond this life you call your own?"

"I've never felt the need to. It's a sucker's way out, to

blame the problems of the world on higher forces, as though we aren't all really at fault. We're what we make of ourselves and our lives, not wooden puppets on strings."

"I disagree."

"Well, that's your prerogative."

"I thought you of all people would understand. Your sister is missing, yes? Is this circumstance of your doing or someone else's?"

"It couldn't be mine. I didn't drive her away."

"So your life is influenced by others, some of them unknown to you. Perhaps entirely unknowable. Things affect you that you cannot see or touch or understand."

There was definitely something to see of Zee by then. He became, while he talked, a translucent silhouette—little more than edges and the suggestion of a round face—pacing to and fro before her. She didn't take her eyes off him.

"Of course," she said.

"Yet still you do not believe in God."

That was more a summation than a question, so she didn't bother responding. There were more important things on her mind. "What do you know about my sister?"

"Only that she is important to you, and that she has stolen your name."

She was struck by his matter-of-fact tone. "That doesn't sound a bit cracked to you?"

"Not at all. Names are important. They reveal much about us that we cannot otherwise see—that we are *hypnotized* not to see. You protest that you are not under anyone's spell, but I assure you that you are. I am, also. The only difference between us is that I know it. That is what makes me dangerous, and is perhaps also why you cannot see me clearly. I am in conflict with the context that you have been given. I am not entirely *of* the world anymore, because I try to see beyond it. Everyone you know has been hypnotized by God. I, perhaps alone, have touched Heaven."

"Does that make you an angel?"

A phantom's crooked smile floated in the air before her. "I fear not."

Her knees were beginning to shake, so she moved across the room to sit on the cot. The protoplasmic Zee didn't try to stop her. The engine noise had grown louder, as though the ship was straining against a heavy current. The crew was more active too. She could hear orders flying in all directions, running feet, and the ringing of bells. The deck rocked and rolled without respite.

"At least one of us is crazy," she said. "Frankly, I'm betting on both of us."

Zee said nothing, just stood by the desk as diaphanously as a silk curtain. She wondered when Monsieur Li would come. The next chapter in her imprisonment might be as impenetrably bizarre as the first, but at least it would be a change. She was tired of this strange confrontation.

Li and Zee. They sounded like a vaudeville duo, which didn't help their credibility. What had Zee said? "Names are important. They reveal much about us that we cannot otherwise see." She wondered, idly, what their names said about them.

Then she thought of the names that had changed while she was unconscious, the anagrammatical transformation of everything she had learned since meeting Mac Grimes, now the ominous-sounding "Saber MacGrim." Even her home address had rearranged itself into something new. If she could remember her own name, would it—or her memory of it—have changed as well? That seemed impossible, but in the middle of a conversation with an invisible man that point was rather moot.

Why anagrams? That question snagged at her mind. Mentally she laid some of them out before her in an attempt to find an answer before she completely unraveled.

Beammer Cigars → Acme Ambergris
Sir Gram Becamé → Sir Graeme C. Mab

Aces "Gimme" Barr → Ace "Germ" Bismar
Craig M. Besmear → Gabe C. Smarmier

Mac Grimes's transformation puzzled her until she remembered that his full first name had been "Macabre," thus providing the missing letters. There were thirteen in all—another ominous note, but one she felt safe assuming was purely coincidental.

Until she noticed that "Acme Ambergris" had thirteen letters too, as did "Sir Graeme C. Mab" and "Ace 'Germ' Bismar."

Her eyes scanned down the mental list. They all had thirteen letters.

What's more, they all had the *same* letters. Everyone she had met or heard about in recent days was linked by this one small fact. "Ma Cigar" Embers, Serge "Crab" Maim, Magic Amberres—and places too, like the torched Cimbaa Mergers offices.

The murdered dancer, Mirage, had taken her stage name from the one she had been born with, which was "Mira G. Embraces." The same thirteen letters. Even S. Mareri matched, because he drove a "Gem Cab" and that made up the difference.

More fell into place as soon as she started looking. Marge Cambresi had worked for "Brice Mars' game." The Crème Bar was on *Sigma* Street. She had heard ads for "E. G. Mamba's McRib" on the radio.

A sick feeling swept through her. Somehow, her life was as much a part of it as anyone's. She had enjoyed a play called *Brag Me a Crime* and lived at the *Iceberg* building on *Rammas* Street, now the Carriage on Bemms. Where did it end?

Names are important.

"Imre Bergamasc" had thirteen letters.

"Monsieur Zee" did not. Neither did "Monsieur Li," "Anthony 'Rosy Tony' Archer" or "Bianca Biancotti."

The feeling that she had been on the verge of some

important understanding evaporated. She put her head in her hands and fought the urge to weep.

"He is here," said Monsieur Zee.

She looked up and through swimming vision saw that Zee had become much more substantial while she had been thinking of other things. A dumpy, unremarkable man dressed in a white suit with a Nehru collar, matching waist-coat and tie, he had a weak chin and receding hair. Fleshy hands hung limp at his sides. Marble eyes stared into infin-ity, while the ship's engines strained and strained beneath them.

She rose warily to her feet. Apart from the two of them, the room was empty.

Seemed empty. She raised her hands protectively in front of her chest and, futile though it was, kept her eyes peeled for another invisible man.

Zee jerked as though he had been stabbed in the back. His face stiffened, but he didn't cry out or fall down. She edged toward the door, figuring she'd rather take her chances with Rosy Tony. Zee jerked again, and his body arched like a tautened bow. His mouth opened, but still no sound emerged. A splitting sound came from his chest, and a red stain spread in a line from his throat to his stomach.

She turned away and pounded at the door. "Get me out of here!" There was no answer. The noises from behind her were becoming louder. Tearing, wet sounds as though Zee was being gutted. She didn't want to look, but she couldn't keep her back to it forever, like a child pretending what she couldn't see couldn't hurt her. She didn't want to suffer the same fate as Zee without at least putting up a fight.

She turned and pressed herself flat against the door in horror. Zee was still upright, but he couldn't possibly be alive. His chest and abdomen were ripped completely open, exposing his internal organs—which at that moment slipped and tumbled messily to the floor. Blood was everywhere. He jerked and swung in the air, wrenched by invisible forces. When something started moving inside his chest cavity, she thought she might faint.

It was a hand, a human hand groping for purchase among the bent and broken ribs. Slick with gore, it clutched lower and found a grip on Zee's pelvis. A second hand appeared and did likewise. Muscles bunched. Zee's shattered corpse shuddered. From the bloody depths of his stomach, something round and black emerged.

A head, followed by shoulders and chest. She cried out in denial as a full-grown man hauled himself bodily out of the dead man and, with a vile sucking sound, splashed to the floor.

The twisted, violent parody of birth was followed by something even more shocking. The man on the floor was neither monster nor stranger. He was tall and muscular, as demonstrated by his unfolding limbs and the height he attained upon standing. His face was broad and masculine. Through the blood, his black skin gleamed. His nakedness hid nothing.

She knew him. He had come to her every night since her sister had disappeared. His name, she guessed, was Monsieur Li.

His eyes opened, dripping blood like tears. He turned to look at her.

"I was asleep, lost to dreams." His voice was exactly as it had been during her sleep—emotionless, dead, ancient. "I was dying in a big machine. Didn't think the voice that called me could be real. Didn't think I'd find the savior in the dark."

Her whole body was shaking. She wanted to scream, to pound at the door, to run, but every muscle was locked. Even when he took a step closer to her, moving like a giant through thickened air, she couldn't make herself budge. His eyes were crystalline and cold. She could only stare at him with visceral terror and awe.

"I am the darkness that crawls into you." His right hand reached for her. "I'll drive a stake through the black of your heart."

Oh no, she thought with renewed desperation, *you won't.*

Falling was just a matter of giving up, relinquishing all attempts to control her muscles and allowing them to go limp. She dropped like a stone to the deck and kicked upward, finding strength for retaliation where there had been none earlier. This wasn't a dream. This was really happening, and she hadn't yet found the answers she needed, or her sister, or her name. She wasn't going to let some well-hung nightmare get in the way of her promise to herself.

Her stockinged feet struck him the same moment the metal door crashed open. Rosy Tony fell backward through it, blown by a hail of bullets into the room. He crashed into Monsieur Li, and the two of them went down. The noise was deafening. She rolled over and crouched with her hands over her ears as men in uniform poured into the room. It sounded like a dozen tommy guns were firing at once. Monsieur Li's grotesque body was torn in half. The air was full of gun smoke and misted blood.

A strong hand took her wrist and dragged her out of the tempest. The hand belonged to a cop, and she sobbed with relief. Someone must have tipped off the police, or they had worked it out for themselves. The trail of bodies was there for all to see. Only dumb luck had brought her to Monsieur Li before them.

The pounding of guns faded behind her. The cop was still holding her by the arm, leading her irresistibly through the ship's tight corridors. The engines were still running, still straining against unknown currents. Blue-uniformed men were everywhere. The ship had been completely overrun.

She was dragged out onto an open deck, where a strange sight greeted her. They weren't on the open sea, but they weren't in any recognizable dock, either. To her right, the water was as flat and transparent as pure ice. To her left hung an impressionistic vision of a city, smeared as though seen through a window streaked with water. Ahead was a bright yellow light, too powerful to stare at, and behind nothing but shadow. There were no stars in the sky at all.

The engines had taken on a sick sound, as though the ship too had been mortally wounded. Glancing behind her, she realized that at least part of the shadow consisted of smoke billowing from the ship's stern. The deck quaked underfoot, and she stumbled. The hand at her wrist dragged her upright again, and she realized only then that she was as much a prisoner as she had been before.

The cop holding her was stony-faced and lifeless. He dragged her onto the foredeck, where a dozen other policemen waited with pistols drawn. Individually they lacked personality, but as a group their hostility was palpable.

"Wait," she said, tugging herself free from the tight grip. "Aren't you supposed to be *rescuing* me?"

Without saying a word, the cops as one raised their weapons and took aim at her.

She didn't have time to think about fingerprints on Grimes's gun. She didn't have time to wonder if she could persuade them of her innocence or talk them out of it some other way. Fighting back wasn't even an option. They had the numbers, and the guns, on their side.

The deck shifted under her again, and the officers swayed, losing their aim. While they were off-balance, she moved. A powerful sense of self-preservation guided her. She had walked knowingly toward the threat of death and survived this far. This time she wasn't going to freeze. Her legs moved with surety, putting all her strength to the task.

Five steps took her to the starboard edge of the deck. One strong leap took her over. From there, gravity was in charge.

Bullets snatched at her but couldn't hold her back. She felt no pain, just weightlessness as the ocean rose to meet her. Its frozen surface was as smooth as glass. Reflected in it, she could see herself, blood-spattered and with arms outstretched as though to embrace her reflection. Or her reflection was rising up to embrace her. Or—

When the two met, they shattered into pieces too small and too numerous to count, and all the world shattered with her.

THIS DARK FACADE

[T]he doom and burden of our life is bound forever on a man's shoulders, and when the attempt is made to cast it off, it but returns upon us with more unfamiliar and more awful pressure.

—**Robert Louis Stevenson**

Imre Bergamasc woke knowing exactly who he was. He didn't know where he had been or what he was doing. They were smaller problems to contend with, later. For the moment it was enough to bask in the knowledge that he was in one piece, and that piece was him.

He was lying in a coffinlike space that felt like a hard-caster sarcophagus, and he had returned to consciousness naked apart from a microfiber skin suit. His body seemed complete, apart from the last finger on his left hand, which was missing, as it should have been. He waited for the lid to open or for a data feed to connect from the outside, a feeling of weariness and morbid anticipation beginning to present itself, as though a dreaded task awaited him upon his emergence and the return of his memories. He wondered what dire situation would prevail upon his attention.

The memories did come, and they didn't belong to him.

A man in an antique suit shot in the back while leaving a dingy gambling hall . . . A dancer strangled in the entrance of her tiny apartment . . . A businessman kidnapped and sealed in an empty oil drum, where he suffocated not long after . . . A detective chasing phantoms through a landscape of urban clichés shot in his office because he had been getting too close to the truth . . .

Imre could barely keep track of all the counterfeit memories pouring into his skull. Under skies as fluid as an oily rainbow, he had been dozens of people in a city with no name—working, eating, sleeping.

Dying.

His ears popped. The sarcophagus broke its seal and slid open. Warily, he sat up. The room he found himself in was much longer than it was wide and contained nothing but a single queue of hardcasters of unfamiliar design. Sleek and curved like seedpods, all were open and empty apart from his. Absent were the thick data and power cables familiar to him. Absent also were any signs of life.

He inhaled deeply through his nose. The air had an ozone tang that wasn't entirely pleasant. He was reminded of attack ships that had been running hard in battles either unwinnable or too costly to wage for long. He remembered with bitterness the *Pelorus* and his long-ago war against the Forts, and the decision that was still haunting him many, many years later.

More secondhand memories poured into him. Not all of them were immediately comprehensible. Some were just emotions, fear, anger, and lust among them. He glanced down at himself, and was momentarily surprised not to see a woman's body through his skin suit. He had been re-created female once before, but why did that thought come to him now? Why the feeling of having lived a thousand lives, but missed the one that mattered most?

The last date he remembered was M1552. In relative terms he was barely two thousand years old, but by the Absolute Calendar he had been around over a million years. Sometimes he felt that old. This time, it seemed, was one of them.

A door opened at the far end of the long room. Air stirred as pressures equalized, confirming his suspicion that he was in a ship of some kind. Footsteps echoed in the distance, coming steadily closer. He peered past the endless ranks of hardcasters to see who had arrived to welcome him back to life.

Atavistic horror caught the breath in his throat. A tall black man was striding with confidence toward him—a tall black man he had never seen before, but whose face and body were vividly familiar all the same. There was no logical reason to be afraid of him, but Imre felt his pulse rise regardless. His palms became moist. A flash of memory crossed his mind—something sexual and bloody—then dropped back into nothing, leaving him wildly disoriented.

Stop it, he told himself. Get a grip. You know who you are. Find out who he is before giving anything away.

Imre slid his legs over the edge of the sarcophagus and dropped to the ground in readiness.

The black man slowed as he approached. He wore a white suit with simple, clean lines—a uniform, perhaps, but lacking visible insignia. He appeared to be unarmed. Imre didn't fancy his chances in a straight fistfight. The man's reach was prodigious and musculature pronounced. His eyes, unlike those of the man in Imre's adopted memories, were a deep, dark jade.

"Are you to blame?" Imre asked him, not letting his disadvantage in height faze him. He had ruled the galaxy, once. He had killed gods.

"For what, exactly?"

Imre wriggled the fingers of his four-fingered hand by his left ear. "For the mess in here."

"I don't understand."

"You got your wires crossed and plugged me into someone else's screwed-up fantasy. If I wanted garbage like this, I'd go back to being a singleton."

The black man came to a halt two meters from him and stood with arms hanging heavily at his sides. "They are your memories, Imre. You should be grateful. It took us a long time to extract them, and you with them."

"Extract me from where?"

"From the city: C20. You were caught in a honey trap. Your plan failed: you were broken down, fragmented, eroding, and wouldn't have lasted much longer. By the time we caught up with you, MZ and Chyro had become entangled too, trying to get you out. Fortunately, I had something the city couldn't defend itself against. I had a guaranteed way in."

Imre remembered C20, a mobile metropolis and exclusive haven for Old-Timers that mimicked the pre–space era's twentieth century. Some regarded it as a legend, like the Wandering Jew, but he had suspected otherwise and proved his hunch true. The tempo of its passengers was maintained at a near crawl while superdense materials in the foundations provided gravity under a dome designed to let in the light of nearby suns. Permanently drifting between the stars, it could observe anything approaching from millions of kilometers away, no matter how small—anything but a wrinkle in space-time, a ghost ship ship called the *Wickthing*.

These memories were real; he could tell the difference. Despite the *Wickthing*, getting into the city hadn't been an uncomplicated process. C20 was a physical place, not a virtual environment. Its inhabitants possessed real bodies and walked real streets. Imre and the galaxy's last-known Fort had tapped the telephone exchange and hacked into the city's contemporary maintenance systems where, below the facade of ancient days, lay machines capable of building him anew. Encased in flesh and blood, with an assumed identity and credible credentials, Imre had begun his search for a woman and the answer he hoped she possessed.

Bianca Biancotti.

The name was as familiar to him as his own, but it came now with a hint of intrigue. To one among the many whose memories crowded his head, Biancotti had been a mystery to be solved. He could not remember his own mission, however, beyond getting into the city and the beginning of the search. From there, he could only guess. If what the man before him had said was true, the city's defenses must have identified him as an intruder. It hadn't killed or expelled him, but it hadn't let him go, either. His sense of self had been dissolved, suddenly and without any chance to resist. The city had overwhelmed him and taken him into itself.

"They are your memories, Imre," the black man had said. Memories of parts of him that had been excised and let loose—to keep him distracted from his quest and to play roles in the city alongside its "authorized" inhabitants. He understood perfectly now. There had been endless anagrams of his own name scrawled on a dog-eared note in another man's handwriting. He remembered the search to find "Imre Bergamasc," who didn't seem to be anywhere. He remembered a song he heard without respite and a woman looking for her lost sister. He remembered feeling alone and fundamentally incomplete in a variety of ways.

Lost names, lost siblings, lost opportunities, lost hope . . .

You dreamed of something like I dreamed of you.

A name swam like a silver fish through the sea of his consciousness—*Vaia Falisa Soulis*—but it meant nothing to him then.

"Tell me who are you and why you rescued me."

The black man regarded him without blinking. "I think part of you already knows."

"I don't see how."

"In the city, my name was 'Monsieur Li.' "

That rang a very loud bell. The Mac Grimes part of him had taken orders from a mysterious figure with that name. "I presume that's not really you. Is it an anagram like the others?"

"Of a sort. A pun, anyway. The city's overseer wouldn't give us complete access, so we had to sneak in by any means available. Because of that, we sometimes arrived mistranslated. It's not surprising you didn't recognize me in the city. I probably wouldn't have recognized myself in that light." The deep, green eyes studied him for a moment. "No? What about 'Monsieur Zee' and 'Anthony Archer'?"

Feeling tested, Imre turned away from the black man and paced four steps along the hardcaster queue. Anthony Archer was better known as "Rosy Tony," the hit man who had killed Grimes and so many others. He didn't know who Monsieur Zee was. None of the names were anagrams of his own. He jumbled the syllables, reassembled them, free-associated with other words and names in his memory.

It came to him at last.

Those three names were the key to everything.

" 'Rosy Tony' Archer is 'Rositano, Archard,' " he said, turning. "Render's real name. That's how you got in. He's an Old-Timer; he's permitted."

That earned him a nod. "He was our route into the overseer. Getting from there into the honey trap wasn't so easy, however. The allegories are difficult to penetrate, and by then the city was aware of our tampering."

"The blockade of the docks," he said. "The intruder from outside."

"Removal from the trap constituted a kind of death, so Render was portrayed as a murderer."

"Killing pieces of me so they could be excised cleanly." It made sense, in a dourly poetic kind of way. His manifold physical bodies remained in the city while the data comprising their experiences were recombined in the new body he wore, one based on a template provided by another of his former companions.

" 'Monsieur Zee' is MZ. He came in after me and must've got a toehold already, which you were able to exploit."

"Something like that. The Forts built C20 to host their former selves in comfort and dignity, with AIs to keep the peace. MZ was able to get partway in before he was caught. Render rescued him first, before we made a move on you."

"And you are Monsieur Li, the ringleader. 'M. Li.' *Emlee.*"

He—*she*, in the body of a man—bowed again, but made no move to come any closer.

Imre turned and leaned against the sarcophagus closest

to him. He felt faint, and he couldn't immediately fathom why. He and Emlee had been lovers, briefly, and his memories of that encounter remained strong in his mind. Commingled feelings of desire and uncertainty distracted him, interfered with thoughts he desperately needed to pursue. How long had it been since he had wished his former bodyguard au revoir on Earth? How had she tracked him down? Why?

Who was she now?

A flash of memory, in a bedroom, of a dark figure with eyes full of stars, caught in his mind like a splinter. He raised a hand to his breast and held it there, clenched into a fist, until the disorientation passed.

"Are you all right?" she asked him.

He dismissed her concern with an irritated gesture. "Forget about it. You brought me out of the trap and put me back together. Now I can get on with my life."

"Don't you think you should thank me, first?" she said, stiffly.

"Yes." Acknowledging his self-absorption, he inclined his head. "All right. Thank you, First Prime."

"Prime Minister, now. There's also the matter of Bianca Biancotti. She wasn't in the city when we arrived here. In fact, she was long gone. The city's records suggest that she left soon after you were caught. I believe your arrival prompted her to leave, perhaps to take action elsewhere. I'm hopeful she gave you information before she left."

"What kind of information?"

"That depends on what you asked her, in the city. Don't you remember? I assumed it would be something to do with the Jinc, since you and I talked about looking for them once. Or the Luminous, or your old obsession."

Himself. Of all his former associates, only Emlee had known the truth about the man he had once been. That had indeed been the prime motivator of his search. Bianca Biancotti had spent many thousands of years studying the broken and submerged text flooding the rewired Line. She must have possessed important data on that front.

Imre's mind was empty of data, however. If there was anything important in there, if he had found Biancotti and she had told him anything at all, it was buried in a mess of memories and lives that barely resembled his own.

"Give me time," he said again. "I'm sure the answer will come."

"Time," Emlee said, "is one thing we're particularly short of."

Emlee granted him a glimpse of the data feed he had been anticipating earlier, a taste of the world outside the hardcaster room. Through virtual senses, he saw the disk of C20 tumbling like a tossed coin through the gulf between stars. Its velocity was considerable, explaining the changeable sky of his fragmented lives. Emlee's maps revealed the location of powerful magnetic field lines protecting the structure from debris. Those field lines presently had more to grapple with than ancient meteorites and dust grains.

A series of complicated glyphs defined ships stationed near the city. A contingent of three was Emlee's, arrow-thin darts of unfamiliar design. He was inside one of them. The rest belonged to a fleet of some fifteen heavy warships maintaining a powered stance surrounding the city. Drive flames burned in naked displays of aggression. Intense signals flashed between them, consummately encrypted.

"Not yours?" he asked Emlee.

"Not remotely. They're Ra MacPhedron's."

His stomach sank. "Well, stall him for a few days, and we'll hardcast into the *Wickthing.* Then he won't be able to track us. Or have the Apparatus kill his drive system to stop him following."

She shook her head. "We can't do either, Imre. Ra's ships are protected against the Apparatus by the same spatiotextural technology that makes the *Wickthing* vulnerable now." She hesitated. "Check the date, Imre. Things have changed while you were gone."

He lifted that tiny detail from the data available to him. Not quite believing it, he checked it again.

Emlee had reassembled him in the 2010th millennium of human history, meaning that he had been in the honey trap for 508,000 years. While his fragments had crawled along at nearly Fort tempo, and the city had tumbled close to light-speed, his Absolute age had advanced half a million years without his noticing.

No wonder the tech looked different and Emlee had changed so much.

No wonder his head ached.

Emlee came close enough to touch him. Her massive right hand gave his shoulder a reassuring squeeze. "We'll outrun them the old-fashioned way."

He looked down at her hand, and froze.

Don't pull away, he told himself. Don't react until you're absolutely sure what you're reacting to.

"Go do your thing," he said, stepping back and waving her ahead of him. "All I ask is for a good view."

She flashed white teeth at him, in something that he supposed was a smile, and led him to the bridge.

Things have changed while you were gone.

If his life had a recurring theme, that was it. His first return had been after the Slow Wave, to the news that every Fort in the galaxy had been killed. Later, his rise to power had been punctuated by whistle-stop tours lasting fifty thousand years or more. Then this new development, the longest gap of all. While he had slept, the galaxy had kept patiently turning; stars had gone out; the universe had expanded a little more; humanity had . . . changed.

Civilization was over two million years old. Imre was amazed he recognized anything at all. The same cultural momentum that had been such a powerful force in his time was clearly still in effect—sustained by long life spans, records stretching back hundreds of thousands of years, and an innate desire by the majority of people to maintain at least the illusion of a status quo. While Old-Timers born in the twentieth century still existed alongside people like

Emlee Copas and himself, humanity's evolution was bound to be sluggish. There had always been fringe dwellers, strange offshoots who burned brightly in the Core or explored new ways of being out in the dark spaces between the arms. Sometimes these mutations were successful, as the Forts and singletons had been. Mostly they died out, though, or diverged so far from the mainstream of human existence that they were never heard from again, by choice or through an inability to communicate with their former siblings.

Changes to the mainstream accrued inevitably, but slowly. It wasn't the ship design or politics that startled him this time, made him reach urgently for the data feed when Emlee had clapped her hand on his arm. Electrons had moved sluggishly along quantum channels as he overclocked to gain time to think. Gates had opened and closed with infuriating slowness. Mountains of data were waiting to be processed and pored over—he had no doubt there was much more hidden behind security screens and filters—but he needed only a quick scan, a handful of specifics, a partial understanding.

It was worse than he had feared.

The being standing before him was definitely Emlee Copas—former signals officer of the Corps, then colonel in Imre's galaxywide army, and most recently Prime Minister of the Milky Way—but she wasn't even remotely the person she had been. She might not, if he was forced to press the point, even be human.

He had raised his tempo before she could become suspicious, and he said nothing to her about it as they walked through her ship. There would be time later, when they had safely slipped through Ra MacPhedron's net—and *there* was a whole other thread of history he would have to unravel before he could even begin to feel like he had found his feet.

They came to a vast, semicircular bridge, whose purpose was undoubtedly more ceremonial than functional.

Walls, floor, and ceiling were angular, with brushed-steel fittings that spoke a language from another time. Thirty duty stations clustered in two arcs around a central command podium. There, three meters above the rest of the crew and standing behind a safety rail, was the one face Imre expected to recognize no matter when he woke up.

An extra half a million years had been hard on Render, and he hadn't been a beauty to start with. His skin had acquired an eroded look, like pitted stone, and his mismatched eyes were simultaneously sunken and mobile, as though the mind within that ancient skull let nothing escape its notice. His scalp was hairless apart from a white half Mohawk leading from the crown of his head down to the nape of his neck. He wore a uniform identical to Emlee's, but black where hers was white. They looked like negative images of each other.

Imre wondered if that was intentional, if Render was deliberately making himself stand out. The rest of the crew also wore white uniforms, and most of them had distinctive black markings on their skins. Few were completely black like Emlee—he wondered if that was a sign of seniority in this strange new society—but most of them were male.

Imre hid all signs of rising discomfiture. He wasn't one to discriminate over superficialities; he would work with people of any race, color, height, age, or gender. That they did their job was all that mattered—and the fact that Render was still associated with this particular crew hinted that they must be doing their job very well indeed.

Emlee led him up a flight of spiral stairs to the top of the command podium. On that vantage point focused the manifold screens of the curving walls. He felt as though he was stepping into a sea of data, as vivid and vital as a coral reef on old Earth. Colors assailed him; ever-changing graphs evolved in split-second increments; real-time images of Ra MacPhedron's ships came from dozens of different angles. For a moment, all he could do was soak it in.

"Say, are you new here?"

Imre shrugged off the information onslaught and forced himself to focus on his old friend. "I might as well be."

"Welcome to the real world."

They shook hands, and Imre was relieved to see that Render possessed none of the black markings of the rest of the crew.

The old soldier noticed him looking and said softly, "Just you and me," answering his unasked question. "Everybody's infected."

Imre nodded, not wanting to talk about it in front of Emlee. "Thank you for getting me out of the city."

"Dreams are cruel." He shrugged. "I suppose it all meant something to you."

"We'll see about that later, when I've had a chance to think about it." He indicated the screens. "Are we going to make it out of here in one piece?"

"Maybe. Watch. Keep a low profile. Don't leave."

Imre assured Render he would stay. He had no intentions of going anywhere until his immediate survival was assured.

"Who's the commanding officer?"

"I am," Emlee replied. She was leaning with her arms splayed on the handrail, watching the screens. Her green eyes reflected a thousand different colors. She looked every inch the commander in her new body and spotless uniform. Imre felt underdressed beside her.

The members of Emlee's crew looked up from their stations as though in response to an announcement. A low buzz spread through the room. Images shifted at an increased rate on the screens. Imre came forward to stand next to Emlee, feeling the energy in the room rise.

"It's started," he said.

"Yes." She didn't turn to look at him.

"Can I talk to the *Wickthing*?"

"Not yet. We're maintaining a strict comms silence so Ra won't know which ship you're in." She did glance at him, then. "Forgive me for keeping you out of the loop.

When we're done here, we can talk about how you and your friends are going to fit back in."

"No need to apologize. I'll just sit back and relax."

"You will definitely need to take a seat." She gestured behind them, where three couches had risen out of the podium in readiness to cradle their frames. The rest of the crew were adopting similar precautions. That was a startling detail: not even the most powerful engine of his day could stretch a Prime or singleton's combat-hardened body.

He did as the rest did, including Emlee, and powerful g forces immediately gripped him. He could barely move his head. From his supine position, though, there was still plenty to see. The trio of arrowships was breaking station around the city, each of them accelerating in a different direction from C20. Ra MacPhedron's flotilla split in turn into three pieces and set out in pursuit. Clouds of drones and independent weapons spread out like a halo around each of the stubby, businesslike ships. They were destroyers, Imre's data feed informed him, and had names to match. The stubby vessel following Emlee's arrowship was called *Wurmbrand. Thanhauser* and *Januskopf* led the other two charges. All three were registered to something called "the Fleet Vanguard of the Host," with numbers linking them to the Round.

The Host. Imre could guess what that meant.

Again, unease rippled through him. It was clear that many things *had* changed. In the old days of the Corps, Imre would have placed copies of himself and all his major officers on each of the three fleeing ships, to maximize the chances that at least one complete set would survive pursuit. That wasn't a luxury he allowed himself anymore, having embraced the philosophies and limitations of a Prime and limiting himself to just one body, forever.

In more recent times, Imre wouldn't have been in a ship at all. Traveling by physical ships through space had been a rarity in the Returned Continuum. Hardcasting along the Line was the norm, so interstellar space battles were rare occurrences. The one commencing before him was the first he could remember for a very long time.

Light flared as batteries engaged. Weapons both subtle and massively destructive added their own spectacles to the diverging battlefield. Imre raised his tempo to keep up. Most of the combat systems were unfamiliar to him, but many of the tactics remained the same. Emlee's ship possessed the advantage of the lead, which meant its drive wash effectively functioned as a weapon. On the flip side, the pursuit vessels were following a highly visible target. Providing they were able to keep up, they could theoretically pursue it forever.

The start of the chase was the trickiest phase, for high-acceleration drones still had a chance of catching up with the lead ship. Swarms of tiny vessels expanding from each of the combatants flashed and sparkled with energies dwarfed by their parent vessels but capable of inflicting significant damage if they hit their marks correctly. Imre studied the diagnostics with a growing sense of amazement. The drones were pulling delta-vees a thousand times higher than anything he had ever seen and reacting with reflexes far beyond human. Whole battles were conducted in microseconds, leaving behind clouds of glowing debris that covered half the sky. Signals were wildly blue- and red-shifted as their sources darted this way and that. For a brief moment, the sphere of vacuum surrounding C20 glowed with the energy of a small sun.

Twice, the couch beneath Imre physically shook, reminding him that the ship he occupied was a physical thing, not an illusion generated by the *Wickthing*. It could be destroyed, he along with it, if his luck turned sour. The crew took their duties very seriously and performed with impeccable skill. Emlee commanded them like a master, which surprised him at first although he should not have expected otherwise. She had much more than just half a million years' experience on him. Her ship and its crew possessed advantages he had never experienced.

Her ship, the *Memory of Markheim*, was gaining a steady lead on the *Wurmbrand* when a chain of impacts struck it from a completely unexpected direction: the front.

Imre swung his attention forward. Seven deep pits pockmarked the *Memory of Markheim*'s tapering nose—entry scars from weapons that must have been seeded by Ra MacPhedron just in case Emlee tried to escape along that route.

A boarding alarm sounded. Anything from nanotech swarms to human shock troops could be spreading through the ship even as he thought about it.

He turned his head against the crushing g forces. Emlee's expression was appropriately concerned.

"Is there anything I can do?"

"You can stop distracting me." She relented. "Here are the protocols," she said, opening command pathways through the firewalls surrounding him. "Go for your life."

He eagerly took the chance to be more than a passive observer in the fight to escape Ra MacPhedron. Counterintrusion systems had already identified the nature of the hostile drones. They consisted of fast-tunneling bombs—tasked with seeking out vulnerable areas and self-detonating—supported by teams of robotic "bodyguards" that kept the bombs functional as long as possible. To counter them, Emlee's ship was manufacturing assassin droids to take out the bodyguards plus bombarding the bombs with viruses designed to disable their trigger mechanisms. Already one of the bombs had sensed the interference and self-destructed well forward of its target. The six remaining bombs were heading for areas relating to telemetry and life support. One passed dangerously close to a crew shelter in which more than a hundred of the ship's personnel lay, unable to move while the ship was undergoing such intense acceleration.

Imre left disarming the bombs to Emlee's software specialists. Taking control of one of the assassin droids, he embraced the spindly machine's lightning-fast reaction times and sent it sprinting along the *Memory of Markheim*'s winding corridors in search of prey.

When he found his first target, he poured an upwelling of frustration and anger into its destruction. For he who had been caught in the riptide of C20 and flung out the far end of time. For the fragments of him who had thought themselves real beings and died in their droves just so he could escape. For the past.

One by one, the bombs were defused or destroyed. Imre helped mop up the last of the bodyguards, noticing Render among those taking an active role in the ship's defense. The old soldier moved with a familiar and utterly brutal efficiency.

When Imre returned to active control of his body, he was sweating and breathing hard, but felt cleansed, part of the world again. His senses rang with the sights, sounds, and smells of combat. As wake-up calls went, there was nothing quite so effective as a good fight.

On the main screens before him, it was clear that pursuit was falling behind. The drones Ra MacPhedron had sent after them were becoming less numerous, and those few remaining were at the very limit of their operating lives, having expended nearly all their mass simply to catch up. Forward sweeps were now on the alert for more ambushes, and several had been neutralized already. The austere visage of the *Wurmbrand* receded steadily into the backdrop, accompanied by a swarm of semi-independent fighters.

The main drive still surged, even though the *Memory of Markheim*'s velocity was now so close to the speed of light that the stars behind barely registered above infrared.

"How long are you planning to keep this up?" he asked Emlee. "The burn must be costing you plenty."

She didn't turn her head. "I know Ra and his ships. He'll break off before we do."

"Are you sure about that?"

"I am. He will."

Imre didn't press the point. Other details were causing

him concern. There seemed to be a whole other conflict taking place on the screens that he couldn't access through his normal senses. Strange sheets and webs unfolded and collapsed in brilliant colors that bore no relation to what was taking place in the real world. They weren't magnetic, electric, or even gravitational fields; they weren't vectors of nanotech swarms too small to see. Something else was going on that he couldn't quite fathom.

That wasn't all. Ahead, where the sky blazed in brilliant ultraviolet, he saw no obvious goal for their headlong flight. "Wherever you're taking me, it isn't Earth."

"No," she said. "We're heading out of the galactic disk."

"Do I get any say in that?"

"Later, I promise. Let me put one problem to bed before tackling the next."

Imre acquiesced, although it seemed very much to him as though they were running, not retreating. He didn't want to believe that anyone formerly under his command would mount an extraction without first preparing an exit strategy. The other two ships Emlee commanded, *Sitwell in Retrospect* and the *Hermiston Memorial* were already well outside the *Memory of Markheim*'s light-bubble. He assumed they were experiencing similar barrages from the ships in pursuit of them.

On the screen, a flurry of activity indicated the sudden dimming of the *Wurmbrand*'s drive halo, indicating that Ra was indeed breaking off the chase, or at least lessening the urgency of his efforts to keep up.

Emlee didn't say *I told you so*, for which Imre was grateful. Instead, she maintained the *Memory of Markheim*'s burn for a further fifty seconds. When an extra few points of velocity differentiated the two ships, she finally called for the mighty engines to be stilled.

Imre's sense of down shifted wildly as the ship reconfigured itself around a central, centripetal habitat and speedily spun itself up to a comfortable one gee. He took that as a sign that they would be coasting for a long time.

The crew relaxed as the threat from behind eased, but they didn't lose their focus. The way they moved, the intense concentration with which they went about their tasks, and the lack of interaction between individuals— all told him that they were most likely frags. None of them looked familiar, which also shouldn't have surprised him. In half a million years, most of the people he had known should have been dead or radically transformed, like Emlee.

He eased himself out of the couch and stood, grateful to be mobile again.

"You want answers," Emlee said. It wasn't a question. "Render will take you to my quarters. I'll meet you there in an hour Absolute, after I've tidied things up here. There'll be time to talk then. Browse through Hard Records while you're waiting. Fill in some blanks. Feel free to call the *Wickthing* and double-check everything." Her green eyes met his for a moment. "I know you'll want to."

Imre understood Emlee. He didn't entirely trust her, and she almost certainly knew why. It would take more than data from her own ship to turn him around on that point.

"Come with me."

Render indicated the stairs leading from the command podium, and he dutifully followed, leaving Emlee and her crew to settle the *Memory of Markheim* into its long voyage wherever. The bridge was eerily silent: no orders, no exclamations, no conversation. He hadn't seen a group of frags so content since the Forts had died.

Render noted the direction of his gaze as they moved past the orderly ranks and headed for a section of the ship Imre hadn't seen before. "Say nothing." The old soldier switched to an encrypted line, using old Corps protocols that had probably been superseded a thousand times over. "Tread careful. Hide your fear. Don't let them know."

"But it's alien—a parasite, a threat—"

"All this is true."

"I told her to think about using it, to consider its strategic advantages. I didn't expect her to infect everyone with it. I didn't expect her to infect herself."

"I know. You and me—we don't like it, but it's too late. This is real."

"You should have done something."

Render shrugged as he led Imre along a perfectly straight corridor that appeared to have no end. "You were somewhere else. It's what she needed."

"So no one stopped her?"

"She said, 'I've nothing to lose.'" Render halted midstride and tightly gripped Imre's right arm. "Look at us. Have we become all that we could be? Where do we belong? *We* are the unknown."

Imre wanted to argue with him. Anger coiled tight and hot in his chest, like a whip ready to strike out. He knew, though, that Render wasn't the source of his temper, and neither was Emlee. It was himself, for being out of the loop for so long, for letting so much time pass in such a fruitless and frustrating way.

"You're right, old friend. I shouldn't judge anyone until I know the full story. Emlee must have had her reasons."

"Okay." Render let him go with a sharp nod. "Did I let you down?"

"No. You did your best. I know you did. You couldn't have changed her mind once she'd made it up."

"Well, maybe . . ."

Imre didn't want to pursue that point. With full control of the Apparatus in her hands, no one could have stood in Emlee's way for long. Imre of all people knew that.

They resumed their walk in silence, until Imre asked, "Any sign of Helwise?"

The question prompted another sharp look. "Don't mention that name."

Imre's curiosity was piqued, but he resigned himself to finding the answer on his own, to that question and so many others.

* * *

The end of the corridor wasn't as distant as it had seemed. It terminated in a blank white panel that slid aside as Render approached. Beyond that point were two doors, one limned in red, the other green. The green door opened smoothly to allow Imre access, but Render didn't move to pass through. They had arrived at Emlee's quarters.

"Do your best," the old soldier said.

Imre nodded. "Once Emlee's finished with me, I might want to talk with you about what comes next."

"Call me. I'll be waiting."

They shook hands. "It's good to be back, I think. I count myself lucky."

"Miracles," Render said, "are never what they seem."

Imre smiled for the first time since his reawakening, as his friend's solid back retreated along the corridor.

Then the panel slid shut, and he was alone. The smile fell away. Behind him, the green door beckoned. He turned and went to see what kind of quarters Emlee favored these days.

They were neither opulent nor unduly extensive, consisting of two rectangular rooms, one clearly a bedroom, the other a study. The walls were dialed to a soft shade of brown, making a welcome change to the bright white of the rest of the ship. What furniture there was favored lean, economical lines: a slim-line desk, two cushioned chairs, a bed set low to the floor, a skinny wardrobe filled with ceremonial uniforms made out of genuine cloth. Nothing that would suit him should he decide to change out of his skin suit. There were no artworks on display. The face the Prime Minister presented to visitors was a minimal one, almost nonexistent, and Imre wondered what was hidden behind it.

"Give me access to Hard Records," he told the bare walls.

"Yes, Imre," said the Apparatus.

The familiar voice didn't put him entirely at ease. That the AI seemed to be moving with the ship, when in the past it had been confined to relatively stationary locations, was another indication that things had changed. "Full access?"

"I am instructed to hide nothing from you."

"Emlee might have instructed you to tell me that." The Apparatus didn't respond to the gentle accusation, and he waved it away. "Doesn't matter. Tell me the difference between Hard Records and any other kind."

"The term is employed to differentiate between standard information-retrieval systems and the one commonly employed by the Host, which I am unable to access."

There was that word again. "What exactly is 'the Host'?"

" 'The Host' serves the same function as 'the Returned Continuum.' "

"It's the galactic government, then."

"Yes. The term can also be used in reference to the citizens of that government."

"And the information-retrieval system they commonly employ is . . . ?"

"The Veil."

He nodded, finding no surprises in that answer. The truth had come to him in that superfast moment of clarity when Emlee had touched his shoulder. He had looked down at her hand and realized that her skin wasn't black at all. What he had initially taken to be skin was in fact the surface of a nonterrestrial parasite he had first encountered on an unremarkable world called Dussehra. In return for the nutrients it stole, it provided certain benefits, principal among them its ability to function as a neuronal analogue, allowing its hosts to expand their memories. The parasite also provided a means to propagate memories from person to person, simply by exchanging samples of the Veil. The Gravamen of Dussehra had used the parasite to bring stability to a culture that had been turbulent ever since the fall of the Forts, and Emlee had clearly performed the same trick on the galaxy as a whole.

As Imre had first suggested she do. He hadn't meant, however, for the parasite to take over. In her shoes, he would have confined its use to Primes alone, since they were the ones in most need of stabilization. Singletons, frags, ge-stalts, and the rest had their own means of preserving what needed to be preserved. It was the short-lived multitudes who raised the turbulence and made governing the galaxy such a thankless task.

Have we become all that we could be?

Render's words were pointed. From the Host's perspective, Primes without the Veil, like him and Render, were throwbacks. Who wouldn't choose a better memory if they could? Who would voluntarily accept to be disadvantaged? That the parasite preferred males over females wasn't necessarily an impediment, since sex was a choice many people exercised, as Emlee had. Surely, by now, the Host must have solved that problem.

He felt an urge to pace as though in a cage.

"What did Emlee say about letting me out of this room?"

"That I am not permitted to do so."

"I'm a prisoner, then."

"She instructed me to tell you that this is only temporary, for your own protection."

"Against what? This is her ship."

"That is correct, Imre."

The Apparatus offered nothing more than that, so Imre was left to speculate about spies or worse. "You'd better give me access to the Hard Records, then," he said, deciding it was time to stop asking fruitless questions and start accessing facts.

"Yes, Imre."

One of the study walls dissolved into an old-fashioned flat screen. He sat in a chair opposite it and tapped into a virtual feed at the same time. The amount of information waiting for him was considerable. He would need help winnowing it down to something he could absorb in under an hour.

"Find me a history of the Host, right back to when it used to be called the Returned Continuum." He wanted to know where he fit into the picture. Had Emlee come looking for him deliberately or had she stumbled across him by accident? "While you're at it, you'd better give me an up-date on Executive Order KISMET. Is that still in place?"

"Yes, Imre. It is."

"Have there been any sightings lately?"

"None for two hundred thousand years."

That should have put him at ease. If Helwise hadn't been seen for so long, that surely meant that she was gone for good.

Again Render stood between him and satisfaction. *Don't mention that name.* What did Render know that the Apparatus didn't? Helwise had a nasty habit of biting when least expected to.

"Tell me about Al Freer."

"The Marshal has retired from active duty," the AI told him. "He awaits you at this ship's destination."

"Where is that, exactly?" he asked, jumping ahead of himself.

The Apparatus provided him with a map. Far from the starry arms of the galactic spiral hung a small red sphere. The name attached told him that it didn't define a star or a drifting planet. The red sphere contained a ship maintained by the fifth ganglion of the Noh exploratory arm. The Noh was a widely dispersed group mind; this aspect of it was known as "the Jinc."

Imre understood then exactly why Emlee had come after him. He might have got lost on the hunt for answers, but she hadn't forgotten the questions. With half a million years in which to ask them, she had been bound to make some progress.

What he felt at that moment, however, wasn't exactly triumph. There was trepidation too, and no small amount of self-doubt. He told himself that both were perfectly reasonable.

The time had come to meet his makers.

With the past catching up on him in more ways than one, the time was also perfect for a history lesson. It wasn't one he was looking forward to. In his day, the galaxy had held an average of one hundred thousand Primes per star system, amounting to a total human population of ten quadrillion across the entire galaxy. The length of a Prime generation had been around 250 years, Absolute, meaning that since his day twenty quintillion people had lived and died, the equivalent of four billion twentieth-century Earths. That figure wasn't unreasonably enormous; just as many had lived and died while he had ruled the Returned Continuum. But he had been there for that; he had been connected to their lives, no matter how tenuously, by the threads of government he had spread through the galaxy. The majority of Primes since then might never have heard of him. How long until his name had been dropped from history texts? How long until all memory of the Bergamasc regime had been expunged entirely from human consciousness?

He was being melodramatic, and he knew it. While Emlee, Render, and Freer still existed, his name wouldn't be completely forgotten. It was, however, a stark reminder that what influence he had once possessed was likely to be much reduced. He was just another Prime lost on the vast tides of time. Like Ozymandias, all his works might one day come to naught.

Even that, he chided himself, was probably nonsense. While he had been absent, his Fort-self had presumably maintained a presence via the Barons, working in secret to further the ends of Domgard. And then there was the Veil. Wherever he was and whatever he was doing, Imre was certain the name was far from forgotten.

Nomenclature was at the top of his research list. He had already made a mistake by calling Emlee "First Prime." She was now Prime Minister, and had been, he soon learned, ever since a constitutional crisis in M1610, during which the government had been overhauled from the very top down. Galactic history up to that point had been volatile, as he had feared it would be following his departure. He had witnessed some of it himself while searching for

Bianca Biancotti and the Luminous. Civil unrest had threatened to undo Emlee's every effort at expansion and reconstruction, until it seemed like she might be toppled from power as Imre had almost been. In the end, she had met the rising dissenters halfway. She had agreed to reconsider the way her empire was run. Once she allowed that much, tensions had eased. Elections, also, had helped.

Ra MacPhedron, Imre was surprised to learn, had risen through the ranks to become President of the Host, elected in a landslide against several well-known opponents, former Marshal Al Freer among them. Primes and singletons alike had voted for him, which surprised Imre even further. The man Helwise had set up to be a successor to Imre's own throne, complete with a genetic kinship establishing a direct lineal descent for those who cared about such things, had been somewhat of an incompetent. Nor had he seemed especially sympathetic to Prime issues. Something had turned him around in the eyes of the masses, something that wasn't articulated in the Hard Records. Perhaps, Imre thought, he had simply improved at the job.

Campaigning had been conducted over ninety thousand years, with platforms and candidates crisscrossing the galaxy in order to strengthen ties and gather support. Singletons had a clear advantage over Primes in that regard, since they could campaign in many different places at once. Few candidates talked about the past, and none referred to Imre's time. The First Church of the Return had been completely removed from the table—as it should have been, Imre supposed, with both its prophet and high priestess deposed. The discussion was about the future and how humanity would respond to it. Under the twin yokes of the Apparatus and the Veil, opportunities existed to talk realistically about such long-term issues as total resource use, expansion beyond the galaxy, and so on.

Calling the poll alone had been a miracle of organization that wouldn't have been possible even in the Forts' time. Encrypted votes had taken millennia to converge on regional centers, then millennia more to reach Earth, where they were checked and double-checked to ensure an accurate result. It wasn't contested. President MacPhedron, son of the former Regent Helwise MacPhedron and First Prime Imre Bergamasc, was sworn into power in the 1750th millennium of human history.

Ra's victory ushered in an entirely new era—one publicized as peaceful, but actually one of overwhelming intra-governmental stagnation, as Prime Minister and President remained deadlocked over critical issues. In that sense, their corule was not so different from that of Helwise and Imre, except for one important detail: this conflict wasn't reflected in the general population. Apart from the inevitable and unstoppable Brownian motion among the Primes, as small powers rose and fell within the confines of individual solar systems, the galaxy as a whole was stable. In the half million years or more since Imre had disappeared from the scene, the communal memories shared through the Veil had such a binding effect that, regardless what happened to the top, a sense of kinship spread across vast expanses of space and time. A low-level empathy had in effect captured the galaxy and brought peace where over a million years of conflict had failed.

Imre scanned through pictorial records of Ra MacPhedron's election campaign and found his son to have become a lionesque figure since their confrontation on Earth, with no trace of his genetic ancestry apart from his mother's gold-flecked eyes. He wore the Veil like the Gravamen of Dussehra, with tattoolike whorls and patterns intricately carved across his cheeks and temples. His lips were black, and his eyes were dark-rimmed as though circled with kohl. He was often portrayed with hair wild and manelike, his pose theatrically aligned with images of humanity's greatness: atop the Citadel of Earth; under the skies of Hyperabad; on the bridge of an advanced warship; in discussion with politicians and philosophers. As far as hagiographies went, Imre thought, this was first-rate.

In the background, attending Ra as a running partner

during his campaign but playing only a symbolic role in the government, was an unexpectedly familiar face.

Vice President Sevaste had changed little, superficially, since Imre had last seen her, although she played a very different role now than when they had first met. They had known each other briefly on Dussehra, birthplace of the Veil. Later, on Earth, she had come to him bearing the memories of her former leaders in a plea to use the Veil exactly as Emlee had subsequently done. Imre had rejected her, fearing that she was being used as a pawn by Helwise MacPhedron—just as he had feared she was being used by the Barons when on Dussehra. Since then, he hadn't spared her a second thought.

For over six hundred thousand years, she had played an active role in spreading the Veil across the galaxy. If any one person could be said to be responsible for the plague, it would be she. That she was one of the few women who had survived Assumption—which Imre couldn't help but think of as *infection*—had only raised her public profile. Every person she brought into the fold carried with them a piece of her, for the rest of their days. That kind of influence couldn't be bought—or easily erased. Maybe that, Imre thought, was how Ra MacPhedron had attained power so easily.

Imre's concern about the parasite returned. His understanding of the Veil, gleaned in passing shortly before his abdication, seemed to be more or less correct. The limitations of its "soft" record-keeping were similar to those of a human brain: extra memory required extra tissue, and there was only so much a Prime body could cope with. Because no one person could possibly contain all the memories of twenty quintillion others, the Veil had brought stability without uniformity, and had worked its way into more human niches than even the long-lost Continuum. The question was: was the end result still humanity?

Imre didn't know how to answer that question. Even if the Veil truly wasn't conscious and had no agenda of its own, the fact that a vast amount of alien tissue was responsible for subduing the human race's self-destructive impulses struck him as troublesome.

Gravine Sevaste had been a priest in the First Church of the Return before becoming Gravine of Dussehra, and he was surprised to learn that she still called herself one, but of a new faith, one with a much gentler face. Calling itself the Revivalist Doctrine, it had no prophet and it promised no restoration of glory days, since the present was regarded by most as comfortably affluent. He skimmed its teachings and found them uninspiring. Vague references to an unnamed savior kept its options open for assumption of a leader, should the Doctrine ever turn militant. That it hadn't found the focus to do so thus far didn't encourage him to worry on Emlee's behalf.

Imre eased himself out of Hard Records for a moment in order to collect his thoughts. Officially, at least, the galaxy was in good shape, despite the squabbling of those nominally in power. If he could bring himself to accept the presence of an alien symbiont, maybe he could sleep at night.

He didn't, however, entirely believe everything he had read so far. The picture was too perfect. Reality didn't work like that. Humanity didn't work like that.

The dark speck of the *Wurmbrand* still dogged the *Memory of Markheim*, as patient as a vengeful shade.

Darker still was the complete absence of the Barons and the Luminous from the official histories he had skimmed over. That worried him more than the Veil, Gravine Sevaste, and Ra MacPhedron combined. The defining conflict of his rule couldn't have disappeared so easily. He had abdicated over it. He had *died* for it. He refused to believe that it had simply vanished into nothing.

"I want to talk to someone on the *Wickthing*," he told the Apparatus.

"I will arrange that for you, Imre."

A minute passed, during which he rose from his seat and walked twice to and fro across the room. His body felt awkward, wrongly shaped. He wished he could find some other clothes to wear, apart from the unflattering skin suit.

The flat screen rearranged the many windows he had opened in order to present a new view, one of a greenly pastoral countryside lit by a pleasant yellow sun. The stately Georgian town house was instantly recognizable to Imre, who had spent some considerable time inside its virtual walls, prior and subsequent to his abdication.

"MZ," he said. "Can you hear me?"

"With perfect clarity," said the ancient Fort.

"Thank you for trying to rescue me from C20."

"The effort had to be made. We were fortunate in the end to have the assistance of your associates. Without them, I fear none of us would ever have emerged."

"I'll be appropriately grateful once I know for sure what kind of mess they've brought us back to." He studied the view before him closely, but failed to see the only other inhabitant of the ghost ship. "Where's Chyro? Lost in another simulation?"

"In a manner of speaking. He remains caught in C20. His pattern was irretrievable."

Imre sat back down to absorb the news. "I remember a book—the Book of Kells." He frowned. "That's a real book, isn't it?"

"It was."

He didn't know where the memory had come from. Something about a library and a man whistling; the rest is obscured. He shivered, feeling again as though his body no longer belonged to him, and cursed the mad ingenuity of the trap's architects. Puns, tangled connections with the outside, fragmentary versions of himself—he did indeed count himself lucky to be in one piece.

"We'll go back and get him," he promised, the loss of his old companion gnawing at him, "or bring him back the cheat's way. You still have his pattern recorded, I presume."

"I do, but you should know that this method of retrieval is strictly forbidden by the Host."

That didn't surprise Imre, knowing that Emlee was in charge. "What they don't know won't hurt them."

MZ disagreed silently; Imre had learned through long association how to interpret the Fort's unspoken messages. "I have been waiting to hear from you," MZ eventually said. "Did you find Bianca Biancotti? Did you learn everything you hoped from her?"

He frowned. "To be honest, my memory's hazy on that point. There's a lot to sort through. You'll have to be patient."

He was speaking as much to himself as to the Fort and didn't really expect an answer. The one he received surprised him.

"Perhaps the Host can help."

An automatic rejection of that idea died on his lips. Perhaps indeed. The Veil had given humanity half a million years of experience with memories. As long as he didn't have to become infected, he was willing to explore the possibilities.

The entrance to Emlee's quarters slid open.

He looked up as she entered, and his pulse involuntarily quickened.

"Are you nervous?" she asked him as he killed the feed to the *Wickthing*.

Imre stood, but that didn't make him feel any less diminutive in her presence. It wasn't a feeling he liked at all.

"I don't know," he said. "You kidnap me. You lock me up. You surround me with people infected by an alien parasite. What reason could I possibly have to be nervous?"

She smiled and began to disrobe in front of him. "What I'm about to tell you won't help. The Veil is sexually transmitted."

He kept himself perfectly still. Emlee's white uniform was several layers thick, consisting of subtle armor, he assumed, designed to protect her against different sorts of attack. Beneath the armor she was hugely broad across the shoulders and chest—like a weight lifter, or a clumsy ultramale of old, the kind he had routinely rejected for positions in the Corps. Her upper arms were thick with corded muscle, as were her thighs. Her stomach was perfectly flat.

Again, something inside him quailed with a mixture of fear and desire.

"Are you coming on to me or converting me?"

"Look closely," she said, holding out her arms and standing as still as he was. Her discarded uniform lay on the chair beside her. "Don't be like Render. You have nothing to fear from me or the Veil."

"You haven't answered my question."

"I want to educate you, not fuck you." She wasn't smiling anymore, and he remembered that the Gravamen of Dussehra hadn't liked being touched. "This is a very old organism that spread among protomammals on Dussehra long before humans arrived. There was a survival advantage in being infected; it increased the animal's experience, gleaned from the parasite's former hosts. Infection usually went from male to female, then from mother to male offspring. The role of the female changed in the human pandemic. Gravine Sevaste told us, correctly, that in her day it was very difficult for a woman to assume the Veil. That's changed now; we cracked the parasite's genome and proteome a long time ago. But the tradition was firmly established by then, and it's easier for me to play the role this way. Apart from the extra mass I need to keep up with demands, I could change back anytime I wanted."

Imre was curious despite himself. He moved closer to study the surface of her body. It wasn't skin, but it covered every square centimeter of her from head to foot, so it might as well have been. It was smooth like cured leather, and lacked the fine hairs and wrinkles his subconscious expected. The illusion of muscles was created by thick layers of the Veil accumulating in areas best able to support the extra mass: shoulders, arms, back. She needed the extra memories, presumably, to give her a commanding edge over rivals; her body therefore had to be physically able to support it.

"Normal biomodifications would be simpler," he said.

"People find this more palatable, and biologically it sits well. Human bodies have been home to parasites as long as we've existed. A lot of Primes prefer it to machines and genetic engineering."

He could see that, but he could also see how such an accumulated mass of memories could be a disadvantage as well as a boon. If they interfered in normal life, if they disrupted the normal sense of self, the Veil might become an albatross of unspeakable proportions.

Emlee seemed unbothered by it. Only her eyes and the inside of her mouth displayed natural hues. She didn't smell alien, though. Up close, she smelled faintly of cloves and cinnamon.

Her breath was soft on his cheek. He wanted to touch her, to see what the Veil felt like, but the feeling wasn't entirely clinical. He backed away.

"Who's in there?" he asked.

She didn't answer until she had walked to her bedroom and put on a robe he hadn't seen before. They sat opposite each other on the two chairs while she tried to explain.

"It's not like having a thousand people in your head. It's more like extending a house. Every room you add on gives you space for more furniture, more books, but the address remains the same."

"You claim it's still you."

"It is me, Imre. Older, more powerful, harder . . ." She nodded. "There's no denying I've changed, but I would in half a million years, don't you think?"

It hadn't truly sunk in yet, that he was a visitor to the galaxy around him, no longer a living part of it. The confused perspectives in his head were making it hard to think clearly about anything, and he was mightily glad Emlee had covered herself up. "The Apparatus says I'm in here for my protection, yet you had Render march me through the ship without bodyguard or armor. On the bridge, you had me standing in front of dozens of people, any one of whom could've taken a potshot at me. Forgive me if I question the reasoning behind your decisions."

The lazy gesture she offered with her left hand was all nonchalance. "Naturally you're suspicious. You have a lot to catch up on—and that's partly your own fault, I have to point out. When you left Earth, you promised to stay out of my way. You did that a little too well, I think. You disappeared completely. There were a dozen times I thought you'd been killed, but rumors eventually trickled in from outposts all across the galaxy. You weren't interested in keeping up with current events. You were too busy poking around in the past."

"That was the whole point," he said. "We needed to find out more about the Luminous and the Barons—or have you forgotten that?"

"Not forgotten, Imre. Not at all." Her green eyes dissected him like surgical lasers. "Did you find anything?"

"Hints and rumors. I presume MZ gave you the data."

"He did, and there was nothing in it we hadn't already learned. Has anything new come to you while you've been waiting here, alone?"

"Anything Bianca Biancotti gave me, you mean, while I was in the city?"

"Yes."

He shook his head, feeling faintly resentful. The jumble of experiences weren't going to settle easily, and it wasn't as if he had been sitting around doing nothing.

"Let me tell you this," she said, leaning forward and resting her elbows on her knees. Her giant hands hung before him with fingers interlaced. "Getting you out of the city was a long and complicated process. No, allow me to finish," she said when he tried to interrupt. "You don't have to feel obliged to me. I just want you to know how it worked. The more of your pieces we pulled out, the more filled-in the jigsaw puzzle became, but we could tell it wasn't complete. There were gaps. Until we were sure we had everything, we weren't going to try to start you up. Who knew what damage we would do?"

"That didn't stop the Jinc."

"Yes, and look what happened. We traced the pieces of you in C20 by following clues relating solely to you. Some of them you noticed yourself: the anagrams, for instance. Occasionally there were physical clues, like white hair, blue eyes, and a missing finger. Behavioral quirks sometimes gave you away too: a dislike of mirrors, say, harking back to when you didn't recognize images of your old self."

As she spoke, he nodded, understanding more about the disparate personae he had been while under the city's spell. He recognized all those symptoms.

"There was a time limit, as you know. Ra was getting closer, and the city itself had started to fight back. We couldn't afford to miss anything, but at the same time we couldn't afford to be subtle, either. The city's immune system mobilized at the end, manifesting as police stamping down on a crime wave. Your names were changed in an attempt to further confuse the issue. We barely got the last part of you out in time."

He remembered only fragments of his final moments. People—parts of him, all of them—had been dropping like flies. Pain and confusion had reigned.

"Now we've plugged all the gaps, and you still don't know the answer," Emlee said, watching him. "I think it was more than just the city working against us."

"What do you mean by that?"

"I think the problem is Bianca Biancotti."

Imre waited for Emlee to explain.

"Look at it from her point of view. She's lying low in the city—maybe hiding—when you appear, wanting to dig up the past again. The city catches you before you can find her, and she's immediately in a bind. Something is calling her away, but she doesn't want to leave you ignorant. If she knows something truly incendiary, she can't just tell part of you because it's likely to be misunderstood, and could be easily extracted by someone following on your heels. She'll want to keep it safe from everyone—outsiders and the city included—until you're able to understand it. You're the only one she trusts. You're the recipient of the message she wants to give, no one else.

"So I think she hid the information inside you, buried deep where even you wouldn't be aware of it," Emlee said, her hands still folded as though in prayer. "I believe she left the city, safe in the knowledge that the secret she had found was preserved inside you, and therefore inside the trap itself. The city would hold that information as long as it survived. You might not be aware of it yet, but it must be there."

"Like what?" he asked.

"Only you can tell us that," she said. "Did any of your final personae have a secret? Were they hiding anything in their minds or under their beds? Was there a puzzle that obsessed them unduly, a mystery or riddle they couldn't solve?"

Imre nodded slowly, unwilling to give in completely to the fragmentary recollections. As the detective on the case of a missing sister, he had asked, "Did she say or do anything unusual before she left? If she left a message of some kind, that'd make it real convenient." It wasn't, however, this viewpoint that he was trying to remember.

"There was something," he said, remembering a photo of a buxom blonde with a fragile smile. "There was a woman looking for a twin sister. She came to another part of me for help. Finding that sister was the most important thing in the world to her."

Emlee nodded. "We pulled her out last of all. Did she find the sister?"

Imre shook his head. "I don't remember. In fact, I don't remember her at all. Just the things she did with other people who were also me."

Emlee frowned. "We definitely extracted her. Maybe her experiences haven't fully integrated yet."

That made sense. So much was still filtering through

the fog of loss and confusion. "The twin was a figment of this woman's imagination. There was no evidence she had ever existed: there were no photos of the two of them together; her apartment only had one bedroom. I think the sister was actually the woman herself, a persona within the persona, and this caused unwanted sequelae like amnesia and other syndromes. The sister theory was probably just an attempt to explain those side effects, which seemed utterly incomprehensible to her."

"That must have been how Bianca kept her knowledge safe from the city, then," Emlee said. "She subsumed one of your personae inside itself, armed with the knowledge she wanted you to find. We have to access it."

"Why?"

She frowned again. "What do you mean—*why?*"

"Why is that information important to you, and why did you go to so much trouble to get it? There's something missing from this picture, and it's not just Bianca Biancotti. It's you."

"I want the same thing I've always wanted," she said in stiff tones. "What's right."

"We've always disagreed on that point."

"Then we're no worse off now than we ever were."

He acknowledged that point with half a laugh. The bitter edge to it was thicker than he had expected.

"Let me show you something," she said, rising from the chair and indicating the door. He hesitated, then followed her out into the hallway. The door sealed shut behind them.

She turned to the second door, the one limned in red. "It opens on your biometrics only, Imre."

He walked forward and the door slid smoothly aside, revealing chambers no more spacious than hers, identical in design except mirrored down the connecting wall between them.

Where hers was sparsely furnished, his was crowded with personal effects. He recognized all of it at a glance: clothes, books, weapons, trinkets—all saved from his private retreat on Earth. There was even a transparent container full of shards of red-stained glass. That touched him, obscurely. For all he knew, the Adytum had been filled in long ago, its former occupation erased along with popular memory of his existence. Something, however, had been saved from it.

"Render did this?"

She shook her head. "He's as sentimental as a screwdriver. It was me, of course. I knew you'd be pissed if we just threw it all out."

"Or put it in a museum."

"Either way."

They stood shoulder to shoulder in the entrance way. He could feel her looking down at him, but he didn't have the courage to look back. His gaze roamed the stacks of items he had once found familiar, locating several he had missed while searching the galaxy with MZ and Chyro Kells. Now he had them back, and Kells was missing. Life never handed him everything at once.

In a corner, almost invisible behind a mountain of books, was the obsidian cabinet in which he had once kept the loop shunt that had given him such strange visions on Earth.

His gaze skated away and found Emlee at last.

"I don't know what you expect me to do with all this stuff."

"I just want you to finish what you started."

He nodded, understanding perfectly well what she meant: Himself, the Barons, the Luminous, the Forts. "And Ra? What does he want with me?"

"That's not so easy to answer. On the one hand, he doesn't want you at all. He's after me because I still haven't given him control over the Apparatus."

"On the other hand . . ."

"You killed his mother. You ruined his plans to take over the Returned Continuum. Then you abandoned him."

"He's done rather well for it, by the look of things. In fact, I told you to involve him in the reconstruction rather than locking him up and throwing away the key."

"He sees it rather differently. One sentence doesn't stack up very well against half a million years of silence."

Another nod. "All right," he said. "I don't know if I can do anything to help, but it's better to understand."

"What about you, Imre?" she asked. "What do you want with yourself?"

Find Himself. Avenge the Forts. That had been his mantra through the years of the Returned Continuum, and he'd done a fine job of both. "First things first. I guess I need to think about the Bianca Biancotti mystery, the answer that's in me somewhere." He didn't let his expression change one iota. "Did you think of asking some of the Old-Timers before you left the city? They might have spoken to her before she disappeared."

"Not likely. The honey trap isn't just for trespassers, you know; it accepts willing participants too. It's a kind of euthanasia for those afraid to permanently end it all. The Old-Timers as a group are too damaged and useless to do or know anything that could help us."

"Does Render agree with that sentiment?"

"He convinced me of its veracity."

Imre believed her on that point. Fragile though his sanity occasionally was, Render had been an active participant in the galaxy's affairs for over two million years. He had little patience for those of his generation who chose an inactive life.

"I need to prepare myself for meeting the Jinc again. How long until we arrive?"

The figure she told him was meaningless. Like C20, the *Memory of Markheim* was traveling at a highly relativistic velocity with a slow tempo on top of that. "One week, relative," she added, giving him the information he really needed.

"Is Ra off our tail?"

"No. Don't worry about him for the moment. The Jinc either, if you can put them out of your mind. Just concentrate on the problem at hand."

He looked away then. The clutter of his room was too much for him, and he wasn't afraid of showing it. "I'd like to go to the *Wickthing* to think."

"Of course," she said.

"You're not afraid I'll slip away from you again?"

Her smile had a challenging edge. "This time, that won't be possible."

"All right. Let's go. My brain is going to explode, otherwise."

The door shut on the detritus of his past, leaving him temporarily free to move forward. He was sure, though, that the gravity of such old and emotionally compacted matter would drag him back before long.

They returned to the hardcaster room via a different route. He was aware of crew members staring at him as they passed. The tattoolike markings revealing the presence of the Veil were different for every individual. Some crew members wore their scarification like symmetrical masks; on others it was barely visible. All moved through the ship with confidence and surety, as unfazed by the recent battle with Ra as they seemed to be by his presence among them.

Their opinion of him was hard to read. Were they disappointed, excited, outraged, or indifferent? Frags were impenetrable at the best of time; frags supplemented by other people's memories were an entirely new beast.

When he and Emlee arrived at the hardcaster room, an unexpectedly familiar face awaited them.

"Alice-Angeles."

"At your service, Imre." The frag who had once been his personal assistant was clad in seamless, body-hugging armor as white as Emlee's uniform. She wore it well. Two thin lines of black stretched vertically down her face from the corners of her eyes, like tears. "I have been assigned to act as your bodyguard."

Imre glanced at Emlee.

"Well, I can't do it any longer," she said.

Alice-Angeles didn't appear to be armed, but neither had anyone else he'd encountered in the ship. "Thank you," he told her. "Where I'm going, I won't need your services. I'll be grateful for them when I return, though."

She inclined her head. "Yes, Imre."

A hardcaster sarcophagus opened, fourth along the endless line, and he stepped inside. Emlee loomed over him as he settled on the yielding surface within. Part of him wished that he could hardcast himself back into the past, to join her on the long journey that he had missed. He suspected, however, that he would have been a reluctant traveler. Her path wasn't one he would have chosen, and he remained unsure about the destination.

"Speak to you in a few days," he told her.

"Hours," she corrected him. "That's another thing you'll have to get used to."

Imre just nodded as the lid swung closed, and darkness consumed him. He closed his eyes automatically, and waited, thinking of changing faces and changing roles. The body he inhabited was the same as it always had been, but now the world around him didn't fit. The disorientation was different than the one he had felt on his resurrection by the Jinc, but just as real. Then, he had changed the galaxy to bring it in line. This time, he didn't know what to do.

He felt nothing as the hardcasting began, none of the mental jerkiness that had come in his day from being stripped back to atoms, then rebuilt from scratch in a different place, identical but interrupted in midflow. His thoughts continued smoothly despite his deconstruction and reassembly in the virtual world of the *Wickthing*.

Only when a glowing oblong appeared in one corner of his vision—an old-fashioned door swinging open, shining light into a darkened bedroom—did he realize that he had arrived.

A silhouette appeared in the doorway. He sat up.

"Hello, Chyro."

The familiar figure of his physician nodded and moved closer. "We have returned, both of us, from improbable fates."

Imre's eyes adjusted to the gloom. Kells's fleshy face was dismally amused.

"MZ brought you back?"

"He did, and he told me what happened." Sharp eyes examined Imre's form for any sign of deviation from the data. "I much prefer life like this than as a book. As a *pun*. You need never fear in that regard."

"Thank you, my friend." Imre submitted to the examination with a feeling of relief. Something about this second awakening—in MZ's virtual embrace, with Kells to ensure the accuracy of his form—settled a clutch of restless memories into place. Together the three of them had hacked coded messages on the Line, interrogated partial Forts driven insane by their isolation, and pursued faint hints of Himself, the Luminous, and Bianca Biancotti. Finding the spoor of C20 was a crystalline memory in his mind now, as was their approach to the city through the vacuum of interstellar space, invisible to material eyes. He could see the three of them plotting their route into the city and preparing contingencies should things go wrong, unaware that their efforts would be useless.

"I'm sorry," he said. "I failed us."

The physician shrugged. "No matter."

"Hardly. Chyro, we could have been trapped there forever. We might have died there."

"No one dies there."

"You know what I mean. The honey trap is as good as death."

Kells stepped away. "You're you again," he declared. "What's to regret?"

Imre raised himself off the bed. MZ had created the illusion of him within the chamber he used for privacy aboard the *Wickthing*. In perfect keeping with the rest of the town house, it could have been lifted from a tour guide of the nineteenth century, with stately furniture and fittings to match. His default attire was a loose gown worn for modesty's sake, not out of any need. The ambient environment was perfectly comfortable.

You're you. Why, then, did he no longer feel like himself? Were the memories of his fragmented self still crowding at his attention to blame for that, or was something more fundamental at work in the back of his mind?

You're the recipient . . . no one else.

Physically he was fine, as was Kells. They walked together through familiar corridors to a library full of books. In the symbolic language of the *Wickthing*, the books were memories, a painting on one wall provided a window to the real world, and data could be accessed by maps and charts scattered across the desk in the middle of the room.

"It's good to be back," he said. "Are we secure in here?"

"Yes." MZ's voice came from all around them. "The Host has gained considerable ground in spatiotextural engineering: we cannot leave without their permission, for instance, and are forced to travel with them wherever they go. They have yet to penetrate my defenses, however. Of that you can be certain."

"Good." Imre nodded. "I don't entirely trust them yet. There's something going on. Until I figure out what it is, I can't be sure Emlee won't throw me out an air lock once she's learned everything I know."

"What *do* you know, Imre?"

He walked to the window while pondering the Fort's question. Through the heavy curtain, he could see the broad, richly landscaped terraces of MZ's virtual world, writ large on a three-dimensional canvas. Flowers and trees grew in a wild profusion of colors and shapes possessing an underlying order that appealed to the Fort's inscrutable sensibilities. Beyond them, the landscape gave way to Chyro Kells's experimental cityscape, one of twisting towers and gracefully curved roofs. Sunlight gleamed off countless angled surfaces, vying with the garden for dominance of the view. The city was empty, an object to be admired from a distance, not inhabited.

Kells had already wandered off, probably to test that the architecture of the *Wickthing* hadn't been interfered with during his absence. Imre resisted the pull of that reality.

This had been their world for a relative century, while outside the *Wickthing* the galaxy had changed in ways he hadn't noticed or anticipated. Emlee's world seemed more unreal to him than MZ's, but it was the one he had to come to terms with. He had to accept it and move on.

"Emlee thinks Bianca Biancotti found me in the trap."

"That is known to us," said MZ. "I was part of the extraction process."

Imre ignored him, thinking aloud. "If the missing sister was actually the woman herself, that would make her like a Klein bottle, hopelessly tangled. I have no memory of ever finding Bianca or of being told anything by her. It's in none of the memories in my head. So that can't be the answer—or, at least, the answer can't be that simple."

MZ didn't disagree.

"I think the missing sister is a distraction," Imre said. "She wasn't the only thing lost. There was a name, too. That's where it all started."

"Do you remember it?"

"Perfectly well. The names of my various parts were anagrams of my own, all except this one. That fact has to be significant."

"That conclusion is attractive."

"Well, her name was Vaia. Vaia Falisa Soulis." The words sounded strange. He had thought them only once, on awakening in the *Memory of Markheim*, and quickly put them out of his mind. They were unusual but not so unusual that they didn't call up tens of thousands of references, from locations on historical Earth to words in obscure languages half a galaxy away. "It doesn't mean anything to me."

The Fort pondered this for a long moment. " 'Foe's value as alias.' "

"I don't get you."

"There appear to be no meaningful anagrams."

"Is that the best you can do?"

"Assuredly not." The Fort sounded smug. "All three are systems located in the Core of the galaxy. Vaia is a world on the Scutum Arm, about forty kilolights from here; Falisa is another system farther in, practically on the bar itself; Soulis is deeper still. The names are old, which means they might well have been known to Bianca Biancotti. Apart from that, they appear to share no other connection. Their orbits about the galaxy's Core are not in resonance; their natures are not similar in any known way; none is known to be inhabited at the moment."

Imre considered that information. "Things change fast in the Core."

"Indeed they do," the Fort admitted.

"And we're heading in the opposite direction."

"Indeed we are."

Imre paced once around the room. "What are the odds of this being a red herring?"

"That depends entirely on Bianca Biancotti's motives, which are currently unknown."

"Could you be wrong about what the words mean?"

"It's remotely possible that another relationship between the words could be found, even by someone of your limited capacities."

"No need to be sniffy. I'm just considering our options." They had one week before the *Memory of Markheim* reached the Jinc's location. Sorting through all the possibilities could take an easily distracted Prime much longer than that. "I reckon it's worth trying while we're in transit."

"Very well. I will review the information available to us and report in due course."

Imre nodded. "And I'm going to sleep on it—not just this, but everything I've learned. Maybe my subconscious will piece it together." He rubbed at his temple and thought about this woman, Vaia Falisa Soulis, who he could no longer remember.

Bianca Biancotti was old and cunning. As a Fort, she had also proved just how ruthless she could be. He didn't put it past her to create a persona purely to deliver three words, unmindful of what happened to it afterward.

Vertigo struck him out of nowhere. So many versions of him, so many meaningless deaths . . .

"Emlee told me to finish what I started," he said, thinking aloud again. "What *did* I start? Which version of me is she talking about?"

MZ remained silent on that topic as he had so many times before.

THIS KILLING OBSESSION

Much of his past was unearthed, indeed, and all disreputable: tales came out of the man's cruelty, at once so callous and violent, of his vile life, of his strange associates, of the hatred that seemed to have surrounded his career; but of his present whereabouts, not a whisper.

— Robert Louis Stevenson

In her dreams she saw half-glimpsed shapes reaching between facts like lines of hydrogen gas connecting distant stars. And what facts they were! Cities adrift in the gulfs of space. Ships that plowed the vacuum as easily as a cutter plied the sea. Weapons so powerful they could have split her world in two. People the likes of which she had never imagined—from fresh-faced, limber beings with eyes like jewels to ancient warriors wrapped in skin as weathered as stone. They should never have seemed familiar to her, yet somehow they did. They spoke of things she should never have understood, and the knowledge was part of her, like a limb she had never known she possessed. She knew them, and they seemed to know her in return.

Did they, really?

Even in the grips of the dream, she wondered. The rush of familiarity was tempered with an undercurrent of disquiet. Some things jarred: the tattoos, her body, and the man in black who still haunted her. The space made for her wasn't the right shape. She felt as though she had picked up a dress from her dry cleaner only to discover that it had somehow become a size too small.

Gradually it occurred to her that she wasn't dreaming at all, that this was the real world and everything else she had experienced was the dream. The city, her apartment, her sister, Mac Grimes—they were illusions in which she had been momentarily caught. No less convincing for being illusions, however, and the moment had felt like a genuine lifetime—had lasted in Absolute terms longer than many—so she didn't consider herself a fool for being fooled that way. She wouldn't let herself. She had to absorb the truth, somehow, and move on.

"Absolute." That was a word she would never have used in the city. She was already adapting, becoming, arriving.

But who was she?

Her new memories told her everything she needed to know. She was part of Imre Bergamasc, the ghost everyone had been chasing in the city, and she was supposed to have dissolved into his personality like a salt grain in warm water. She could sense that the other fragments of him had done exactly that: the capable impotence of Mac Grimes; Ma Cigar's black-market practicality; Serge Maim's viciousness. All were inside him with her, part of the architecture of his mind.

She remained apart, perhaps because of the way her life had been folded in on herself in order to hide the clue, the name that had meant so much to Bianca Biancotti. Perhaps that made her indigestible, in which case it was arguably her responsibility to give herself up and make things right, to force herself to disappear into the never-ending flow of Imre's being and let him get on with things. What valuable qualities did she personify that he was now missing? What subtle lack would she engender in him by remaining apart?

Try as she might, she could not see it that way. She was more than just a single quality. She was a complete person, with memories of her own and the capacity to wonder, hope, and fear. That he didn't believe she was real wasn't her problem. Her architecture was sound, whereas his always seemed on the brink of collapse.

He slept, and she dreamed alongside him—of C20, of the ancient soldier called Render, of other wars. When he woke, she immersed with him in the *Memory of Markheim*'s telemetry feeds. Together they endured the ferocity of the universe as long as they could. Powerfully distorted by the ship's velocity, infalling photons bunched together into a blazing light directly ahead. Somewhere in that furnace was a human gestalt called the Jinc. They might have been flying directly into the sun for all Imre could tell. Behind them, shrouded in darkness, came the *Wurmbrand*, implacable, relentless—and between the two extremes drifted grey, distorted stars, like ghosts passing them by.

His life and hers felt exactly thus: rushing away from a gulflike past into an all-immolating future. In between, details.

One week was nowhere near long enough to reassemble the pieces of a broken mind, let alone a jigsaw puzzle as large as the galaxy and over a million years in the making.

Within an hour of an ill-fated attempt to spy on Emlee, Imre received a note from her saying, "Perhaps this is what you're looking for."

Accompanying the note was a densely packed file, full of data. He didn't read it immediately. His head was still aching from the Apparatus's retaliatory strike. Every time he moved, his senses roiled, plunging him into a vertiginous panic. Until the virtual world calmed down, he was good for little more than cursing.

"How can they be better at this than you?" he asked MZ. "You're a Fort. You helped invent this technology. You should be able to think rings around a bunch of frags."

MZ didn't respond, perhaps out of pride, or perhaps

because the weapon had shaken up his thought processes more thoroughly than those of a mere human. Imre would accept either, and remain healthily skeptical of any future claims of impregnability on the Fort's behalf.

"The frags can't have formed a Fort without the Luminous noticing," offered Kells. "Or the Barons."

"Could the Veil be influencing them, somehow?"

"I fail to see the mechanism. The individual parasites aren't linked in any way."

"Not even through bioelectric fields?"

"Too weak," Kells said. "The background in a ship like this would swamp anything they could possibly generate."

Imre accepted that. Besides, a thought had occurred to him. "Depth, then, rather than breadth. That must be the key."

"In what sense?"

"Q loop technology gave frags the ability to connect with many other frags, operating in parallel. The Veil gives them access to past memories, so they're operating in series. Could that be enough?"

"It could well be, making each one a miniature Fort."

That was an intriguing speculation—and a worrying one, too, if frags ever came under fire again from the Luminous. This time it would take a lot more than the Slow Wave to render them harmless again. Imre imagined plagues, killer viruses, and nanotech. He shuddered.

"Their viewpoint has to be different," he said. "Part of the point of being a Fort is taking the long view. Modern frags might be able to see into the past, but they're still living in the present, with Primes and singletons. They're not true Forts." He thought of Alice-Angeles, happy to serve as his bodyguard in Emlee's stead. "They're something different."

When the walls of the map room had stabilized, he opened the file Emlee had sent him, perfectly reproduced as a cloth-bound book in the *Wickthing.* And there it was: everything he had been seeking in Hard Records, but which had been either hidden or excised from view. This was what he had sensed hidden in the background, rendering the official story incomplete, and for which he had searched unsuccessfully for almost a week.

He felt like shooting her a terse query: Why the hell didn't you give me this days ago, when I arrived? Why leave me in the dark?

He could guess the answer: to keep him busy, to remind him who was boss, and to demonstrate her technical superiority beyond any possible doubt.

Or perhaps she suspected that he was withholding information from her, and she was letting him know that she knew.

Chastened but unrepentant, he began to read. Emlee had arranged the summary in an easy-to-scan list with bullet points and an economical style. Within moments he came up with a fourth reason for keeping this data from him: to spare him disappointment.

The Barons and the Luminous hadn't just been forgotten or swept under the carpet. There had been no undisputed sign of them for a quarter of a million years. The cessation of proto-Fort experimentation following the adoption of the Veil had reduced attacks by either party to zero. Despite extensive searches and thorough investigations of every site in which they had previously been encountered, no confirmed trace had been found of their activities, whereabouts, or identity. Indeed, hints of their presence in the galaxy had been minimal after Spargamos, when Imre's Fort-self had used him as bait.

Imre still seethed at the thought of that confrontation. He had witnessed his own death secondhand, upon Emlee's resurrection of his hardcast data, and what he had learned from it barely balanced out the sacrifice—that dark matter aliens had taken such offense at the Fort's exploration of their domain that they had wiped them out for good. The lack of evidence for the existence of such aliens made that hard-won theory pale in his eyes.

He read the data once through, then again. Absence of

evidence wasn't evidence of absence, he told himself—and he knew that if there was truly nothing to find, Emlee wouldn't have given him the data at all. She would have let the Hard Record stand. There had to be something deeply entombed to reward his persistence.

Over the course of a day, a half-seen shape began to arise out of that tomb. It wasn't a shape he recognized, but he could sense that it was there. The human mind in all its forms was an adept pattern-recognition system, and his was highly trained at teasing form out of chaos. He had no doubt that the seemingly unconnected data points he isolated as significant were indeed exactly that. Three in particular stood out.

The number of Line fragments was increasing. This ran counter to the accepted understanding that such fragments were leftovers of the Slow Wave—when the galaxy-spanning thoughts of the Forts had been abruptly severed by the Slow Wave's insubstantial guillotine—and remained unexplained.

The second concerned the number of gravitational anomalies in the galaxy, which had peaked fifty thousand years after the incident on Spargamos, then declined to approximately double the usual background rate since then. Such anomalies were often ascribed to the movement of cosmic strings and other arcane but natural artifacts through the subtle weave of the galaxy, but no theory had yet been found to account for either the sudden peak or the failure to return to normal levels.

Thirdly, the failure of nine out of ten extragalactic missions was worrying. That was something he remembered from his day. If it was significant, it was a problem that had taken a long time rising to prominence. The distances and the unavoidable light-speed lags involved made timely reporting impossible. Ten out of ten could have been destroyed and it might take another half a million years to know for certain.

In his mind, strange and sinister figures moved. The galaxy might have become used to stability, but chaos was ever only a thought away. If things were ever to change, upon the return of a long-forgotten leader, perhaps—a warrior with a gutful of suspicions . . .

Imre made a note to ask Al Freer if he was behind the Revivalist Doctrine. It had the scent of a Corps tactic, played subtly for long-term gain. Were Emlee and Ra ever to come to blows on an interstellar scale, the need for a third option might become paramount.

The thought filled him with weariness. He had abdicated for a reason, and everything Emlee intimated suggested that the reason was still in play. Until the Fort that had once been him was atomized, he would never believe that Domgard or the Barons were no longer a threat. The same went for the Luminous. He had to focus on the bigger picture, whatever that was.

His headache was growing worse. Sleep never helped, but he resorted to it in snatches all the same, needing respite from consciousness.

In his slumber he walked C20's streets in search of lost loved ones, lost hope, lost dreams. The stars swayed and turned overhead, defying any attempt at analysis, astrological or astronomical. It would be a devil of a job, he thought, backtracking the city through its long journey by the skies alone.

A snatch of song came on the night air—"What's this feeling? What's it for?"—and he staggered, suddenly uncertain of his balance.

There was a woman standing in front of him, indistinct in the dream logic of the fake city but recognizably the blonde who had lost her sister, the person who was not supposed to be a person at all.

Startled, he took a step backward. She followed him, determined, dressed in a sand-colored overcoat and holding her shoulder bag tightly with both hands.

"You're Imre Bergamasc," she said. It wasn't a question.

"And you must be Vaia Falisa Soulis."

She shook her head. "That's not my name. Don't call me that."

"All right," he said. "What do I call you?"

"I was hoping you would know."

"Because you're a figment of my imagination?"

She smiled tightly. "Less threatening than a fragment of your identity, I suppose."

"What's that supposed to mean?"

"Don't you understand already?"

He looked down at his hands, which were as blurry as hers. "Between the two of us, we don't seem to know much."

"That's because you and I don't add up to two."

He didn't want to think along those lines.

An exceedingly complex star system glided by overhead: one giant, fat sun orbited by eight smaller stars, each with its own planetary system. He recognized the arrangement instantly: this was Hyperabad, where he had found his old friends and launched his campaign to restore the Continuum. The years since then weighed heavily upon him. History was relentless, and there was no turning it back.

His memories of those days were clear. His mind had been broken, then, riddled with holes he had barely begun to plumb, but he had known what he wanted. His mission had been clear. It struck him now that he couldn't say the same thing. He couldn't even be sure that all the holes in his mind were completely healed. Here he was, after all, talking to a part of himself that should have dissolved days ago.

"Are you the woman in white?" he asked her.

She shook her head. "That's your ghost, not mine."

This only mystified him further. Ever since his arrival in the virtual spaces of the *Wickthing*, he had been glimpsing a woman dressed all in white, hooded, her face perpetually hidden. She was never visible straight on. He only ever caught her out of the corner of his eye, blurry, unmoving, and gone in an instant. She appeared in the house and in the garden, but never in the map room.

When Imre had asked MZ and Kells about her, they had

professed to know nothing. He had tried to put her out of his mind, but his mind had other ideas. She persisted, his own private haunting.

Now he had this.

"This place," he said, looking around at the city, its stark, star-painted lines. "It's more beautiful than I remembered it."

"Why wouldn't it be?" she asked him. "It's a throwback to an idealized past, like the medieval in bygone ages. This was the cradle of our civilization; our oldest citizens lived on streets just like these. We cling to the memories like children."

"It's a bedtime story, then?"

"Not really. Nostalgia was once considered a disease, you know."

"I do know that," he said, returning some of the vitriol in her voice. "You're playing the part well."

"I have no choice, in here. In your head."

"It's more crowded than I like it to be. Why haven't you gone away like the others?"

"Gone where?" she said.

"Been absorbed. Vanished."

"Would you submit to that?"

"No."

"Why should I, then?"

"Because—" He stopped himself from arguing semantics with a person who either didn't exist or was ultimately part of him. "What does it feel like to be you?" he asked instead.

"Like I'm dreaming you."

"Do you want to take control?"

"Why would I?"

"Well, it must be frustrating, unable to do or say anything, being dragged around from place to place."

"It's not like that. We're not fighting."

"Then what are we doing?"

"I think we're finding a way to be."

"Aren't I already *being* just fine?"

She tilted her head as though trying to understand him, not the other way around. "Do you really think you could ever be caught in something like the honey trap unless part of you wanted to be?"

He stared at her, shocked, but finding nothing within himself to refute that insight.

Before he could pursue the suggestion, MZ mentally prodded him from the dream. The city dissolved into watery grays and blues. The cream oval of her face was the last to disappear. The stars of Hyperabad spun like the model of an atom, faster and faster, until he was whirled back into full awareness.

His eyes were open and staring into darkness. His mind was full of confusion. Had he dreamed the encounter between himself and a restless fragment, or was a very real part of him waiting to be . . . what? Understood? Liberated? Avenged?

"Ten hours to deceleration," the Fort told him. "The Prime Minister requests that you attend in person."

Imre rose reluctantly from his virtual bed. However many there were of him in his head, he had to act as one. "All right," he said. "Call Chyro and have him meet me in the map room."

"He is there already."

Imre forwent the usual role play of dressing, although his stomach roiled at the thought of stepping out of his contemplative sanctuary and reengaging with the real world. The necessity would not be denied, and he was beginning to wonder if contemplation was doing him any good at all.

That fear was reinforced by a flash of white out of the corner of his eye as he ascended the stairs. When he reached the top, there was no one visible.

"You'll have to stay here," Imre told Kells when he reached the map room. "Emlee won't approve of your existence, and I don't want to push her too hard now she's in charge."

"I understand." Kells inclined his bald head in submission. "But how will I ensure your pattern's fidelity?"

Imre glanced at the map on the table before them. Ink dots were shifting at minute increments across a mostly empty page.

"In C20," he said, "I was lots of different people. Dozens, maybe hundreds. Still, Emlee had no trouble picking me out from the rest—the criminals, the outsiders, and those willingly losing their minds for the rest of eternity."

"What are you saying, Imre?"

"That maybe fidelity isn't all it's cracked up to be."

Kells looked worried. Imre had no reassurance to offer him. Transmission errors weren't going to make things any easier, but they were arguably the least of his problems.

Do you really think you could ever be caught in something like the honey trap unless part of you wanted to be?

"The Prime Minister is waiting," MZ said.

"All right," Imre said, quelling his uncertainty. "Send me back to the *Memory of Markheim*."

"The transfer will commence in a moment."

Imre had barely long enough to hope that he could leave all his problems behind with one jump—his headache, the ghost, and the woman with no name—when the *Wickthing* winked out—

—and he was lying flat on his back in a hardcaster sarcophagus. The air was perfectly tasteless and temperate. Small variations in gravity revealed that the *Memory of Markheim* was still under spin. Presumably Emlee would revert to an acceleration configuration when the time to burn came closer.

The lid of the sarcophagus opened. Tentatively, testing every muscle and joint, he sat up.

Alice-Angeles was waiting for him. "I will guide you to the bridge," she said crisply, before he had fully emerged.

He regained his feet and moved nowhere, clad in light

armor that had been added by the receiving end of the transmission. In every other respect he appeared unchanged. His headache persisted.

"What's going on?"

"Our objective approaches," she said.

"We are approaching it, you mean."

She didn't argue the point. "I will guide you to the bridge," she repeated.

"Let me ask you something, while we walk." He matched her step along the line of empty hardcasters, pursuing another detail left out of Hard Records rather than be mired in his thoughts again. Indicating the Veil-traces adorning her cheeks, he said, "Whose memories do you possess that weren't yours originally?"

"That is considered an impolite question," she answered, stiffly.

"I didn't mean to offend you."

"You have not. I am simply informing you. The Prime Minister has indicated that my role is to educate you as well as to protect you."

"Well, thank you, I think." They left the hardcaster room and followed a broad thoroughfare through the heart of the ship. The centrifugal gravity keeping their feet on the deck was flawless. "Are you going to answer my question?"

"No. In this I am exercising my own judgment. Acclimatizing you to disappointment comes under the rubric of education."

He studied her youthful-looking, fine features for a moment. "Alice-Angeles, was that a joke?"

"If you have identified it as such," she said, "then I am pleased. It was my intention to be humorous."

He rewarded her with a laugh, and he didn't need to fake it. The former frag had been in his service for tens of thousands of years, from the invasion of Earth to his abdication, and he had never once heard her try to be funny. "This must be Render's doing," he said. "Are you two still together?"

"I believe this to be the case," she said without a hint of self-consciousness.

"That wasn't considered an impolite question?"

"Not when you could have deduced the answer for yourself, in time."

"Is that the only difference between the two questions?"

"No. My memories are more intimate and precious possessions than the affection of another."

"Even though the memories once belonged to someone else," he said, "and could probably be stolen by taking a tissue sample?"

"The mutability of memory is what makes it so valuable." She led him through a cluster of seven crew members, two of whom watched them pass with unaccountable intensity. "You used to say that information was the backbone of the Returned Continuum. Both the medium and the content have changed since then."

He nodded, wondering if people in the Host bought and sold memories on a black market, or if carefully cultured experiences of indiscretion could be used as insurance or blackmail. "Can you take specific moments from one person's life and give them to someone else? This moment, say. Could you excise these few minutes and give them to Emlee?"

"No, Imre. The architecture of the Veil, much as with the natural human brain, does not permit that kind of precision."

He nodded again, vaguely reassured by that. If the Host had gained so precise a control over people's minds that they could add or subtract memories at will, who would he ever be able to trust?

"I'm sorry I was impolite," Imre told her. "I asked the Prime Minister the same question, and she didn't answer me either. I won't ask it again."

"If the information is volunteered," she told him, "it is acceptable to listen."

He smiled, amused by her childlike pedantry. She took her duties seriously, as she always had. "Thank you, Alice-Angeles. I'll remember that."

The bridge was humming with activity when they arrived. Information ebbed and flowed in waves across the screens. Few paid attention to it, concentrating on their own internal vistas. Eyes rolled beneath closed lids; lips moved silently; fingers twitched in time to unheard rhythms.

Imre studied the frags with greater understanding of how the Veil had changed them. Instead of minds joined in the moment, thinking different parts of a single thought, they were individuals united by a common past, a bedrock on which they could rest with absolute solidity. Singletons occasionally employed such methods to shore up a sense of commonality, but this was different. The exchange of biological material was intrinsic to the nature of the Veil. It made the frags offshoots of a single organism, not different iterations of the same being. This truly was a different way of being.

Emlee was waiting for him on the dais, an ebon statue surveying her complex domain—much reduced from the vistas she would be used to on Earth, Imre was sure. He went to her side, confident that he understood the situation better than he had before. The Veil made frags happy and brought peace to the galaxy—but did that justify the infection of the entire human race? He remained unsure on that point.

"Tell me what's going on," he said, nodding at Render, who stood at ease by Emlee's side.

"We're about to decelerate." Emlee's words were echoed by the displays, which projected structural diagrams of the *Memory of Markheim*, vector diagrams, and three-dimensional charts. The ship's route was a mess of curves and arrows focused around the red dot of the Jinc, which was visible at the tip of a region of unusually stressed space-time. The fringe of the galaxy attracted such things, along with slow-tempoed explorers like the Jinc. Among the bustle and bump of solar systems closer in, such fragile anomalies were soon destroyed. The Jinc was, Imre assumed, examining the anomaly much as they had examined the ruins of the Drum, seeking questions masquerading as answers.

"You're deliberately overshooting," he told Emlee. "To throw Ra off, I presume?"

"Yes. He doesn't know our precise destination. He'll use the data from our main burn and several small course changes to project ahead, and he'll be wrong. That'll give us a small amount of time to loop back and rendezvous with Al."

"Energy expensive."

"Only by past standards." Her green eyes were amused. "In your day, nothing flew like this."

He wasn't prepared to abandon old methods without a fight. "If we'd hardcasted here, Ra would've had no way of following us."

"We only hardcast in emergencies," she said.

"Why only then? It's cheaper, faster, more efficient—"

"And not as safe. We couldn't very well have hardcast into C20, for instance, without ending up in the honey trap with you."

"How often is that a risk, exactly?"

"More than you might like to think. When something is used a lot, as hardcasting was, people always find a way to subvert it. It's human nature—and the nature of war." She glanced at Imre and lowered her voice slightly. "That's not the whole story, of course. People are suspicious of hardcasting—perhaps superstitious is a better word— because they're afraid of damaging their Veils. The meme is so prevalent in the Host that it would be impossible to govern if we forced people to travel that way. So we fly ships, and we keep hardcasting for crises. Does that seem crazy to you?"

"A little," he admitted.

"Good. It means we're still human."

He couldn't tell if she was joking or not. He didn't know if she should have been.

"Look at the speed," Render said, indicating the screen. "I like this motion."

Imre was glad for the change of subject, and relieved to see the gleam in Render's eye. "It's almost a shame to stop, isn't it?"

The old soldier nodded, and smiled. "You've nowhere to go, so go as fast as you can."

"At last: a philosophy I can fully endorse."

Behind them, acceleration couches had extruded out of the floor. A faint rumble sounded through the ship, and Imre took that as his cue to assume a prone position. Emlee and Render did the same. Alice-Angeles had joined the other frags on the bridge's lower level with no overt sign of affection for Render. How their relationship worked, Imre didn't feel it was his place to wonder.

The rumble became a roar as the *Memory of Markheim*'s mighty engines woke from their long sleep. Energy forcibly ripped out of the vacuum plowed back into the space around them, furrowing space-time for light-years around. The waves of the ship's passage spread at light-speed, meaning that the *Wurmbrand* wouldn't detect the alteration of its course for some years, Absolute, but that would seem mere moments at their tempo. Imre watched the screens and the data feed trickling into his senses, waiting for the first signs that their pursuer was doing as they did.

The *Memory of Markheim* was decelerating at hundreds of gravities by the time that evidence arrived. Ra left his run late, presumably to give him the advantage of velocity when they crossed the same future point. Ra didn't have to come to a full halt in order to attack, and would undoubtedly launch weapons made more effective by that excess momentum long before the projected rendezvous.

Imre acknowledged Emlee's understanding of her enemy. Ra's speed would work against him, with the *Memory of Markheim* not planning to come to a full stop. He would overshoot them and have even greater distance to make up before reaching the Jinc. He could, however, still deploy matter rams and independently powered weapons while he went past Emlee's ship, so their run wouldn't be smooth all the way. Imre braced himself for developments he could neither foresee nor have any control over.

The minutes crawled by, even at his reduced tempo. By the Absolute clock, more years passed. The *Memory of Markheim* and the *Wurmbrand* grew closer until the latter's drive wash began to become a serious concern. The deck shook beneath Imre's couch. Warning lights flickered across all the displays. Emlee kept the ship's arrow-sharp nose pointed into the wash and brought the weapons systems on line.

Salvo after salvo fired into their pursuer's blazing engines, prompting immediate retaliation. Swarms of energetic darts came in clouds, apparently moving at slow motion but with immense energies, pockmarking the *Memory of Markheim*'s superheated hull. Signals flashed backward and forward between the ships—not communications, but attempts to penetrate semantic defenses that might have been left vulnerable during the long burn. Some screens showed nebulous shapes grappling for control of the space around the ships, similar to those he had seen at war during their first encounter. Belatedly, Imre realized that these weren't physical beings at all, but entities like the Apparatus and the *Wickthing*, agents composed entirely of spacetime, doing battle with each other while the world of matter passed by around them. It was like watching a war among ghosts.

The red sphere denoting the Jinc drifted by, practically invisible at the tip of the gravitational anomaly. The two Host ships must have looked like fireworks on a stellar scale, spraying energy in all directions. On the very edge of the galaxy, nothing rivaled the display.

Imre wondered what the gestalt made of it. He pictured the wizened, monklike faces of those absorbed into the collective blinking myopically at the unaccustomed light.

He wondered if they knew that the man they had created from a cloud of dust was heaving to nearby, and would soon be among them again, demanding answers.

The *Memory of Markheim*'s velocity dropped steadily. Imre knew that the moment of greatest vulnerability would come when they were at rest, and Ra was still coming at speed. Emlee released a flood of defensive agents into the space around them in preparation for a relentless bombardment, and her efforts weren't in vain. The *Wurmbrand* loomed large in the screens, as ugly and squat as it had seemed around C20; the swarm of missiles it launched was so dense it almost completely occluded the drive wash.

The channel allowing Imre access to the ship's counter-intrusion systems was still open. He took advantage of it, gaining control over three of the assassin droids he had earlier employed. He did so not a moment too soon, for a spray of impact alarms spread rapidly across the ship. The crew huddled in heavily shielded bunkers as battles tore through corridors and halls, leaving long, black scars in their wake. A tang of smoke threaded into the bridge. The sound of explosions was distantly audible, conveyed from one end of the ship to the other by its skeleton.

The *Memory of Markheim* held its own. Not without cost and not without struggle, but even as it approached its most vulnerable alignment, Ra revealed no new tactic or weapon that the crew couldn't eventually repel. He showed no inclination to ram, either, which relieved Imre but didn't surprise him. Even Ra, he supposed, would realize that there would be no point sacrificing one of his ships out here, where no other versions of himself existed for thousands of light-years. Should Emlee and Imre survive a ramming attempt, he might never track them down again.

Imre lifted his awareness out of the assassin droids for a moment when their forward momentum reached zero. The space around them was empty of anything they hadn't brought with them, and he wondered if Ra was beginning to realize that he had been duped. If he did, it was far too late to do anything about it; he could only watch as Emlee moved off elsewhere. That thought gave Imre a small amount of pleasure.

Emlee, however, looked only worried. He could glimpse her profile from the couch next to hers if he strained forward against the g forces of deceleration—turning to acceleration now, the ship having passed their point of rest and begun powering toward the Jinc. She didn't look triumphant or confident.

She looked as though she was waiting for disaster to strike.

He watched her as the seconds ticked by. The ship's velocity grew, and the distance between the *Memory of Markheim* and *Wurmbrand* shrank. Soon, unavoidably, would come the instant when the two vessels passed each other broadside on, and the prospect gave him no small reason to worry. Imre had never fought in a maritime battle; he would never have involved himself in a campaign so small, either as a mercenary or as First Prime; but he had read about them in conflict histories. His mind was momentarily occupied by corsairs with full sails bringing cannon to bear and sailors preparing to board—updated by two million years of investment in lethality.

Before he could ponder what tactics Emlee might best employ, the deck lurched beneath him, and with alarm he realized that the *Memory of Markheim*'s engines were stalling.

The timing could not have been worse. As the forces of acceleration pressing him into the couch eased, he checked the information available and saw a cluster of warnings around the ship's engine-control systems. Not the engines themselves—not a lucky shot from the *Wurmbrand*, then—but a more subtle kind of damage. However this had happened, the injury to the *Memory of Markheim* wasn't going to be permanent.

The bridge rattled and shook. The ship's resilient backbone flexed as insistent acceleration unexpectedly ceased. Although the thrust took hours Absolute to ease, those hours passed in less than a second at the crew's current tempo. By the time Emlee and the rest had started over-clocking, the *Memory of Markheim* was effectively adrift.

Emlee was the first out of her couch, finding her balance with aplomb in the sudden free fall. Orders barked over numerous channels at once as the ship rearranged itself into yet another configuration. Walls flexed into complex, curving surfaces and extruded handholds every meter. Corridors tightened to reduce unnavigable spaces. Chairs became saddles with abdomen harnesses, and air currents brushed against Imre's face. There was no time to spin up for centrifugal gravity, and too great a risk of doing so during battle. Free fall it would have to be.

Imre extricated himself from the couch and kicked lightly to join Emlee. His muscles burned, consuming chemical energy stores at an increased rate in order to allow his superfast movements.

"Someone wants your ship intact," he said.

"I know," she replied.

He leaned in close. "Do you think it's possible—?"

A missile flashed past Imre's left ear and exploded into the bulkhead behind him, peppering his back with shrapnel and throwing him into free air.

For a moment, he was helpless. Instincts noted his trajectory and identified the first handhold he would reach. He drew his legs in close, preparing to kick away from the wall as soon as he was anchored. The missile had been aimed at either him or Emlee, and he wasn't about to stay still and find out the hard way if it was he.

He had been about to ask if Emlee had a traitor on board. He didn't need to now. Someone had sabotaged the drive systems; a different someone had thrown a bomb in the bridge. There could be more, and they had to be found swiftly. With *Wurmbrand* bearing down on them, every second's delay brought disaster nearer.

He reached the wall and instantly kicked away, straining his thigh muscles and wishing he had more than just light armor on his side. Another missile exploded nearby, sending him into a wild tumble. Smoky air billowed around him in slow motion. Through it he glimpsed Alice-Angeles coming up to meet him against a backdrop of fighting frags.

He didn't believe the evidence of his eyes. The bridge had dissolved into a riot of violence. Frags fought frags in hand-to-hand combat, exchanging blows with the cold efficiency that was characteristic of their kind. He couldn't immediately tell who was fighting who—whether the combat had simply snapped their Veil-infested minds or there was some order to the madness—and not knowing the answer to that question was dangerous.

Alice-Angeles' expression as she approached was grimly determined.

To help or harm him, Imre wondered.

He kicked off another wall, aiming right for her.

Alice-Angeles looked momentarily surprised but recovered quickly, even as a third missile whizzed between them. She reached for him and twisted, putting herself between him and the blast. He felt the strain she put her body under; he felt the shock wave as the explosion struck her back and limbs.

They rolled together through the air. Another missile exploded near a group of frags, tearing one of them to pieces and filling the air with misted blood. Imre reached for the first available handhold and brought him and Alice-Angeles to a jerking, painful halt. Once such an impact would have snapped his wrist and shattered his shoulder. Primes were clearly made tougher in this strange new galaxy. Neither the impact nor the explosion had left him harmed in any serious way.

He checked Alice-Angeles next. Her armor was blackened and scarred, but she too seemed no worse than superficially injured, a fact for which he was extremely grateful now that the issue of her loyalty was resolved.

Over her shoulder, he saw Render wading into the fight, wrenching and twisting, using his long experience in zero-gee combat to terrible effect. Emlee observed the battle from the dais, the only person on the bridge holding a conventional weapon. Imre didn't recognize the slim handgun's make or model, but its lethality was without question. As he watched, she raised it, took aim, and fired.

The frag she had targeted was one of two floating in a protective sphere of other frags. The shot went through his skull just above his right eye, taking a quarter of his head with it. A store of unexploded missiles presumably strapped to his midsection simultaneously discharged, exploding powerfully into the chaotic bridge. Imre had time only to close his eyes and tighten his grip on both the handhold and Alice-Angeles before the shock wave hit them, thrusting him heavily into the wall. The noise was deafening. Debris punched him, ricocheting from the curved walls at considerable velocity. Only when he opened his eyes a crack did he realize that the debris consisted mostly of body parts.

Life support kicked in an instant after the blast, straining to suck out the corrosive gases and oxygen both, to quell any incipient fires. Imre held his breath, knowing that breathable air was low on the list of his requirements at that moment.

His ears were ringing, but Alice-Angeles and he didn't need audio to talk.

"Who's behind this?" he asked her.

"I don't know, Imre." Her brow was dimpled into a rare frown, and he believed her without question.

Asking Emlee the same question, he received only a brisk "Later" in reply.

But she knew. He didn't doubt that for a second. Furthermore, she had been expecting it. The worried expression he had seen on her face as they had approached the *Wurmbrand* told him that. She might not have known exactly how the attack would come, but she had known it was on its way.

An attack aimed at him, originating in her own crew. Was that why she had paraded him through the ship on his arrival? Had she been trying to provoke the attack rather than let it come at a time when she was vulnerable? At that, at least, she had utterly failed.

The atmosphere in the bridge slowly cleared. His hands shook with the strain of overclocking for so long, and he eased his tempo back to a sustainable level, hopeful that Emlee had excised the main, immediate threat. There had been no more missiles since the ringleader had been shot, and judging by the wreckage left where the frag had been standing, all of his allies had been effectively taken out too. Half of those loyal to Emlee had been lost with them. The pristine whiteness of the walls had become uniformly red, with darker clots where more substantial tissue had splattered.

Render waded through the mess of tumbling bodies, holding a bleeding left hand under his armpit, his black uniform lustered a deep red. He looked fresh from a slaughterhouse.

Emlee was visibly relieved to see him. With Alice-Angeles shadowing him, Imre kicked off the wall and joined them on the dais. Emlee glanced at him but didn't offer any kind of explanation. He didn't press her. Later, yes, he promised.

The bridge was a blackened, bloody ruin. Nearly half the workstations had been damaged by the blast. No doubt the ship could still fly, but it wasn't going to get far without engines. Forgoing the spattered screens, Imre glanced at virtual telemetry and confirmed his worst fears.

Pockets of rebellion had flared up all over the ship, delaying the repairs and actively engaging in new sabotage. Holding the pistol by her side, Emlee shouted orders over secure links to repair crews working on the ship's drive-control systems.

Meanwhile, the *Wurmbrand* had passed them long ago, heading in the opposite direction, and was even then coming about, passing its own point of zero velocity and beginning to accelerate toward them. The advantage Emlee had gained by overshooting the Jinc was being eroded fast. If the engines weren't running soon, there would be no point—and every imaginable disadvantage—to stopping to rendezvous with the gestalt.

It seemed absurd that they could have traveled so far for nothing. Not just absurd, but wasteful and indulgent in a particularly grandiose way. It reminded him of his own long-distance flight to Spargamos, where he had learned little but rumors and been shot by his Fort-self's hand. Was Emlee suffering the same failure of judgment and losing her grip on the galaxy exactly the same way he had?

The frags were making progress. The rebellion appeared to have been quashed throughout the ship, and the drive-control systems were starting to respond. The bodies had been cleared from the bridge. Imre could feel a new determination spreading through the *Memory of Markheim*'s sterile interior. Frags could access their tasks virtually from anywhere inside the ship's hull, and plenty remained to take up the slack of those who had died. They simply worked at a faster tempo than they had before. With the disloyal element now purged, the campaign continued.

A communications channel opened in his mind at Emlee's instigation. She wasn't talking to him, but the conversation was clearly one she wanted him to overhear.

"There's been a slight hitch," she said.

"I figured," replied a familiar voice after a three-second delay. "That boat is bearing down on you pretty fast."

"We see it."

Imre paid closer attention. Al Freer's voice was thickly layered with static but instantly recognizable.

"We're going to Plan B," Emlee asked him. "Are you ready?"

"Anytime you are."

"Good. Stand by."

"Don't keep me waiting," said Freer. "Ensure your engines and guns stay silent."

The line closed. Imre glanced at the ship's trajectory. The Jinc lay dead ahead; even if the engines were never restarted, they would reach their target eventually. Stopping, however, was a different story. At the back of his mind he began planning contingencies revolving around the gravitation anomaly: if it was strong enough, they might be able to use it as a slingshot, either to capture or accelerate the *Memory of Markheim*'s elongated frame. That would still leave the *Wurmbrand* to deal with, though, and without full maneuverability, Emlee's ship would remain at a profound disadvantage.

Ensure your engines and guns stay silent, Freer had said. The advice was decidedly out of character for Al Freer, especially to people in their position. How were they to avoid a close-quarters fight with the *Wurmbrand* if they couldn't get their engines running?

"Tell me about Plan B," he said Emlee. The ringing in his ears had faded enough to talk normally.

"It's the only sane one we have left," she said, "so keep your fingers crossed."

Imre steadied himself as the bulkheads shook around him. Tugging on a handhold, he swung himself closer to the dais and arrived with barely a second to spare. The engines coughed back into life and thrust their precious cargo forward. A clattering sound resounded through the ship as debris and bodies settled toward the rear. Inertia pulled him "down" too.

He kept a close eye on the ship's condition and was puzzled when the engines reached 80 percent capacity, then dropped back to 70. A moment later it reached 75, and hovered in that vicinity with occasional variations. No acceleration couches extruded anywhere on the bridge.

"Are the engines damaged?" he asked Emlee.

"No."

"So you're faking it to keep Ra misinformed?"

She nodded.

"We're not accelerating fast enough to get away from

him. Misinformed won't matter when he's right on top of us. What difference is it going to make? We can't stop."

"Just watch. I know what I'm doing."

Imre kept his eyes simultaneously on views to the rear and the fore. The *Wurmbrand*'s ugly nose was approaching at a decreasing rate, but approaching it still was. Ahead of them, the red sphere delineating the Jinc's location had been replaced by a three-dimensional crosshair, at the center of which only a faint, fuzzy blob was visible. Imre watched it closely, waiting for it to resolve into something familiar.

It never did, and he told himself not to feel wrong-footed by that fact. Too much time had passed. The Noh vessel now looked like three bulbous neurons connected by slender threads into a scalene triangle visible broadside on at their angle of approach. Numerous secondary vessels clustered like ships around an island. The conglomeration as a whole was keeping conspicuously quiet.

Behind it, visible only as a slight dimpling of the starlight, was the anomaly detected by the *Memory of Markheim*.

"No sign of life," said Render, coming to stand beside him as the view grew larger in the data feed. His uniform and wounded hand had both been cleaned up, but he still smelled of blood. "Is that surprising?"

Imre shook his head. The Jinc in Imre's day had been contact-averse, preferring to ply the empty skies beyond the galactic arms alone, if not always in peace. He didn't expect a trap. What could a functionally stationary habitat do against two well-armed ships bearing down on it at an increasing rate?

His mouth, however, was dry, and he knew better than to write off the wily gestalt. As the distance shrank between the Noh vessel and the *Memory of Markheim*, he steadily increased his tempo in turn, bleeding each remaining moment dry.

Emlee was going to pass at a very close distance. If she didn't kill the engines soon, she would tear the structure apart.

A tinny alarm alerted him to a change. Something had launched from the side of one of the three habitat cores—a skinny transport or missile moving with considerable and increasing velocity away from the Noh vessel. Imre tracked it in minute detail, looking for control signals on all frequencies and seeing none. The transport was self-directed, then. Possibly still a missile, even though it seemed for the moment to be heading in the wrong direction, toward the galaxy's distant heart.

When its course curved to intersect the projected path of Emlee's ship, striving for an asymptotic approach, he modified his opinion.

Instead of warming up the defenses, however, Emlee extended an invisible tracery of magnetic vanes ahead of the *Memory of Markheim*. At the same instant, she killed the engines, throwing the interior of the ship back into free fall. The transport strained ahead of them. There was no way it could match the mighty ship's headlong speed, not without thrusting for hours. Then it met the vanes and activated its own smaller version. Magnetic forces grappled and snatched at each other, snapping and tangling field lines across hundreds of meters of open space. Caught, the missile surged with new acceleration.

Like a shark bringing a child close to its belly, the *Memory of Markheim* guided the transport into an oval docking bay and sealed the fluid hatch tightly behind it.

"In," came Freer's static-filled voice over Emlee's secure channel.

The vanes snapped off.

Imre braced himself for the engines to restart, but they remained silent. The *Memory of Markheim* was still too close to the Jinc for them to be activated without tearing the relatively fragile structure apart.

That concern didn't bother the *Wurmbrand*. Haloed by its energetic afterwash, Ra's ship powered hugely at the *Memory of Markheim*'s slender heels. The President of the Host issued no detectable warning and changed tactics not one iota as the Jinc loomed large in his telemetry. Imre stiffened, knowing what was coming but unable to change a thing. The *Wurmbrand* would tear the Jinc apart, then steamroll over the *Memory of Markheim* without a second thought.

Then a strange thing happened. The backdrop of distant stars behind the *Wurmbrand* shifted as though seen through boiling water. Gravitational sensors went wild. Eerie tides swept through the *Memory of Markheim*, rocking Imre and Render from left to right. Creaks and groans echoed through the battle-weary ship.

That was the worst of it, though. The larger effect was aimed directly at the trailing ship.

Telemetry tracked the *Wurmbrand* as its nose tipped wildly off course. Its hull twisted as though gripped at either end by giant hands and turned in opposite directions. Huge rents opened up, belching air from pressurized compartments within. The engine died almost immediately, sending one explosive ripple through space-time in all directions that briefly spiked all the *Memory of Markheim*'s sensors.

Imre could only stare with a mixture of fascination and horror as the data rolled in. Space itself seemed to have reached out and knocked the *Wurmbrand* from the sky.

"Don't look back," Render intoned. "The vengeance of God will make you blind."

A feeling like déjà vu lit his mind like a nova. The Jinc had been obsessed with the search for humanity's origins. He remembered that clearly. "We trawl the outer edge of the galaxy," it had told him, "for clues to the nature of God." What Imre had seen just then wasn't a clue, and he was sure it had nothing to do with a deity of any kind. It was a force the like of which he had seen before, in a recording taken by Emlee after he had "died" on the surface of icy Spargamos.

"The Jinc were looking for God," he said aloud.

"Looks like they found it," said Emlee.

He glanced at her. She couldn't turn pale, but her hands were gripping the rail around the dais with greater fierceness than the zero gee demanded. The muscles in her jaw were knotted like rocks. She was obviously as surprised as he by the attack on the *Wurmbrand*. Clearly she had been planning on simply running headlong once they had scooped up Al Freer.

Freer, however, had known, and his warning had saved them. The *Memory of Markheim* had coasted by, presenting no threat at all to the Jinc. Ra MacPhedron's haste had killed him.

"There will be survivors," Emlee said.

The sky was still moving behind them, but the *Wurmbrand*'s tumble grew no more severe. A cloud of weapons still accompanied the stricken ship, its disposition chaotic.

"Is that really our problem?" Imre asked.

"The Jinc will take them. Assimilate them."

"That's not a fate worse than death."

"Some might think so," she said. "You would have."

"Are you trying to talk yourself into turning back?"

Render shook his head. "She won't turn. She won't stop."

"He's right," Emlee said. "I won't. I don't feel good about it, though."

"It's not your job to feel good about anything," Imre told her. "It's your job to get it done."

Her eyes were hot. Her tone was bitter. "Well, I guess I did just that. We have you, safe and sound. We have Al, too. Maybe we can make some sense out of this fucking mess, finally."

"What good do you think Al will be, without the Jinc?"

Emlee didn't answer him. The *Memory of Markheim* had reached a safe distance from the Noh vessel. Slowly, so as not to bring down upon them the same wrath that had destroyed the *Wurmbrand*, the ship's engines came back to life, and the illusion of gravity returned. Imre's feet lightly touched the deck. The muscles of his back and shoulder tensed, preparing to assume the weight he had been free of, just for a little time.

* * *

She watched and learned, feeling the long years of Imre Bergamasc's life accrete around her like layers of sediment. Every thought he had, every emotion, triggered long chains of memory that were only slowly beginning to overlap. The explosive battle with the frags had prompted a powerful series of associations that she recognized from her dreams: of burning worlds and conflicts sprawling across the galaxy, of blood and smoke in vast profusion. When Imre remembered Al Freer, she thought of capability, ruthlessness, loyalty, and strength. And rigidity, self-interest, dispassion, and ice.

"We need a destination," Emlee said, as they hurried through the ship's smoke-blackened corridors once the hard burn was finished. Freer was waiting for them in a meeting room near the air locks. This was the first time Emlee had spoken since the *Memory of Markheim*'s engines had reignited. The black man's voice sent a shiver through her entire being. "We can't blaze a trail across the galaxy without having an actual destination in mind."

The phrase *Vaia Falisa Soulis* sent ripples through Imre's thoughts, but he repressed them as he continued to repress everything to do with C20, as though they meant nothing to him.

"Inward," he said. "That's the only possible direction from out here."

"Do you want to be more specific than that?"

"Not until you tell me why your crew mutinied back there."

"That's done with," she said. "We're clean now."

"I'm supposed to take your word for this?" A hint of betrayal flavored his thoughts. "You used me as bait. That doesn't fill me with trust, Emlee."

"Not bait," she told him. "A catalyst."

"Either way, you could have told me in advance that some of your crew had it in for me. Do you plan on telling me who was behind it?"

Emlee was tight-lipped.

"Ra?" he pressed. "The Barons?"

She winced at razor-sharp memories of the confrontation on Spargamos. Being shot by another version of himself didn't qualify as suicide, exactly, but the existential crisis it had precipitated was yet to be resolved. His fragility remained, for all his bluster.

"The Revivalist Doctrine," was all Emlee would say.

Imre took that small piece of information and tried to slot it into place. The jigsaw was growing more complex, not less. His half-formed theory that Freer had established the Doctrine in order to prepare the way for Imre's return certainly made no sense in light of what Emlee had told him—unless the Revival referred to a very different iteration of Imre Bergamasc, to which the one she haunted would be nothing but anathema . . .

They arrived at the place Al Freer was being held, a surprisingly large room that had been hastily cleared for the new arrival, and all thoughts of the mutiny were pushed from her mind.

Alphin Freer was supposed to be a lean, tall man with steel grey eyes who rarely laughed aloud. In the Corps, he had been the perfect executive officer: possessed of all the abilities that made for a good leader except the desire to be ultimately in charge. He was happiest when given orders and helpless when cut off from his chain of command. She saw in Imre's mind a moment long ago, when Freer had practically pleaded for direction. "There's nothing more useless," he had said, "than a soldier without a fight."

Freer had become Imre's Marshal in the Returned Continuum and played a very important role in maintaining both security and stability. A singleton rather than a Prime, he had been multiplied many times over and positioned as conduits between new, potentially rebellious governments and the administration on Earth. From the privileged position of the long view, he had manipulated, deposed, executed, or converted trillions of people, all in the name of propagating Imre Bergamasc's vision. He had been one of the all-important trinity underpinning the First Prime: the

Regent, Helwise MacPhedron; the Marshal, Al Freer; and the ghostly Apparatus.

Imre knew (and therefore she knew) little about what had happened to Freer since his abdication, except that he had campaigned for the role of President of the Host with battle-hardened determination, but that somehow he had lost to Ra MacPhedron.

What awaited them in the meeting room shocked Imre deeply. And the shocks kept on coming.

Al Freer was a bloated mass lying face upward in a sophisticated sling from which numerous tubes and wires led into the nearest wall. He didn't appear to be wounded; the medical equipment seemed to exist solely to sustain the disproportionately large amount of the Veil drawing sustenance from his body. His eye sockets were dimples set deeply in bulging, tumorlike growths projecting from his forehead and cheeks. Grotesque folds of dimpled black tissue rolled from his neck down along his torso. His arms and legs were nearly indistinguishable from the rest of his body, and his digits were completely subsumed. The hugeness of him, and the alienness of his flesh, filled Imre with an immediate and involuntary revulsion.

Only his eyes were the same: hard and flat, staring at Imre with cool dispassion. She felt Imre trying to match that stare but finding it difficult.

"You look disappointed," Freer said through virtual channels. His mouth looked as though it hadn't moved for centuries.

"I thought—"

Imre interrupted his own thought and moved to take one of three utilitarian seats facing the bedridden figure. Render and Emlee stood behind him, while Alice-Angeles watched by the door. The room was spare and functional, like every other public space on the *Memory of Markheim*. It looked like a medical suite, but most of the equipment was unfamiliar to Imre. There were several tubular tanks at the rear of the room. One of them glowed a warm yellow.

"I thought you'd resist the temptation," Imre finished.

"Why?" Freer's eyelids flickered. "You were gone. The age of war was ending. I had no purpose."

"Except to be yourself." For hundreds of thousands of years, Freer had been accruing experiences across all his manifold bodies—too many for any ordinary mind to hold, even that of a singleton. To contain them all biologically, the Veil would be an essential prosthesis. "You went on a pilgrimage, picking up all your other selves as they retired from office. It must have taken you—"

"A long time, yes. And I'm clean, I assure you."

Something about the way Freer spoke tickled Imre's radar. "Clean" was the same word Emlee had used. "Clean of what, exactly?"

"You haven't told him?" Freer asked Emlee.

"Things have only just come to a head," she said. "There hasn't been time."

"How long does it take to say it?" The cool gaze returned to Imre. "She doesn't want to tell you because she's unreasonably afraid of what the Apparatus will do. Executive Order KISMET is still in effect, and we know the spook has struggled with the definition of what it means to be a person or not. So when I tell you that a certain batch of memories has been spreading through the Host, and that those memories are behind the trouble you've just gone through, perhaps you'll understand why I can't be more explicit."

Imre's muscles locked. His mind worked so fast she could barely keep up. KISMET . . . memories . . . the frag revolt. There was only one way all three could connect. Still, he resisted the conclusion. Yes, Helwise had been on Dussehra. Yes, she could have Assumed the Veil before he ordered her killed through the Apparatus. Yes, he had known at least one other woman who had been infected and survived . . .

Gravine Sevaste. Shock waves rippled through his psyche. Sevaste had carried the memories of Helwise

MacPhedron to Earth and deliberately spread them with the Veil across the galaxy. Those memories were behind Ra MacPhedron's rise to power, and they were surely behind the uprising in the *Memory of Markheim*. Emlee must have suspected that they had been carried aboard the ship by her frags, but she couldn't tell how many had been infected until they were provoked into action—and who best to do that than the man who had ordered Helwise's death?

The Revivalist Doctrine. Imre repressed an audible groan. No wonder there was a vacancy at the top of that organization. Helwise couldn't be named. Her lingering existence couldn't even be implied lest the Apparatus changed its mind and wiped out half the people in the galaxy, thinking that it was obeying Imre's second-last order—an order that couldn't be countermanded.

Behind him, Emlee radiated tension like a bomb about to explode.

Imre forced himself to nod calmly, although his insides seethed. "I understand—but she's not really still alive. They're just memories; aren't they?"

"Of course, but I'm told they're pretty persuasive." Freer's stare wasn't unsympathetic. "You'll have a hard time undoing them."

She wondered what they contained. A condensed version of Helwise's dealings with Imre—if such a thing was possible—from the Corps right through to the last days of the Returned Continuum, or a random selection of memories plucked at random from her long life? Either would be explosive. Helwise had seen him at his best and worst, many times over. She had no doubt that the memories could be as damning as Freer said they were. Imre hadn't even been himself for some of them.

"Who said anything about undoing them?" His voice seemed to come from far away. "The more I learn about the way things are, the less relevant I seem to be."

"Don't be so sure about that. There's someone I want you to meet."

The walls of the glowing tank became transparent, revealing a human body within, suspended in a dense, translucent gel. At first glance, it appeared to be unconscious. Wizened and hunched, it looked barely alive.

Then its eyes opened, and its limbs twitched. Skeletal fingers clutched at the walls of its cylindrical cage. Its face loomed closer, slightly magnified by the curved membrane.

Imre stood up, resisting the urge to run. She recognized with him the physiognomy of the Jinc. The component was something more than a frag but less than human, valued as a living brain, a mouthpiece, and a mobile pair of hands rather than for any lingering individuality. Imre had almost become one himself, only escaping forced assimilation with the help of the silver sphere the gestalt had collected during its search for God. But for that good fortune, the story of Imre Bergamasc's resurrection and return could have ended right then.

"What good will this do?" Imre asked Freer, feeling a mixture of pity and disgust for the creature. "It's useless without the rest of the gestalt."

Its lips moved. "We are not here," rasped the same staticky voice Imre had heard over the comms while the *Memory of Markheim* had approached the Jinc. "We are not here, but I am. I am here, and I am complete."

Imre stared harder at the figure in the tank. Its shriveled features were unrecognizable, but the voice left no room for ambiguity.

He was looking at another Al Freer.

"Jesus," breathed Render

Imre glanced at Emlee. She was unmoved. Obviously, she had known about this in advance. She might even have planned it with Freer before he had undertaken the mission. Freer was a singleton; it wasn't the first time one of his selves had met with a grisly fate.

Not a fate worse than death. The words sounded especially hollow now.

Imre successfully swallowed his revulsion. Moving closer, he placed himself between the corpulent Al Freer on the sling and the wizened version in the tank. Their eyes followed him, and he felt the weight of their diverse experiences heavily upon him.

"What do I call you?" he asked the tank version.

"We are the Jinc," came the crackling response. "I am Al Freer," it added with a pained look. "There is a distinction."

"How long you been part of the Jinc, Al?"

"I do not know. We record events, not time's passage."

"How much do you know about its activities?"

"Everything." Thin lips pulled back in something that might have been a smile. "We have been studying you."

"From out here?"

"We rebuilt you. You escaped, so we rebuilt you again." The grimace widened. "This time you did not escape."

Anger more pure than any emotion Imre had ever felt rose up inside him. All he could see—and she could see through his eyes—was the leering face before him. All he could hear were the words it had just said. All he could feel was fury.

"Why?" Imre hissed.

"We thought you were connected to the mysteries."

"I wasn't. That was just a coincidence. You and your fucking test—" He stopped to take a deep breath. She could feel him losing control, or fearing that he might. She braced herself for actions that she could not prevent. "You put words into my head. I reacted to one of them because of something that happened on your ship. It had nothing to do with who I was, before you brought me back."

"I disagree," said the Al Freer in the sling.

The cool voice of Imre's old friend punctured the expanding bubble of emotion. "Why?" Imre asked again, in a calmer voice.

"The word you reacted to was 'luminous.' You told me that in the Cat's Arse."

"Yes."

"We also know," said tank-Freer, "that your reaction was triggered by the phrase 'persistent luminous archaeoglyphs.' "

"Don't think I haven't wondered what that means, ever since." Imre rubbed at his aching temple with his left hand. He had gone from needing answers to having too many of them at once.

Tank-Freer said something, but she didn't hear it. Imre had frozen with his left hand in front of his face, and was staring with shocked blankness at it. There was no room left for surprise, but that was all he felt, rising up to subsume every other thought in his mind.

Where his little finger had once been, a lump had formed. Half a proximal phalanx in size, it protruded from the truncated knuckle like a child in the midst of adults. Already there was a suggestion of a nail.

His little finger was growing back. Not perceptibly, but definitely. It hadn't been visible at all in the *Wickthing*, just hours earlier, but already the nascent digit was near the first joint.

Hours relative, she reminded herself. That could have been centuries, Absolute, plenty of time to grow new cells, knit new bone, and weave new skin.

Imre's first coherent thought was to call Kells, immediately, and reverse the change.

Put this into perspective, she wanted to tell him. What's a finger when we're talking about the fate of the galaxy?

Some of that thought must have penetrated. His knee-jerk panic subsided. It wasn't as if he was being radically rebuilt before his eyes. He was still him.

"I'm sorry," he said, lowering his hand to his side. "I didn't hear you."

"We seek evidence of the works of God," said tank-Freer. "Persistent luminous archaeoglyphs comprise part of that evidence: 'persistent' because they survived the transition from energetic plasma to the Dark Ages of the post–Big Bang era; 'luminous' because they radiate light;

'archeo' for ancient and 'glyphs' for signs that are the work of intelligence."

The other Freer stirred heavily. "The Jinc believe—"

"Wait, Al. I want to hear it from its own mouth."

"We believe these signs to be evidence of God's work during the early days of creation," said tank-Freer. It twitched all over as though hit with an electric current. "The ages of light were chaotic and furious. Life as we know it could not survive then. There was intelligence and purpose, however, and we exist today because of it."

Imre shook his head. "I thought you were searching for evidence of exospermia," he said. "Why else would you be scouring the edge of the galaxy for trace material?"

"It is all part of the same mystery," said tank-Freer. "The inhabitants of the Light Ages are the first of which we have obtained evidence, but that by no means rules out the existence of earlier beings."

Imre's grasp of astrophysics wasn't comprehensive, but he did know the basics. Three seconds after the Big Bang, the basic building blocks of matter had formed—protons, neutrons, electrons—and the fundamental forces of nature were already in play. However, many tens of thousands of years passed before the matter such as that humans encountered in their everyday lives was able to form. The energy of the Big Bang had filled space with a storm of photons so intense that it would take three hundred million years of cooling before stars and galaxies could exist. Conventional wisdom ran that no forms of life could have evolved before then, let alone thrived.

The Jinc had never boasted of possessing conventional wisdom.

"You think something lived during the Light Ages?"

"We know it. The evidence of their handiwork is recorded in the fine details of the cosmic microwave background."

"So what happened to them? Why aren't they around today?"

"They might well be." Tank-Freer twitched again. "By what name do you call the perpetrators of the Slow Wave?"

The Luminous. "But for something that evolved in the Light Ages, today's universe would be certain death for them. The center of even the hottest sun would freeze them solid."

"Then they are dead. It makes no difference. God's work is accomplished by many hands."

"What is God's work?"

"Life."

"Whose life?"

"God makes no distinctions."

"So why does it matter if there was life in the Light Ages or not? Why do you care if we're here because of evolution or something that happened billions of years ago?"

"We do not care," said the thing in the tank, "but others appear to. I—you are not the only ones coming to the Jinc for answers."

She thought of the gravitational anomaly and the way it had flexed to destroy the *Wurmbrand*—clearly protecting the Jinc from harm.

"To what questions?" Imre asked.

"What humanity is. Where humanity stands. What humanity wants."

"That's what brought on the Slow Wave," Imre said. "The answer to one of those questions."

"I believe so." Again, Freer in the sling had spoken. "If someone outside the galaxy noticed us, the Jinc might be where they first stopped to take stock. Imre, you said you were contacted and helped by something the gestalt had found; it gave you the word 'luminous'—"

"It never claimed to be one of them."

"Regardless, it was observing and interacting with humanity, just as identical copies were also observing and interacting with anyone trying to re-create the Forts—by blowing them to kingdom come, specifically. It connects."

"Maybe," Imre admitted, "but I still don't see where I

come into the picture. Why did the sphere talk to me? Why do I matter to something that might be fourteen billion years old?"

"You know why," said Freer in the sling. "Because you betrayed us. You sold us out to the Forts in order to become one of them. The Jinc found that much in your memories when they assimilated you into the gestalt, but they never worked out what your reason was—what great venture led to your change of heart."

"Do you know?"

"No." Freer's gaze didn't budge. "Emlee never told me. But I've been thinking about it. Whatever it was, it was big. That's why the pattern you were made from was destroyed. You didn't want anyone to know what you'd done, just in case someone went hunting for it. The best evidence we have that someone did go hunting is that the Forts were killed—but I think that might be looking at it about-face. Someone noticed the end result, stomped on the Forts, then began the slow and painful process of working out the backstory."

"They also made sure Domgard was never repeated," put in Emlee, speaking for the first time. "Don't forget that."

"I won't."

Tank-Freer was twitching. Imre ignored it. His weariness went bone deep, and she felt it keenly. "So the sphere talked to me because the Luminous had already worked out some of the backstory. It knew my name. It also knew that my memory was fouled up. There was no point interrogating me directly. The best it could do was let me go and see where I went. That's why it helped me escape." He half turned to address the agitated tank-Freer. "What happened to the sphere after I left?"

"You—we—" The wizened thing was unable to speak for a moment. Tremors rippled through its gnarled flesh. "I will answer. It left us. We did not recognize it for what it was. We did not know."

Something it said rang a distant bell. Imre searched

though his own extensive memories until he located the reference.

On the verge of leaving Hyperabad, he had encountered a version of Himself who had played a recording detected by the Barons in the Line.

"You were old when the universe was young," the Jinc had broadcast. "You are the creator and the destroyer. Heed the prayer we commit to the void." Like most prayers, it had sounded as though an answer wasn't expected. Then, however, the prayer had talked about the absence of God's emissary, which Imre had taken to be a reference to him. "The one who called you was found and is now lost. Your angel has departed." But they had rebuilt a new copy of Imre as soon as he had left, so that meant they hadn't been talking about him at all. "Your emissary is gone. You gave us evidence, and we did not recognize it."

They could only have been talking about the sphere—one of the "rebel" spheres such as the one he had encountered in Spargamos, which claimed to be not entirely at one with the Luminous's aims.

The closing words of the prayer echoed in Imre's memories: "We beseech you, our God, to shine your light upon us once more. Illuminate our sacred path that we may know the road toward you. Hear our words, and grace us with an answer. We are patient. We sift the darkness for your guidance with rapturous hearts. We dedicate our quest to you and to your mighty works. You are master over all levels of creation. Your seed created us, and your wrath destroys us. We worship you in your absence."

Imre might never know exactly how long it had taken, but the Jinc had clearly received a reply to that entreaty.

"There's a place," he told the Freer in the sling, "called Spargamos. It was Volume Zero when the Slow Wave hit; that's where Domgard was based. I met my Fort-self there. Did Emlee tell you this?"

"No." The answer came evenly while tank-Freer, ignored, scrabbled weakly at the glass. "She couldn't have done so without revealing your secret."

Imre was beyond feeling gratitude for that, or worrying if Freer was offended.

"I met something else there, too: one of the Luminous spheres, like the one who helped me escape from the Jinc. It told me that Domgard was an experiment involving dark matter—something MZ had already suggested, but for which we had and still have no real proof. The sphere said that inhabitants of the dark matter universe were trying to stop us from making the leap. It implied that the threat was alien."

"That fits."

"It also said that this wasn't the whole story, but that it wouldn't tell me anything more until we trusted it and its kind."

"A big ask."

"I agree. My Fort-self used me as bait to test weapons he's developed against the Luminous. I don't know who won."

"He's still out there, working on the problem."

"He was. I presume he still is."

"Gearing up for war," Freer said. His voice was very solemn. "We're the noncombatants, for a change."

"I—we did not know," exclaimed tank-Freer. "We—you were not aware!"

All eyes turned to him. There was silence for a long moment.

"Od's balls," Freer breathed. "If the Jinc find out about your Fort-self, they'll tell the Luminous."

Imre nodded. "And that will be the end of us. They've spent one and a half million years knocking out the proto-Forts, and still we attack and plot against them. At some point, they'll decide we're more trouble than we're worth and kill us all."

"What *are* we worth to them?" asked Emlee.

"They created us," tank-Freer grated. "I—we owe a debt of veneration."

"We don't owe them anything at all," said Imre, rounding on the wizened creature with reawakened fury. "So what if they were around in the Light Ages? That doesn't mean they created us. The stuff they were made of isn't anything like DNA. It was cosmic strings and quarks or even stranger stuff. We can't imagine the kind of things they were, or the environment they inhabited. There were no suns or planets; there wasn't even space. It was a soup, and they might have been the only thing going.

"They built things we can see echoes of today. So what? The entire universe is an echo of that age. Hell, maybe they made *everything*, not just us. Maybe their machines caused the plasma to clump into stars and black holes. Maybe without them there'd be no galaxies or solar systems at all. We're just an accident in an entire universe of accidents—and who knows how they feel about that? Maybe they regret the way things have turned out. Maybe they wish they could go back and smooth out the clumps, so there'd never be anyone else to disturb their peace. Well, it's too late for that. We're here, and they've got no right to fuck with us."

Imre slapped the side of the transparent tank, close to the wizened thing's face. It recoiled as though actually struck.

"Your—my thoughts are blasphemy," it crackled.

"Your beliefs are insane," Imre said. "God ignored you until we got in its way. It's using you now to spy on us. It'll wipe us out if it gets the chance."

"It's probably too late to contain everything," Emlee said, coming up beside Imre. She could see her dark features reflected in the curved surface of the tank. "The Jinc will have picked up survivors from the *Wurmbrand*. They'll suspect you're aboard this ship. That alone might be enough to rouse the Luminous."

"So they'll come after us. They'll try to stop us." He turned his attention back to tank-Freer. "Do they have anything that could catch up with this ship?"

"Time is on God's side. You'll never outrun your fate."

"If these things have survived fourteen billion years, I'd

say you're right about the first point. As to the second, that remains to be seen."

Imre turned away from the tank, dismissing the thing inside physically as well as mentally. The confusion had been swept away. She could feel decisiveness crystallizing his mind like ice spreading through supercooled water.

"Kill it," he told the Freer in the sling. "Dump the body out an air lock. If the Luminous are coming after us, let them know what we think of those who follow blindly."

Tank-Freer thrashed and beat at the glass, but the Freer in the sling answered coolly, "It will be done."

Imre turned next to Emlee. "You said earlier that we need a destination. I have one for you, if you're willing to hear it."

"I'm open to suggestions."

"It's a place called Vaia. You'll find it in the Hard Records."

"What's there?"

"I don't know," he said. The time for dissembling was long past. "It's part of the message Bianca Biancotti left me in the city. 'Falisa' and 'Soulis' comprise the rest of it, and they're places too. I think it's a trail, one she intended us to follow."

"She'll be at the end of it?"

"I don't doubt there'll be someone."

"Waiting for you to come home," said Render.

Goose bumps lifted the fine hairs on Imre's arms, but he didn't respond to the aside.

"There's a choice you need to make," he told Emlee. "You're not going to like either option, I'm afraid."

"Go on."

"If letting the Jinc know about my Fort-self is dangerous, letting the information escape into the Veil would be catastrophic. You know that. Am I right in guessing that you've kept your memories to yourself for just this reason?"

She nodded.

"Well, the secret is out now—unless you kill the two other people in this room to guarantee its safety."

Emlee glanced at Freer and Alice-Angeles. Both of them were infected with the Veil. Neither showed any emotion, but Imre could tell that Freer was overclocking, ready for anything.

"Or?" she asked.

"Or you call Ra and tell him to rendezvous with us at Vaia."

Emlee exhaled sharply through her nose. "All or nothing, eh?"

"Exactly. Two lives to save quadrillions, or all the quadrillions on your side. There's no middle ground. Which is it to be?"

"Life is never easy when you're around." Emlee put her hands on her hips and looked down at the floor for a moment. When she raised her head, her expression was cheerless. "I'll draft a message and signal Ra immediately. There's a chance he might not come. You know that, right? Or he might bring a fleet and blow us out of the sky."

"A fleet might not be a bad idea," Imre said, "since we'll be arriving with the Luminous hot on our tail."

"Do you really think that's likely?" she asked. "If these things are as old as the universe, they'll be working on a tempo even slower than Forts. It could take them millennia to decide what to do about us."

"Want to take that chance? What happened to the *Wurmbrand* proves they can move quickly when they want to."

"Don't forget the spheres," said Freer. "That's what they're for, I think. They interface with us quick-thinkers so their masters won't have to muddy their feet."

"All right," said Emlee. "I will call him. Don't expect a response anytime soon, though. The next time we hear from him, he'll probably be right on top of us."

Imre nodded distractedly. The reference to the silver agents of the Luminous made him wonder again about dissension within their ranks. If it did come to a stand-up fight, he hoped they could rely on help from the inside.

At the back of Imre's mind, something worried at him, something he had either forgotten or not entirely noticed yet.

I am telling you the truth, the sphere in Spargamos had told him. *Not the whole truth but part of it.*

Somewhere ahead of him, or behind him, or conceivably all around him, the whole truth was waiting. Until he had it in his possession, he could never rest.

That's what I want, he told himself. That, and no more. Is it too much to ask?

No, she replied, not knowing if he could hear her but hoping that her agreement counted for something. It's not.

He thought something bitter about things that wouldn't die—Helwise, the Luminous, *her*—but she couldn't quite make it out and was glad for it.

The thrashing of tank-Freer had ceased. It floated limp in the fluid, its wrinkled face downcast and mouth agape. It had posed no real threat while physically separated from the rest of the gestalt, and Imre felt a moment of shame for allowing vindictiveness to overcome good sense. He should have asked that it be put in hard storage for a while, just in case it was needed again, and spared it an ignominious, unnecessary execution.

No one had stopped him, though. Al Freer had lost many iterations of himself down the millennia, and the Jinc could spare any number of its many components without even noticing. Even if Imre's motives were suspect, the consequences were the same.

You'll never outrun your fate.

Too late to take those words back. Despite his misgivings, he wished he had killed the thing before it had uttered them.

"I need to talk to MZ," he said. "I'll do it from my quarters."

Emlee nodded. "I'll flag you the course details once they're finalized."

"I'd like to talk with you too, once this mess is cleaned up," said Freer.

"All right. What about you?" Imre asked Render. "Do you want a shot at me too?"

"I'll say it if I feel it." The old soldier smiled like a cracked statue. "Nothing, for now."

Imre felt a rush of gratitude. Out of everyone in the Corps, Render was the only one who had known the truth about his Fort-self all along. He had kept that truth to himself since the Mad Times. If anyone deserved to berate Imre, it was him.

Emlee left to put the ship back together. Imre lingered a moment, wanting to bring some kind of resolution to his first meeting with Al Freer in half a million years. The words wouldn't come, and Freer himself didn't offer any. In the end, there were none. They were three ancient combat veterans—counting Render—who had all seen better days. There might not be enough left to waste on small talk.

Gathering up Alice-Angeles, Imre went back to his quarters. The corridors of the ship were silent apart from the distant murmuring of the engines. No one looked at him oddly any more. The taint of Helwise had been expunged without his even knowing it had been there. That didn't reassure him in the slightest. Her ghost permeated the entire galaxy—so who had won, really?

A sudden stab of pain in his abdomen caught him in midstep. He paused to catch his breath with Alice-Angeles standing by, ready to lend him assistance if needed. The pain was needle-bright and unexpected, as though something had torn deep inside him.

It wasn't an unfamiliar pain. He had felt something similar on Hyperabad, not long after his first meeting with Chyro Kells. That wasn't reassuring. That wasn't reassuring at all.

Vaia Falisa Soulis, he thought. The words shone like a light in his mind.

That's not my name, she replied.

What are you doing to me?

Define "you," "to," and "me."

Imre laughed aloud. It sounded almost like a sob.

The pain came again, sharper and more penetrating.

She was as surprised by it as he was. His legs gave away, and the ground came up to meet them.

The last thing she saw before consciousness fled was Alice-Angeles leaning over him with her lips moving. The words were inaudible. A siren of agony drowned out everything, and she was glad for the moment for both of them to let it go.

THIS NEW ANGER

●

And still the figure had no face by which he might know it; even in his dreams, it had no face, or one that baffled him and melted before his eyes . . .

—Robert Louis Stevenson

He dreamed of a large black man bursting out of the body of another. The process was messy and visceral and horrible to behold, and even as it unfolded, he understood the metaphor: not just dead things, but dead things wanting to come back to life, killing the living in the process. The past and the present didn't coexist easily.

There was an edge to the dream, however, that suggested it was more than just his imagination at work. The imagery was too graphic, too immediate. It felt like a memory.

Not one of his, though—and he shied from that thought, as he had shied from so many in recent days.

Time passed. He could not measure it. Eons might have swept by, and he would be oblivious. On waking, slowly and with a great wariness, he wondered if that was deliberate. He had tried physically running by abdicating from the Returned Continuum, telling himself that he was leaving Earth to fight the battle head-on. The truth was, though, that the front was impossible to find. It was all around him. It was inside him. It was nowhere at all.

When he opened his eyes, he was in the quarters that Emlee had provided for him, surrounded by the looming mounds of his personal detritus. His body ached in a thousand small ways. The last thing he wanted to do was find out why. That he had five fingers on each hand was impossible to ignore.

At least his mind appeared to be entirely his. There was no sign of the presence that had haunted him since his escape from C20. His thoughts echoed along empty halls and through vast, hollow chambers.

He rolled onto his stomach and closed his eyes. Complicated skeins of data awaited him, some new, some very old. He wasn't ready for any of it.

"Apparatus?" He spoke aloud, knowing that his muffled words would be easily understood by the AI. "Clear the room for me."

"I don't understand, Imre. You are alone."

"I'm not talking about people. I'm talking about things. Take it away—all of it, except for a robe for me to wear. When I open my eyes again, I want everything else to be gone."

"Very well. I will place it in storage elsewhere."

"No. Get rid of it for good. Burn it, ditch it, dissolve it; whatever you do these days. Just keep the books and the other museum pieces. They have value."

"All of it belongs in a museum," said Emlee, butting into the channel from elsewhere in the ship. "You included."

"It's a waste of energy dragging it around," he said, unsurprised that he was being monitored. "No one needs it anymore."

"Let me be the judge of that."

The line fell silent for a moment. Imre assumed that she was giving the Apparatus orders of her own. The end result was the same. He kept his eyes closed as the walls of his quarters began to move around him. With myriad soft sounds, the paraphernalia Emlee had carefully preserved for him were absorbed and taken away.

"Thank you," he said, when the sounds ceased.

"MZ sent you something," she said.

He rolled back over, gingerly. "He did?"

"He says it's private. Would you like it delivered to your room?"

"Yes." He could guess what it was, and wasn't entirely surprised that the Fort had preempted him. "Don't look at it."

"Your one remaining possession? I wouldn't dream of it."

The channel closed. He folded his hands behind his head and opened his eyes. A single white robe hung like a ghost from a hook on the wall. The towers of detritus were gone. Apart from a lingering smell of dust, they might never have been there at all. The neatness appealed to him although it didn't put him entirely at ease.

His mind was a crowd of thoughts. Aliens from the dawn of time who had created humanity by accident and now wanted to destroy it; the ghost of Helwise spreading like a disease through the galaxy; Himself, and his ongoing role in the fortunes of the galaxy.

The puzzle was slowly assembling, but holes remained that hadn't been filled in. What did the Luminous care about humanity? If they had really been civilized during the Light Ages, they could span the universe now. Killing the Forts would be like the Host slapping the face of a child that had annoyed it. Why would they bother? What threat could the Forts possibly have been?

Al Freer signaled him. He got up and quickly shrugged into the robe, ignoring strange twinges in his body and unfamiliar sensations as he moved. His balance was out. The robe fit loosely around him, hiding him safely in its folds.

When he was suitably disguised, from himself as well as Al Freer, he lay back on the bed and took the call.

"I heard you were awake," Freer said. A virtual image of him as he still looked in Imre's mind—tall, angular, economical in movement—accompanied the voice, making it easier to forget the bloated mass of Veil-stuff he had become. "You've been out four days by the ship's clock. Are you feeling yourself again?"

Imre was already regretting taking the call. *Four days.*

He checked the time; it was correct. Whatever had been going on inside him, it had taken much longer than he'd realized.

As for feeling himself . . .

"It's not that simple, Al."

"I guessed."

"Is that what you wanted to talk about?"

"Principally." Freer didn't waste any time. Folding his arms behind his virtual back, he stood at the end of Imre's bed and spoke directly at him. " 'My Fort-self.' That's what you called him—the version of you who betrayed us."

"He betrayed me too, Al. If it wasn't for Emlee, I wouldn't be here now."

"So I hear. We've been playing catch-up while you were snoozing."

Imre nodded. Freer would have requested a thorough debriefing now that the veil of secrecy had been drawn back. "What's your point, then?"

" '*My* Fort-self.' "

"It's a turn of phrase."

"Not the way you really think of him?"

"Why would it be?"

Freer's image frowned and walked two paces to one corner of the room. There he appeared to lean against the wall with his arms folded across his chest. "You didn't ask me what happened to the other Imre Bergamasc the Jinc made, the one they assimilated into the gestalt."

Imre thought back. He remembered being angry when he had learned about the existence of the Jinc version of him, taking the news even more personally than he did word of his Fort-self's activities because, for an instant, he and that version had actually been the same person: the incomplete records from which they had been created had borne identical errors. He still felt an echo of that fury, when he thought about what must have happened to it. His twin had endured all the horrors that he had managed to avoid—like the mental rape to which Al Freer had willingly subjected himself in exchange for data.

Imre's willingness to take out his ire on the Jinc version of Al Freer was something he wasn't proud of—and now it turned out that he had entirely forgotten what had prompted it.

That he could see where Freer was heading didn't help.

"Would I call him my Jinc-self? I don't know. Tell me it's running around out there, causing trouble, then I'd start to feel some kind of kinship."

Freer shook his head. "You don't have to worry about that. Once they had sucked it dry, the Jinc threw it away."

The news affected Imre, but not deeply. There, but for the grace of God—or the Luminous, if there was a difference . . .

"I'm Imre Bergamasc," he said. "The one the Jinc killed stopped being me the moment they plugged it in and took what they wanted. Even if I thought he was me, I remember being a singleton. I'm used to the idea of losing parts of myself."

"Is your Fort-self Imre Bergamasc too?"

Don't be so sure you know who I am, the Baron had said over the prison moon Kismet. *That could be a fatal mistake.* "I'm sure he doesn't think of himself that way anymore."

"That's not what I'm asking."

"He's the one who changed, not me."

"Are you trying to emulate him?"

"What? No! How could I when I don't know anything about him?"

"We have only your word about that."

"He tried to kill me—not just on Spargamos, but on Hyperabad as well. Remember?"

"That tells us how he feels about you, Imre. I have no idea how you'll react if you come face-to-face with him again."

Imre gave the question the consideration it deserved. He could squirm and dance around it, but Freer had a point. If Imre still thought of Himself as an extension of his own being, then what would happen if they ever met?

You'll know how to contact us when you work out what you want, his Fort-self had also told him. *I can't promise we'll take you in, but that is an option.*

Their relationship—if such it could be called—had gone downhill since then.

"We're back where we started, you and I, just like when we hooked up again at the Cat's Arse."

"It seems so."

"Is that why you came out to the Jinc in the first place, to dig more deeply into my past?"

Freer's image shrugged. "We only had your word for what happened to you. It seemed sensible to check it out."

"How long did it take you to find the ship?"

"Don't ask."

Imre could imagine. The edge of the galaxy was a vast and empty vacuum sea. Finding one ship would have taxed the Host considerably, especially if the search was conducted under the President's radar.

"Well," he said, "we're left at something of an impasse. Just be glad I'm not asking you to follow my orders anymore."

"Emlee is listening to you."

"Only so long as I'm making sense."

"Really? So what's at Vaia that's so important?"

Freer had him there. "I don't know. No one knows."

"It could be a trap."

"Bianca Biancotti wouldn't be party to that."

"Bianca might have fallen for it herself."

There was nothing Imre could say to that. It was indeed a possibility. "Then I'm triply glad Ra might be there too."

Freer's image displayed nothing. He unfolded his arms and walked to the far opposite side of the room, by the door. His attention appeared to be solely on where he placed his feet.

"Here's a thought," said Imre. "What if he's dead? The Fort version of me, I mean. Himself. What if the trap he laid on Spargamos turned against him, and the Luminous kicked his sorry arse? All this paranoia could be for nothing."

"The Barons are still out there. I'm sure of it."

"We know less about them than we do about him. Is it wise to assume that he was the only member of that organization? That it couldn't re-form even if he had been destroyed?"

Freer nodded and returned to stand at the end of the bed. "The echoes of the Slow Wave have been reassembled," he said. "Ninety percent of it makes no sense, and the rest is perfectly mundane. There's no evidence in there that you were involved in a deliberate attempt to murder the Forts, so that's one conspiracy theory laid to rest."

"Good," said Imre, not sure how this new line of conversation answered his question. "Didn't I read somewhere that fragmentary Line traffic is on the rise again?"

"You did. Thirty percent of the traffic is anomalous."

"That seems like a lot."

"It is a lot. The black traffic looks like noise, but we've discovered a pattern to it, the first layer of what looks like very deep encryption, much deeper than anything we could generate. We're gathering what we can and working constantly to penetrate the next layer. We're also trying to find the source. At the moment, it looks like it's coming from everywhere, which, of course, doesn't make sense, so we're hunting ordinary traffic for signs of a response, since all encrypted transmissions have to be decoded somewhere."

"Anything yet?"

"Just one phrase stands out." Freer's grey eyes were as sharp as knife points. "'Imre-F.'"

Imre absorbed this. "'Imre' isn't an uncommon name, Al. A lot of Primes gave it to their children when I was in charge."

"That's true," Freer acknowledged. "They're dead now, of course."

Another good point. "It could be a reference to this version of me, or nothing more than a coincidence."

"That's true too."

Freer clearly didn't give those possibilities much credence, though, and neither did Imre.

"If there's an Imre-F, what happened to A through E?"

"Maybe Imre-A is the one we knew in the Corps and Imre-B is what he became when he took the deal with the Forts. Imre-C survived the Slow Wave, and Imre-D is you, rebuilt by the Jinc. Imre-E could be the second version the Jinc made, or another one we don't know about." Freer didn't seem convinced by that either. "Maybe the 'F' just stands for 'Fort.'"

Imre shook his head. "I think you're applying a very mundane logic to all of this. You're suggesting that the black traffic has something to with the Fort version of me—which I'm happy to call Imre-F since we need a name for him, if only to separate him from *me*—but Forts don't think like us. They have their little puns and jokes. It's been a long time since you've had to deal with them, so you've forgotten that. We should run it by MZ before coming to any conclusions."

"We already have," Freer said.

"And?"

"He thinks we're idiots."

"We probably are, compared to him, but he still needs us if he wants to retire to Earth unmolested." Imre remembered the package that the Fort had sent from the *Wickthing* and wondered where it had got to. "You're looking for patterns in the wrong places, Al. Instead of trying to make me as part of the conspiracy, why not find out what the conspiracy is, first, and see what pieces are missing? I've been out of the picture too long to be a serious player, on either side. Remember that. For good or ill, I—this version of Imre Bergamasc—is just a bit part."

"Bianca Biancotti didn't think so. Emlee doesn't think so. Ra doesn't think so." Freer thought for a second. "I don't think so."

"Thanks for the vote of confidence, if that's what it is, but I'm inclined to disagree."

"That's your prerogative. You don't have to believe it for it to be true."

Imre dismissed him with an irritated gesture. "Get out

of here. You're messing with me—and I've been messed with plenty already."

Freer offered a shallow incline of his head and disappeared. No arguments, no farewell. Just perfect compliance and passive aggression, the soldier's first resort when faced with irrational authority.

Imre fumed until a virtual chime announced that someone had come to the entrance to Imre's chambers.

He checked. It was Emlee, balancing a sealed white box in both hands.

"Is that what I think it is?" he asked her.

She nodded. "I decided to bring it myself."

He couldn't ask her to leave it outside. The door hissed open at his mental command, and she strode purposefully into the room.

She seemed very tall from his position in the bed. Her physicality was astounding. He thought about standing, but knew that would make very little difference to how he felt. He sat up instead, leaned his back against the wall behind the bed, and tried to look more relaxed than he felt.

"Where do you want it?"

"Here, next to me. And for God's sake, sit down. You're giving me a crick in my neck."

She brought the box to him and eased onto the mattress beside it. "Care to share what's inside?"

He considered saying no. If Freer found out about it, he would only become more anxious. There was no point hiding from Emlee, however. She could probably guess what he had wanted from the *Wickthing* given the destination he had given her—as MZ had, ensuring it was ready for him when he awoke.

The box opened at his touch, revealing what looked like a translucent glass eye with two pupils looking in opposite directions. The loop shunt that had once been part of his body seemed harmless enough on a bed of black velvet, little more than a bauble he could have picked up on any of a billion worlds, but he knew its potential. The last time it had awoken, the visions it had shown him had torn his mind apart. He had also very nearly ended up with a shot through his skull from Emlee's old pistol as a result.

"Don't ask me what I'm going to do with it," he said, "because I don't know yet."

"You think there's something left for it to connect to?"

"There was the last time."

"On Earth, yes. It makes sense that there would be some kind of network there, lying low so the Luminous won't find it. Out here, though?"

"Maybe we can use it as a Fort detector: when we get close to something, it'll wake up." He shrugged. "I don't know." Shutting the box, he put it to one side of the bed so nothing lay between them. "Where are we, exactly?"

"Following the course you suggested. We'll be at the world called Vaia in two days, relative."

"That soon?"

"I've dropped the ship's tempo now repairs are complete. There's nothing to do until we arrive or word arrives from Ra."

"No more revolutions to worry about, anyway, now you've killed half your crew."

Emlee slid her long legs onto the bed and crossed her ankles. The mattress extruded a cushion and shifted under her weight, adjusting its resistance so they were balanced equally atop it. The two of them sat side by side, he still in the robe, she in her usual white uniform, unbuttoned around the collar. He could see the darkness of her chest between the folds of stiff fabric.

"The ship still isn't entirely clean, you know," she said, leaning her head back and closing her eyes. "I'd hate you to be misinformed on that point."

He watched the hard lines of her face settle into a weary mask. *Don't mention that name,* he remembered. "I thought that was the whole point of triggering the revolt. To bring you-know-who out and reveal—ah." He stopped, understanding. "It only brought out those infestations you weren't already aware of. And you, like any good soldier, understand the importance of knowing your enemy."

Her expression didn't change. "You taught me too well, Imre."

"Don't blame me on that point. Every book on the subject will tell you the same thing."

"Do they warn you about getting too close?"

"Only if you're determined never to change your loyalties." He waited a beat. "Is doing that a possibility?"

"God, no." She laughed without humor, deep in her throat. Her Adam's apple bobbed. "She was a crazy old bitch at the end. I'd never take her side."

"I think you're being a little hard on her."

"Do you?"

He said nothing.

Emlee's eyes opened, green against black, and she said, "She loved you. That's pretty clear from the memories she left us. But there are different kinds of love, and hers was of a fundamentally dysfunctional kind. It's clear she loved for power rather than pleasure. She gave herself completely in times of crisis, and in exchange received—not security, exactly, but complicity. She liked to be close to the source of conflict. She liked to be caught up in the flow. She was physical, and instinctive, and very much in the moment. She understood strategy, but it didn't interest her as much as the organic nature of combat. Sex *was* combat to her; that's why she loved it. That's why she loved you, because wherever you went, conflict was close by—and that's what killed her, in the end.

"You went too far." Her green eyes were depthless, shining. "You betrayed her. You disengaged from her. You wouldn't play the game. She had to look elsewhere for what she thought of as love. You know about her and Ra; those experiences are in her memories too—but that's only part of it. The coup was less about taking control of the galaxy than trying to get your attention. She was a woman scorned then murdered by the man she loved.

"That's what's in here, calling for revenge," Emlee said, tapping her head. "That's what Ra will use to destroy you. The details don't matter—how she schemed, where and when you fucked, who disagreed with whom, although a lot of that is in there too. Most people won't care. The emotional truth is what matters. Fucked-up love and betrayal is her legacy to the galaxy."

Emlee's gaze wouldn't release him. He wanted to defend himself—although against what he didn't know. Emlee wasn't accusing him of anything; she was merely relaying Helwise's version of events, and there could be no denying that. Not with the woman who had laid them down effectively expunged from humanity. There was nothing left to confront except the echoes of her, converging on him from all corners of the galaxy. He could never shout them down.

Guilt, likewise, wasn't so easily silenced.

"You're wondering what it's like, having her in my head," Emlee said, as though he had accused her of something.

"Yes," he admitted, "but I'd never dream of being impolite."

"Just like I'd never come out and ask you what's under that robe."

He felt a tangled knot of emotions tighten inside him: fear, dread, curiosity. "Don't you already know?"

"Tempting though it was to peep while you slept, I let the Apparatus have that honor. It would've sounded the alarm had there been a problem. I had other things to think about."

"So you keep saying. If you're so busy, why are you here?"

"Because I *am* curious about what's happening to you. Because I think it matters."

"Why? The galaxy doesn't care if I grow four arms and extra head. You're the Prime people look up to now."

"Who said anything about people?" She looked away. "Whatever. Changing the way you look is probably a good idea, if you're ever to dodge Helwise's wrath. You don't want to live in a box the rest of your life, however long that might be."

"Do you think that's why I'm doing this?"

Emlee didn't say anything for a moment.

When he realized an answer wasn't coming, he got up from the bed. Facing the wall, and thinking of the time that she had undressed to let him study her Veil, he unfastened the robe and let it drop from his shoulders. As the thick material pooled heavily around his ankles, he stepped free and turned around.

There were no mirrors in the room. Emlee knew him well enough to be sure of that. He couldn't tell, therefore, exactly what she was seeing, but he could look down, finally, and see rather than feel the changes that had been wrought upon him.

He was female, or something approaching it. His breasts had returned, and his hips had widened, accounting for his altered balance. Penis and testes had retreated into his body, but without exploring that area by touch he couldn't be sure what, if anything, had grown in their place. He could tell that he had changed internally, though, his Prime body mimicking an ancient genetic template that hadn't evolved naturally for two million years. *He* had changed.

So quick, he wanted to say, but of course the four days relative he had slept might have been thousands of years Absolute. While his internal clock ticked slowly over, the laws of physics and chemistry had maintained their usual progression.

He wanted to be appalled by the change in gender. He certainly had been the last time, among the Jinc, and he had taken swift steps then to begin the reversal back to maleness. But his skin had always been hairless, apart from that on his head, and he retained the musculature he was familiar with. He was no shorter or slighter than he had been before. His voice was the same pitch. His transformation from male to female was, therefore, largely symbolic.

Of what, he wondered. Of his rogue fragment's absorption and the legacy she had left? Was that the price he had to pay for being left alone at last?

He doubted it would be so simple. Nothing stayed dead

for long anymore, no matter how he tried to keep them down. What had Mac Grimes said? *When ghosts start multiplying, you don't pinch yourself. You get an exorcist.* When that failed, you ran, and you kept running as fast as you could, as he had run by abdicating, by becoming a Prime, by turning his back on Himself and everything he stood for, and by letting himself dissolve into C20 where he—he—

—she—he—Imre—

—*she*, still Imre, had emerged, and now wanted to run from the giant black man of her memory, even though she knew she was Emlee in male form and retained none of the priapean excesses of her dreams.

"I dreamed of you," she said.

"When?"

"In the city—the trap."

"Any particular kind of dream?"

Emlee was looking at her in a way she didn't entirely like. It stirred something inside her, touched places she tried but wasn't able to ignore.

"You always appeared after a memory of one of our old campaigns: Davos-Platz, Ballantrea, Tusitala; I didn't know what they were at the time, but I recognize them now, looking back on them from this perspective. You appeared just like this, but more . . . more sexualized. Very threatening. You never called me by name. You said that you were looking for me, that you were my savior. You talked a lot about heaven, a dead heaven, and choices I had to make. You—" She stopped. Emlee was nodding. "What?"

" 'Dead Heaven' is C20's code name in the back channels of the Line. That's how we tracked it down."

"Well, great. I wasn't losing any sleep over that detail, but I suppose it's good to have the answer." She knelt on the bed diagonally opposite Emlee, facing her but keeping her legs carefully together. "You were a nightmare. I was afraid of you—and what you represented too, I guess. Should I be afraid of you now—now I know what you have in your head, urging you on?"

"There's nothing to be gained by harming you. Or do you mean sexually?" Emlee folded her arms behind her head. "For all I know that's exactly what you want. Helwise wasn't the only one with a fucked-up relationship to sex."

Imre couldn't argue with that.

"Well, you have nothing to fear on that score," Emlee said. "If I wanted to infect you with the Veil, there are more efficient means. Besides, what happened between us half a million years ago was, well, half a million years ago." She smiled. "Frankly, at the moment, I'm just too tired to think of anything like that."

Imre nodded, not entirely convinced that Emlee's lack of interest was genuine, or that her own feeling wasn't disappointment. "You should know in return that that's not why I've changed either. It wasn't my plan to seduce you so you wouldn't betray me."

"Why are you changing, then?"

That was harder to answer. "Maybe because I need to. Because there's no point holding back when everyone and everything has moved on and left me behind."

"Except Render."

"Except him, yes."

"He's getting paranoid in his old age. Have you noticed?" Emlee closed her eyes and settled lower on the mattress. "I'm not paranoid, and I don't care why you've changed, Imre. I'm just going to stay a while, in case you try anything stupid with that loop shunt."

"Who says *I'll* be staying?"

"Fine. Then I'll just lie here and get some sleep. It's been over two hundred thousand years Absolute since I last took a nap."

"Looks like it, too."

Imre waited to see if Emlee had anything else to say. One minute passed in silence, then another, and eventually, when it became clear that Emlee had actually gone to sleep, her expression as open and vulnerable as a child's, she—

—he—

—Imre moved slowly off the bed and stood still for a full minute. A switch had tripped in his head, and he didn't entirely understand what had happened. One moment he had been himself, and the next he had been, not someone else, but *herself.* She had a raft of new memories that dovetailed where his ended, explaining much that hadn't made sense before.

Why did Emlee trigger such strong reactions in him? Because *she* had dreamed about her. Why had he dreamed of Emlee bursting out of a man's chest? Because *she* had seen it with her own eyes.

Her eyes were his eyes, and her memories were his memories, whether he wanted them or not.

He felt himself trembling on the brink of dissolution, as though at any second he might crumble into dust. It was inconceivable to him that he could be so undone by something so small, so insignificant.

Unless, a dissident part of him murmured, there was something about her that made her significant—and if that were so, couldn't ignoring or trying to get rid of her actually make things worse?

When he moved, it wasn't to call Kells and ask him to change him back, but to go about finding some clothes. He could live with his body the way it was if it meant that he could think clearly. That was the ultimatum he offered himself. Or herself. The moment, though, that he experienced fugue states and started doing things he couldn't remember later, all bets were off.

The corridors of the *Memory of Markheim* were as quiet as a tomb. Emlee hadn't exaggerated about running the ship down while they were in transit. The bridge contained just calm crew members whose sole function was to double-check the function of the navigational AI—and to maintain a close watch behind, in case the Luminous were indeed following. Thus far, there was no sign apart from suggestive occultations and double images. If a cosmic string or something similar was snaking after them from the fringes of the galaxy, it was keeping a very low profile.

Alice-Angeles dogged Imre's heels as he strode from one end of the ship to the other. She never spoke, and seemed perfectly content to remain silent. Frags didn't hold on to things the way Primes and singletons did—something that had always made Imre slightly envious. Unless emotions came under their monomaniacal focus, trauma slid right off, leaving them untouched.

Fucked-up love and betrayal is Helwise's legacy to the galaxy.

Do you think you could ever be caught in something like the honey trap unless part of you wanted to be?

I'm used to the idea of losing parts of myself.

Imre walked through halls where battles had been fought with the followers of the Revivalist Doctrine and saw no signs of the conflict at all. All battle damage had long been erased from both the ship and its frag crew. He wished his traumas were as easy to erase.

"I'd like to explore ways of counteracting the Helwise meme," Imre told MZ. "It's going to destabilize the galaxy unless we hand total power to Ra MacPhedron. If we don't, the risk of the Apparatus's slaughtering half the people in the galaxy will always be there."

"One option that springs immediately to mind," MZ said, "is to allow me to merge with the Apparatus so I might unpick the Executive Order from the inside."

Imre almost stopped in midstride, surprised. On the face of it, the idea was simple and obvious, but Forts were rarely so straightforward. He wondered if MZ had been listening in on the conversation regarding his motives. "I thought you just wanted to go back home."

"By this means, I can do that and many other things at the same time."

"True. Aren't the two of you incompatible, though?"

"Operationally, at present that is so, but you know firsthand that form does not dictate function. The technology I stole from Earth was a prototype. I can transfer to a lepton-based system with only a modicum of difficulty."

"The Apparatus was ordered by its creators to ban you from Earth. Would operating on the same system create conflict?"

"That would depend on the instructions of the Prime Minister."

Imre nodded. "So you want me to talk to Emlee about it."

"I believe the proposal has merit."

"It might be a hard sell." Imre was unsure which way he would fall if the decision was left up to him. "I'll talk to her when the opportunity arises."

"Thank you."

Footsteps sounded from a side corridor. Imre slowed his metronomic step and waited to see who was approaching.

"The picture's changed," said Render on seeing Imre. His mismatched eyes missed nothing, even through several layers of clothes chosen deliberately to be ambiguous. "Give me a reason."

"Do I need one?" Imre retorted, ignoring his own internal misgivings. "All things change. You might try it sometime."

"Age shows no kindness to me." Render screwed up his nose. "I've got a face like metal."

"At least think about replacing the rivets."

With a simple gesture—not the one Imre expected—Render indicated that Imre should follow him. "I know that I'm not all that pretty, but I don't care. Do you?"

Imre was more interested in where Render was leading him. "As long as you don't shoot me or lie to me, you can look any way you want."

That earned him a smile. "I'm a pure and perfect lie."

"We'll leave it at not shooting me, then."

Render led them through a narrowing maze of corridors that were even less inhabited than the rest of the dormant ship. Several times they stopped to pass through thick security doors that opened only to Render's biometrics. The ceilings became lower; the flavor of the air itself changed. It seemed to Imre that they were approaching the heart of the ship, where few humans went.

They came to a narrow dead end. There Render opened a final, concealed door.

"Here we are," he told Imre, waving him through the door. "I've got something to show you. In here."

Imre stepped into a long, dimly lit chamber lined with a dozen transparent cases. Each case was a cubic meter in size, constructed from layers of glasslike material and resting on plinths of pure black. The air was alive with energy and stank of ozone, suggesting that the function of the cases was far from ornamental.

Imre barely heard the door close behind him as he approached one of the cases and peered inside. A complex heads-up array of data appeared in the glass as he approached, defining numerous characteristics of the object within. At first, he couldn't identify it: there seemed little more than a cone of metallic ash with several fragments scattered haphazardly nearby. Only when he moved to the next one did he begin to understand.

The second case contained a section of curved, shell-like material as wide across as Imre's hand. Its edges were ragged, and its concave surface pitted and blackened as though by fire. Its other side—the exterior of the object it belonged to, presumably—was silver.

If the shell formed part of a sphere, it would have been roughly the same size as a human head.

"This is a secret," Render said, unnecessarily.

Imre's gaze jumped along the line from case to case. His breath caught in his throat on spying what looked like a complete sphere at the far end of the room. With hurried steps, he approached it and leaned in close.

The sphere cast a distorted image of his own face back at him.

Imre started at it, waiting.

Nothing happened.

He frowned, disappointed, and wondered if the sphere was playing dead. Then it occurred to him that the Host's technology was considerably more advanced than that of the Jinc, over a million years earlier.

"Can you open this for me?" he asked Render.

"Why? There's no one home."

"If you're so sure, why the precautions?"

Render came closer. With a series of delicate chiming noises, the case began to unfold, layer by layer, until the sphere was exposed to the open air.

Still nothing happened.

"See?" Render said.

"I don't see much of anything. If it's so harmless, why wasn't I shown this earlier?"

"Give me a reason."

"Don't play games with me, Render. This is Emlee's collection, I presume—and her decision to keep it from me."

"No. It was me."

"So why?"

"Afraid of the truth?"

"Never."

The old soldier came to stand on the other side of the sphere. "It feels like something dead and cold. Old news."

"Like me?" Anger made Imre's heart beat faster and harder. That was exactly what he had been trying to convey to Emlee and Freer. It was one thing, though, to confess; another thing entirely to be accused. "I thought we'd covered this five times over. You saw the thing back there; you saw what it did to the *Wurmbrand*. If it's relevant, then this is too, no matter how old and cold it is." He indicated the sphere, lying passively before them. "So am I."

"Nothing's ever quite what it seems. You must know that."

"Maybe you don't trust me yet. Is *that* what you're saying?"

"Well, I was never gonna trust you too far." Render shrugged like a man out of answers. "Who are you? How are things with you? I know what you've been doing, but now that's all I have." He shook his head. "No safety in old glories."

"I'm sorry there haven't been more lately. Glories, I mean. And I'm sorry I can't make you believe me when I tell you that I'm trustworthy. I'm trying to do the right thing."

"What *are* you gonna do? Anything?"

"Is that your problem? Because I got lost in the city and didn't come out with guns blazing?" Imre's mood softened slightly. Render was showing him his secret stash, and that demonstrated a degree of trust he hadn't shown the rest of Veil-infected humanity. The chances were that Render hadn't trusted anyone at all for a very long time. "Maybe you're right: maybe I am getting on a bit."

"Us all," Render said, softening in return, "I suppose." Imre saw the skies of C20 in the old soldier's eyes and knew that he was talking about more than just the two of them.

"Old news like you," Imre said, "not me. That's why you've been collecting these things. You feel a—a kinship?"

Render laughed. "I'm out of my class."

"All that talk about billions of years might not be true. You'll always be the oldest man I know."

"And you would change me?"

"Hey, I was joking."

"I am not a man who laughs."

"I don't know how Alice-Angeles puts up with you."

"She comes and she goes," Render said, with a wink like that of an ancient reptile. "Isolation is good for the heart."

Imre was happy to leave the conversation there. The tension that had passed between them had abated, thankfully, and he felt frazzled by trying to decode Render's increasingly bizarre attempts at communication. In another million years, he wondered, would they be able to talk at all?

They looked down at the sphere.

"I don't suppose you have a second whole one tucked away somewhere," he said. "Two of the Luminous have talked to me so far. I was hoping for third time lucky."

Render looked regretful. "There are no more."

"Well, it was worth a try. Seal it back up, and I'll take a look at the data you've gained from it. I presume they've been analyzed."

The transparent panels began swinging back into place, and a flood of information poured into Imre's mind, far too much even to glance at without becoming quickly lost. Render was already moving to the door, his cache of Luminous artifacts revealed, and Imre went to follow.

The darkened room turned even darker, with deep crimson highlights.

"Sound the alarm," spoke the voice of the Luminous into Imre's mind, "do anything at all to draw attention, and this conversation will immediately cease."

Imre was caught in midstep, his mind moving at speed in the body of a statue. He was unable to suppress a slight turn of his head. At the movement, the air singed his skin.

"This cloak-and-dagger routine is beginning to annoy me," he said. "Give me a reason to talk to you first, and I'll weigh the alternatives."

"You have questions."

"Until you start providing answers, you'll have to do better than that."

"We have saved your life twice, now."

"Yes, from the Jinc and from your fellows on Spargamos—and I'm still wondering why you did that."

"We are allies."

"I think you're using me, and I only like being used if the arrangement is reciprocated."

"You must earn our trust, Imre Bergamasc," said the sphere. "Ask me how."

"Forget how. Try why for a change."

Imre's right foot made contact with the floor of Render's secret hideout, sending ripples of force up his newly modified shin. The noise made by one of the sphere's protective layers clicking back into place sounded like the chiming of an enormous bell.

The sphere said, "You are who you are. Your name is important. The Jinc recognized you, and so did we. Even damaged, your existence had currency. You were encouraged to escape in order that you could be followed. From the moment of your rebirth, we observed your movements and puzzled over your motives. You are our window into a much greater mind."

"My Fort-self."

"Yes. What lies beyond this imperfect pane of glass is knowledge we must possess."

"Why?"

"The war between our species began over a million years ago. It will be waged for millions more. The opening salvos are crucial."

Imre examined the cards falling on the table. They outlined a complex and incomplete divination for him.

"Let me see if I can map this out," he said. "You guys were watching the Jinc because, well, because they were looking for you. You allow one of you to be found, and you study them from the inside. When the Jinc stumble across me, all sorts of alarm bells go off. Instead of turning me over, the Luminous start to poke around in my head, looking for the connection. You, you're playing both sides of the game. You want me free so I might lead you to the rest of me, who might or might not still be a player in this galactic soap opera. You help me escape, in a ship you've probably bugged, and you set me loose. I'm contacted a couple of times by the rest of me, but it's nothing conclusive, insufficient to bring anything to a head. And so time passes."

He stopped to think, and the sphere let him. "The Returned Continuum keeps me distracted for a long time, during which you guys lay a trap for me on Spargamos, knowing I'm bound to go there eventually. Traps within traps within traps. My Fort-self is waiting there too, hoping to catch big game of his own. You talk to me there, but

I don't escape: I die, or so it seems, and the battle is on. A resistance has formed, with new weapons and a willingness to fight. The gloves are off."

Another protective layer boomed home around the sphere.

"Here's what I think happened next. The Barons were beaten on Spargamos, pounded to dust. Even with new weapons, they were outgunned and outclassed by a civilization capable of building galaxy-sized Fort-killers. That should have been that. Everyone thought I was finished—until I popped up again on Earth, only to abdicate and disappear again. That threw everyone off. Suddenly I wasn't dead, and I couldn't be followed. Suddenly I was a threat again, and you spread yourself thin, planting yourself far and wide to catch a glimpse of me should I reappear in person, one day."

His left leg started to rise. His hips were aching. "I guess your net caught something now. A small fish in a big ocean, but you think I can work as bait again. You and I are both wondering if the defeat at Spargamos was faked, a ruse to gain my Fort-self more time. Data too. Maybe he was testing your defenses. He might have been lying low ever since, building bigger weapons still. And you want to get to him in case he plans to burst out of wherever he is and try again. You think I'm going to take you to him."

The sphere said, in a voice that had become a degree more indistinct with each closing layer, "You are correct. That is what you need to do in order to earn our trust."

"In return for . . . what?"

"The whole truth."

"Is that the best you can offer me? There's a lot to be said for a comfortable lie."

"This isn't a time for comfort, Imre Bergamasc."

"When has it ever been?" He was conscious that at any moment the conversation might be cut off by the shutting of the last security screen. "Let me ask you something. You know about the Apparatus now, I presume. It's no secret, after Helwise's attempted coup. Writing data onto space-time was a trick the Forts pulled that no one seems to have predicted. Why not? If you guys really are fourteen billion years old, I'd have thought you'd be all over that kind of technology."

"Environment dictates need," said the sphere, "and need dictates the means by which we manipulate the environment. One predicates the other. That law is inescapable."

"So you never had a need? The environment never suited? I don't understand."

"There is no such thing as idle curiosity. The Forts of Earth foresaw a time when such technology would be needed, and that time is not now. Although it has undeniably helped you, it is not the front on which this battle is currently being fought. That particular war is not expected until the visible universe is eight times its present size."

"You keep schedules for these things?" Imre couldn't help his incredulity. "You *plan* them?"

"We anticipate and we prepare. We are not so different from you in that respect."

With one final boom, the containment screens surrounded the sphere, and Imre's tempo returned abruptly to normal. He stumbled, caught off-balance—

—and she—

—forced herself to walk normally, on feet reassured of their balance, even as she considered going back to open the screens again. The chances were the sphere wouldn't talk to her again. If its cover needed to be kept so badly, it would do nothing while attention was focused so squarely on it. Besides, the chances were it had already told her everything it was going to.

The sphere's words turned rapidly over in her thoughts. *You are our window into a much greater mind . . . What lies beyond this imperfect pane of glass is knowledge we must possess . . . There is no such thing as idle curiosity . . .*

The sphere wanted to make contact with his Fort-self for reasons it would only hint at, and then direly. She hadn't told it that the Luminous were likely following the

Memory of Markheim, and she wondered what difference that might make. If it was a representative of a breakaway faction among putative aliens, its motives were doubly difficult to interpret.

Short of tossing it out an air lock, she supposed the sphere would be going with the *Memory of Markheim*, wherever it ended up.

You are who you are.

She was who she was. Her name was Imre Bergamasc.

Render glanced over his shoulder at her, catching Imre square in the vision of his blue eye. If he suspected anything, it didn't show.

"Take me to the bridge," Imre told him. "I want to watch our approach firsthand."

Render nodded and, with Alice-Angeles joining them in the hallway outside, led her away from his sinister secret.

Vaia was a small, wandering orphan on the fringe of the Core, scantily depicted in Hard Records as possessing internal heat thanks to an overabundance of radioactive elements in its core but cold compared to in-system worlds and not regularly inhabited. It had looped past several suns in its long lifetime, and each atmosphere-melting spring had brought it a brief reprieve from obscurity. The most recent survey, conducted hundreds of thousands of years earlier, had confirmed the existence of several ruined installations buried under meters of frozen gas and water ice, along with layers of organic material, either permanently dead or in natural suspended animation. Since that survey, the orphan had experienced spring just once.

"There are no records of its being occupied then," said MZ, who had patched into the bridge's comms in order to participate more fully in the approach. The Fort had no official role on Emlee's staff, but the Prime Minister wasn't averse to using his abilities to back up her depleted crew. "It is possible that the information was simply never recorded."

"Or Vaia was interfered with later, after it froze again," said Imre, watching the screens impatiently for their first glimpse of the tiny world. She had opened the outermost layer of her armor down the front, unafraid of what people thought of how she looked. She was surrounded by frags and people who had undergone much more severe changes in their time. Any discomfort she detected in them was probably nothing but a projection of her own lingering uncertainty.

Still, her right hand frequently found her left behind her back. The fact that she had five fingers on both hands was a novelty, thanks to the full range of experiences she now possessed. She was she and he was he, and it didn't matter to her when the switch in her head occasionally flipped.

"If I were the one doing the interfering," she went on, "I doubt clement weather would be a factor."

"Probably the opposite," said Al Freer. He had joined them physically, propped up in a portable truss to one side of the command dais. "There's no reason to do anything on a world like this unless you don't want to be found."

"Like Spargamos," Emlee said.

Imre nodded, bracing herself against finding more ruins. The *Memory of Markheim* was coming in hot and bright, hiding nothing. They had bypassed the nearest habitable system, looking for any sign of Ra's presence, but everything had been quiet, suggesting that the President of the Host was either lagging behind, not coming, or lying implausibly low. Emlee's sensor arrays were much faster than Imre had ever seen. Not even the *Wickthing* could have escaped detection.

"We're picking up some stray EM," Emlee said. "It's coming from where the planet should be."

"What kind of EM?" Imre asked her.

"Nothing I can unpack. The fringes of something big, though. A lot of data, coming fast."

"I have an infrared image," MZ announced.

All attention turned to the picture coalescing on the main screen and through personal feeds. It showed a cool, patchy oval, undistinguished by drive flames or washes, point power sources or gas vents.

"At least it's there," said Imre. "I was beginning to wonder if the charts were wrong."

"They're not entirely correct," said Emlee. "As far as fact checks go, location is just the first and most obvious. We know the albedo to be wrong, for starters. We should be picking up pictures in the visual spectra by now, and we're not."

Imre pored over what data they did have: numerous occultations against the dense starscape; parallax measurements; patchy images in several other frequencies. As high-speed probes converged on the planet, a more detailed picture began to form—of a world displaying some very faint signs of recent occupation, mainly in the form of warm spots rather than hot spots, and the continued leakage from a powerful comms source. The lack of a detailed visual continued to puzzle. For something to have such a low albedo, it had to be almost black.

Insidiously, a horrible idea began to form in Imre's mind.

"Stop decelerating," she told Emlee. "If I'm right, we won't want to stay here long."

All eyes turned to her. "Don't you dare tell me we came here for nothing," Emlee began.

"Oh, no. This is something all right. It's something we're not equipped to deal with." She drew her audience's attention to the leaky data stream. "That's a Line junction," she said. "A big one, which makes sense when you know what it's connected to."

"There's nothing there for it to connect to," said Freer. "Maybe Vaia had a population once, but it's definitely uninhabited now."

"I think you'll find that's wrong," Imre said. She wasn't surprised that Freer hadn't guessed. "Vaia is home to someone. Or part of someone, at least. Someone's memories, to be specific."

Emlee realized first. She turned back to the screens,

blurring around the edges for an instant as she overclocked to check the data and think the proposition through.

Imre needed no further thought. She knew she was right.

The reason why they couldn't see Vaia was because the world was black.

The reason why Vaia was black was because it was covered in the Veil.

It made more and more sense, the longer she thought about it. The world had a hot core and layers of frozen biomass for raw material. A small infestation growing on artificial or cloned tissue could have taken root with ease, absorbing data flowing in via the Line through organs of cognition that didn't need to be entirely conscious in order to fulfill their function.

Back before the Slow Wave, Imre had seen with her own eyes some of the rumored and reviled "frag worlds": planets inhabited solely by the components of Forts, with no Primes or singletons to be found anywhere. They were usually employed as temporary measures if fast reaction was required and had been of key strategic importance to his enemies during the Mad Times. Occasionally, though, they had been symptomatic of a Fort equivalent of mental illness. Obsessions took on physical dimensions as the need to process so many thoughts prompted rapid, localized increases in frag numbers. Without careful oversight, such agglomerations of frags struggled to support themselves. Frag worlds had been typically chaotic, polluted planets, with disease rife among an uncaring population. It wasn't uncommon to find graves as big as cities, where bodies were left to rot uncovered. The rest of humanity regarded the practice as abhorrent, while Forts looked on it as throwing away fingernail cuttings.

A Veil world was different in several important ways, but performed a similar function. There no were frags to manage; this tissue was immobile and constantly connected to the rest of the "body." So long as nutrients were available and waste didn't build up, Imre supposed that a

Veil of this size could continue growing indefinitely. Weight might eventually become a problem, he decided, unless the mass of the upper layers rested on internal supports or skeletons. There was, otherwise, no limit to how many memories could be amassed.

The question was: who did all those memories belong to?

A free-fall alert sounded through the ship as Emlee followed his suggestion. The *Memory of Markheim* ceased its fiery deceleration and readjusted its course to fly by the small world, not seek orbit around it. Imre was glad that Emlee agreed, even though it only delayed the decision they would still have to make. She was sure they were all thinking about it.

Al Freer dispelled any hope of uncertainty by putting it into words. "We should at least hail it."

"To what purpose?" Emlee asked.

"To find out who it is, of course."

"You really think there's someone in there?"

"It's not impossible."

"It's unlikely. This is a dump, maybe even a backup. The real action is elsewhere."

"Falisa," said Imre, "or Soulis."

"You think there are three worlds like this?" Freer asked.

"I'm sure of it. Maybe more." Imre held tight as the ship rearranged itself. "Bianca Biancotti tracked them down, and she left me the data for us to follow. There's no point trying to hail anyone until we reach the last name on the list. We've probably already set off enough alarms by coming this close."

"There's another reason to keep moving," Emlee said. "We don't want to draw attention to this place, just in case something is following us. Not until we're certain what's going on here. If this is an offshoot of one of the Core civilizations, and Bianca Biancotti got it wrong—well, I've enough on my conscience already."

"What about Ra?" Freer asked.

"We'll leave a beacon, one he can't possibly miss. If he's come this far, he'll go the rest of the way."

"He'll suspect a trap," Freer said. "And who could blame him?"

"If this is a trap, we're not the one laying it."

"That's no comfort at all for us," said Imre, "since we're rushing headlong down the same path."

The engines fired. Inertial gravity returned. A tiny autonomous beacon fired out of a launch tube and fell rapidly behind. The *Memory of Markheim* began its long journey to Falisa.

"You think they're your Fort-self's memories," said Freer. "I'm surprised you don't want to stop."

"I don't on both counts," she said. "How could they be his? You don't need a planet to remember everything that might be important. Look at Render: he gets by on nothing but what's between his ears."

"Sometimes," the old soldier said in deadpan tones, "I remember how to feel."

"Let me guess what *you're* thinking, Al," Imre said. "You're thinking of the black traffic on the Line. You think you've found the source."

"That's a possibility, isn't it?"

"More likely, I'd have thought, it's the endpoint. Valuable though it might be to tap into that endpoint, the source is what we're after."

"Do you think that's what Bianca found?"

"There's only one way to be sure."

"Short of taking a sample of the black stuff on Vaia and injecting it into you."

Imre couldn't tell if Freer was joking or not. "That is not an option," she said, turning pointedly to study the new course Emlee had plotted. The ship would continue on a faster tempo until they were sure they hadn't triggered any defensive reactions or that Ra wasn't about to show up. Falisa was barely one hundred light-years away. At a full gee's steady thrust, the journey would feel like only a matter of hours once the crew hit its cruising tempo.

To avoid both a long wait and torturous exploration of the possibilities implied by the existence of one Veil world, Imre dropped her tempo down further and sat through the journey in subjective minutes rather than hours. Stars became denser as they approached the galaxy's central bar. The constantly shifting Core population mixed ancient white dwarfs with hot blue newcomers in a way that was brilliantly disorienting. The Forts and their dependents had made a habit of avoiding the chaos at the heart of the galaxy, leaving it for faster, more fleeting civilizations that rose and fell with unpredictable consequences. Considered effectively ungovernable, it was nonetheless a rich source of experimental science and art. Reliable suppliers rarely stayed in business for long, and physical haulage was prohibitively expensive outside the close-packed Core, but the melting pot of the galaxy had produced numerous items prized by collectors elsewhere.

Twice on the way to Falisa, the *Memory of Markheim* crossed the intense beam of data lancing along the Line out of Vaia. The automatic relays passing on the signal were of a design unfamiliar to Imre and also to Al Freer, who had worked briefly on the Line during the chaotic post–Slow Wave era. Like Vaia, the relays appeared to be undefended, but Imre advised against putting that to the test. If her Fort-self was indeed behind the arrangement, she was certain he would have prepared for every eventuality.

"The environment dictates need," the sphere had told her, "and need dictates the means by which we manipulate the environment. One predicates the other. That law is inescapable."

She wondered what need had driven her Fort-self to such extreme ends. Or were they in perfect accord with the environment he now occupied? A world or two were, after all, insignificant on a galactic scale. What could she read into this about the person he had become?

Falisa was identical to Vaia: a former hot ball smothered with featureless, black material. On arrival, she—

—he mentally stumbled, as though the confirmation of his guess had undercut something important about his own sense of self, leaving him uncertain of everything. His Fort-self had changed, just as he was changing. Would it ever stop? Once the whole galaxy had known who he was. Now even he was entirely unsure.

The *Memory of Markheim* coasted by the dark world on a slow half-gee burn. Nothing interfered with them; no alarms sounded. Emlee probed the surface of the planet with radar and found it to be approximately ten meters below the outer layers of the Veil. Imre performed a series of quick mental calculations and was surprised by the result. There were approximately one million cubic kilometers of tissue clinging to the surface of the tiny world. A human brain came in at just fifteen hundred cubic centimeters, for a Prime. Even allowing for internal structures—skeletons, veins, and digestive tracts or their analogues—that accommodated a formidable number of memories.

Although he had dismissed Freer's suggestion that those memories might belong to his Fort-self, he found himself wondering if he hadn't been too glib about it. He didn't know what had been going on behind the scenes since Domgard had fallen. Sufficient frags overclocking at a superfast rate for a million years might just be able to amass that many experiences.

The temptation to claim them—or at least test them—was nonexistent. He didn't want anything to do with them. They belonged to someone he had never been and didn't want to become. Besides, he would need a brain as big as a planet to process the data, and he wasn't about to force-evolve himself that far anytime soon.

Emlee dropped another beacon for Ra as they cruised out of the planet's vicinity. The ship's instruments detected no sign of pursuit, be it by Host ships or something more exotic. Imre was beginning to feel hypnotized by the passing of two similar worlds without event. Only the stars ahead changed as they headed for Soulis. Their destination was the Core proper and navigation at speed became a concern as a result. At the slowest tempos available to him, stars glided by three to a minute. His dazed incomprehension increased.

"I need to stretch my legs," he said, pulling away from the dais rail and heading down the steps. When it became clear that he intended to leave the bridge, Alice-Angeles fell in behind him. He waved her back, but she insisted, and he knew better than to argue.

He walked in silence up the long spine of the *Memory of Markheim*, relishing the feel of putting one foot in front of the other. He hadn't physically left the ship since he had been pulled out of C20. His only excursion had been to MZ, and that hardly counted. The body Emlee had had made for him was a state-of-the-art Prime body, seemingly identical to but evolved by increments from the others he had inhabited in past times. The fact that he was walking so easily while the ship was under thrust and his tempo was so low spoke volumes. By far the most difficult extreme tempo to maintain was the slowest, since every movement—no matter how short it seemed to the instigator—could take a thousand times longer to complete at Absolute tempo. Each step he took lasted hours, perhaps even days, and by various sophisticated means his body was able to maintain the illusion that he was walking no other way than he normally would.

When he reached the end of the corridor and faced the green door leading to his private quarters, he hesitated. Days Absolute rushed by as he wrestled with his conscience. Yes, he had asked MZ for the loop shunt for just one possible purpose, but even in such strange circumstances, had the time truly come for such extremes?

He could feel fate pressing in on him from all sides. So many invisible forces conspired to move him around the galaxy like a pawn on a chessboard. Was he to be sacrificed when some unknown plan came to fruition, or did another crowning await him on the far side of the board? He was certain he didn't want either. That it would all be over soon was the summit of his ambition, but neither was he tired of life. The galaxy had changed; he was changing too.

You'll never outrun your fate.

Fair or foul, perhaps he was better running toward it than away, or at least ensuring that the option remained open to him.

"Wait out here," he told Alice-Angeles, opening the door and stepping into his quarters. Even though only seconds had passed from his perspective, it felt entirely novel to be moving again.

The white box was still on the floor next to the bed. He picked it up and unsealed the lid. The glassy cool grey sphere slipped into his hand. He cradled it lightly for a moment, wary of any kind of unprompted activity, but it remained inert.

He considered slipping it into a pocket but decided that Emlee, Freer, and Render deserved to know everything. If they chose to stop him, he told himself, there was a chance they would be doing exactly the right thing.

Alice-Angeles hadn't moved a millimeter when he emerged. She stirred on his reappearance with no sign of boredom. The twin lines of the Veil stretching down her cheeks gave her a somber appearance, one at odds with the deceptive youth of her features. Imre wondered if it was deliberate, and that made him wonder in turn if the hosts of the alien parasite had any choice over how the Veil manifested. The black patches seemed unique to each individual, ranging from solid blocks to complex fractal designs that no human hand could have drawn. Subtle physical or even psychological properties might influence the way it grew— or it could have been completely random. Without looking into the matter more deeply, he might never know.

He and Alice-Angeles began the long walk back to the bridge, with feet unintentionally marching in sync. The loop shunt didn't warm in his hand, no matter how firmly he gripped it. He had speculated once that loop shunts and the Luminous spheres might use the same technology to communicate, since neither means had been hackable by ordinary humanity. That would also explain how the Luminous had been able to detect the Forts and knew how to cut the links between their component frags. The exact mechanism remained unknown, but he wouldn't be surprised if it connected to dark matter, somehow. The arcane, clouded physics governing that complicated realm had produced the occasional boon for humanity down the millennia, for dark matter was not just one species of matter but many, intimately entangled with dark energy. Q loop technology could have been another such spin-off of the Forts' research, and who knew what bizarre primordial physics the Luminous had access to?

"Imre, I am worried."

For an instant, he didn't credit that it was Alice-Angeles who had spoken. She so rarely initiated conversation, especially ones about her internal state. "About what, Alice-Angeles?"

"About Render," she said. "Increasingly he is incommunicative, inflexible, erratic, and fragile."

"Hasn't he always been that way?"

"It is becoming pathological. I worry that he is reaching the limits of Prime endurance."

"I don't know, Alice-Angeles. He seems normal to me—normal for him, anyway—but I suppose you know him better now."

She nodded. "Around you, he is more like his old self. Your return reminds him of who he once was. But now that you have changed, he has lost his last anchor to the past."

He wanted to explain that his change wasn't voluntary, but knowing her straightforward mind, he realized that she would only ask why he didn't take steps to reverse it. He didn't have a good answer to that.

"What about you? Don't you help, just by being around?"

"I have assumed the Veil. Our relationship is not what it once was."

Imre thought about that and remembered how conspiratorial Render had been when Imre had first arrived. *Tread careful,* he had said. *Hide your fear. Don't let them know.*

His feelings of suspicion had been exactly the same as Imre's, but where Imre was beginning to see that maybe the Veil did have a valid place in the governance of humanity, at least where frags were concerned, Render had nursed his feelings unchanged for hundreds of thousands of years. Imre could imagine how that could poison a relationship, especially when the parasite could be conveyed by sexual contact.

He really didn't want to know any more than he had to about Render's private life, but it seemed there was no avoiding it.

"Do you love him?" he asked.

Alice-Angeles didn't flinch from the subject. "Yes. Does that seem strange to you?"

"No. I know independent frags sometimes form relationships. Where I was going with this was: have you talked to him about it?"

"I have tried. He knows what I tell him to be true, but will not act upon it. I find that . . . difficult."

Imre could understand that. Alice-Angeles was nothing if not pragmatic and self-aware. She had had plenty of experience dealing with the rest of humanity's illogical ways, but that didn't mean she liked her face being rubbed in it.

He remembered a conversation with Emlee not long after he'd first returned from C20.

The Old-Timers as a group are too damaged and useless to do or know anything that could help us.

Does Render agree with that sentiment?

He convinced me of its veracity.

"Do you really think Render's at risk of breaking down like the other Old-Timers?"

Alice-Angeles glanced at him. " 'I want to be, to overdose on time.' "

She was quoting Render. Imre had heard him say that before, a very long time ago.

"I think he's been alive so long," Imre said, "that he's forgotten how to—"

"Die?"

"No. Live."

The end of the corridor was approaching. If they were going to continue the conversation, they would have to raise their tempo closer to Absolute in order to have time. Imre followed her lead, however, and her expression was, as always, impossible to interpret. Her steps came like clockwork, unhesitating, unflinching.

As they neared the entrance, she turned to him and took his arm.

"If anyone must remind him," she said, "it should be you."

He could only nod.

Without another word, she led him back to the bridge, where the others were blurs moving back and forth. The ship was approaching the third of Bianca Biancotti's enigmatic destinations.

Imre's fist closed tight around the loop shunt as he stepped up to the dais and adjusted his tempo to match the others'. Emlee and Freer were arguing about long-distance telemetry from Soulis's location. Against a backdrop of crowded stars and hot gases, several bright emission spikes had been detected. Emlee had killed the *Memory of Markheim*'s steady thrust and delayed the expected deceleration burn in order to maintain as low a profile as possible.

"We don't know who they are," she said, as the ship reconfigured itself to zero gee. "Until we're close enough to get a definitive fix on the source of the spikes, we'd be foolish to give ourselves away too soon."

"You think they're the Barons," Freer said, "but back at Vaia you were worried about implicating an innocent civilization. Don't you think you're being inconsistent?"

"I'm trying to cover as many bases as possible," she said, unmoved. "Besides, there's no such thing as an innocent civilization in the Core. Just because they might be uninvolved in any of our problems doesn't mean I want to rush around waving my hands over my head."

Imre studied the telemetry. The data was scant but

suggestive. What should have been empty space looked like a dozen operational ships, maneuvering in a cluster. There were no sharp flashes or sudden dropouts indicating a battle under way, but if the spikes did originate around the distant orphan world, then the ships they came from were big.

"What about behind us?" he asked.

The view on the primary feeds changed. Several occultation or lensing effects had been recorded. Still not conclusive, but worrying all the same.

"Tick-tock-tick," said Render, as Imre thought it through.

"Do you want my opinion?" he asked Emlee.

"You're going to give it to me regardless, I suspect."

"I think you're doing the right thing," he said. "I also think it'd be a wise move to peel off some decoys, just in case we need them."

"Three launched an hour ago, relative."

"Good." He nodded. "I also think you're not telling us everything."

"Why?" The muscles in her broad, masculine face barely moved. "What would I be hiding from you?"

"I don't know." For a communication specialist, Emlee had always been a poor liar. "I guess we'll find out when it becomes important."

She turned back to Freer. "We're coming in quiet, and that's the end of the discussion. When we know more, we'll reconsider our options."

The attention of the crew was firmly focused on the data trickling in through the *Memory of Markheim*'s powerful senses. They were now well within the bright ring of new stars surrounding the galaxy's central regions, and moving into the bar of old, red stars that led like rivers into the dark heart itself. Ferocious knots of starbursts surrounded the dangerous regions closest to the galaxy's singularity, but they had no intention of going that deep. Travel became exponentially more difficult as concentrations of stars, stellar remnants, and dust increased.

Imre watched with the rest of them as the view ahead clarified. Ten ships, maximum, four of them likely as large as the *Memory of Markheim* with six smaller support vessels. There might have been more in the latter class if they weren't currently under power—or hadn't been when the light they radiated had left the vicinity of Soulis. As the *Memory of Markheim* drew closer, the lag between emission and reception steadily decreased until suddenly, without warning, the emissions ceased.

"They haven't left," said Freer. "We would've seen the drive flares."

"They've gone silent," said Emlee.

"Out of sight," said Render. "Out of mind."

"Someone told them to expect visitors," Imre said. "They're lying low."

"They'll be looking for us now." Emlee sent a flurry of commands to the crew, who began signaling the decoys via ultratight bursts. "We'll give them something to track."

Imre waited impatiently as signals propagated through space at light-speed, to and from the distant drones. They were simple machines, consisting of little more than a noisy drive and basic control systems. When their drives activated, they would light up the sky like supernovae. It was a simple ploy that would most likely fool no one, but the watchers would be forced at least to check it out.

One drone flared, angling its burn toward Soulis like a ship decelerating for a close approach. Minutes later, relative to Imre's internal clock-rate, a second drone also appeared, mimicking the same motions from a different segment of the sky. The third waited longer, then followed suit. A trio of new stars converged on Soulis's location from slightly different angles, presenting the illusion of a small fleet arriving from the galaxy's outer arms.

Emlee said nothing until enough time had passed for the light of the three drive flames to reach the watchers and for evidence of their reaction to reach the *Memory of Markheim*. Nothing stirred in that distant patch of space.

"Well, they're not launching intercepts." Emlee drummed the fingers of her right hand on the dais rail. "They're taking their orders seriously."

"They'll wait," said Render, "and won't make mistakes."

"Time for us to join the party," Imre said.

"Yes." She nodded. "I agree." Another flurry of orders swept through the crew. Acceleration couches extruded behind all stations.

Imre sank back into his, hating the feeling of lying in an open coffin while they rode a sword of fire toward the unknown. He stared at the bridge's ceiling and counted down the seconds to the burn, wondering how many times he had been in similar circumstances: approaching target systems from the outside; juggling the element of surprise over the operational constraints of attacking at speed; second-guessing the thoughts of unknown enemies when news of every action took days to arrive. Casual mistakes could cost whole worlds.

Weight returned like a giant sitting on him, forcing him down into the elastic membrane of the couch. He took a deep breath and closed his eyes, letting the virtual feeds envelop him—

—her—

—and had a brief but startling flashback to the dream she had had the night Bianca Biancotti had placed the fantasy of her missing sister into her mind. Her strange adventure down through the underbellies of both C20 and her own psyche had begun with a dark shadow of Emlee whispering sinister words as she pressed her down onto the bed. The sexual feelings inspired by the dream returned with a startling intensity, distracting her for a moment from the immediacy of her situation.

Such had it often been, she realized, for the old Imre Bergamasc. Sex and danger, power and pleasure—all entangled in a horrible mess. She wondered if he had killed Helwise as much for fucking their son as for her betrayal of him. It was impossible to tell now, with so many years between the past and the present. Guilt and personal transformation made it increasingly difficult to translate the motives of one Imre to another. Even the current one was proving to be something of a mystery.

The dream image of Emlee had become entangled with a more recent one: of Emlee drifting to sleep on Imre's bed, huge and masculine but in search of peace she was likely never to find.

Sparkling lights appeared around the world ahead. The *Memory of Markheim* was so close that Soulis itself could be seen, bathing in the light of the ships nearby. Widely scattered probes—far enough from the *Memory of Markheim*'s drive flame so as not to be blinded by it—relayed the copious data they were gathering. Four large ships and eight in support: Imre's estimate had been roughly correct. They were deploying in response to the three drive flames, half breaking orbit and swooping out to meet the intruders and half forming a defensive cordon behind. Tentative pictures of Soulis revealed a world with features: low hills and sharp-edged cliffs of atmospheric ice surrounded black lakes of the Veil. Approximately 50 percent of the world lay exposed to the bright starlight.

"The Veil hasn't completely taken over," Imre said aloud. "Soulis is a work in progress."

"That makes them Baron ships," said Freer. "That makes them you."

Imre raised her clenched right fist up to the swell of her chest and held the loop shunt close.

"Don't be so sure," said Emlee. "Those drive flames are familiar. They look like Fleet Vanguard to me."

All attention returned to the telemetry. Imre didn't know what to look for, having only the barest outline of the Host ships' designs, but she believed what the crew's analyses were telling her. One of the larger ships was soon comprehensively identified, and two more were considered likelies. *Mamoulian*, *Vandegrift*, *de Mattos*—the names meant nothing to her, but they clearly did to Al Freer.

"Od damn it. How did that son of a bitch get here before us?"

"That's your President you're referring to," said Emlee with a dark expression.

"Ra?" Imre asked, surprised. "How can you be sure it's him?"

"He's on every Fleet Vanguard ship," she told him. "It's his private navy."

"To hell with that," interjected Freer. "Ra can't have reached Vaia, followed the relay to Falisa, and overtaken us. It's simply not possible."

"So either he was here already," said Imre, "or someone else is flying those ships and wants us to think it's him."

"Do you like the odds either way?" Emlee asked her.

"I'm hoping a third option will present itself."

The bridge fell silent as the ships and drones laid in courses toward each other. Imre reviewed the data at a slightly higher tempo, making sure there wasn't something they had missed. Emlee had signaled Ra on Earth shortly after the *Memory of Markheim* had left the Jinc behind. The signal would hardly have traveled in a straight line along the Line, so even allowing for the fact they were traveling sublight, there was, as Freer had said, no way a fleet could have tracked them down and beaten them to their destination. It was distantly possible that Ra had access to the same data as Bianca Biancotti and had been able to extrapolate their final destination from the first port of call—but that didn't explain the sudden comms blackout they had detected on approaching the tiny world. It was most likely that a message had arrived from someone elsewhere, warning the Soulis contingent to expect visitors soon.

The *Memory of Markheim* was detecting a similarly leaky Line transmission, so the operation was presumably no different than that in Vaia and Falisa, except that this one wasn't complete. Ra—if it was Ra—had been caught in the act.

Emlee knew her ship and those coming toward her. She decelerated hard at them, using the forward-pointing drive wash as a shield in case the system had been mined. Apart from the decoys and baseline probes she had launched to investigate what lay ahead, she issued no advance hardware, nothing that might signal a hostile intent. Her expression was controlled apart from one small muscle dancing in her cheek, visible even through the Veil.

When they had halved the distance to Soulis, Emlee opened a communications channel and broadcast a brief message, relayed through all the drones and timed so the transmissions were simultaneous.

"This is Diplomatic Expeditionary Force One. Provide immediate identification and authorization."

Imre waited out the communication lag with impatience. The approaching ship—tagged the *Vandegrift* by the spectra of its drive halo—was growing brighter by the second.

A voice crackled out of the void.

"Rogue elements will stand down and surrender by order of the President of the Host."

It wasn't Ra's voice. The flattened inflection suggested a frag.

"Playing tricks," said Render.

Emlee nodded. To the approaching ship, she said, "Prime Minister Copas surrenders to no one, least of all a fellow officer of the state. Put the President on the line."

Another long and tense wait. Although Imre knew that Render was right about Ra's playing psychological games, their effectiveness could not be doubted. She resisted the urge to fidget or to drop her tempo any lower than it already was. When two ships were hurtling toward each other at high velocity, things could change in a second.

"This is President MacPhedron." Ra's voice boomed through the bridge, resonant and deep. Imre would not have recognized it. "You stopped being my ally, Emlee Copas, when you junked the *Wurmbrand*."

"I'm not here to fight you, Ra. The *Wurmbrand* was attacked by forces inimical to both of us. We need to plan a unified response, not squabble like children over who did what."

The communications lags were shrinking. "If you're not here to fight me, Emlee, then what are you doing here?"

"You tell me," she shot back. "What is this place? Why have I never heard of it before?"

"I'm saving the human race," he said, "while you jump at shadows and waste resources hunting ghosts. Stand down, and we'll talk."

"I'm not surrendering anything to you, Ra. We share authority."

"That depends entirely on who you have aboard your ship—and how much authority you're sharing with him."

"Who are you referring to?"

"You know very well who. Is he there? Is he listening in?"

Imre bit her tongue.

"What would that matter, Ra?" Emlee's response was terse. "He is irrelevant, and so is your ridiculous grudge."

The ships were slowing, and Soulis was growing larger in the forward displays. One of the drone decoys had been snuffed out by a well-aimed salvo. The others were sure to follow before long. If Ra entertained any doubts as to which ship contained Emlee and the others, they would soon be dispelled.

"Hand him over, Emlee," came Ra's equally brusque reply. "If you won't give me control over the Apparatus, at least give me that."

Another piece of the puzzle clicked into place. Ra didn't want the Apparatus for the unbreakable control it would give him over the galaxy. If he had developed his own spatiotextural technology, he could theoretically attain that on his own. His aspirations were more prosaic: the Apparatus was the force behind Executive Order Kismet. The memories of Helwise MacPhedron would be hidden forever until that order was rescinded.

Reversal of the Executive Order, or revenge. Imre could understand how the latter might seem a temporary panacea, but she also knew that it wouldn't satisfy Ra for long.

In time he would be scheming again, and dreaming perhaps of a day when Helwise could be reborn in a cloned body, free to live once more.

Imre had no intention of turning herself in, except as a last resort. The stakes were too high.

"You can ask all you want," Emlee told Ra. "I can't give you what I don't have."

"You're saying you didn't find him in C20?" Disbelief was naked in his voice. "You're saying he wasn't the reason you hightailed it out to the edge of the galaxy?"

"The city is a graveyard," she said, "and Al Freer was my reason for visiting the Jinc. You can ask him about that yourself if you don't believe me."

"I don't believe you," Ra said. "I won't believe you until you've opened your locks and let me search your ship from nose to stern."

"Will that really satisfy you, Ra? Won't you still wonder if he somehow slipped through your fingers? Put it behind you and concentrate on problems that matter."

"My mother's murderer matters to me," Ra said. "He matters to a great number of our constituents, too. Bear that in mind when you offer him shelter."

Imre frowned, not just at the sentiment, but the jar she felt every time Emlee and Ra used the wrong pronoun. She didn't know where exactly her identity was going to settle, but for the moment she was put on edge by the mismatch.

The *Vandegrift* was altering course, no longer powering forward as though about to ram but rotating its drive flame to decelerate. It would overshoot the *Memory of Markheim* by a large margin. A second ship, the *Mamoulian*, was angling to intercept as the approaching ship eased back its burn slightly. Some of the crushing pressure eased.

Imre indicated that Emlee should kill the comms so they could talk.

"Give him what he wants," she said. "Let him into the ship."

"No." Emlee's expression was adamant.

"You're outnumbered. Besides, do you really want to spark a civil war over this?"

"It's been a long time coming. I'd be relieved to have it out in the open."

"Sure. That'd save the Luminous from having to lift a finger." She couldn't hide her irritation. "I'm not talking about giving Ra me. Just the ship."

Emlee studied her for a long moment. Her mind was visibly working. Emlee's green eyes searched her face as though reading invisible words.

Eventually she nodded. "All right. I see where you're heading. There's something you should know, first."

It was Imre's turn to study Emlee. "Are you about to tell me what you've been hiding?"

"I won't need to. You're about to find out all on your own."

A rush of telemetry data distracted Imre. Fearing that Ra's ships might be making a preemptive move, she called up a map of the drive flares around Soulis, noting their dispositions and vectors. All the drones were dead. The Fleet Vanguard ships responsible were coming about and returning to the planet. Before long, the *Memory of Markheim* would find itself facing not just two capital ships, but four with a full complement of support.

Only . . . She studied the data more closely. New signals were flooding the ship's sensors. Four more drive flames had appeared in the dark gulfs around Soulis; four capital ships were decelerating at crushing rates to join the many gathered around that cold, orphaned world. Staggered by light-speed delays, they appeared one by one out of the void. The *Memory of Markheim*'s crew promptly identified their emissions: *Perpetual Franchard*, *Evocation of Underwood*, *Osbourne Recalled*, and *Balfour Anamnesis*. Clusters of smaller drive flames accompanied the larger burns like fireflies dancing around a pyre.

Imre laughed with something approaching delight. They were Emlee's ships. They had to be. Furthermore, there was only one way they could have arrived so quickly.

"You called them," she told her. "You called them when I told you to send for Ra."

She shrugged. "It seemed sensible."

"It was. It was indeed." Imre reached out of her acceleration couch to grip Emlee's broad shoulder. Had they been standing up, she would have kissed her.

"He won't like this," said Render, indicating the approaching *Mamoulian*.

"Ra can feel anyway he wants," Emlee said, "but there are witnesses now, and an even chance of us beating him." She turned to Imre. "You should know that I still like your plan. With the cavalry, we're only delaying the inevitable. Putting you out of the picture would give him cause to reconsider his assumptions."

"Which are spot-on, by the way," said Freer. "You haven't gone out of your way to keep your head down."

"That's been a low priority," she said, "until now."

Imre nodded. "We need to know what he's doing out here and why he's doing it. We won't find that out while he's trying to shoot us out of the sky." She checked the rear view again. Still no obvious signs of pursuit, but their wake wasn't entirely clear either. "There are a couple of things I'll need before we go through with it," she said. "First—"

Imre stopped, unsure at first why she did so, but certain once again that something had unexpectedly changed. She glanced at the telemetry, but this time the source of the distraction wasn't coming from there. The crew were busying themselves with their usual tasks: no sign of another rebellion.

Emlee was rising out of her acceleration couch, muscles straining in her shoulders and arms as she levered her considerable weight. She was staring at Imre in puzzlement, then concern.

An ultraviolet glow played eerily across Emlee's face.

Imre realized only then what had caught her own attention: the loop shunt was growing warm in her hand. Automatically but uselessly, she tried to open her fingers. Her muscles had locked. A distant numbness was spreading up her arm. She tried to stand but could do little more than lurch spastically forward, out of the couch and into the heavy air.

Emlee was shouting orders she couldn't hear. Simultaneous feelings of weightlessness and incredible pressure rose up in her, and she fought them as best she could. Emlee's lips said something about turning back. She tried to tell her not to—to press on, not to worry about her—but she couldn't tell if the message was getting through. Her vision broke up like a faulty video link. Blackness consumed her—

—the essence of black: velvety, cold, depthless, and impartial. He was simultaneously lifted up and pulled down, crystallized and dissolved, torn apart and recombined in an entirely new way.

Glowing specks of white light appeared in the darkness, and he realized that he had seen this before. The light spread and took on colors, painting the void with every shade of the electromagnetic spectrum. Dots joined into lines; lines bunched together to form sheets; sheets overlapped and became volumes. What had been a far-flung disparity of points evolved into a complex, unified structure, beating and vibrating with life.

A dark shape slashed through the structure, rending and tearing everything it touched. Truncated surfaces peeled away from the blackness and retreated into themselves. The web remained, but it was damaged, blighted, scarred.

He reeled under the emotional intensity of the vision. The last time he had connected with the loop shunt, he had experienced a similar mental invasion. A series of powerful sensory packages had completely overwhelmed him, leaving him feeling like a sandbank pounded by a tsunami. The mind that had briefly touched his had been far beyond anything he had ever experienced before.

A Fort, he had assumed. His own Fort-self.

Not *hers*. He was beginning to suspect that the difference was more than semantic. There was nothing he could do about the rest of him, but he could change himself.

Hello?

His voice left hardly a ripple in the sea of information pouring through him.

I'm back, and this time I need to talk to you!

Fiery light erupted all around him. Sound shocked every cell in his body. Roaring, burning, shaking him, it smashed him flat against space itself. He might have cried out, but could never have known if he had. He could barely think. He barely was.

Process. Order. Even in the hellish furnace, something moved. Nothing material in the way he understood matter, but capable of sustaining itself in the brilliant superplasma nonetheless. Transmission, reproduction, evolution. The fire of creation didn't need to wait billions of years for its fruit to ripen. Life was impatient. Life was tenacious. Life, once sparked, would never die.

I saw this last time, he shouted into the fire, but didn't know what it meant. I do now. You're showing me where the Luminous came from. They were born in the Light Ages. They're creatures of the primordial fire. I've worked it out. Tell me something new.

The fire faded. Individual sparks separated and danced through space in an untidy spiral, whirlpooling about a central point like a Catherine wheel. Each individual spark was a mind. He remembered this vision too. He was seeing the Milky Way galaxy from without, and each long-dead Fort was a star.

He knew what was coming, but still he tensed and felt dismay.

A shadow appeared, close to the center of the spiral, and spread across its ever-changing face. Where the shadow passed, the lights went out. One by one, they were extinguished until finally, despairingly, the galaxy turned dark.

Spargamos, he said. That's where it started. I've seen

what's left over. You saw me there. Why are you telling me this all over again?

The first time he had assumed the mind he had tapped into was testing him, probing the extent of his knowledge while he was distracted by the fireworks. He felt a similar questing urgency now, but he wondered if he hadn't misinterpreted it all along. What else could the loop shunt be linking him into? What other purpose could the repeated images serve?

The Slow Wave.

Three words emerged from the darkness. He remembered them too.

The Slow Wave.

The voice was full of recrimination and anger—the combined voice of an entire caste of humanity, slaughtered with one fiendish gesture.

The Slow Wave!

Imre rode the surge of emotion with greater facility this time. Instead of being subsumed into it and losing himself entirely, he let it carry him on its back, neither fully accepting nor fully denying its message.

What's next?

A scattering of glowing points returned, fuzzy and indistinct against the backdrop of infinity. With the patience of ages, they danced like glaciers to music inaudible to his ears. He drifted among them, invisible, immeasurable, as time's heartbeat stretched out, and out, and out . . .

I don't need a history lesson, he said. I want answers. If you won't talk to me, I'll find someone else who will.

Bright light flared again, and he was back at the dawn of time. The battery left him cold.

The rending of colored webs didn't touch him.

Even the death of the Forts was beginning to pale.

You can rail about the Slow Wave all you want, he hollered into the impassive distance, but at some point I'm going to stop listening!

Galaxies danced at the end of time, and a voice whispered:

(i hear you, imre bergamasc)

He pursued the voice, wondering if he was imagining it. The words were softer than the brushing of molecules, the sigh of light itself.

Hello? Hello?

(interference)

A dark knife slashed through rainbow strands. The images were repeating, shuffling order each time. He was becoming adept at ignoring them. What he had initially assumed was the message was perhaps something else. Not quite interference, as the whisperer said, but a beacon. An SOS, or a warning, endlessly cycling for the benefit of anyone who could listen.

(traitor of *pelorus* . . . architect of Domgard)

The whisper arrived in fragments, chopped up by the wild excess of the repeating broadcast.

(got my message)

A chill went through him. Now he knew who was talking to him.

The Butcher of Bresland, he said. None other.

(a long time ago)

The voice of Bianca Biancotti spoke like a ghost from another age, barely using words at all, barely recognizable as human.

(old and cold)

Are you part of this? he asked as the Fort-bedecked galaxy turned before him. Is this your message, or someone else's?

(not my message)

(not *one* message)

The Forts disappeared under a spreading shadow, and Imre understood. The loop shunt was picking up two overwhelmingly powerful transmissions: one decrying the death of the Forts, presumably from Domgard and his Fortself; the other from the Luminous, to an end he couldn't immediately fathom. Why reveal their origins so openly, and why do it via a means no one was listening to?

Unless, he thought, the transmission coming in over the loop shunt wasn't from the Luminous, but *of* the Luminous. Just as the Forts hadn't used Q loop technology to communicate, but to *be*, so too might the alien force that had destroyed them use the same bands to think their ancient, mysterious thoughts.

Or maybe Q loop was so far beneath the Luminous that all he was tapping into was a basic subroutine, a memory, a neural analogue that in a human might be equivalent to the mindless beating of a heart, or the insensate filling and emptying of lungs.

The vision shifted again, became the dancing of galaxies. How that linked to the other visions, he wasn't entirely certain. Two gargantuan thoughts beat through Imre like mistuned notes, garbling both of them in the process—and through the discord slipped one feeble transmission.

> (are you still angry?)

With you, Bianca?

> (no reason to be angry at me)

Well, your message could have been clearer.

> (too clear and everyone would be here)

Everyone *is* here. What's the story?

> (you should be angry, imre)

Fine. I'll be angry. Who with, if not you?

> (don't you know?)

There are plenty of candidates, starting with myself.

> (there are reasons to be angry)

Yes. Yes, there are.

> (that's what he wants)

Soul-stripping white light exploded through his mind, but he ignored it: just the universe being born, again.

If you've got something to tell me, Bianca, do it now. I don't want to stay plugged into this thing too long. If the Luminous picks up the signal—

> (too late)

Then why are we sitting around making small talk?

(people are going to die, imre)

(nothing you can do about that)

At least let me warn them.

(they know)

(the war has begun)

If Emlee dies—

He stopped. Through the discordant double transmission, Bianca Biancotti was laughing at him.

(whatever it takes)

(be angry)

A new image pressed into his mind: *Space tortured and twisted, dragged in a tight spiral around the heart of the Milky Way; stars ripped apart, dying with X-ray screams bright enough to light up the universe; a violent ecosystem that made the bar of the galaxy look like the fringes inhabited by the Jinc; the realm that took its name "Abaddon" from an ancient legend of Earth: a place of destruction, a realm of the dead.*

That was both too obvious and too unlikely. Nothing could survive in that maelstrom. Not even Imre's Machiavellian doppelganger.

The image shifted slightly: *To one side, dwarfed by a factor of three thousand by the central singularity but a heavyweight in its own right—1,278 solar masses, dragging a motley collection of giant stars with it—circling Abaddon at almost three hundred kilometers a second, little more than a light-year from the event horizon from beyond which no matter or energy returned—*

Gabriel. Largest of Abaddon's smaller siblings. Destined to be absorbed at a point unknown in the galaxy's future, and for the most part overlooked by those staring aghast at the monster nearby. Gabriel, the left hand and messenger of God, and occasional angel of death.

Gabriel.

(come)

What's waiting for me there, Bianca?

(just come)

(you are invited)

And if I say no?

    (then you're not the man i thought you were)

    (watch)

The image winked out. Bianca's deathless whisper fell silent. The massive beating of the thoughts of gods ceased, and Imre was flung back into the real world with the force of a cannonball.

Too late he asked: What kind of man do you think I am, exactly?

With that, he was released.

The first thing she heard was someone screaming.

"Get away from it! Get away from it!"

G forces tilted the deck under Imre's back. She was lying with limbs splayed as though left where she'd dropped. Engines whined and snarled. Every sense—real and virtual— was full of strident information. This was, in its way, worse than the loop shunt's transmission. This was uncontrolled, panicked, desperate. It smelled like smoke and tasted of blood.

"It's coming!"

The source of the voice wasn't nearby: it came over a comms line from one of Ra's ships. Distantly, with a numbed mind, Imre took the data into herself. The *de Mattos* was trying and failing to avoid a flaw in space-time that boiled like a crack through planetary crust. Energetic vibrations sang along its length as it curled and uncurled, its tips moving at relativistic velocities, snapping like the whip of a god. Gravity waves twisted and warped the starry backdrop and tugged humanity's fragile vessels back and forth. As she watched, the whip caught the *de Mattos* across its stubby bow and collapsed a significant percentage of it into degenerate matter. The rest of it sprayed across the sky like a comet, glowing blue and purple.

The voice died with a deafening snap.

"He is awake."

Alice-Angeles was leaning over her. Imre tried to focus

on the frag's Veil-marred features but found that the full use of her eyes hadn't yet returned. She felt utterly debilitated and helpless in the middle of a battle with a weapon not of humanity's making.

Render's face came into view. "How are you?"

"Could be better," she said, trying first with uncooperative lips, then via virtual channels. "You?"

"Don't ask."

"We've lost three ships," said Alice-Angeles. "*Evocation of Underwood*, *Osbourne Recalled*, and *Balfour Anamnesis*. Ra is down to one, the *Vandegrift*, and it has been damaged."

The war has begun.

"It's a cosmic string, right—the thing the Luminous are hitting us with?"

"We don't know for certain. There hasn't been time to conduct detailed observations."

Alice-Angeles' reply was perfectly dry, with no trace of rebuke, but Imre accepted it as such anyway. While she had been chatting with an old friend, her companions had been fighting for their lives. They still were, judging by the pitching and roiling of the deck.

"How long?" she asked. "How long have I been out?"

"Days," said Render.

"Sixty hours, Absolute," Alice-Angeles qualified.

Not long, then. The string must have been hot on their heels to have struck so quickly. That unnerved her. They had actively looked for it, but it had been barely visible. There could be thousands of such things scattered through the Milky Way's dusty arms, waiting for the signal to strike.

Sensation was returning to her limbs. She could feel the loop shunt between her fingers, glassy and smooth. It was cool once more, apparently harmless, but still she was tempted to hammer it down on the deck and smash it into a million pieces.

Instead she sat up, relying on Render and Alice-Angeles to keep her balance. With a grunt, she made it to her feet.

The bridge was energized and active. Frags pursued their tasks as overclocking blurs all around. Al Freer lolled in a corner, examining the data with deep-set, worried eyes. Emlee stood tall among them, obsidian and strong, calling directions as needed. Imre felt a wave of admiration, even as the facts of their situation sank in.

Six capital ships destroyed, another damaged. The remaining ships were doing their best to fight back, but every attack was an experiment. There were only so many left to make before the Luminous mopped up all resistance around Soulis.

People are going to die, Bianca Biancotti had said. That prophecy was coming abundantly true.

Imre felt anxiety but no fear. Her architecture was sound, and she trusted her instincts. She was expected elsewhere. Someone had an ace up their sleeve that had yet to be revealed.

"Back away from it," Imre called out as the *Memory of Markheim* powered in for another attack run. "Get well clear."

Emlee turned her great hairless head. "You want us to run?"

"Temporarily disengage. Something's coming. Trust me."

"Like Spargamos?"

"In principle, except this time they want witnesses."

"Why?"

"I think they're trying to send another message."

The war begins here.

Emlee took a second to think about it, then nodded. Commands flashed through the remaining ships and were relayed to Ra's surviving vessel. It had limped out of range of the string in order to patch itself together as best it could, and was using the orphaned world of Soulis as a shield. The powerful gravity of the string stirred the frozen atmosphere of the cold world every time a loop of it swung close by. How that was affecting the Veil-stuff growing in the icy soil was impossible to tell.

Light-speed lags made it difficult to take a momentary snapshot of the battlefield's disposition, but it was clear looking back on it that Emlee's ships had been trying and failing to protect the *Memory of Markheim*, the source of the Q loop signal, while Ra's ships had engaged in a futile defense of the world below. As data from the present trickled in, Imre eased herself into her acceleration couch and let it take the weight of her weakened limbs. She felt as though every cell had been stripped of their enhanced mitochondria, leaving nothing but limp tissue behind. Closing her eyes, she embraced the virtual data and left her physical self behind.

Don't wait forever, she said to herself as the remaining ships set about increasing the distance between them and the roiling space-time defect in their midst. It looked like a Chinese dragon, coiling and uncoiling and spitting primordial fire.

Bring it on, already.

A black dot streaked across the starscape, a fast-moving hole in the chaotic backdrop. The ship's sensors barely had time to register it before it struck the dragon midcoils, liberating an immense flash of energy. Imre flinched from the microsecond burst, even though it had passed before the impulse to recoil had even reached his nerve endings. The *Memory of Markheim* was quicker to recover. It recorded the arrival of another black dot, close in the wake of the first, and a third after that. Two more flashes expanded out from the locus of the strikes, painting the debris of the dead ships every possible color. The dragon writhed, cut into four unequal segments and spraying the sky with energetic blood.

Exotic radiation scarred the hull of the *Memory of Markheim*, triggering strident alarms. Engines surged to increase the distance from the stricken enemy as three more dots struck it. The second trio came from a different sector of the sky; either the source was moving implausibly fast or there was more than one of them, invisible against the starscape. The effect on the string was no less dramatic. One of its truncated sections sparkled all along its length like a burning magnesium wire, then exploded, sending the rest flying. A second fragment whipped past the *Perpetual Franchard*, tearing it and its occupants to ribbons. A third struck the planet, buckling and shearing its crust under unimaginable gravitational stresses. Rock turned instantly to steam; a bright red scar spread across its dark face.

Black dots lanced out of yet another sector and picked off the remaining threads. They dissolved one by one, sending sheets of light in waves through the volume of space around Soulis. No fragment was left unaccounted for. Those dots that missed their targets vanished in a shower of multicolored sparks well out of harm's way. Gravitational detectors aboard the *Memory of Markheim* registered sharp spikes every time one self-destructed. Imre clutched the sides of her acceleration couch as space-time roiled and foamed.

Gradually, the tumult subsided. Radiation alarms sounded for another minute, then ceased. She opened her eyes to see Emlee looming over her.

"We're not guinea pigs," she said. "How do I pass *that* message on?"

Imre looked down at the loop shunt lying inert in her hand. "I think that window might have closed."

She turned away with a disgusted look.

"It worked, didn't it?" Imre heaved herself out of the couch and followed Emlee down to the crew deck, where the overclocking of the frags made the air seem full of ghosts.

"Not without significant collateral damage," she snarled. "And what have we got out of it?"

"A weapon."

"Wielded by people we can only assume are the Barons against something we assume the Luminous sent. There are no certainties, Imre. It changes nothing."

"It changes everything," Imre said, indicating a transmission incoming from the *Vandegrift*. The stricken ship was broadcasting an SOS and requesting assistance.

"You want me to—?" She stopped and rolled her green eyes. "Well, you can't be here when I save his unworthy hide. You know that, don't you?"

"I do know that. If you let him on board, and he doesn't find me, that'll get him off my back once and for all. I'm willing to be elsewhere. The *Wickthing*, if I have a choice."

She opened her mouth and closed it, warring inside. "All right. Get to the hardcaster bays and wait for me there. I'll be right behind you."

The deck was settling underfoot as Imre headed for the exit. Alice-Angeles accompanied her, and Render watched them go. The old soldier's expression was intense and unreadable.

He knows, Imre thought. I can't hide anything from him.

She opened a secure comms channel.

"Time to leave, I suppose?" Render broke in before she could say anything. "Here it comes again: that old familiar pain."

"Don't be such a drama queen. I'm not abandoning you."

"I've heard it all before."

"Come along for the ride if you don't believe me."

"I don't know. Give me a reason to stay."

Imre hid her relief. Render was as wary of hardcasting as Emlee and the rest of the Host. "That collection of yours: you need to keep an eye on it. It's not as dead as you think."

"But you—"

"It's not the sort of thing I'd advertise, right?"

Render was silent for a second or two. "I want to believe."

"So believe me. Have I ever not come back to you?"

"Nothing is the same. Change your colors, change your mind, change your rules. I'm trying to learn the rhythm. I'm trying hard—never tried so hard before. The change disturbs me."

Render's internal struggle was difficult to listen to

dispassionately, especially in light of what Alice-Angeles had told him. "It's not easy, old friend," she said. "Remember what you said to me when I first came back here: 'Tread careful. Hide your fear.' That's all we can do. We might not like the way life is now, but it's real, and there's no point fighting it. That's one war we'll never win."

Render took a deep breath, audible over the virtual link. "I'm so tired. Get out of here—don't look back—before I change my mind."

"All right. You do as I told you. Watch those relics carefully."

"You'll see me again."

"I'm sure of it."

"Come back to haunt me," Render said, "like a gangster in drag."

Imre let that parting shot lie. They had reached the hardcaster room, with its endless row of unused sarcophagi. "For crises," Emlee had said, but Imre wondered how many of the frags on the destroyed ships had managed to transmit to safety. If they considered damage to their Veils to be analogous to brain damage, maybe they had chosen death willingly—but still, it struck her as absurd. That was the only point, it seemed, on which Render and the Host agreed.

Then she thought of what Al Freer had told her about anomalous data on the line. Would she trust her pattern to a corrupted medium over any great distance? She had to admit that she probably would not. Perhaps that harsh truth lay behind Emlee's willingness to let perfectly good hardware lie idle while people died in their droves.

The third sarcophagus along was open and ready for her. Alice-Angeles left her alone while she waited for Emlee. Memories of her loop-shunt-inspired visions percolated through her thoughts, no matter how she tried to put them from her mind. She had so much to think through and absorb; she couldn't afford to be distracted by things she already knew, or at least felt that she could accept for the moment. Aliens born in the fire of the early universe had taken offense at the Forts' tentative exploration of the dark matter universe, and killed them all. From there, so much remained unknown. What was the purpose of the Veil worlds Vaia, Falisa, and Soulis, and how did Ra MacPhedron expect them to save humanity? What was waiting for her around the black hole called Gabriel? Why did Bianca Biancotti want her to be angry?

The deck was rock-steady beneath her feet by the time Emlee strode through the door. "We're coming about to pick up the survivors of the *Vandegrift*," she said, "Ra among them. He'll want to conduct a search, but I'll stall him as long as I can. The record of your transfer to the *Wickthing* will be buried so deep, he'll never find it."

"Thank you," Imre said with a grateful incline of her head. "I'm sure it'd be easier for you just to hand me over."

"Where would be the fun in that? It's good to keep the little twerp guessing."

They exchanged a smile, but it was forced. Despite facing each other across the open sarcophagus, unequal in height and political stature, they seemed for a moment to be standing eye to eye.

"I'll take Ra to Earth," Emlee said. "Do you want to tell me where you're going?"

"No." Imre wasn't surprised that she knew, like Render. Of course she did. "Do you want to ask me?"

"Yes, but I don't need to, this time. I'll find out."

"You can track the *Wickthing*?"

"Something like that."

Imre hadn't considered that possibility. "You'll bury that information too, I trust."

"As long as I must."

She caught the word Emlee chose: *must*, not *can*.

"Here." Imre held out her right hand. "Take this."

Emlee offered her left hand, palm up.

Imre dropped the loop shunt into it.

"Won't you be needing this?" Emlee asked, challenging her with her jade eyes.

"I sincerely hope not," Imre said, but that didn't satisfy her as he had hoped it might.

The difference in their heights returned.

"Just finish it," Emlee said.

"I will," Imre promised her.

"Don't show your face again until you can say 'I have.'"

She turned and walked for the door, and didn't look back.

THIS NAME

It is one thing to mortify curiosity, another to conquer it...

—Robert Louis Stevenson

Imre waited in the sarcophagus for the hardcast to begin, knowing as she knew well by then that it would come painlessly and without sensation. One moment she would be real; the next she wouldn't. That the technical wizardry was invisible to her didn't concern her at all. Technology at its most powerful freed people to deal with the problems that most concerned them—more often than not other people.

In her case, that person was Emlee. Something unnamable had passed between her and the giant man she now fully accepted as the woman Imre had once known—an inappropriate desire that simply would not die. Part of her wanted exactly the same kind of connection that she had dreamed about in the C20, and she wondered if Emlee had come intending to confess to the same desire.

Half a million years ago, she wanted to say, but it must mean something.

It took one person to say something, two to remain silent. So the moment had passed, leaving her tense and frustrated, and angry at herself in a way that Bianca Biancotti would surely find next to useless. Whatever might have happened now never would. The chances were they'd never meet again, let alone feel the same way if they did. It was over.

The light altered, and so did her clothing. She was lying gowned as she usually was aboard the *Wickthing*, atop a linen sheet in her private chamber. Thick curtains obscured the artificial daylight of MZ and Kells's consensual illusion, allowing just a faint yellow radiance around the edges. All physical sensation relating to the *Memory of Markheim* had vanished. With determination, Imre told herself to leave all thoughts about Emlee behind as well.

Out of the shadows stepped the woman in white. Imre sat up in surprise, ready to raise the alarm. The woman's face was obscured, but she was in perfect focus and as solid as a real person. Even in the gloom, Imre could discern the finger she urgently raised to unseen lips. Moving quickly, purposefully, she came to the side of Imre's bed and leaned close.

"Say nothing of my presence," she whispered, pressing her back with one small hand against her breastbone. "They must not see me until we are well under way."

"But—"

"Get rid of them, and we will talk again."

The woman kissed Imre quickly on the mouth, then backed into the shadows once more.

The door opened, allowing a cascade of blinding light into the room. The rounded silhouette of Chyro Kells stepped into the frame, peering in at Imre with exaggerated myopia, almost suspicion.

"We expected you in the map room," said the surgeon. "This is not the first displacement we have experienced."

Imre didn't need to feign concern. "If it was dangerous for me to come here—"

"I was monitoring the transmissions carefully."

Imre had yet to test her virtual body, to see if it had changed during the execution of the hardcast. If she was hallucinating, that wasn't a good sign. "Do you have anything to report?"

"Are you you, do you mean?"

"Isn't that what you usually tell me?"

Kells didn't answer. He looked flustered and unsure.

Imre spared him the answer. Physically, she felt fine. "MZ?"

"I am here, Imre."

"Set a course for Abaddon," she told them, reluctant to reveal anything about Gabriel until she absolutely had to—especially with the woman in white lurking nearby. "Don't tell anyone where we're going. Don't even ask permission to go if you can avoid doing that."

"The Apparatus has been given approval for our departure," the Fort said immediately.

"Then let's get moving."

There was no perceptible change to the virtual environment: no inertial g shifts or roaring engines. Imre could only assume that the Fort had obeyed his command.

"You didn't bring up my request with the Prime Minister," MZ said.

She had to think for a moment to remember what that had been. "To merge with the Apparatus? The opportunity didn't arise. I'll talk to Emlee when we return—or you could always ask her directly, you know."

"You have influence over the Prime Minister that I do not," the Fort said. "I have yet to earn her trust."

Imre remembered her parting words—*don't show your face again*—and wondered if MZ wasn't imagining trust where none remained.

Her lips still tingled where the woman in white had kissed her.

"Leave me alone for a while," she told MZ and Kells, who still hovered in the doorway like a slope-shouldered obelisk. "I've got a lot to think about."

That wasn't a lie, and she felt no guilt as Kells closed the door on her. The vision from the loop shunt had added turbulence to all manner of issues that already needed sorting.

"That's not an entirely crazy idea, you know," said the woman in white as she reemerged from her adumbral nook and tugged back her hood. The face beneath was familiar—shockingly so, for Imre had convinced herself that she would never see it again.

Was it her, though, or a convincing simulation? Her skin was flesh-colored and crinkled in all the right places—but verisimilitude was easy. There was only one way to test whose intelligence lay within.

"Which idea is that?" Imre asked.

"Merging MZ and the Apparatus. It'd give us an edge that Ra doesn't have."

"It would also turn MZ into a god."

"Better a smart one than an idiot, don't you think?"

"And if the minds of Earth designed it dumb for a reason?"

"I'm sure they did just that: the Forts didn't want any competition. We, however, need to be as competitive as we possibly can." She grimaced. "Ra's copy of the Apparatus is no better than ours, you know; it has no initiative, no independence. It's useless without orders."

"Does it have a name?"

"He calls it the Godmother."

A ripple of disgust went through her. "And what does he think he's doing in Soulis? Do you know?"

"I suspect—strange as it might seem—that he might be telling us the truth."

"About saving the human race?"

" 'Saving' us in a very different sense from the way you obviously took it. There's enough Veil on those three worlds to contain the memories of every person alive today."

"A memory bank," Imre said, groaning at the pun. Then the fact that it was a pun sank in deeper. "I bet it wasn't originally Ra's idea. Someone else is behind it."

The woman in white shrugged. "We'd need to be surer of our facts before we started pointing the finger."

"I'm disinclined to be so cautious."

"Some things never change."

They stared at each other. She was real. He was sure of it.

"Emlee, what are you doing here?"

The fullness of her lips curled up in a smile. "When we disentangled the *Wickthing* from C20 and put you back together, I knew you'd want to come back here. I couldn't stop you, but I could cover my bets, so I piggybacked a hack on your hardcast and trickled this version of myself in byte by byte."

"This is what you meant when you said you could track the *Wickthing*."

"Yes." She looked appropriately self-satisfied. "It took ages for me to be fully confident of the simulation. The hack—one of the toughest I've ever worked on—keeps me hidden from MZ, but I can't hide completely from you or Chyro because you're part of the simulation too. I think Chyro has spotted me a couple of times. He's acting suspicious."

Imre had noticed that. "I saw you too," she said.

"I guessed. And more besides."

"What does that mean?"

"Looked in a mirror lately?" She tilted her head onto an angle, sending her sandy blond hair askew. "No, of course not. Here. Work it out for yourself."

A woman appeared next to Emlee that could have been her twin sister. Economically muscled and slight with it, she was hairless from the neck down and had no visible tattoos or Veil markings. There were differences between the two of them, but they were small: a whiter shade of blond, blue eyes rather than green, and a more triangular chin among them. A casual glance might not have been able to tell them apart, especially when Emlee put them in identical outfits: old-style Corps skin suits, black with red trimming and insignia.

Imre didn't need to look under her gown to make the comparison. Emlee looked like her, and she looked liked Emlee. The revelation shocked her profoundly. She had imagined herself as she had been in C20: more rounded and buxom, and taller as well. Emlee's doppelganger didn't resemble that image at all.

"I dreamed you in C20," she said in wonderment. "Are you saying I became you, here?"

Emlee made a show of checking out herself out. "I take

it as a compliment." She turned back to Imre. "Seriously, I do."

"Don't be ridiculous," Imre said, feeling a flush rise to her cheeks. Emlee's gaze was entirely too direct. "I needed a pattern to model myself on; yours just happened to be handy. Did you ever think that the way you infiltrated the *Wickthing* might have caused you to bleed into me? I say it wasn't a conscious decision at all."

"You sure know how to flatter a girl."

The image vanished. Imre was relieved to see the back of it. Her hard-won sense of self didn't need the beating.

"Anyway, this is irrelevant," she told Emlee. "It doesn't explain why you've willingly duplicated yourself, or why you look like this, like you used to."

"I told you. We're suspicious these days about hardcasting the Veil. I'm not above that, so here I am without it." She perched herself on the corner of the bed. "As to the duplication issue—well, you weren't the only one feeling out of sorts. The Veil made me a better Prime Minister; it gave me a depth of experience I never could have possessed without it. But it's heavy, literally, and I missed the way I used to feel. It was surprisingly easy to break my principles just to become myself again. You understand, right?"

She did, all too well. Emlee wasn't just talking about the Veil. Imre had experienced gender dysphoria at the hands of the Jinc; she knew what it felt like. The Emlee before her seemed infinitely more comfortable in her body than she had in the real world, and that spoke volumes.

"We both chose to look this way," Imre said, "consciously or subconsciously, for our own reasons."

"We both like it, I guess. I honestly won't read anything into it."

"Good." Again, Imre couldn't look at her.

"Yes, why would I? You had me naked once and in your bed another time. If you'd been at all interested in me, you would've let me know before now."

Imre vividly remembered those occasions. "You were waiting for me to make the first move?"

"I didn't say that."

"You practically threw yourself at me—and you did kiss me just then."

"I did." Her gaze was frank and unflinching. "I don't apologize for doing that, by the way. It got your attention."

Imre nodded. She could think of nothing to add that didn't sound awkward, or that she might regret later. The opportunity was before her to reveal everything she had thought about while waiting to come to the *Wickthing*, but the thought of doing so made her liquefy inside. What had happened to all that certainty? The desire was still there; of that, at least, she was completely certain.

"Why don't we try doing what doesn't come naturally, just this once?" Those were the words Emlee had used on Earth, the one and only time they had slept together. "Why just once?" she wanted to ask now. Why not a thousand times, until it became natural?

They said nothing until the silence started to become uncomfortable. Imre, clutching at the genesis of their conversation, managed, "I guess we'd better talk about what happens next. You're helping Ra, back in the *Memory of Markheim*, and convincing him I'm dead at last, but it won't lead to more than a temporary truce. That you think we'll need the edge MZ could give us speaks volumes about what's to come."

"I'm afraid it does," Emlee said, leaning back onto one elbow. "Can you imagine what a war between the Apparatus and the Godmother could look like? Perhaps we should hammer out some thoughts on what we'll do if we get back in one piece."

"We're on the same side, then?"

"We've always been on the same side, Imre, even when you didn't know it."

They talked for an hour, relative. Outside, the angle of the light shifted slowly, as it would have on a real world. Imre didn't dare think how much time was passing beyond the *Wickthing*'s virtual walls. MZ's temporal yardstick was long compared to the rest of the galaxy. Thousands of years could have passed since they had left the *Memory of Markheim*; they could already be deep in the galaxy's darkest wildwoods, for all she could tell.

The discussion was animated and occasionally heated. This Emlee looked like the one Imre had known half a million years earlier, but she spoke with the authority of the First Prime of the Returned Continuum and Prime Minister of the Host: older, more powerful, and harder, as she herself had said. She was different, however, from the giant they had left in the *Memory of Markheim*, although they were technically the same person. Imre read them differently. They read themselves differently too, and it showed.

She wasn't the only one. In the mess and tangle of recent events, the Barons had taken on a new face, still shrouded by secrecy but less hostile than it had been. Bianca Biancotti or Imre-F or whoever was behind them persisted in shuffling ordinary humanity about a chessboard to their own ends, but at least those ends were coming into sight. The weapons Imre and Emlee had witnessed over Soulis had been designed for one purpose: to strike at the Luminous. They hadn't been used against the Host, and Imre took some hope from that. The Barons were "gearing up for war," as Al Freer had put it. It was up to the Host not to be caught in the cross fire.

Emlee, on the other hand, regarded with suspicion anyone who failed openly to declare a common cause against the enemy. In a war that had been forgotten by most people, she remained a hardliner. For or against, she needed to know. In a world of shifting lines, she ached for clarity. It was naked on her face, but on that front Imre could not provide.

Neither of them wanted to be a spectator in what was to come. That was the only thing they agreed upon.

In the middle of an argument about whether Ra was crazy or not for trying to create a massive backup of humanity—no matter who he was working for—their hands collided, cracking with wincing force in midgesture.

Emlee's eyes widened in surprise. "Well, you're still

clumsy. Couldn't you have fixed that as well as your face?"

"What do you mean? I was never clumsy." Imre shook her hand, driving blood into her bruised knuckles.

"At least you'll admit to the problems with your face." Emlee snatched playfully for Imre's hand, and, catching it, held it up for examination, front to back. "They're the same, too."

"As yours, or as they used to be?"

"Either."

"Can't you tell?" Imre twisted in her grip, but Emlee was holding on too tightly for her to slip free. The challenge was irresistible. Imre reached for her shoulder with her free hand and wrenched her sideways onto the bed. She kicked up with her left knee, and Imre caught her other hand and *twisted*. Emlee gasped.

Imre abruptly let go and leaned her weight back. "No," she said. "It can't be like this."

"No. But it cuts through the crap, doesn't it?" Emlee sat up and leaned closer. Emlee was still holding her hand, but the pressure on her fingers had eased. Imre could easily have pulled away, but she didn't.

They kissed softly at first. Emlee's lips were exactly as she remembered, but nothing else about the moment was familiar. Both hands came up to touch Emlee's face. Her skin was warm and soft against her palms, her slender form moving closer, welcoming the embrace. Emlee touched her throat, her right breast, the small of her back; each contact was gentle, intimate, and sure. Imre welcomed it, the tension in her body reaching new places, demanding release in new ways.

It wasn't that she was female. She knew that, even as a flood of novel sensations cascaded through her. The last time had been a guilty and traumatic experience, a brief war conducted against her suddenly alien self. Now, she embraced it in a way that simply had not been possible for her before—as a broken human being created by the Jinc, in the doubt-racked role of the galaxy's First Prime, or with the gargantuan figure Emlee had become on the *Memory of Markheim*. Who she was had changed at least as much as her body. She embraced herself, and that was an entirely new point of departure.

They made love as virtual dusk descended in the world beyond the curtains, led by Emlee's greater experience with her body and its needs. Their passion became more urgent, more all-involving. Imre wondered if she had ever truly embraced sexuality except as a means to generate and release tension. With Helwise it had been a battle. With Gravine Sevaste it had been a power play. Even with Emlee, before his abdication, they had been exorcising demons rather than engaging with each other. She couldn't remember a sexual partner that hadn't been an enemy or a conflicted ally. The people behind those masks had been absent—on both sides.

The night grew older, and Imre realized that euphoria was making her exaggerate. She must have felt this way before, and she had surely had such feelings returned many times throughout her long life. Such was a natural state of affairs for all humans, be they frags, Primes, singletons, or even Forts. Emlee had loved the proto-Fort called Ampersand, and there was no doubt those feelings had been mutual. Alice-Angeles loved Render, in her own autistic way. Love was part of being alive, and Imre had, in all things, embraced exactly that.

She simply couldn't remember those other times. Her former self had let them slide.

"Do you still have the memories?" Imre asked Emlee in one sweaty, tangled pause. "The memories of the memories?"

"The Veil, you mean?" Emlee's lips were soft against her ear. "You can't help them," she said, "but you can stop recalling them. I'm clean, if that's what you're asking."

Imre hadn't been. She had simply been curious about how it felt to have the Veil, then give it up. Was Emlee shrugging off the weight more figuratively than literally? It was nothing but a technicality until Emlee pointed out that

Helwise's memories were effectively gone too. She could look at Emlee and know that only Emlee was looking back.

They kissed more deeply. Time passed in waves. Imre resisted the urge to adjust her tempo in order to prolong the night indefinitely. Her unwillingness for the moment to end was heightened by the knowledge of what an end it would be for them—in the heart of the galaxy, where space-time itself was shredded and torn, and flesh sizzled under powerful X-rays. She told herself to be sanguine about it. Without the desert, there could be no oasis—and without forgetfulness, there could be no new beginnings. It didn't help.

They slept for a time in each other's arms, then woke to make love again, with more surety this time, and no less urgently.

Only when MZ intruded to tell her that they were nearing the stormy regions surrounding Abaddon did Imre overclock to gain a few extra minutes. What light there was turned crimson. She and Emlee lay face-to-face on their sides, barely touching. Emlee's green eyes deepened in color until they were almost black.

"I think I chose your face," Imre told her, "because I missed it."

"It's not so bad, I guess." Emlee took her left hand in both of hers, and squeezed it. "Thank you for saying that."

She could have stayed there for years. "We need to go."

"I know. And you know what appalls me? For all your talk, you have no idea what's waiting for us out there. I've always assumed that part of you knew what was going on, even if it was buried so deep you didn't know it was there."

Imre didn't have the heart to say that she felt any different. "Life would be simpler if I did," she said, thinking of everything she had thought she'd lost in C20: friends, a job, family. None of it had been more than a fantasy, even though who she had been then was making her strong now.

"Simpler, but not better. The time has come, Imre. Time to finish it."

Emlee's other self had told her not to return until she had done exactly that. There was no withdrawing now.

"I'm afraid," she confessed.

"Good." Emlee patted her cheek. "I like you better this way."

The light returned to normal. They got up and dressed, Emlee by willing herself back into the white dress she had been wearing earlier, Imre by slipping into a light-armor sheath she pulled from the room's virtual closet. The illusory fabric felt tight and rough against her skin, helping her reacquaint herself with what needed to be done. *Find Himself. Avenge the Forts.* The pledge was age-worn and weighty around her neck, but there was only one way to be rid of it forever, and that was to make good on it.

She opened the door to the room, giving MZ and Kells their first glimpse of the stowaway in their midst. Emlee was unapologetic, and Kells almost relieved to have the mystery solved. By the time they convened in the map room, she had managed to turn MZ's automatic huffiness to reluctant acceptance of her presence.

"Besides," she told him, "if you behave, we'll talk about that deal you mentioned earlier. The Apparatus, wasn't it? I may be an uninvited guest, but I still have the succession codes."

"Yes, Prime Minister. Forgive me for mistaking expedience for philosophical inconsistence."

"The two of me, you mean?" Emlee didn't dodge the point. "Today I don't have a philosophical bone in my body."

The magic picture frame through which the occupants of the *Wickthing* viewed the outside world showed a scene almost surreal in its violence. Abaddon itself was invisible, hidden by a vast bubble of superheated debris and mutilated stars. Here the detritus of the galaxy converged for destruction and conversion into energy for another universe. No natural human in recorded history had seen more than a glimpse of the ghastly horizon and returned to tell of it.

Yet it was nothing, Imre thought, compared to the primordial fires of the early universe, where the Luminous had been born.

It struck her then as strange that the aliens responsible for the death of the Forts lived beyond the edge of the galaxy rather than in climes they would surely find more comfortable. Was it something to do with the technology they employed? Cosmic strings, unless carefully controlled, would be dangerous in any decent stellar populace. The reason might be as simply expedient as that, or there could be more to it than she realized.

There was always more, Imre told herself. She was peering through a keyhole at a room as large as a city. Slowly, painstakingly, she was combining individual glimpses into a comprehensive snapshot.

The maps on the desk charted the *Wickthing*'s careful passage through the densely crowded environment. Gabriel was a small circle tracing a geometric route around the empty void that was Abaddon.

"There," Imre said, pointing at the moving circle. "That's where Bianca told me to go."

"We must be cautious," admitted MZ. "The *Wickthing* is not indestructible."

Imre had never heard MZ admit to any kind of limitation. It made sense: the *Wickthing* was written on space itself, and nowhere else was space deformed as much as around a black hole. Sturdy matter might survive where their fragile patterns failed.

She took the note of caution on board, but it didn't touch her. She felt revived, confident, and centered, as well as afraid of what lay ahead. It was a thrilling mix.

"Bring us as close as you can," she said. "Don't take any risks you think are unnecessary."

"It's all relevant down here, isn't it?" Emlee radiated the same indestructibility. "We've gone way beyond the normal scale."

"And we're still going." Imre watched closely as Gabriel neared, represented by visual data overlaid with complex schematics since it couldn't be seen directly. The backdrop was nearly solid radiation: stars and plasma filled every wavelength with unimaginable noise. Imre resisted a sudden impulse to translate it into an audible signal, just to hear what it sounded like. She was sure it would be exceedingly unpleasant—the chorus of stars screaming their last.

MZ was incapable of broadcasting, so all observations were passive, relying on infalling radiation and gravitational waves. It was easy to forget in Abaddon's shadow just how large its smaller sibling was. MZ charted four blazing giants in orbit around it, pumping steady streams of electrons and photons into an already turbulent whirlpool of superheated gases. If they had once possessed worlds, they had long been slingshotted away or reduced to rubble. Dense currents of plasma curled like snakes around them, lending the entire scene a surreal air. Pockets of gas were moving at close to the speed of light in places, creating shock waves and intense X-ray bursts. At times the density of gas around the *Wickthing* approached terrestrial levels.

Something hard and round loomed out of the maelstrom—the one solid object MZ had found amid so much liquid chaos. It was dense and reflective, like a ball of mercury, but clearly artificial. Its lines were too perfect, and remained so even in the face of the storm around it. Its mass was also much higher than expected for its volume, suggesting that at least part of it was made from degenerate material. Imre remembered Kismet, the iron prison in orbit around a dead star from which they had rescued Render long ages ago. This was orders of magnitude stranger.

MZ matched orbits without being asked to. Gabriel's shrouded bulk rose like a bruised star over the too-smooth horizon.

"No obvious way in," Emlee noted.

Imre nodded. The surface of the ball was an unbroken mirror, reminding her of the Luminous's silver shock troops. MZ was unable to dock with anything physical. He interacted with the wider universe only by means of gauge bosons.

"Look for a Line feed," Imre said. "That should be our first priority."

"I detect no leakage," said the Fort, "but such would be quickly swamped in this environment. I will attempt to find the transmission by trial and error."

Imre let MZ work unimpeded, keeping an eye on the background charts for any changes. The sky was shifting with unnatural rapidity, making her nervous. The usual laws of celestial mechanics simply didn't apply.

"This would be the perfect place," said Emlee, "to hide a weapons-testing zone. Anything could go off down here—you could even use stars as target practice—and who would notice?"

"Instant disposal for your mistakes, too," Imre agreed. Apart from Gabriel, there were numerous other black holes orbiting galactic center. "You wouldn't assemble an army here, though, or use it as a headquarters. It's a bolt-hole at best. A bunker."

Emlee nodded. "No bursting out en masse and saving the day, then. That's a bit disappointing."

Imre could see that she too was unnerved by the spectacle. If this was the headquarters of the Barons, Domgard's replacement, what hope did it hold for humanity?

A flicker of white noise rolled through the *Wickthing*, making Imre momentarily uneasy on his feet.

"I have located the outgoing Line feed," MZ announced. "The signal is exceptionally strong, as it must be to reach the first relay."

"Which way should we go?" Imre asked Emlee. "To the relay or straight into the lion's lair?"

"Relay," she said. "We don't know what kind of defenses they might have."

"I agree. Do it, MZ."

Their point of view pulled away from Gabriel as the Fort followed the fringes of the Line feed to the first relay station, a tenth of a light-year away. During their journey,

MZ sampled random packets from the stream of data and tested against known codes and ciphers.

"I know those algorithms," said Emlee, as the data scrolled down a sheet of paper in front of her. "I don't know what it's saying, but I recognize it. It's black traffic."

"The clutter you've been picking up on the Line?" Imre asked.

"Yes, but here there's nothing else. That's all this transmission consists of. Nothing *but* black traffic in both directions."

The sky roiled as the relay hove into view. It was a miniature version of the Barons' headquarters, equipped with a complicated array of dishes and beamers. There was no sign of human habitation: no ships docked; no visible life support; no doors or windows. If any kind of intelligence was responsible for maintenance, then it was purely artificial.

"Get in close, MZ," Imre told the AI. "Do your thing."

Imre had only the sketchiest understanding of how the Fort's "thing" worked. That it had many times in the past was all he needed to know. With Emlee watching closely, the Fort glided through the relay's outer layers, invisible to matter, and began searching for an optical circuit through which it might gain access. The guts of the relay were tightly packed and utterly dark. Flashes of bright light came and went, indicating when they had located a candidate circuit. Five times, MZ tested and rejected the possibilities he found. The sixth he liked.

"I'm not familiar with the protocols," said Emlee, as MZ began probing the relay's semantic architecture. "Parts of it look like Fort code but heavily edited, with sections I've never—"

Emlee was cut off by a blast of static and a noise as terrible as a cracked bell tolling directly behind Imre's head. She reeled, jerking like a damaged film, and felt her consciousness dividing once more into discrete fragments. The *Wickthing* juddered; the illusion shattered; the sound grew louder, until it subsumed everything.

Then the map room returned, snapping back into place as though nothing had happened. Imre was standing at the table with Emlee beside her, staring at a schematic diagram of the relay's code. Kells was opposite them, glancing at the ceiling, momentarily caught like a statue by the glitch.

"—ssssseeeeeen before."

The end of Emlee's phrase completed the transition back to normality, and they were able to move again. Emlee recoiled from the table, taking stock of her and Imre's appearance with a series of quick, alarmed glances. "What the hell?"

"I don't know what just happened," Imre said, "but I suspect we're about to find out. MZ?"

There was no answer. Imre was about to ask again when she saw Chyro Kells staring at the doorway.

She turned. A woman with spiky brown hair and brown eyes was standing in the entrance to the map room. Her face was heavily lined, with hollow cheeks and a slightly protuberant jaw. She wore clothes more practical than stylish and carried herself with a surety born of long experience. There was a hardness in her stare that reminded Imre of Render. She would have guessed this woman for what she was even had she not recognized her instantly.

"You shouldn't have come here like this, Imre," said the Old-Timer Bianca Biancotti.

"Hello to you too," Imre said, covering her alarm as best she could. The illusion flickered around Biancotti's presence, as though reacting to it, trying to erase it. "How did you get in here?"

"We're not stupid. We thought you might repeat your trick on Spargamos, and we prepared defenses in advance. MZ triggered one of them. He's caught in a Hyeres paradox—not permanently, but long enough for me to get in through a chink in his armor. I'm widening those chinks as I speak. And you—" She turned her attention to Chyro Kells with a sudden widening of her eyes. "You had better stop what you're doing right now, or I'll erase your pattern for good."

The surgeon raised his hands. The flickering ceased.

"Thank you." She turned back to Imre. "I'm leaving in a moment, and I'm taking you with me."

"You invited me here, you even gave me directions, then you tell me I shouldn't have come here. Make up your mind, Bianca."

"You were invited—but not *like this*."

Bianca Biancotti's dark eyes took in Imre's new appearance, and she—

—he—

—she bristled.

"This isn't about me," she said, feeling the last struts of her former architecture fold away to nothing. "It's about *him*. Imre-F, or whatever he's called now."

Biancotti nodded. "You know what he's like."

"Don't be so sure about that. I'm not taking anything for granted, not after all he's done to me down the years."

"You probably won't be surprised to learn that he sees it quite differently. Becoming a Prime was bad enough; he took that as a personal affront. This he'll probably read as defiance—blatant, deliberate, and directed once again at him. It's bad enough that you won't stay dead. For every step he takes forward, you keep taking one backward."

Imre suppressed a corrosive laugh. What had she thought earlier about Imre Bergamasc and things that wouldn't die? "I have no idea what you mean, Bianca. He and I have nothing to do with each other anymore. I'm my own person. We're tackling the same problem in different ways—and that has to work to everyone's well-being."

Biancotti's expression didn't soften. It became only more skeptical. "Well, you try telling him that and see how it goes. Are you ready?"

"I'm going with him," Emlee said, stepping closer to Imre's side.

"No, Prime Minister, you're not—but do stick around. You'll be needed later."

Biancotti gestured, and the contents of the *Wickthing* froze again. Imre struggled, but she could do nothing more than think and feel as, bit by bit, her pattern was forcibly excised from the illusory world. It felt as though she were being unpicked by needles. The pain was excruciating, and made much worse by the spreading tide of nonsensation that accompanied it. Gradually, inevitably, Imre was ripped from the *Wickthing* and taken elsewhere.

That elsewhere was, for the moment, nowhere. She railed against the void, feeling nothing, sensing nothing, doing nothing but screaming with her thoughts. Frustration and anger fueled her determination to break free, but she was unable to vent that energy. She felt it building up inside her like heat in a faulty space station, until she felt like she was going to choke.

Then she was falling onto her hands and knees, gasping for breath and tasting metal on cold air. The surface beneath her was hard and unyielding, and curved under her fingers, rising up around her as though she were caught inside a giant bubble. She stayed down, concentrating on getting her wind back and taking the measure of the space around her out of the corners of her eyes. It was a sphere nearly fifteen meters across.

"We don't use hardcaster sarcophagi anymore," said Bianca Biancotti from a point behind and slightly above her. Her voice echoed off walls as unyielding as pure iron. "The Host may no longer invest in hardcasting technology, but we've kept working at it."

Imre was still wearing the armor sheath, and her body was unaltered. Relieved on both scores, she stood up, keeping her eyes open and wary of any odd gravitational anomalies. She reasoned that they were inside the object orbiting Goliath, using its degenerate shell for artificial gravity. The effect was disorienting and difficult to get used to; she had experienced it only once before, while subduing a gestalt for the Forts, and it had been messy in the end, with high-density shrapnel flying in all directions. No one resorted to such gross methods unless their capacity for exotic engineering was exceeded only by a paranoiac desire to discourage attack.

With a sinking feeling, Imre ticked both boxes.

Biancotti was standing an eighth turn around the sphere, her head pointing calmly into the structure's center of gravity. Imre had to look up in order to see her properly. She was exactly as she had been in the *Wickthing*, standing at ease with both hands tucked in the waist pockets of her work uniform—which looked, unless Imre was very much mistaken, like one of the old Line maintenance suits from after the Mad Times. The last time anyone had seen her was on a relay station near Hyperabad. Among the people who had visited her was Himself, as his surviving frags attempted to reconnect into a functioning Fort. She, a notorious trawler of the Line, was an obvious contact for anyone looking to find out what had happened to the Continuum.

So she remained, Imre thought.

"Tell me what he wants."

"What makes you think he wants anything from you?" Her smile was faintly mocking.

"The fact that I'm still alive."

"Well, let's start with that," she said, putting her weight onto her back foot and walking around the curving floor toward Imre. "From your point of view, it must seem that it would be easier to kill you than to bring you here. You forget, though: he's a Fort now. It takes time to attract his attention. That's what we're here waiting for, if you hadn't already guessed. And once you do have his eye on you, well—" Her hands came out of her pockets and cupped the air. "He might yet countermand my order, once he realizes what you've become."

"I think you're lying."

"Funny how the hubris never changes, no matter what package you come in." She shook her head. "It's not you he's after, not specifically."

Her stomach sank farther. "Emlee."

"She's part of it. He wants MZ and the Apparatus too. Ra and the Veil he already has, so that completes the set."

"I don't know what Ra has agreed to, exactly, but Emlee

won't give in. Neither will MZ, and the Apparatus is useless without the succession protocol."

"Don't be so sure about MZ, Imre. He's bored and looking for a challenge. But don't worry about that. There's no need for anyone to give in. Quite the opposite, in fact. That's how he got me on board. That's why I led you here. Your curiosity was the lure. I thought we might be able to convince you once we finally had you in front of us. That you brought everyone here with you is an unexpected bonus. Thank you, my friend, for that."

Biancotti tipped Imre a casual salute that made her feel sick. Standing still was killing her. She had to move, to burn off some of the energy pent up inside her. Turning her back on Biancotti, Imre began to pace around the waist of the sphere, determinedly ignoring the disorientation that caused her.

"He came to you," she said, "after the Slow Wave."

"That's right," Biancotti said. "He was looking for directions, first, and answers, later. I helped him as best I could, just as I helped Al Freer. How is Al, by the way? I lost track of him after the election."

Imre waved the question aside. "Keep going."

She didn't press the issue. "He sought me out once he'd got his shit together. He wanted me to Fort up for battle, but I told him to get a grip. I Graduated once already; I remember how hard it was, and these days I'm too tired to be anything but a Prime. But I agreed to help out. It's an important business, and it needs doing. Just like the Luminous, he needs someone on the ground, keeping up with you fast talkers."

"That's what the silver spheres are to the Luminous," he said. "They're an interface as well as a vanguard."

"Effectively, yes. I'm not a vanguard, obviously, but we're not trying to invade or commit genocide, either."

"Just sabotage, assassination, subterfuge—"

"Distraction," she said, "and necessary pruning. The less attention humanity drew to itself, the better—particularly in the early days, before he was sure of himself. Every

proto-Fort threatened to bring on a second wave, something
more deadly and thorough than we could have imagined.
The Luminous don't muck about, Imre. You had to be kept
in line, or you'd kill us all."

The two women stared at each other as Imre strode by.
"You know they're aliens, I presume."

"Of course."

"And that all this has something to do with dark matter."

"It has everything to do with dark matter, Imre. There's
still so much we don't know about it—and dark energy, too.
We're not fighting a turf war over the Milky Way. We're
fighting for the entire universe, for our future."

"Isn't that a bit melodramatic? After all, we've hardly
come close to exhausting one galaxy's reserves of ordinary
matter. What do we need the rest for?"

"You're thinking like a Prime. The long run is longer
than we can imagine. Bigger minds than ours have seen
what lies ahead, and what they've seen is the reason we
fight."

"On his say-so?"

Biancotti's smile had a crooked quality. She knew Imre
was trying to rile her. "I may only be a Prime, but I can
follow the principles. I still make my own decisions; I'm
not his slave."

"You are a Baron. You do as he tells you."

"There's no shame in that—and if you don't understand
that yet, then you don't fully understand the situation. You
do know why we call ourselves the Barons, don't you?"

Imre shook her head.

"It's a pun. Forts can't help themselves. *Baryons*, Imre.
That's what we're made of, and that's what we're named
after. But that's not what we're fighting for. There's much,
much more at stake now." She tilted her head, as though
listening to something. "Okay, he's here. Get ready. This is
the moment you've been waiting for all your life."

Imre stopped walking. Her heart was suddenly in her
throat—and for no good reason, she told herself. Imre

Bergamasc—Imre F, or Himself, or whatever he called himself now—was just another Fort. That they shared a common past meant nothing. She was just rattled by her experiences in C20, watching Monsieur Zee burst apart after announcing the arrival of Monsieur Li.

Unable to hide her nervousness, she looked around, seeking the route by which Imre-F would come to her. No hatches had appeared in the seamless surface surrounding them. She could hear no mechanisms whirring, no motors humming. The gravitational field surrounding them didn't shift one iota. She half expected her own voice to boom out of thin air, like God announcing His presence to the high priest of a false religion, and she steeled herself against feeling anything approaching awe.

Something tickled the back of her gloved left hand. She ignored it.

"Is he giving me the silent treatment?" she asked Biancotti.

She shrugged. "He moves in mysterious ways, like all Forts."

"Only when they don't want to communicate."

"There are ways to talk that don't involve words."

"I think I'm getting the message." The tickle became an itch that she rubbed absently at through two layers of fabric. "Well, you don't intimidate me," she told the echoing walls. "I'll wait you out. Do you hear?"

She turned in a full circle. Silence was her only reply.

"He hears you," Biancotti told her, "but I don't think you're intimidating him either. Waiting is his strong suit."

The itch was starting to burn. Imre could ignore it no longer. Tugging at the seals of her glove, she pulled it free and looked for the source of the irritation.

A black, star-shaped spot was growing between the veins on the back of her hand.

She stared at it in horror, knowing instantly what it was. Her horror grew as the spot sent out tendrils through her skin, finding and following the radial nerve up to her wrist to where the musculocutaneous nerve began its long journey up her arm. The ancient pathways of the nervous system, retained as a blueprint by her entirely artificial Prime body, gave the invading tissue a convenient route to the seat of her consciousness, and from there to the rest of her body.

Black traffic, she thought, feeling feverish as the invader made tracks for her brain. Dark matter, dark energy.

The Veil.

"This is unacceptable," she said, hoarsely. "Take it out. Take it out of me now."

"It's there for a reason," Biancotti said, looking both unsurprised and unconcerned. "Get used to the idea."

Imre shook her hand, but the black spot didn't budge. If anything, the increase in blood flow made it grow faster. "I reject it. I refuse to accept any memories that aren't mine."

"I'm afraid you won't have any choice about that."

Imre looked up at her. Biancotti's skin seemed clear, but there was no way to tell what the uniform hid. "Don't tell me you're infected too, Bianca."

"I've become used to the idea of forgetting." She came closer, watching him as though following the progress of a fascinating experiment. "Don't you want to know what it contains, Imre? Couldn't this be exactly what you were looking for when the Jinc made you wrong?"

"I'm used to forgetting too, now."

"Clearly there's something he wants you to remember."

Imre became more desperate by the second as thin lines of black spread rapidly up her arm. Her pulse was quickening, making her light-headed. If she'd had a pistol, she would've shot her hand clean off in order to get rid of the contagion.

With a snarl, she lunged at Biancotti. The Old-Timer was taken by surprise. Imre knew her history; before the Mad Times, Biancotti's background had been in administration, not combat. Her Fort-self had been deadly, but she was as slow now as she had ever been.

Imre caught her about the throat and flung her bodily to the surface of the sphere. Their combined weight made the metal surface ring like a bell. Biancotti kicked and struggled, but Imre had her pinned.

"You can't kill me," she gasped.

"Of course I can't," Imre snapped. No one had ever died in hand-to-hand combat that she could remember; even Prime bodies were built too tough for that. "I can make you uncomfortable, though." She brought up her violated hand and held it up in front of Biancotti's face. "Why shouldn't I give you a taste of your own medicine?"

Biancotti struggled. "Because you know that's just being vicious. You're on our ground. I have access to all the antibiotics I need. It'd be out of my system before it came close to taking a hold."

Biancotti was telling the truth, and Imre knew it. Imre had been naturally exposed to the Veil on Dussehra and fought the infection with no difficulty at all. The experience had been so mild and unremarkable that she hadn't even recognized it for what it was.

Impotence burned in her like acid. She couldn't tell if the giddiness came from dread or because her body's resources were being burned at an accelerated rate by the alien invading it.

When she tried to call Emlee for help, all she received was silence. Unauthorized communications from the habitat were jammed, of course.

She let go of Biancotti and let the strange gravity take her. The curved metal floor was hard and cool. She slumped onto her back, stared up at the opposite floor, and tried not to think about what was to come. Would a wave of foreign memories crash over her, burying her under their weight? Or would they insinuate her being without her conscious awareness, only making themselves felt when she inadvertently accessed them?

"Which Imre does this make me?" she asked aloud, refusing to watch the black stain's progress through her flesh any longer.

"What?" Biancotti was still lying next to her, rubbing her throat.

"If the Imre who did this to me is Imre-F, am I A, B, C, D, or E? Or something new? Imre-G, perhaps."

Biancotti chuckled. "You're looking at it the wrong way again. Think like a Fort. Until you do that, you'll always be one step behind him."

Like a Fort. Imre frowned. He had rebuked Al Freer for making the same mistake. Forts liked puns and word games, as Biancotti had already demonstrated in the last few minutes. There were only so many possibilities where names were concerned. What was there about "Imre-F" that Imre hadn't considered?

She rearranged the letters. She rotated them. She searched for meanings in ancient dictionaries and alphabets.

Then she read it backward.

IMREF

Despairingly, she too began to laugh. The echoes were mirthless and cutting in her metal cell, and there was no ceasing them once they had started. Her body was racked by them. Tears flowed freely from her eyes. Sensing Biancotti's gaze on her, she rolled over and pressed her face against the floor.

She stopped laughing, but the echoes grew louder and louder until they sounded like the cries of wild animals or a chorus of braying voices. She covered her head with her hands and tried to burrow away from the sound. Escape was impossible. The hideous racket was coming from inside her head.

"Make it stop," she moaned. "Make it stop!"

"Don't fight it," Biancotti said. "It's easier that way, I'm told."

A memory struck her, but at least it was one of her own.

I trained for the Assumption for fifty years before I was allowed to take the Veil. Women are usually forced to change their gender because the Y chromosome is an essential part of the match, but I insisted on being myself. I was only the second woman for ten thousand years to make the attempt and to survive.

Gravine Sevaste's words were as clear to her as they had been the day they were spoken, over seven hundred thousand years earlier.

"Assumption," she ground out through tightly clenched jaw. "Months of preparation and trials. Always been that way." Helwise had been the first to survive, and now Imre was following in her footsteps. "The wrong sex," she gasped. "The wrong sex."

"Maybe that's what he wants to tell you." Biancotti's voice was unsympathetic. "The Gravamen were barbarians. The Host has had a lot of time to refine the process, so now any gender can Assume the Veil. Superstition remains rife, however."

Imre kept hearing that. It made her angry, and for a blessed moment the ghastly clamor diminished. It angered her because cultural maladaptions could only be enhanced by the Veil. When knowledge was absorbed like vitamins, who was to say what was reinforced and what fell by the wayside? The everyday fashion of people's lives would propagate fast, leading to cultural homogenization, and to the peace that Emlee had so rightly craved but so wrongly achieved.

"Look at us," Render had said. "*We* are the unknown."

Imre was out of the loop. She didn't speak the language. The prodigal son had returned, and she had turned out to be an alien.

She understood, though, that the Veil was neither conscious in its own right nor stultifying consensus. It was much more complicated than that.

The clamor began to rise again—deferred, not defeated. Imre tightened her hands about her head and felt a shift in tempo roll over her. She was involuntarily overclocking; they clearly wanted her processed fast. To what end, she didn't know, but she supposed she should be grateful she hadn't been killed outright. If she could only hold on to her mind while another person's memories flooded through her, hope remained—hope of getting away and having the infection removed. She vowed that nothing entering her mind would change that thought, not after everything she had endured to find herself at last.

Intention was a fine thing. As the sensory hallucinations plaguing her worsened, she found herself beginning to slip. The auditory clamor had been joined by powerful smells and flashes of impossible colors. She was rapidly losing touch with the real world. The metal beneath her could have been stone, ice, wood, or even air. She could have been floating, weightless and bodiless, in an infinite space—one filled with every sensation possible to imagine.

Perhaps every sensation her Fort-self had ever experienced, all at once . . .

Cling to something, she told herself. Find an anchor and hang on to it for dear life.

FERMI

The letters danced before her, tumbling in and out of focus—

—and became a name on a virtual screen. She was thirteen years old and doing her homework. The Ancient History and Philosophy of Science had always bored her, but it was a required subject on New Esperance, the Prime colony to which her parents had moved in order to procreate. Their home town of Shizaru was especially conservative when it came to sticking to curriculum. She didn't understand why it mattered to anyone whether Albert Einstein had invented Special Relativity or Quantum Chromodynamics. Who cared if Karl Popper was born on the Earth or the Moon? That was old news of the worst possible sort. She was more interested in singletons and Forts. She wanted to be a reverse engineer like Andavan Carvanan and travel the galaxy, stealing from those considerably more advanced than common-as-muck Primes.

Of course, that was just an entertainment, both the show from which she stole the dream and the dream itself. She was smart enough to know what was likely and what wasn't. Secrets weren't stolen; they were doled out to goad the masses in the direction the Forts wanted them to go. Nosy reverse engineers mostly likely ended up spitted on incomprehensible weapons or absorbed into gestalts. Real life was always more boring and deadly than fiction.

Still, she was determined to do more than live, breed, and die, as her parents seemed content to do. She was a backward kid on a backward world, and only an extraordinary effort on her part would lift her out of it. That meant doing her homework, whether she saw the point of it or not. "Stab with the point and miss," as she had read in an old book on warfare once, "and the battle is over. The sword is sharpest closest to the hilt."

The first ship that came along looking for interns, she swore to be on it.

"Enrico Fermi," she dictated, "was a prespace physicist best remembered for building humanity's very first nuclear reactor. This legacy is a mixed one, since without nuclear power, it is unlikely that we would ever have lived in space and reached the stars, but neither would our ancestors have been burdened with the nuclear pollution that poisoned life on our home world until clean technologies were invented.

"Fermi was considered remarkable in his time for being both a theoretician and an experimentalist. (The short life spans in those days made it very difficult for people to follow up on the inspiration of their youth before they died.) Although many of his theories now seem outdated, one of his propositions troubles philosophers even today. The Fermi Paradox, as it is known, asked the question: why, if life is as probable as it seems to be here on Earth, isn't the galaxy full of it? 'Where is everybody?' Fermi wondered if civilizations destroyed themselves before contacting their neighbors. Later speculators devised complex theories to explain why Earth's siblings were somehow unable to make their presence known. These theories were all debunked by the exploration of the galaxy, which uniformly turned up no evidence of extraterrestrial life more complex than plants and slime molds, anywhere.

"These days, the Paradox remains, although the emphasis has shifted from interstellar to intergalactic civilizations. We fill the Milky Way from end to end. There must be other species out there doing the same in their home galaxies. Why haven't we heard from them yet? The question, perhaps, should not be 'Where is everybody?' but 'What happened to them?'"

Her mother interrupted her the old-fashioned way, by yelling from the kitchen to say that dinner was ready. Imre saved the essay and sent it, even though she knew her teacher wouldn't approve. Paranoid speculations were frowned upon in a history class; she'd heard that line before. She couldn't help it, though. It seemed obvious to her that absence of evidence sometimes *was* evidence, just not of absence. If you walked into a city and found it empty, you'd wonder what had happened to everyone. Wasn't it the same here? Wasn't it worth at least thinking about what would happen when humanity did stumble across someone?

"You're too young to worry about this," her mother chided her when she complained over the simple meal. "Besides, you'll hear plenty about it in the history of the Expansion, next semester. I remember being bored of hearing about planet-wreckers and death-seeders or whatever they were called. Just be patient. All your questions will be answered soon enough."

"Aren't there always questions?" Imre protested. "The Forts don't know everything. It's impossible to know everything."

"That's not what I'm saying, dear. I'm talking about all *your* questions. We only have a finite number in us. When they run out, we can get on with life as we're supposed to."

By growing old and dying, she wanted to say, full of scorn and bile for her parents' lack of ambition. She looked at them and wondered if they had ever questioned anything in their lives.

"I'm off to Kikazaru tomorrow," her father said through a mouthful of naturally grown beans. "Want to come with me? We could look for that new guitar you've been asking about."

She couldn't contain her excitement, even though she knew she was being bribed for compliance. The instrument she had been playing was an old virtual thing, full of glitches and odd harmonics. She dreamed of a genuine Gibson acoustic made from maple grown on Earth. That was a dream worth having, albeit another one likely to remain out of reach, for now.

After dinner, she went for a solitary walk through the plantation forest neighboring their home. The evening was cool and windy. Pinprick, New Esperance's bright blue primary, was almost completely occluded by its yellow companion, giving the dusk an autumnal feel. Soon the light would be completely yellow and shadows fall sharp-edged again. It made her feel, for the first time in her life, like she was getting old.

It didn't help that her brother still called her "kid" when he came home to visit. It certainly didn't help that Clay Michailogliou had turned down her advances, saying she was too young to experiment with anything too "odd." Just because they were mucking around sexually, Clay said, didn't mean they should form a gestalt. Perhaps they could change genders for a while instead, experiment at being two boys for a while, instead of two girls. Or find a third to spice things up a little—perhaps someone their parents didn't approve of, just to see what would happen.

It wouldn't be enough. Imre knew that. Clay was as stuck in Shizaru's conservative mire as Imre's parents. She renewed her pledge to get off New Esperance as soon as she could in order to see what else was out there. She would become a singleton and live for thousands of years in thousands of bodies. She would take lovers and do things that would turn her parents' hair green. She would even go to Earth one day and play guitar for the oldest minds in the galaxy. If she wanted to.

By the time she returned home, chilled and refreshed by her walk, the grade for her essay had arrived. It was acceptable but not outstanding. As expected, she had been penalized for speculating too much. At least it wasn't a fail, which meant that her Ancient History and Philosophy of Science unit was safely on track. Next week she had "The Naïve and the Macabre," a tract on what had passed for modernism in the twentieth century, followed by a primer in Old-Timer society. Both were on her wish list: to see a real Mondrian and to meet someone who might have been alive when it was painted.

Not only was anything possible for citizens of the galaxy, but it seemed to her, on the outside looking in, that anything was perfectly permissible as well.

Imre returned to herself, briefly, shocked and moved by the immediacy of the recollection. It was a window into a life she had completely forgotten, apart from names and facts. Her parents' faces had long since slipped away; the people in the photos she had owned in C20 had borne no relation to the ones she had just seen. Clay Michailogliou, her first "serious" lover, might as well have never existed. As for playing guitar . . .

She wept, thinking of the massive sculpture from which the four capital cities of New Esperance had taken their names. It was modeled after a similar monolith on Earth, except that this one commemorated monkeys instead of United States presidents. Their names were almost as old as humanity itself: Mizaru, Kikazaru, Iwazaru, and Shizaru.

See no evil.

Hear no evil

Speak no evil.

Do no evil.

The rebuke was as harsh as a slap across the face.

It could have been much worse, she told herself. She could have experienced something much more regrettable than this glimpse into a forgotten past. So she had been born female: didn't that reinforce her decision to turn back? She had also been interested in Enrico Fermi, once. That revealed nothing about the Fort whose name he had referenced. It was nostalgia, pure and simple.

People had once considered nostalgia a serious disease, one capable of causing death. Perhaps, she thought, for citizens of the galaxy, that was a possibility she had foolishly not considered.

"It doesn't add up."

Spargamos swooped a quarter turn around the core of the Milky Way before Factotem responded.

"This isn't mathematics, Imre."

"Don't be coy. You know what I mean."

Unusually for Forts, the rest of the conversation was conducted by individual frags using technology even Primes could have grasped. Some topics were so large they could only be discussed in the smallest circles. Imre's frag had called the meeting, but he was under no illusions that this gave him the upper hand.

"There are anomalies in the data," Factotem admitted.

"They're not your concern. Tell me about Domgard instead."

"You know everything about Domgard. It's running to schedule, producing data as expected, and experiencing no cost overruns. Did you ever think I wouldn't deliver?"

"Not once. Still, I watched you before you Graduated, and I know restlessness when I see it. You haven't changed as much as you like to think. Why exactly have you sent parts of yourself back into the wild?"

Imre's frag knew there was no point denying the charge. "To keep the Corps distracted."

"Some say it's because you're having second thoughts, that your commitment to the project is wavering."

"They think I'm going to go back on my word?"

"Your reputation precedes you, Imre, in more ways than one. You possess unique capabilities, yes, but you are also unreliable. You follow your own counsel. You are not a team player. You have a habit of changing your mind that some find—"

"Disconcerting? Well and good. You lot have been too comfortable for too long."

" 'Flighty,' I was going to say." Factotem hesitated, then said, "You are one of us now, Imre. Don't let youthful impulsiveness distract you from that fact. Focus on the long view, and remember why you signed on."

The frag had full access to the memories of Imre Bergamasc, prior to his Graduation. He remembered that hurried meeting on the *Pelorus*, when he had sold his soul to the fledgling project, later called Domgard. "It's getting crowded in here," Factotem had said then, and there had been no arguing with that. "It's a natural function of humanity: to expand and spread, to create and multiply networks." No arguing there, either. "We are thinking in the long term, Imre Bergamasc. The juncture we have reached today will seal the destiny of all humanity, not just the Forts. You are invited to join us in that great venture. Are you interested?"

"The view is different," Imre's frag said, "depending on where you're standing. Where you see only opportunities, I also see threats."

"It's in your nature to do so."

"It's in your nature to assume that you're among the top dogs. That's justified in the Continuum, where there are only Primes, singletons, and gestalts to push around, but what if there's something out there bigger than us?" He attached a packet of data to his words, to emphasize his point. "What if this *is* mathematics, and you're ignoring what comes after the equal sign?"

The packet contained information with which Factotem should have been very familiar: maps of the vast web of neutral hydrogen left over from the Big Bang that crisscrossed the visible universe from one side to the other; interlaced nets of ultradense cosmic strings filling the gaps in the web; behind both, filaments of dark matter millions of light-years in length that, although invisible, influenced the movement of galaxies and distorted light still echoing from the dawn of time.

Humanity had been studying this vast structure for barely a blink in the lifetime of the universe—not even a million years—but to Imre's eyes it seemed to be very much more than the random accumulation of matter. It was a vast resource, and neither nature nor intelligence was prone to leaving resources unutilized. Sometimes he played the data accumulated at preposterously huge rates, simulating a tempo beyond anything even the Forts could reliably enjoy. Through this dusty, occluded keyhole into the vast history of the universe, he thought he glimpsed something moving with purpose and intent.

"We are the top dogs," Factotem said, "and there are no wolves out there. Put that fear from your mind and get on with the job you have to do. For all our sakes, including your own. Remember that Domgard isn't a luxury; it isn't an idle experiment; and it isn't a favor we're asking of you until you think of something better to occupy your time. It is the single most important thing humanity has ever undertaken to ensure its survival."

"You're fools if you think there'll be only one more phase change."

"We're not fools, and we don't think that. We'll work out how to cross that particular barrier when we see it looming ahead of us."

Imre, even as part of a Fort, could barely imagine such timescales. It appalled him that Factotem could discuss them so glibly—as though the only challenges awaiting humanity were ones of keeping house.

"You should know," Imre told him before the Line transmission closed, "that sometimes I do feel doubt. I betrayed my allies and turned on my self for a reason; sometimes it's unclear whether the exchange was worth it."

"You're still you," said Factotem. "The fact that you

cling to your old name is proof of that. You doubt, question, and occasionally change your mind, and my job is not to stop you from doing any of that. It's to convince you we're still right."

"I have no desire to be your conscience."

"Rest easy on that score, my friend, and go back to your sums. When both sides of the equation balance, we'll talk again."

The frag let Factotem go, feeling less than reassured. Everything he had experienced would automatically be shared by his loop shunt with the rest of himself, once the signals had time to reach Domgard, but he felt an irrational urge to hurry to Spargamos and convey his conclusions in person. Factotem wasn't listening to him, which meant none of the Forts would listen. They were dangerously overconfident, which meant they would have taken no precautions. The stately dance of hydrogen, cosmic strings, and dark matter outside the galaxy was regarded as a curiosity at best, which meant that any attack coming from that direction would take humanity completely by surprise.

With Domgard's fifth stage due to come online within the century, that seemed a dangerous state of affairs.

The frag took control of the Vespula and instructed it to take him away from Spargamos rather than toward it. Imre Bergamasc might not be able to buck the will of the Forts in toto, not as they were on the verge at last of meaningfully exchanging information between ordinary matter and dark matter, but he could at least take precautions for himself.

She was done with feeling sorry herself by the time the second memory clouded and fell away. This one had taken place immediately before the Slow Wave, if she read the final moments correctly. Half a million years had passed since her early childhood and her former, male self's secret Graduation to a Fort. Although she had glimpsed the wider arc of his thoughts through the filter of a frag and had received no real insight into the way his mind worked, the information was important. He had seen the threat, and no one had listened. She could only speculate what might have happened had the Forts been less cocksure of themselves.

It would be appropriate, she told herself, to feel sorrow for the uncounted masses that had died in the crash of the Continuum, but their numbers were too great to grasp. Her Prime mind could only deal with them in the abstract, and in the abstract they meant as little to her as the thoughts of a Fort.

The meeting took place on a world called Saranac, located a safe distance from Sol in the Crux Arm and thirty thousand light-years from the new installation near Gabriel. As always, secrecy and security were the highest concerns. Black-uniformed frags, their faces carefully obscured by visors and face masks, manned doorways, patrolled the streets, monitored airways, and watched the skies. The safety of their guest was paramount—or had, at least, to seem so.

She came veiled, as always, and clad in the finery of a dozen worlds. The Regent of the Returned Continuum had expensive taste and wasn't afraid to show it. Accompanied by a retinue of cloned acolytes, alike in dress, expression, and obedience, she breezed into the Grand Antechamber of Henley Hall, where he, one frag standing apparently alone, awaited her. The echoes of her footsteps took half a minute to subside. She waited until the chamber was completely silent before cutting straight to the point.

"Who do you think you are," she said, "and what the fuck do you want?"

He took off his mask and indicated that she should do the same. He was dressed much more economically than she, in light armor covered by a ceremonial robe. "I know who you are, Helwise MacPhedron. I have always known, since Mother Turin first appeared on Hyperabad. Let's not play these games anymore."

For a second, she didn't move. His face might have turned her to stone, for all the animation she showed. Her gold-flecked gaze didn't leave his expression.

Then her right hand came up and tugged the veil away. Her too-beautiful features were exactly as he remembered them. They hid a bottomless well of cunning.

"All right," she said, "but my questions remain on the table. I know that's not your real face because you're not wearing it right. And you haven't lured me here to talk about trade with the Axenian worlds; they've been a spent force for ten thousand years. So what really gives? Here's your chance to tell me. I'll admit you've piqued my curiosity."

"As have you mine," he said, "by defying the First Prime's warning to steer clear of other versions of yourself." She opened her mouth to protest, but he waved her silent. "Yes, that you are not the real Regent is also known to me. She is still on Earth, where my spies have her undergoing a deep-cell rejuvenation treatment. You are taking her place, as you have done at least once before. You are in league with yourself, and I naturally wonder why."

A slow, reptilian smile crept across her face. "I asked first."

He turned from her and paced to the nearest window. Through one-way glass he could see airships gliding through the big world's stratified cloud layers. It pleased him to be out among people again, at least to pretend to have a conversation. Abaddon was an environment hostile to human habitation. He couldn't remember the last blue sky he had seen with his own eyes.

"It is true," he said without turning, "that I am not the same man who used to wear this face. Neither am I the man calling himself the First Prime. My name, however, is still Imre Bergamasc, and I speak with considerable authority."

"Invested by whom, exactly?"

"By experience. By the fact that I'm still alive. Does it matter?"

"As long as you deliver, I suppose it doesn't. I'm an ends-justify-the-means kind of girl."

"I remember."

"Do you remember the Casco Campaign, Imre?" She came up behind him, swaying like a cobra under her robes. "The Colvinites used orphanages as human shields. You—"

"Do not try to trap me," he said, turning. "I also advise against casting judgment upon me or attempting to seduce me. Until we reach an understanding, there is only one thing to discuss."

Her smile didn't falter. "The ends you are offering in exchange for my means."

"Correct."

"So let's do it: show me what you've got. Then, when you're finished, I'll tell you whether I believe you or not—because unless you can convince me that you're really who you say you are, we're never coming to any kind of arrangement."

"I believe that I can convince you."

He talked then, telling her frankly and in great detail everything that had been kept hidden from the human race since the Slow Wave. The nature and purpose of the aliens who had excised the threat contained by the Milky Way. His fears that just such a thing might happen, and his survival, alone out of all the known Forts. His retreat to the center of the galaxy, where natural interference hid his efforts to regroup and pursue means of gaining revenge. His ongoing campaign to ensure that humanity did not emerge as a threat that the Luminous would have to prune once again. Until he was ready to retaliate, he would not give the enemy reason to act.

Of course, such reasons arose thanks to natural curiosity and ambition. He couldn't easily dispose of every instance. The forgotten scrap of his past that had escaped erasure and become, somehow, the ruler of a galactic empire was his greatest concern. If the First Prime became too curious, he could attract exactly the wrong kind of attention.

"So take him out," Helwise said in a voice as sharp as glass. "You'd be doing us both a favor."

"The political upheaval—"

"Temporary, manageable, and worth it. I'd do it myself, except I'm the obvious suspect."

He watched her closely, as he had watched her throughout his account. Her smile had faded on the discovery that he was a Fort—had indeed been a Fort during much of their latter association, prior to the Slow Wave—and she assumed a deep-etched frown upon his admission that he was behind the saboteurs and spies that so plagued the Returned Continuum. That came as no surprise. The revelation that he had systematically lied to her and betrayed her was unlikely to curry her favor.

Yet here she was, trusting him with the truth about her political aspirations and freely admitting the lengths she was willing to go to in order to pursue them.

He didn't like to believe that she had lost all reason. Better to assume that she was testing him, as he was still testing her.

"I am not proposing to replace the First Prime with you," he said flatly.

"With you, then?"

"No. Render would immediately see through the deception."

"So take him out too."

"That is not an option."

Some of her suspicion evaporated at that. "All right," she said. "No assassinations or impersonations. What *do* you want?"

"You to resign as Regent and join me in the defense of the human race."

She physically reacted to the suggestion, pulling away from him as though he had shoved her. Her arms came up to cross in front of her chest, and her brows dropped. Years fell from her. She looked like the young recruit he had co-opted into the Corps, ages ago, because he would rather have vicious killers like her on his side than fighting against him.

She turned away and walked, as he had earlier, to stare out the window. He knew, though, that she wasn't looking at the view. She was seeing only her reflection in the glass.

Her laughter, when it came, was cruel. "You sad, lonely fuck." She turned, and her expression was almost triumphant. "Take your fantasies, whoever you are, and get the hell off my planet."

"I am not a fantasist—"

"Well, you're sure as shit not Imre Bergamasc." She rounded on him as though he had insulted her personally. "He would never ask me to do that."

"To resign, or to join him?"

Her laughter returned. "Oh, don't you dare try to guilt me into anything. You faker. You liar." She pointed at him with one sharp-tipped nail in time with each accusation. "Did he send you? Is this the First Prime's idea of a joke? Maybe he's testing my loyalty, seeing how far I'd go before turning on him. What would happen if I failed your test? He'd accept my resignation while you quietly buried me in your bolt-hole, I bet. Nice one, Imre." She spun away from him and shouted at the ceiling. "I never knew you were such a prick."

"There's a lot about me you don't know," he said, mentally signaling his other frags, "or are at least failing to accept. I could make you a Fort. We could work together as true allies, not the farce you currently endure. In time, nothing could stand in our way."

She turned back to him with disdain in her eyes. "I'm afraid the only person refusing to accept anything, here, is you."

He swallowed his disappointment. "I am nothing if not pragmatic, Helwise. If you tell me that an alliance is out of the question, I will believe you."

"Not just out of the question, buddy, but off the entire page."

"Very well. This conversation is concluded."

A stream of blurs swarmed into the room: black-clad, overclocking guards that had disposed of Helwise's retinue of guards silently and efficiently just moments before. Helwise's acolytes fared no better, even though they, like her, were armed to the teeth with weapons not immediately visible to the eye. He himself pulled an antique Surflen Systems sidearm from under his robe and pointed it at her.

She recognized it and started to say something.

He shot her three times before a single syllable emerged.

It was over in less than a second. The cleanup was well under way a second after that. Within minutes, there would be no evidence that a slaughter had taken place in the Grand Antechamber of Henley Hall, and there would certainly be no evidence that he had been there. The only people who had known that, however briefly, were now dead.

He had no doubt that the Regent would cover up the murder, as she had covered up such mishaps in the past. There had been assassination attempts before, and he would make sure they continued long into the future. He didn't want her, of all people, to feel comfortable.

He would also keep asking her until one day, finally, she said yes. The alliance between her and the First Prime couldn't last forever. He would make sure of that, too, if he had to. The very second the First Prime outlived his usefulness, he would be disposed of, and that would be that. There would be no more resurrections for that irritating scrap, Imre-Prime.

And if Helwise didn't come around . . . ?

There would be someone else, he told himself. There had to be. He couldn't do this on his own.

You sad, lonely fuck.

As Helwise's body was taken away, he wondered if he really had seen acceptance in her eyes, at the very end. He was certain that she had believed him when the gun had been on her. When it was entirely too late.

She had always underestimated how ruthless he could be.

The smell of smoke and blood hung in the air. He

breathed deeply of it, his natural atmosphere, and walked away.

Another piece in the puzzle, set a further half a million years after the previous. More plans that went awry. Her Fort-self sounded less human than he had in conversation with Factotem, struggling to maintain conversation at the level of even a singleton. Also, Helwise had said that he wasn't wearing his own face correctly. The Slow Wave and his survival had clearly damaged him, left him scarred and more desperate than ever.

His schemes, however, were all Imre Bergamasc. She could see the beginnings of the plan that had killed her on Spargamos; she could see how he might ally himself with Ra MacPhedron, the closest thing to Helwise he could find after Executive Order KISMET had removed that possibility from the board. His certainty that the uneasy alliance at the heart of the Returned Continuum was doomed dismayed her. How had she genuinely thought it would last?

How had her Fort-self genuinely believed that Helwise would ally herself with him?

Some flaws, she supposed, were perennial, and the memories they spawned were relentless.

An image of the Milky Way filled the installation's core, but it wasn't one with which many people would be familiar. It showed no stars or nebulae, no plasma lanes or clusters. The arms of the galaxy were indistinctly outlined, and there were patches of particular brightness that didn't match any material densities. The map might almost have been one of humanity's spread through the galaxy, except it wasn't.

"That's the Apparatus, isn't it?" his prisoner asked.

"Yes."

To speak was difficult, now. He had been isolated for so long that he had forgotten how to use words. A long

time ago he had occasionally practiced conversation between his frags, but the sad futility of that exercise had
quickly worn him down.

"Remarkable," she said. "I mean, I know it's everywhere.
You can guess where it is by how the Host reacts to things,
and there aren't many places Emlee and Ra haven't got to,
by now. To see it, though . . ." She walked around the spher-
ical chamber rather than rotating the image herself, the sort
of archaism displayed by Old-Timers that he had once found
equal parts charming and frustrating. "It looks like a cell or
an amoeba, ready to divide."

The analogy satisfied him. "Why are you here, Bianca?"

"I could ask you the same question," she shot back. "It
wasn't easy tracking you down, you know."

"That is because I do not want to be found." He had
caught her sniffing around the Gabriel installation in a ship
not much younger than she was, making no attempt to hide.
He had taken her on board without resistance and placed
her inside the secure heart of the installation, from which
there could be no escape. That she appeared to be unin-
fected by the Dussehran parasite called the Veil reassured
him, irrationally.

"Sure, except I'm not sure you're really here, even now.
Gabriel is just a Line relay like all the others. This isn't
your home; it's not where the thoughts of your frags com-
bine. This is just where you conduct your weapons testing.
Which begs the question: are you anywhere at all?"

"I must be somewhere," he said, "in order to be."

"Yes. Yes." She folded her arms and walked a meander-
ing line around the sphere, her gaze directed at her feet,
deep in thought. Bianca Biancotti had never been one to
shy away from the truth. "I got it completely wrong. I
wasn't following the trail of your frags, was I? I was following your thoughts inward, but they lead outward too.
There's no one spot you belong. That means you're everywhere. You're in the Line itself. You are the black traffic."

He didn't deny the accusation, but neither did he want to
dwell upon it.

"This is not the only conclusion you have reached," he said. "Tell me them all."

"Why?" she asked. "Are you going to find out how much I know before you squash me like a bug?"

"That is an option," he admitted.

"Well, I want you to know," she began, then caught herself with a laugh. "Actually, no, I don't care. There are no records secreted away in a vault somewhere, destined to see the light if I never come back. There are no partners in this mad venture, waiting for my word before going to the Prime Minister with what I've discovered. I fully expect not to return—so if you kill me, it won't come as a great disappointment. Just promise me you'll tell me whether I'm right or wrong before you do anything drastic. I'd hate to die not knowing how clever I've been."

She seemed completely unafraid. For that, he allowed her what she wanted.

"All right." She stopped walking and sat cross-legged on the metal floor. Holding up five fingers, she tipped one over and started: "Humanity is a Type III civilization under attack from a Type IV or higher."

"Correct."

She tipped over a second finger. "We are an accidental creation of that superior race—probably replicators that got tangled up in a dust cloud somewhere and hopped from galaxy to galaxy, seeding life in their wake."

"Correct."

"The irony." She rolled her eyes and curled up a third finger. "The Domgard experiment had something to do with dark matter, and whatever you did back then triggered the first shots in the war, the Slow Wave. The attack completely set back your experimentation, but it wasn't the end of it. You tested a range of anti-Luminous weaponry a while back, for instance, and some it was successful."

"Correct."

She nodded. "Good. Now, this one's a little more speculative. What we call the Luminous—the silver spheres—are autonomous scouts sent into the galaxy to keep us in check. The real bosses are in the gulfs between the galaxies, thinking at tempos that make Forts look positively impetuous. A million years have passed since the Slow Wave, but that's nothing to those beings. Humanity's only hope is that it can catch up with the Luminous by virtue of being quicker to react, to bounce back."

"Correct."

Four guesses. Four correct answers. Only her thumb remained. "You've changed your plan of attack at least twice down the years, but this seems to be what you've settled on: to abandon frags except where absolutely necessary and continue catching up with the Luminous very much on the QT. When you have everything you need, you'll spring into action and save the day."

Her tone was faintly mocking, but of herself, he suspected, not him. She knew as well as he did that this plan was hopelessly naïve.

"Incorrect," he said, "for the most part."

"Well, thank goodness for that. I'd hate to be right all the time." Her hand came down, and she leaned her weight easily upon it. She actually smiled. "Now I want to change the terms of our agreement. Tell me what I'm getting wrong and I'll leave you in peace. Will you do that much for me, Imre?"

Her question unexpectedly threw him off guard. "In peace," she said. He had dedicated his life to the one course open to humanity, willingly but not without cost. What peace awaited him now, except that of an empty tomb?

"This is more, Bianca, than a puzzle to be solved and discarded."

"That's all I have left to me now."

"You have your life."

She shrugged. "I'm two million years old now, don't forget, and counting."

"You think I will spare you."

"I'm not thinking anything right now," she said. "I'm waiting for you to tell me what I guessed wrong."

He reached a surprisingly snap decision, for a Fort. "I will tell you," he said, "but only if you advise me afterward."

That surprised her. "Me advise you? That'd be like a mouse helping a lion."

He detected the literary allusion and surmised that she was agreeing with his terms, in a roundabout way.

"That is our agreement," he said.

"So be it." She made herself more comfortable. "Give it to me."

"You must understand," he said, "that we are not the only species to change during its evolution. We advanced from plains-dwelling mammals in Africa to minds as large as the galaxy in much less time than it takes for Sol to orbit the Core. The Luminous have changed too, and no less dramatically. For them, the universe is not a static place. It is lively and full of alteration. They have seen it transformed at least once before—when the Light Ages gave way to molecules and dust. Before then, they were fast-lived creatures of pure light. Now they are vast, slow minds adrift on intergalactic gas, similar to that which dominated the universe before the first stars and galaxies evolved. Had they not changed themselves to live in the new environment, they would have died out. They evolved, as we have evolved, and they are willing to keep evolving in order to survive."

He paused to make certain she was following him. The argument wasn't complex, but on it rested everything: Domgard, the Slow Wave, and what must come for humanity to have a future.

"That's one sign of intelligence, isn't it?" she said when she realized a response was expected. "The unshackling of evolution from chance, so we choose our own mutations?"

"Or not, as the case may be. The human race has been extraordinarily static since the Forts," he said. "Some blame Old-Timers such as you for preserving too much cultural memory. Fast as we have been, compared to the Luminous, we could have moved more quickly."

She snorted. "You've been talking to too many core civilizations, if that's what you think."

"It is not what I think," he said, "but I do believe we must proceed more efficiently toward our goal. Some of us, anyway."

"I presume your goal is something nobler than finding a new way to knock Luminous heads together."

"No less than staking our right to exist on the far side of the universe's next great phase change," he said.

She nodded slowly. "Which is?"

"Inevitable. Those who fail to evolve will die."

"I'm getting that message clearly already. The last phase change was when the light of the Big Bang dimmed enough so that matter as we know it could form, and the Luminous in their original forms couldn't survive. What's the next phase change going to be, Imre? What's it like on the other side? How far away are you talking? These are the questions I want answers to."

He said nothing. She had all the information she needed. He was confident she would work it out eventually, and he had the patience to wait her out.

"Dark matter," she finally said. "The next phase change is to a universe dominated by dark matter and dark energy—when the stars have gone out and the galaxies are dead. My God—can you really be looking that far ahead?"

"It is all a matter of perspective," he said, knowing that of all things to be true. "The Luminous were masters of the universe until they created us by accident. Now they have a rival, and their plodding pace may not be quick enough. It is a race between us fast, fleeting things and the glacial gods who spawned us. Before the days of subtler stuff than matter are at hand, they would snuff us out—and that is why the legacy of Domgard must continue.

"In the world of matter, outside the galaxies, the Luminous are clearly dominant. Here among the stars, though, we have a chance. If we beat them to the dark-energy phase change, then we will beat them to the future and threaten their dominance. So that is what we, without question, must do."

"Or?"

"Or we languish here and die. As a civilization and as a species. Forever."

"Wait," she said, raising her right hand in the universal "halt" gesture. "Didn't you imply that I was wrong on this point? That you're not about to spring forth and save the day?"

"I did. The Luminous have suspected that I survived the Slow Wave ever since the former First Prime was resurrected by the Jinc. For me to show my face risks immediate reprisals, perhaps bringing down yet more punishment upon the human race as a whole. When I had no other options, I was willing to take that risk. Now, I am not."

"Because you have other options that don't involve springing anywhere and saving anyone."

"I have chosen my fate. Now I can only wait for it to arrive."

"Your fate? I still don't get it. What's the point of sitting here building weapons if you plan never to use them?" Then a light seemed to go on behind her eyes. "Unless you're building them for someone else to use. That's it. You're waiting for the right person to finish the job you started." Her eyebrows went up. "It's not me, is it?"

"No, Bianca."

"Good. Your other self, then? Is that why he's disappeared?"

"No."

"It can't be Emlee, because she's just a Prime, and I'm not sure how you feel about Ra. He doesn't seem like a very safe bet to me. Al Freer would be a certain disaster." Her head tilted in puzzlement to look at the map of the galaxy again. "You can't be thinking of the Apparatus, surely."

"Not exclusively."

"Ah. A combination of it and someone else, then." She drummed her fingers on the metal, making it ring. "Are you going to let me keep guessing, or are you planning to give me the answer anytime soon?"

"'Soon' is a relative term," he told her. "I am accustomed to waiting, and I will do so until you have reached the same conclusions I have."

"Cocky bastard."

She hummed to herself for a minute. He couldn't tell if she was annoyed or continuing to think the problem through.

"You know," she said, "there's rumored to be another Fort out there, someone the First Prime recruited before he disappeared. What's stopping me going after him and asking him the same question?"

"Me," he said. "I would stop you."

"By keeping me prisoner or killing me?"

"I would prefer the former."

"Why?"

"Because I still desire your counsel."

"You really think I have something to offer?"

"Yes." On that point he was completely sure, but he wasn't about to tell her why. Admitting that Helwise MacPhedron was right—and that he missed her—still galled him.

Bianca Biancotti smiled. "Well, I guess it's better than the alternative."

Imre opened her eyes. The influx of memories wasn't over; she could feel more trembling on the far side of a mental membrane, as heavy as an avalanche. But she needed a moment, and the moment, it seemed, needed her.

"Here's what we want from you," Biancotti said, looming over her like a cenotaph.

"Wait." She wasn't ready to hear that yet. She needed a moment to think, a small reprieve in which to work out what, exactly, was desired of her, before she had to be asked.

The last revelation had taken her a long way toward

knowing everything, but it left her dangling just short of full comprehension. She could see how his Fort-self was wary of engaging the Luminous directly. He was regarded, correctly, as a threat and would draw immediate reprisals. She could see how he therefore needed allies like Bianca Biancotti to move among the inhabitants of the galaxy, negotiating with people like Ra MacPhedron and finding his lost "scrap."

To what ultimate end, though? Simply out of hopeless loneliness in the face of an overwhelming force?

That didn't sound like Imre Bergamasc, in any iteration. It was neither decisive nor tidy. There had to be more to it. Imre-F and Biancotti couldn't have lured her all this way for nothing.

A very simple fact occurred to her then, opening the door on a world of speculation.

The Luminous didn't see Primes and singletons as threats unless they built more Forts or directly engaged with the Luminous. That was their blind spot—and it could be exploited.

Imre-F had admitted that the Apparatus was part of his long-term strategy. Capturing the memories of the human race was part of it too. So, presumably, were the weapons he had been developing.

Imre-F had given her the image of the galaxy as a vibrant, living cell, on the verge of replicating. Perhaps that had been the most important message of that memory, not the conversation with Bianca Biancotti. That image of the Milky Way as a unity, filled with a vast potential, waiting to be tapped. What if his plan was less a plan than a confluence of necessary parts, a grand conjunction that would, as a whole, become what was required?

The Apparatus, she thought, was analogous to a mind, but as everyone knew, it had no true independence. It had a rival now, in the form of Ra's Godmother, but this development changed little, essentially.

The Veil was nothing but memory—fragmentary memories that united individuals into the illusion of a whole, *much as she had been after her resurrection by the Jinc, plus the summary of individual experiences accumulated in Ra MacPhedron's memory farms.*

The Line, in certain lights, looked like a nervous system.

Imre-F was building weapons capable of destroying cosmic strings.

Everything was coming together nicely, if the plan was to make the galaxy one single vast, intelligent, well-armed, and pissed-off individual.

"You've skipped well past Forts," Imre said. It sounded absurd spoken aloud, but she knew it was true. "You're building a gun that will aim itself at the Luminous, and pull its own trigger. You're weaponizing the entire human race."

"We are, yes," said Biancotti. "Unashamedly, that's what we're doing. And you're going to help us."

"How?"

"By surrendering, but not to either of us. To the situation. You do understand that, don't you? We need you, and you need us. It's not a marriage of convenience. It's reality."

"You need the succession codes for the Apparatus," she said. "You don't need me."

"We need you to convince the Prime Minister to surrender too. If you don't—remember that reality I talked about? We'll here's a taste of it. In response to the weapons test at Soulis, Luminous scouts are converging on Earth and the Round, even as we speak. They know we can hurt them, so their gloves are finally off. The longer you delay, the more damage they will do."

Imre bristled at that. "You won't send help unless I submit to you?"

"Oh, we're sending the weapons. They were on their way before you reached Soulis. But humanity won't fight as effectively unless it's united. That is the dilemma for you. We're facing an enemy that spans much more than the galaxy. We need to be that big too in order to fight back."

Imre didn't answer immediately. She looked down at her hand, at the black threads that spiraled like seaweed around her fingers and wrist. There was no way to tell if more than memories had gotten into her as well. Imre-F could have twisted her mind in a thousand subtle ways if he had wanted to. He could be rewiring her brain even as she thought, making sure she did as he wanted.

How could she possibly make a decision under such circumstances?

She was standing on the metal floor of the secure room, and she was everything Bianca had warned him she might be, and might not be. She wasn't *him*; she never would be.

He wasn't himself anymore, either, so he didn't feel he had the right to complain.

"Is he giving me the silent treatment?" Imre Bergamasc asked Bianca Biancotti.

"He moves in mysterious ways, like all Forts."

"Only when they don't want to communicate."

"There are ways to talk that don't involve words."

"I think I'm getting the message. Well, you don't intimidate me," she shouted. "I'll wait you out. Do you hear?"

Looking at the woman called Imre Bergamasc, the Fort called Imre-F felt homesick for the first time. He had survived by moving forward, by adopting everything he needed to survive from the environment that threatened him: the Forts; the Veil; even the technological prowess of the Luminous. His discarded self, on the other hand, had proceeded only backward, to places he could no longer go. She was much closer to the person he had once been than he would ever be again. Not in his wildest dreams could he ever return.

"He hears you," Biancotti told Imre Bergamasc, "but I don't think you're intimidating him either. Waiting is his strong suit."

Biancotti and Bergamasc fought and traded accusations. Defiance became not resignation, although it could be mistaken for that, but a state he understood well: opportunistic calm, a willingness to see what happened next and how it might be put to one's advantage. That was exactly how he had spent the last seven hundred thousand years; he could recognize it on the face that used to be his.

A black stain spread like recrimination across reborn skin.

"If the Imre who did this to me is Imre-F, am I A, B, C, D, E, or F? Or something new? Imre-G, perhaps."

"You're looking at it the wrong way again," said Biancotti. "Think like a Fort. Until you do that, you'll always be one step behind him."

That was the hardest lesson to learn. Knowledge only went forward: Enrico Fermi had once said that, or words to that effect. There was no use trying to stop knowledge, and it was always better than ignorance. Yet Fermi was best known for the paradox named after him, and he had also said that the search for knowledge only resulted in confusion at a higher level—so what did he really know about anything?

Imre Bergamasc was succumbing to the Veil. Her Assumption was far from complete, but the end of the beginning was near. It was time to finalize the communication he would deliver, in order to bring her around. Days she had forgotten; days she had speculated about; days she had never known. She had to see reason. She had to understand.

"Don't fight it," Biancotti said. "It's easier that way, I'm told."

A name was just a name—and the opposite of a paradox wasn't necessarily a certainty, readily comprehended and acted upon.

Let it go, he wanted to say. Let it go and let me *fight*.

That was all.

She surprised herself by thinking about it. After so long railing against the manipulation of her Fort-self, she actually considered doing as he said. Imre-F saw the bigger picture. He seemed so sure of himself. If submitting to him would save the human race, wasn't it worth considering?

"I can't do it," she said.

"You can," Biancotti said. "He has."

"But I'm not him, and I don't want to be him. He hasn't fought as long as I have to be who I am—and he can't ask me to give up that fight now, just when I've worked out what that means."

"What does it mean, Imre? Maybe if you can answer that question, we'll let you go."

"You don't really mean it."

Biancotti almost smiled. "I do know that 'who we are' is a moveable feast."

"Said the Prime to the Prime."

"We're not the ones humanity is relying on to get the job done."

Second and third thoughts didn't change her mind—and that made her more certain than ever that she was making the right decision. Her will had not been poisoned by invading memes, and blackmail meant nothing to her. After so long fighting to be herself, she would rather die than forget who she was again.

"There's no point winning, Bianca, if we lose ourselves in the process."

Biancotti's expression became stony. "All right. You've made your decision, and now you have to live it. Don't blame me if you come to regret it."

"What's the worst you can do?"

"You wouldn't believe it."

"Emlee—"

"Forget her. Humanity has a fight on its hands." Biancotti held out her hand. "Come on."

She didn't move. It was inconceivable that she could ever forget Emlee Copas. Or were Biancotti's words intended more sinisterly? "What are you going to do to me?"

"Make you see what happens, of course. Killing you would be the easy way out, for all of us. He wants you with

him when it ends, whether you choose to be there or not. He wants you to know you how wrong you are."

Imre stared up at Biancotti in despair. An age of loneliness stretched ahead of her. Victory and defeat were irrelevant. She was losing everything that mattered to her in exchange for her silence—which was all he had ever really wanted . . .

Doubt touched her with a cold hand, then.

"It's neater this way, he says." Biancotti's arm remained outstretched. "And crueler too, I think."

With as much dignity as she could muster, Imre reached out and took the Old-Timer's hand.

PALINGENESIA

In time, all history becomes legend, all biography doctrine, and all words syllables in a rite devoid of meaning.

Imre-Prime watches delicate forces converge from the perspective of her Fort-self, and wonders at the sense of omniscience it brings. A bare instant after the creation of the universe, the fundamental forces of the universe devolved from a single unified force and sowed the seeds of the Luminous. Fourteen billion years later, here is Imre-F, metaphorically rolling back that process. It is like watching stars in collision. A nova is inevitable.

With a godlike view comes godlike guilt. The first victims of that expanding shock wave are the inhabitants of the *Wickthing*. One of the many weapons developed around Gabriel reaches out and erases the strange wrinkle in spacetime before word can spread of what happened at the center of the galaxy. Imre-Prime feels an ache of loss that no amount of war will assuage. She is angry now, but it is too late to change her mind.

Bianca Biancotti's promise to the Prime Minister—that she would be needed later—is not unbroken. The other Emlee Copas has returned to Earth with Ra MacPhedron, where many internal matters are due to come to a head—catalyzed in part by the Prime Minister's wild search for a lost madman and the President's apparent pact with a subversive force. These matters are destined not to be easily resolved, for the Luminous choose that moment to break the uneasy truce that has existed in the Milky Way since the spat over Spargamos. Everywhere, without warning, waves of silver spheres attack in retaliation for the Soulis incident.

The concentrated assault sorely tests human civilization. Uncounted numbers die—trillions, possibly, but no one will ever know for certain. Entire systems are laid waste. Earth itself is besieged. When resistance forms, however, it does so in force and with great determination. Al Freer respawns a multitude of himself and propagates through the Host, doing what he does best: fighting without conscience until one contagion is excised, then moving on to the next. Ra MacPhedron mobilizes legions of recruits, buoyed by the memories of his mother and the vehemence that lies buried just beneath humanity's civilized veneer. Emlee Copas authorizes the Apparatus to merge with the Godmother, giving humanity a weapon subtler than anything in the silver spheres' arsenal. Slowly the sources of these deadly vanguards are tracked down and destroyed. The tallies on both sides approach equity.

Emlee Copas knows, however, that humanity has only seen the beginning of the Luminous's capabilities. A civilization that spans the universe has muscle unimaginable. She waits anxiously for the next phase.

It comes, as it must, and Imre Bergamasc provides.

Wave guns and gravity weapons were only the beginning. Developed in secrecy over a million years by the only mind large and determined enough to take on an enemy this daunting, technologies unimagined propagate through the Line from the galaxy's core. Intelligence flows freely, giving humanity the knowledge and strength required to fight back.

Just one piece of intelligence is withheld: the identity of

humanity's greatest benefactor. This crisis is beyond egos, beyond individual credit—and besides, the anger of the Veil must be directed always outward, not inward. If humanity is to survive, it must unite. There isn't time or energy to waste on anything else. Primes in their quadrillions may wonder, but only two know for certain, and they remain carefully silent. For fear of tearing the galaxy apart, Imre Bergamasc's name mustn't be mentioned in connection with the weapons he is building. Imre Bergamasc must be forgotten in order that he might work most effectively toward the long-term liberation of humanity.

This, the harsh truth that Imre-Prime could not accept, she still feels is too stringent. Perhaps with enough time the murder of Helwise could be cast off her back and both she and her Fort-self freed. Through dark millennia, when the future seems particularly melancholic, she asks herself if she can possibly endure all of eternity unknown and unacknowledged. She abdicated once, yes, and more or less willingly allowed herself to dissolve into C20's mind-shattering trap—but that isn't the same thing as vanishing entirely. Not when there is so much work left to be done.

She thinks of her bizarre dreams in C20 and the giant specter of Emlee Copas, which asked her once: *Would you like to pay for all humanity?*

She wonders if Bianca Biancotti seeded that thought in her mind too.

(Somewhere, faintly, an alarm sounds.)

The Milky Way turns about its axis. Wars of this nature are not fought quickly. Attack breeds retaliation, which in turn breeds a kind of stalemate, but one in which each side frantically assesses its opponent and rearms appropriately. It is the intake of breath before an escalation. Everyone knows what is coming, what is inevitable unless an alternate path can be found.

Experimentation into dark matter continues on both sides. Both have made inroads; neither has mastered the transition entirely to that strange new state, and neither is ready to forsake "traditional" matter, either, until the phase change is truly upon the universe. The war must be fought using conventional physics, even as the way is prepared to secede from it. The Luminous have done that before, but humanity has not. Factions arise within the Milky Way calling for the abandonment of Imre Bergamasc's ultimate vision. Couldn't the two species learn to live alongside each other, one within the Milky Way, the other without?

Neither version of Imre Bergamasc has ever shied from changing the minds of others. Imre-Prime knows that certainty is temporary, that nothing is permanent. She also knows that factions within the Luminous have attempted to contact her in the past, and that in such factions lies the hope, however small, of a diplomatic solution. By increments and degrees, Imre-F makes overtures to those factions. Relations are formed and understandings reached. Plans are made.

Conspiracies form. Betrayals are enacted that cost both sides dearly. Nearly one million years after Soulis, the Gabriel installation—by then a vast research complex responsible for much of the munitions innovation in the galaxy—falls in a single act of sabotage. Fortunately, humanity has other such centers ready to take the load. Increasingly, the burden is spread across all the arms of the galaxy, and the idea of losing the center, while difficult for morale at times, is one that can be accepted. The human superorganism begins, truly, to take shape, and it is a wondrous thing to behold.

Imre-F upgrades the Line on a regular basis, enabling a clear oversight across the galaxy. To Al Freer, for a time, falls the responsibility of internal security: he becomes analogous to humanity's immune system, seeking out and purging all signs of cancerous insurrection. He descends without hesitation upon every threat, willing to erase whole subcivilizations in order to ensure the integrity of humanity's vision. Imre-Prime watches him, unnamed and in silence, making sure that such actions are justified—for self-analysis and dissent are critical. Humanity must not become rigid lest it shatter under further attack. It must continue to evolve, or it will never reach the next phase change, let alone survive it.

Ra MacPhedron falls in a single-handed defense of his home world. Not one of his singletons survives. The galaxy mourns, and retaliates once more, pushing the Luminous out of the starry lanes forever. Emlee Copas and Render pursue a mission to survey what is happening outside the galaxy, for information from that arena is worryingly sparse. The Luminous were destroying extragalactic missions long before war was declared, and that ban on expansion has been even more vigorously enforced since. Their mission is time-consuming and dangerous, but the data they bring back is crucial.

Instruments of the Luminous have gathered around the outer arms of the galaxy like wolves encircling a campfire, waiting for the embers to die down. Cosmic strings and other arcane artifacts radiate from that besieged island universe for hundreds of thousands of light-years, conveying information and thought outward in return for energy and matter required for the vast blockade. The slow, momentous thoughts of the Luminous give them the edge on such battlefields. The siege will be long and the castle, Imre-F decides, must fall. Humanity endures the wait with patience and industry, knowing that release will come.

All it has to do is last three billion years.

(The alarm is growing more urgent.)

Tempos steadily slow, until one complete circuit around the galaxy seems like an old terrestrial year. Stars die and are born. Uncounted Primes blur through their lives like neutrinos passing through ruined Earth, and their combined cultural memory remains the lifeblood of the Veil. Humanity is increasingly an informational artifact rather than a biological one, given life and vitality by the goal that unites it. A growing proportion of that information is historical. Change is inevitable and necessary, but the foundations beneath are secure. Some Old-Timers remain among quadrillions of descendants. English is still spoken alongside millions of variants. Life flourishes in wartime, as it always has, galvanized by the threat and promise of release.

Imre-Prime watches restlessly as the Milky Way spins toward collision with its larger sibling, the Andromeda galaxy.

Once, this might have seemed an intractable problem; now it is an opportunity. As the two mighty islands collide, vast masses of gas compress and reach incredible temperatures, triggering blinding waves of stellar formation. Solar systems are disrupted in their millions, flinging planets in all directions and tearing clusters apart. There are few actual collisions, but those few are spectacular. The massive black holes at the center of each galaxy begin a long dance that will inevitably end in matrimony.

The disruption around the Milky Way at last brings the Luminous's siege to an end. Nothing adapted to life in the depths of intergalactic space can endure such turmoil with absolute efficacy. The human superorganism surges through holes in the enemy's ranks and escapes the tangled concentration of stars that gave it birth. From the wreckage of the two galaxies, Emlee Copas and her allies lead the charge into the void, seeking not to circle around and attack the Luminous's flanks but to find new places to defend their brand of life, new oases that will hide them for a time from the universe's first inhabitants. The human seed propagates in all directions, seeking maturation elsewhere—and, ultimately, saturation everywhere.

The vast majority of those seeds are intercepted and destroyed. Perhaps 95 percent fail to escape the combined Andromeda-Milky Way gravity well. Those who stay behind—unwilling to make such a dramatic change, such as the Old-Timers Render and Bianca Biancotti—are lost forever. The remainder power on, aiming for the Magellanic Clouds and other dwarf galaxies still trailing the Milky Way. Some have more distant targets in mind, the larger galaxies in the Local Group among them, while others yearn farther still. All carry with them, like shards of a hologram, a complete record of the human race: its history and its knowledge; its culture and its conversations; its essence, recorded organically and pervasively in the descendants of the original Veil.

The Apparatus-Godmother, too, sends out tendrils unseen, defying the attempts of the Luminous to disrupt the spatiotextural entity from expanding beyond its galactic confines. The alien aggressors know that when space-time itself is corrupted, humanity's toehold on eternity will be all but assured.

(And still, ever-ringing, the alarm insistently calls.)

Humanity's reach expands as rapidly as Imre-Prime's tempo slows. She has lost touch with Emlee Copas and Al Freer, who commandeered their own seeds to far-flung destinations. The Milky Way swirls like a drop of cream in black coffee behind her, becoming fuzzy and indistinct. Sol is long dead, Earth now only a memory. The occupation of the galaxy and the abandonment of all she loved took an eye blink compared to the ages that pass before even a fraction of the expanding universe is colonized. All that remains of her are memories. They are encoded in cold vacuum and sewn into living cells. Some of them are literally written in stone, although stone erodes much faster than it takes her to complete single thought. She is the idea of Imre Bergamasc, the essence of who she used to be— and she has just one question left to be answered.

When will she be allowed to let go? When humanity has reached the cusp it has fought for, or when they are on the other side? When they determine the nature of the *next* phase change and make concrete plans to survive it, or out the other side of that one too?

She doesn't know, and Imre-F won't tell her. If he is waiting for her to admit that she was wrong, he will wait forever. "Be angry," Biancotti had told her, and that emotion has sustained her through the ages. It is her lifeblood; it is the air she breathes; it is the beating of her stellar heart.

The fight for the future spans vast volumes of space as humanity learns how to manipulate astronomical artifacts of its own, cosmic shear points and pion stars among them.

Other life-forms are discovered—also knockoffs of the Luminous in danger from their inadvertent creators—and they are co-opted into the battle. Aftershocks disrupt whole galaxies, but they are much-reduced things from the days of old, surrounded by huge tracts of unlit space. Most battles are fought in this lightless void—which only seems a void to those without the eyes to see what exists there. Slowly, interminably, humanity and its allies rise to stand before the Luminous as equals, crowding the way to un-challenged domination of the universe to come.

Imre-Prime remains—former mercenary, Fort, First Prime, fugitive and captive. She remembers the dance of galaxies glimpsed in an ancient vision, and the slashing of rainbow webs. If she views the war at one million years a second, that is exactly how it looks.

The message has been received.

The source of that message remains with her, the one whose history has devolved beyond legend but whose phi-losophy has shaped the fate of an entire species. The one whose name has been for a very long time something less than music and something slightly more than silence.

I who was Imre—with or without the F, but B always for Bergamasc.

(That damned alarm!)

I who will always be.

DOOM AND BURDEN

His past was fairly blameless; few men could read the rolls of their life with less apprehension; yet he was humbled to the dust by the many ill things he had done, and raised up again into a sober and fearful gratitude by the many that he had come so near to doing, yet avoided.

—Robert Louis Stevenson

Imre Bergamasc awoke knowing exactly who she was, but where and when confounded her. Her mind was full of eternity, of wars conducted across millions of light-years, of colliding galaxies, and of millennia flowing by like microseconds. Once she had struggled with memories of C20 and the idealized past. Now she couldn't think through memories of things to come—memories that couldn't possibly be real if she was in this body, in this place, hearing those voices.

She opened her eyes and found herself in her private chamber in the *Wickthing*. The voices came distinctly to her from the map room, along with the sound of an alarm ringing over an open line.

"Listen to me," Bianca Biancotti was saying. "This is neither the time nor the place. Leave before you get yourself killed."

Emlee joined her entreaty. "I'd do as she says, if I were you. They've got Imre. I couldn't bear to lose you too."

For a moment there was just the alarm, then Render

said, "Keep your tears. All things change. Everything will be decided here."

Imre was moving without thinking, throwing herself off the bed and down the hallway. She didn't stop to wonder how she had come to be there or ask how she could be wearing the same armor she'd had on billions of years earlier. All she had room for in her mind was the broken voice of her old friend.

She burst into the map room shouting, "Don't! Whatever he's about to do, don't let him do it!"

Chyro Kells literally jumped with surprise. Emlee spun around, reaching for a sidearm that wasn't there.

"Where the—?"

"He sent me back," Imre said, raising trembling hands in both their directions. The truth of it was only beginning to sink in. "Or I never left. It doesn't matter. What the hell is Render doing? How did he get here?"

She approached the desk and the mess of charts scattered across it. Emlee's shining stare didn't leave Imre's face for an instant, and the hand that had reached for her sidearm gripped Imre's shoulder instead when she was within range.

"Render followed us," Emlee said. "He says—well, he's not very clear about anything, actually. Something told him to come, he says. He thinks he needs to prove himself, somehow."

Imre studied the maps she indicated. The modern-day equivalent of a Vespula was a small, fast-moving point aimed directly at the Gabriel installation. The *Wickthing* was still stationed nearby. Only moments seemed to have passed since Bianca Biancotti had forcibly ripped her from MZ's illusion, but relative time was inherently flexible. She could have been gone for years Absolute.

The alarm was coming from an open channel leading to Render's ship, signaling that the installation's defensive systems had locked onto the tiny craft.

"What are you doing here, Render?" Imre sent down the open line.

"I heard it in my sleep," the old soldier said. "I don't know its name, but it sounds like my voice, lost and old."

"We don't know who he's talking about," said Emlee to Imre as an aside.

"I think I do," Imre replied with a terrible certainty flowering in her gut.

"It said, 'He lies,'" Render intoned. "It said, 'We are betrayed.' It said, 'Don't let me down.' It said, 'Time to leave.'"

"You're talking about your collection, aren't you?" Imre broke in. "You were curious. You opened the containment fields and talked to it. When it realized I came here without it, it decided to work through you instead."

"It said, 'You can choose.'"

"I know," she said, thinking of Imre-F and wondering. "It's always your choice. Don't ever think otherwise."

"I think he intends to ram," Biancotti said. "That's one option I'm willing to take away from him."

Close examination of the telemetry confirmed that Render was firing like a bullet right into the heart of the Gabriel installation.

"If he doesn't change course," Biancotti insisted, "we're going to shoot him out of the sky."

"It won't come to that. I'd never allow it," Imre said, understanding then that this was why she had been sent back. "He's talking about a silver sphere he hid aboard the *Memory of Markheim*. I promised I'd bring it here, to talk to my Fort-self, but I left it behind. Understand, Render," she said down the line, "that I made that promise not as a traitor to everything we believe in, but in the hope that a rebel faction within the Luminous exists and that we can use it to our advantage. It might be the only way to get an edge over the rest of the Luminous." *I've seen it,* she wanted to say, *or a pretty good projection thereof.* "I don't break my promises."

Emlee was looking at her oddly, but she didn't interrupt.

"Render, can you hear me? Talk to me."

"I don't believe in long good-byes," came the reply down the line.

"Who's talking about good-bye? I'm talking about cooling things down a little. The Prime Minister must have told you where we were going. She knows I'm not betraying anyone, so why don't you?"

"I want to believe—in you."

"I'm not stopping you, Render. It's going to be all right."

"Nothing's ever right; nothing's ever wrong. I've heard it all before."

"And I've been right as often as I've been wrong."

"Too late. I'm losing my faith."

"Well, that's not necessarily a bad thing. No one wants unquestioning obedience, especially from a friend." She waited for a moment, then talked on into the empty line. "I understand how it looked when the sphere started talking. I understand how you came to the conclusions you did. In your shoes, I might not stop to give me a chance to explain either. I fully appreciate how you'd want to dispose of the problem, once and for all. But this isn't the way. This won't solve anything. Why are you persisting when I tell you it won't do any good?"

"I want to feel." Render spoke with rising agitation. "Do you remember the last time you cried? I don't. Something's wrong. I don't remember the feelings. I've been fighting for so long, I'm like a dead man." His voice choked for a second. "I'm dead, and no one can help me."

Imre thought frantically. If she let Render slip away, the galaxy would lose another connection to humanity's origins—and from there it would be one less step to losing humanity itself. The weight of memory wasn't just an albatross: it was an anchor too. Without it, what was the point of striving so hard and so long for the survival of the species?

Genes were cheap; culture *mattered*. She had seen that in Imre-F's version of the future, too. With Old-Timers losing their minds in C20's self-imposed isolation, the situation was already critical.

Render wasn't losing his mind, though. Imre was sure some complex logic lay behind his threat to blow himself and the sphere to kingdom come, a logic masquerading behind a conspiracy uniting Imre, her Fort-self and the Luminous.

When she asked herself what that might be—something more immediate and personal, worth dying for—it came to her at once.

"I'm only going to say this once," she said, "then you have thirty seconds Absolute to change your course. If you don't, I'm going to ask Bianca to fire on you. Do you hear me?"

"I hear you."

Emlee and Kells were staring at her. She leaned over the desk and wished she could see her old friend's face

"What's happening here is more important than you and your problems, Render. It's more important than mine, too—but that doesn't mean that what we do doesn't matter. It's not good enough just to keep fighting and believing. We have to fight the right battles at the right time, and we have to fight the right enemies. Otherwise, we might as well give in and save ourselves the trouble.

"I'm telling you now, Render, that you're going about this all wrong. The enemy isn't me or the guy you think is in that base you're about to hit. If you stick around, I'll show you that it's not Ra, either, or the Veil, or what's left of Helwise. It might be the sphere you've brought here, it might be the Luminous—and it might be immutability above everything else. But you'll never know if you go through with this. The only way to be sure about *anything* is to stop asking questions entirely. If you do that, you're as good as dead.

"I understand, Render, and I sympathize. We've been tangled up in our memories so long it's hard sometimes to move forward. That doesn't stop us wanting to, and I see you making exactly the same mistake I did, over and over: trying to prove something to someone who isn't around and going about it entirely the wrong way. I was trying to prove something to my Fort-self, and we all know how that worked out. You—well, a suicide mission is just a suicide mission. It's not change; it's not evolution. It just stops the questions being asked. If you really want to demonstrate something to Alice-Angeles, there are better ways to do it."

Render was silent.

"What do you say?" Imre pressed him. "Are we going to sweep up your bits with a vacuum cleaner and take them back to her in a jar, or are you going to change course and make your point another time? That you want to make a point is a good thing," she added, "and we can find another time to make it. You may not have noticed, Render, but no one's shooting at us today."

"For now," came the reply.

· "Yes," she said, leaning her weight on both hands and staring at the chart. "I want you at my back when it starts up again. Meanwhile, the clock is ticking. How long did I say, again?"

Render didn't respond. Imre raised her tempo so the seconds crawled by, watching the dot move steadily toward the terminus of its journey.

"Do you want me," Render asked, "or redemption?"

"Just you," she responded. "Just you, my old friend."

"More dead than old," he said, "but not insane. I'll stay, if you want me to."

"I do. Please."

"Good. I'm scared to die."

The dot began, by tiny increments, to shift from its headlong course.

Imre waited until there was no chance it would hit the installation before letting go the breath she was holding and easing back on the overclocking. A moment later, the alarm ceased its clamor.

"Thank you," she said down the open line.

"I don't want to talk about it. I'll just sink or swim with you, if that's the way you want to play it."

"And the sphere?"

"You can have it."

"You're doing the right thing."

Emlee stood close to Imre, but her words were for Render. "We need you to keep Imre honest."

"I don't believe that honesty pays," he said with more life. "It's down to who you know."

"Well, our connections are good," said Imre, thinking of everything she had seen in Imre-F's vision of the future. It may have been an illusion, but it wasn't conjured from nothing.

"You'd better be right about that," said Emlee, sotto voce. "I want to know exactly how you turned him around— or vice versa."

"We've always been on the same side," she said, quoting Emlee's words back at her, "even when we didn't know it."

"That's the best you've got?" Emlee frowned.

Imre looked down at her left hand and found it to be unmarked. All she had left were memories of memories, and they belonged entirely to her, along with Hyperabad, the Returned Continuum, and everything she had been in C20. How could she capture her relief at being back while at the same time conveying the certainty with which she had returned?

I couldn't bear to lose you, either.

From that sure knowledge, everything else flowed.

"It's only the beginning," said Bianca Biancotti from behind them.

They turned as one.

"You've got a fucking nerve," Emlee told the Old-Timer. "You kidnap Imre and threaten to kill Render. The least you could do is knock."

Biancotti was entirely unapologetic. "We gave your Imre a taste of the kind of decisions mine has to make. Be glad we sent him back. The long haul would be pretty bleak without Render."

"Fine," Emlee said, "and now that's done, are you here to take her away again?"

Imre stared at Emlee. That was the first time anyone had used the feminine pronoun in reference to her for a very, very long time.

"Are you saying that's what you want me to do?" Biancotti asked Emlee.

"No," she said. "That's not what I'm saying."

"Good. 'We must proceed more efficiently toward our goal. Some of us, anyway.'" Biancotti was quoting Imre-F and speaking to Imre, now. "Your usefulness isn't at an end. We knew long before Render arrived that you've been contacted by the dissenting faction within the Luminous. We think that faction might be trying to talk to us, and we very much want to talk to them in return."

"So why don't you?"

"It's the right fight on the wrong front. Better to do it through you, if you're willing. You can be the first diplomat between the human race and the Luminous. You will speak on humanity's behalf, with the full weight of the Apparatus behind you."

"Assuming I agree," said Emlee. "You've forgotten Helwise. A large percentage of humanity might not like the idea of Imre talking for anyone."

"We haven't forgotten Helwise. We will prepare an antibody from Imre's memories, taken through the Veil, and release it into the wild. The two memes should interfere with each other in interesting ways."

That was an understatement of the highest order, Imre thought. It was, however, a suggestion she would never have considered had she not already been forced into it. Was that the real reason she had been infected?

"We can meet the Revivalist Doctrine halfway," she said. "If we merge MZ with the Apparatus, he can unpick the Executive Order forever."

"And create another weapon in the process," said Emlee.

"That's the way war works," Biancotti said. "You hold out one hand while keeping a fist behind your back."

"And I get to keep my name?" Imre said.

Biancotti smiled. "You can call yourself whatever you want, just so long as you keep your head down."

Imre leaned her weight backward so the desk took some of it. Her head was spinning. "So all that was a lie, then—everything you showed me before."

"A credible projection. Not a worst-case scenario, but we're hoping you'll find this one a lot more attractive. Noble, even. I know you like to think of humanity that way. This is your big chance to prove yourself right."

"You're pretty cocksure," Emlee said, "for someone holed up in the center of the galaxy."

Biancotti smiled, and Imre knew exactly what she was thinking. Imre-F wasn't holed up anywhere: he was sprawled out across the entire Milky Way, riding the Line like a boat on a sea. "Listen to Imre," Biancotti said. "Talk to MZ. Do what seems right. I'm sure you'll come around to our way of thinking and do the job well."

"To avenge the Forts," said Imre, mentally ticking the check box of the other half of her mission: *find Himself.* That ordeal was behind her at last.

"To own the future," Biancotti said with a slight rising of her jaw. The challenge was unmistakable. "Together."

Imre thought of everything that lay ahead of them—not just repelling the silver-sphere incursion but patching things up with Ra, educating humanity on the true nature of the threat, and making certain the first steps along a very long road were sure, unfaltering ones. The prospect was daunting—she didn't know now if she would see the end of the road on which Imre-F had placed her—but it was a worthy one. It gave her a new sense of purpose.

A deeper truth was that she was glad—glad to be spared her Fort-self's burden and the doom of his long, long fight. That was one fate she could outrun.

Chyro Kells caught her eye. Her former physician had remained silent through the entire confrontation, from her appearance in the map room to Bianca Biancotti's return. He gave nothing away, but his cool, emotionless eyes took in everything.

You're you again.

Imre had been running too long. It was a flight she could not sustain because she had been running from herself just as hard as her Fort-self, in turn, had been running from her. No wonder it had taken them so long to find each other.

It was time to make a stand. She would be the counterweight of Imre-F's universe-spanning ambition, the Imre Bergamasc to his growing alienation. She would go backward while he went forward. Between the two of them, something would survive that remembered being her.

What's to regret?

"Emlee, I think we should be on our way."

"What about Render?" Emlee asked.

"He'll tag along, of course, with the sphere."

Emlee hesitated. "All right," she said. "MZ, coordinate with Render, then set a course for Earth. You're about to get everything you ever wanted."

"Thank you, Prime Minister," said the Fort. "Thank you, Imre."

"You have to earn it," Imre said. "Don't forget that. There are two Forts in the galaxy now, and if I'm not mistaken, the other one just had you over a barrel."

"A Hyeres paradox would not contain me permanently."

"No, but I doubt that's all he has in his arsenal. Bianca—"

She stopped. Apart from Emlee, Imre, and Kells, the map room was empty.

Emlee put a hand in the small of her back. "Nothing left to say, apparently."

"Maybe she's right." Imre nodded to herself. "Let's go be heroes."

That earned her a mocking noise from Render's open line. "I'm not a hero."

"Why not? Think of the perks."

"Heroes always get the best girl," Render said, "and then die."

The old soldier's mood was definitely improving. "So die happy."

"Sound effects of mayhem."

Imre laughed. It felt good.

Nothing felt better than the warmth of Emlee's hand and the promise of a life regained.

Map of the Milky Way

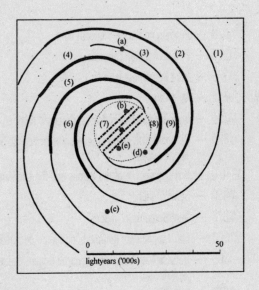

1. Outer Arm
2. Perseus Arm
3. Local Arm
4. Carina Arm
5. Crux Arm
6. Norma Arm
7. Bar
8. Scutum Arm
9. Sagittarius Arm

a) Sol
b) Spargamos
c) C20
d) Vaia
e) Soulis

Appendix A: Absolute Calendar

· ·

C20 — Render and Bianca Biancotti born

M220 — Fort domination complete

M275 — Imre Bergamasc born

M550–722 — Mad Times

M725 — Imre Bergamasc Graduates; Domgard founded

M820 — Domgard fifth-stage experimentation begins; Slow Wave epicenter

M840+ — first appearance of the Barons and the Luminous

M850 — Slow Wave hits Sol

M878 — Imre Bergamasc "reborn"

M1000 — Earth conquered; Returned Continuum declared

M1095–1300 — Helwise MacPhedron pronounced Regent during whistle-stop tours

M1355 — Imre Bergamasc arrives at Spargamos

M1380 — Helwise MacPhedron deposed; Imre Bergamasc abdicates

Appendix B: Glossary

• • • • • • • • • • • • • • • • • • ......

Absolute: see Tempo.

Apparatus: Only given name of an AI found on Earth and conscripted by the invading forces of the Returned Continuum; occasionally referred to as the "spook" or "ghost," it has no material existence, consisting of code written via zero-dimensional topological-frame defects directly into the quantum foam, and is able to interact with the material universe solely via leptons (electrons, muons, tau lepton).

Assumption: Common term for the adoption of the Veil by a human host.

Barons: The name of the organization considered responsible for much of the unrest and sabotage endured by the Returned Continuum.

Bianca Biancotti: An Old-Timer known to Imre Bergamasc by reputation as the seed personality of the Fort "2B"; also called the "Butcher of Bresland."

Cat's Arse: The long-term hideout of the Corps formerly located in a spatial anomaly in Mandala Supersystem.

Continuum: The term used to refer to the sum of human civilization, from the fiftieth to the eight hundred and fiftieth

• •

millennium; includes all civilizations within the Milky Way and some efforts at expansion beyond.

Corps: Mercenary force founded in the 250th millennium that proved influential in the Mad Times owing to its intimate dealings with the Forts, against which the Corps' then leader, Imre Bergamasc, defiantly turned. Last-known members are: Imre Bergamasc (commander), Emlee Copas (signals), Alphin Freer (resources), Helwise MacPhedron (intelligence), and Archard Rositano (aka Render, combat specialist).

Domgard: The name of an experiment occasionally linked to the Slow Wave and Imre Bergamasc; claimed by some to have had something to do with dark matter.

Dussehra: Ninth destination of Imre Bergamasc's fourth whistle-stop tour of systems not yet aligned with the Returned Continuum.

Executive Order KISMET: An order issued by Imre Bergamasc instructing the Apparatus to kill on sight all iterations of Helwise MacPhedron; it cannot be countermanded.

First Prime: Ceremonial name of the leader of the Returned Continuum.

Fort: see Tempo.

• •

Frag: A Fort component, resembling a Prime or singleton but possessing little true individuality; a frag may be separated by light-years yet firmly connected by Q loop technology to its parent mind; Forts regard frags as functionally expendable but may display affection toward particular frags in the same way that Primes keep pets or look after their hair.

Graduation: Common term for the evolution of a collection of individual beings to the status of a Fort.

Gravamen: Former ruling party of Dussehra.

Hardcaster: Generic name for the expensive and power-hungry system of nonmaterial transportation preferred by Returned Continuum worlds to physical space travel. Individuals are "dematerialized" into information, transmitted via the Line or other means to their destination, then "reconstituted" on arrival.

Hyperabad: Capital city of the Hyperabadan regime; also a planet orbiting the star Chenresi; also the regime of the same name, which dominated Mandala Supersystem after the 864th millennium.

Jinc: Component of the gestalt commonly referred to as the Noh; one of seven similar components that function as far-sensing organs on the fringes of the Milky Way, searching

• • • • • • • • • • • • • • • • • • • •

for the source of life in the galaxy, which is presumed to be of exogenic origin.

Kismet: High-security prison of Mandala Supersystem; see also Executive Order KISMET.

Line: Common term for individual legs of the vast electro-magnetic telecommunications web spanning the Milky Way.

Loop / Loop shunt: see Q loop.

Luminous: The name of an organization associated with the Slow Wave, about which little is known.

MZ: This devolved Fort is written on space-time using an abandoned method employing gauge bosons (photons, W and Z bosons, gluons) to connect to the world around him.

Old-Timer: Common term for a living individual born during the twentieth century; usually refers to those who have lived continuously, in one form or another, since their births.

Overclocking: see Tempo.

• • • • • • • • • • • • • • • • • • • · · · · · · ·

Pelorus: Flagship of the anti-Fort Sol Invictus movement; destroyed at the climax of the conflict known as the Mad Times.

Prime: Common term for an individual whose identity and values closely conform to those of Old-Time humans, particularly those of the twentieth century, when the first Old-Timers were born; most Primes function as a matter of principle at Tempo Absolute.

Q loop: Means of communication employed by Forts to enable long-distance, untraceable communication between component frags and each other; loop shunts are devices requiring little power and possessing extremely high signal-to-noise characteristics.

Returned Continuum: The name of the galactic government instated by Imre Bergamasc and Helwise MacPhedron upon the annexing of Earth; closely related to the First Church of the Return, whose followers swept them to power.

Round: Common name for the systems closest to Sol.

Singleton: Common term for an individual that is neither a component in a gestalt nor a true Prime; it is common practice in the Continuum to possess several singleton copies that exchange, merge, or overlap memories at regular

• •

intervals throughout an extended life; tempo is flexible among singletons, ranging from very fast to near-Fort states of existence.

Spargamos: The Core world on which the Domgard experiment was founded.

Tempo: Usual term employed to describe the perception of time at varying rates. "Tempo Absolute" refers to time as experienced by Primes and Old-Time humanity and is widely held as a default referent; "overclocking" is the practice of fitting more seconds than one into a single second Absolute, thereby experiencing time at an increased rate; the most-evolved human individuals known as Forts experience time at an extremely slow tempo, with individual relative seconds sometimes spanning centuries.

The Veil: Common term for an alien parasite first encountered on Dussehra; when symbiotically linked to human nervous tissue, it increases the host's memory and also allows the physical transmission of specific memories between individuals.

Vespula: Common brand of interstellar fighter employed extensively during the Mad Times; millions remain in active service, scattered across all arms of the Milky Way.

Wave guns: Experimental weaponry observed for the first time on Spargamos; wielded by Barons, they were capable of disabling the silver spheres associated with the Luminous.

Wickthing: Name of the virtual vessel created by MZ to house less-evolved passengers.

Appendix C: "My Last Words"

. . . .

Many people, alive and dead, knowing and unknowing, have contributed to this series, and I see no elegant way to thank them all. Here, then, is a list of those to whom I owe a debt of serious gratitude: Danny Baror, Marcus Chown, Richard Curtis, Jay Lake; Ginjer Buchanan, Cam Dufty, and Bob and Sara Schwager (Ace); Bernadette Foley, Tim Holman, Darren Nash, Bella Pagan, Nicola Pitt, Samantha Smith, and George Walkley (Orbit); Chris Robeson and Allison Baker (MonkeyBrain Books); Beth Anderson, Michael Charzuk, Steve Feldberg, Art Insana, and Christian Rummel (Audible); and Cat Walker and Gary Helsiger (Universal).

My wife, Amanda, suffered through my suffering at the hands of this final novel, and I wish to thank her especially.

Lastly I am compelled, once again, to acknowledge the generosity of Gary Numan and Tony Webb, without which this project would have been much less challenging: compelled by my own conscience, not out of any legal sense of obligation, and challenged not by the process of dealing with music publishers but by the act of creating something new from another's words.

To abbreviate Saint Jerome the Presbyter, whose letter to Pope Damascus I is quoted elsewhere in this book: "Is there any learned man, who when he picks up the volume in his hand, and takes a single taste of it, might not instantly raise his voice, calling me a forger, that I might dare to add, to change, or to correct anything?"

"Pious work"? Perhaps not. But "perilous presumption" indeed.

* * *

The Gary Numan albums appropriated for *The Grand Conjunction* were: *Berserker* (1984), *Dance* (1981), *Exile* (1997), *The Fury* (1985), *I, Assassin* (1982), *Jagged* (2006), *Machine + Soul* (1992), *Metal Rhythm* (1988), *Outland* (1990), *The Plan* (1984), *The Pleasure Principle* (1979), *Pure* (2000), *Replicas* (1979), *Sacrifice* (1994), *Strange Charm* (1986), *Telekon* (1980), *Tubeway Army* (1978), *Warriors* (1983).

"1930's Rust," "A Dream of Siam," "A Prayer for the Unborn," "A Question of Faith," "A Subway Called 'You,'" "Absolution," "An Alien Cure," "Basic J," "Before You Hate It," "Berserker," "Bleed," "Blind," "Blue Eyes," "Call Out the Dogs," "Crash," "Crime of Passion," "Cry," "Cry, the Clock Said," "Dance," "Dark," "Dark Sunday," "Dead Heaven," "Deadliner," "Devious," "Devotion," "Dominion Day," "Don't Believe," "Dream Killer," "Emotion," "Exhibition," "Exile," "Face to Face/Letters," "Fadeout 1930," "Fold," "From Russia Infected," "Halo," "Heart," "Hunger," "I, Assassin," "I Can't Breathe," "I Can't Stop," "I Wonder," "In a Dark Place," "Innocence Bleeding," "Jagged," "Love and Napalm," "Machine & Soul," "Magic," "Miracles," "Moral," "My Breathing," "My Car Slides (1)," "My Car Slides (2)," "My Centurion," "My Dying Machine," "My World Storm," "New Anger," "One Perfect Lie," "Out of Sight," "Outland," "Play Like God," "Poison," "Pray," "Pressure," "Prophecy," "Pure," "Respect," "Rumor," "Scanner," "She Cries," "Sister Surprise," "Slave," "Slowcar to China," "Soul Protection," "Strange Charm," "The Angel Wars," "The Hunter," "The Iceman Comes," "The Monday Troop," "The Need," "The Rhythm of the Evening," "The Seed of a Lie," "The Skin Game," "The Sleeproom," "The Tick Tock Man," "This Disease," "This Is Emotion," "This Is Love," "This Is New Love," "This Prison Moon," "Time to Die," "Tread Careful," "Unknown and Hostile," "Voix," "War Games," "Warriors," "We Take Mystery (Early Version)," and "Young Heart."